As a private investigator I meet all kinds of people and hear all kinds of stories. Most people want me to find somebody - a missing daughter, a cheating spouse, a thieving employee. This is what pays the rent and buys the groceries. Still, there are some who come into the offices of Grace Investigations whose stories would not be run on tabloid TV on a slow news night. Me, I believe them. I believe them all, at least for the first ten minutes. When they walk through my door, I always start out believing them.

When a woman came in and told me that she was God and bade me go forth and prove it, I worshiped her, for the first ten minutes. And for ten minutes I believed the guy who wanted protection from the space aliens who watched him from light sockets. I even believed the couple who told me that Elvis was buried in their basement. So when a woman walked in and told me that her baby, who had died at birth, was still alive but had been stolen, I was ready to believe her, at least for the first ten minutes.

OTHER PADWOLF BOOKS FROM JOHN L. FRENCH

BAD COP, NO DONUT edited by John L. French
  -Coming 2010!

PAST SINS
AND OTHER STORIES

The Matthew Grace Casebook

John L. French

PADWOLF PUIBLISHING INC.

WWW.PADWOLF.COM

PAST SINS AND OTHER STORIES: *The Matthew Grace Casebook*
© 2009 John L. French

Publishing history

By the Sword- Weird Stories 6, March 1997, Fading Shadows Publications

Cashing In -Classic Pulp Fiction Stories 24, May 1997, Fading Shadow Publications

Child's Play- Alfred Hitchcock's Mystery Magazine, April 1995

A House Divided - DIME, Futures Mystery Anthology Magazine, 2004 (An alternate version published in Futures Mystery Anthology, May/June 2005)

Lady Killer- Strange Worlds 9, October 2001, Wild Cat Books; - Detective Mystery Stories 26, June 2002, Fading Shadows Publications; - ThrillerUK 18, April 2004

Open And Shut- Alfred Hitchcock's Mystery Magazine, July/August 2003

Past Sins - Hardboiled 13, March 1993, Gryphon Publications; - 100 SNEAKY LITTLE SLEUTH STORIES, Robert Weinberg et al; (eds.), Barnes & Nobles 1997

Serving Justice- Classic Pulp Fiction Stories 41, October 1998, Fading Shadows Publications

Ten Minutes at a Time - Double Danger Tales 10, November 1997, Fading Shadows Publications (as "Changeling")- ThrillerUK 6, April 2001 (published as "The Changeling")

Tipping the Scales- Hardboiled 27/28, December 2001, Gryphon Publications

A Walk in the Park- Alfred Hitchcock's Mystery Magazine, October 1998

COVER ART © 2009 PATRICK THOMAS

All rights reserved. No part of this book may be reproduced or transmitted in any means electronic or mechanical, including recording, photocopying or by any information storage and retrieval system, without the written permission of the copyright holders. Unauthorized reproduction is prohibited by law.
This is a work of fiction. No similarity between any of the names, characters, persons, situations and/or institutions and those of any preexisting person or institution is intended and any similarity which may exist is purely coincidental.

ISBN: 10 DIGIT 1-890096-40-7; 13 DIGIT 978-1-890096-40-3
Printed in the USA
First Printing

To C. J. Henderson,
A great writer and a better friend.

TABLE OF CONTENTS

SHELL GAME	9
CHILD'S PLAY	20
A WALK IN THE PARK	31
OPEN AND SHUT	50
LAST OF THE LATIN ALTAR BOYS	63
TIPPING THE SCALES	75
THE GUILTY ALWAYS PAY	80
PAST SINS	99
BY THE SWORD	105
CASHING IN	117
TEN MINUTES AT A TIME	124
SERVING JUSTICE	133
LADY KILLER	135
A HOUSE DIVIDED	149
MESSAGE IN THE SAND	163
HOW THE STORY GOES	177
THE CHOICES WE MAKE	199

SHELL GAME

"It's called a Baltimore Burial, Grace," Detective Alexander Klein explained. We were in an alley in a part of southeast Baltimore called Canton, looking at a body that had been dumped there the night before. The deceased was wrapped in what looked to be layers of old bedsheets. The first officer on the scene had loosened the bundle just enough to determine that there was a body inside, then had called Homicide and the Lab.

I'd been working for the Baltimore Police Crime Lab for about three months and I'd been flying solo for less than half that time. This was the first dead body scene I'd handled by myself. Klein knew this and was educating me on the finer points of death investigation.

"Probably dumped here from a shooting gallery. The junkies find themselves a vacant house, or someone volunteers theirs, and that's where they shoot their dope. Sometimes one of them gets too much of a good thing and checks out. It may take a while, but sooner or later somebody'll notice he's dead. Now they're not about to call the police. Believe it or not, they're laws against drug use in this city. So the dead guy gets wrapped and bagged and left in the alley."

"And sometimes," came a voice from behind us, "the victim is found dead, wet and naked."

We turned. "Morning, Sergeant," Klein said. I added a greeting, not knowing who this man was.

"Nothing better to do then stand around chatting, Detective?"

I spoke up. "All done, Sergeant. Photos are taken, sketch is drawn and the alley's been searched. Right now we're just waiting on the Medical Examiner."

The sergeant gave Klein a "who is this?" look.

"Sarge, this is Matthew Grace. Grace, Detective Sergeant Joshua Parker." So that was the guy everybody talked about, the one they called the Deacon.

"Pleased to meet you, Technician Grace. New to the Lab?"

"Yes, sir."

"Let me see your sketch." I handed him my clipboard with a rough drawing of the alley. He looked it over then said, "I'm sure it will look better when it's finished. Did you search the alley yourself?"

"No, sir, but the uniforms ..."

Parker cut me off in voice that somehow combined patient instruction with biting sarcasm. "Mr. Grace, despite your lack of experience, you are the crime scene expert here, you are the one with all forensic training and it is your job to search the scene for ... remind me, Detective Klein, what is it they look for?"

"Clues, Sarge."

"Go look for clues, Technician Grace. It's what you're being paid to do. And Detective Klein,"

"Yes, sir?"

"Since you have nothing better to do, why don't you help him?"

Parker stood watching as Klein and I walked up and down the alley.

"Just what are we looking for?" I asked. "From what you tell me, it seems that whoever dumped this guy carried him in, dropped him and left."

"So it would seem, but Parker's right. Always check a scene out for yourself. Don't rely on the uniforms or detectives to do your job."

"Yeah, that makes sense," I admitted. I looked up and saw Parker walking away. "My new best friend is leaving."

"Don't take it personal, Grace. He's like that with everyone. And if you're going to be doing this job for any length of time, you better develop a hard shell."

We finished walking the alley. I didn't have any more evidence than when we started.

"Dead, wet and naked?" I asked Klein when we were done.

"When a guy OD's, his friends will sometimes strip him and put him in a tub full of cold water. If he's still alive the shock's supposed to jumpstart his heart."

"Does it work?"

"It's supposed to, but the only time I see them is when it doesn't."

The ME's van pulled up about then. With the victim wrapped up the way he was, there would be no preliminary investigation. That would have to wait until the body got down to the morgue where it could be examined in controlled conditions. Klein reminded me that I was supposed to be there.

"It's like Christmas," he said, "Half the fun is unwrapping the present."

Which took a while. Under the bedsheet was a shower curtain, and under that another sheet that had previously seen service as a painter's tarp. Each layer had to be photographed, both by me and the ME's photographer. Then it was removed, carefully so as not to disturb any trace evidence, and in the case of the shower curtain, fingerprints. Watching the process was Detective Klein and Darryl Kates, another homicide detective and Klein's current partner.

"Maybe some prints on the shower curtain," Klein said as that item was removed, folded and wrapped in brown paper.

"Keep dreaming, Alex," Kates said. "That only happens on TV. And if it does happen, prints won't match in the computer. Of course, it does have potential, so does the tarp."

"How? Oh yeah, I see."

"You'll still need a suspect, but that'll tie him in."

By now we were down to the victim. He turned out to be a white male in his twenties, dressed in a pullover shirt and jeans. Any hope that this case would turn out to be a drug overdose ended with the rather obvious discovery of a stab wound in his upper left chest.

"Check his pockets," Klein said needlessly, since the ME investigator was already doing that. Keys, change, lottery tickets, comb and handkerchief, and a wallet. The wallet had the usual, along with a driver's license in the name of Randy Fairweather.

"That gives us a start," Kates said. "Let's just hope he wasn't killed at home."

Stripped of everything but what the Lord had provided, the body of Randy Fairweather was wheeled into the autopsy room and met by Dr. Eileen Herrick, the forensic pathologist who would make the official determination as to cause of death.

Talking into her headset, she began with an exterior examination of the body, noting all distinguishing characteristics before moving on to the knife wound — apparent knife wound as she called it. She wouldn't say for sure until she completed her exam.

"Note that the apparent angle of entry is such so as to rule out suicide," she said into her mike. "No defensive wounds are obvious," she picked up one hand then the other, "but the nails will be scraped and removed should they contain any tissue from the assailant. It should be noted that the subject's hands bear a rust-colored residue and," here she leaned close to the victim and sniffed, "smell of vinegar and spices. Crab seasoning." Dr. Herrick looked up at us. "Gentlemen, Mr. Fairweather was a true Baltimorean, he died eating crabs."

This was a joke only funny in Baltimore. Steamed crabs are a local delicacy. It's not summer until you've gotten your first dozen or so hardshells, dumped them alive and kicking into a pot and steamed them until dead and delicious.

The preferred method of eating a crab is a throwback to our barbarian past. The legs and shell are ripped off and the internal organs removed. What remains, the mustard, is scooped out with a finger and eagerly sucked up. The body of the crab is then cracked in half and split with a table knife to reveal the meat. Once this is eaten, the legs are smashed with either the knife handle or a wooden mallet and the meat in them consumed. It's messy and enjoyable, and even better with cold beer.

"Crabs," Sgt. Parker said at the next day's case review. "That at least gives us something to work with. Mr. Grace, what does the Lab have for us?"

Any evidence?"

I'd been to these reviews before, but only as an observer sitting off to the side. This was my first time at the grownups table.

"Nothing from the scene," I said, "except of course the victim himself. The ME sent over the fingernails and scrapings, the Trace Evidence Unit has them and will look 'em over, just in case there was anything there other than crab meat. Trace also has the bedsheet and tarp. They're working on the shower curtain now and when done they'll send it to Latent Prints. When those results are back I'll forward them to Detective Klein." I passed around copies of my finished sketch (which did look much better than the rough, thank you) and the photos of the crime scene and ME's exam.

"Thanks you, Mr. Grace. Detective Klein?"

"We checked Fairweather's house. No signs of a struggle, no crab shells in the trash, no ransacking and nothing missing. He wasn't killed there. We're trying to trace his movements, and known associates now."

"Any record?"

"Just the usual for a Canton kid — drunk and disorderly, DWI, urinating in public, resisting arrest."

Parker turned to Officer Joe Banks, the primary uniform on the case. "When does trash get picked up in that neighborhood?"

"Wednesday and Saturday, why?"

Parker ignored the question and addressed us all. "The victim was found on Sunday morning. Presumably he was killed after a Saturday night crab feast. Today is Monday. You have the rest of it and all day tomorrow to find the suspect or suspects, or else Wednesday morning you and your fellow detectives will be wearing Department of Sanitation overalls and helping them collect the garbage. Now then, anything else?"

No one had anything, and Parker closed the meeting. The rest of us stayed behind after he left.

"What's with the garbage collecting?" Banks asked.

"No one knows the mind of the Deacon," answered Kates. "Ask Grace, I hear tell he's the crime scene expert."

"How about it, Matthew," Klein added, "any ideas?"

I had the feeling that Klein and Kates both knew what Parker had in mind, but it was play with the new guy day. I thought a moment, "Well, I can only guess that Parker thinks that we can match the bits of shell found in what Fairweather was wrapped in to some of the shells we might find in the suspect's home."

"Can we?"

"In theory, but it would be one hell of a jigsaw puzzle for whoever gets to do it." They all looked at me. "You don't think ... he wouldn't, would he?"

"Think of it a job security," Kates said as he left. Banks followed him, leaving me alone with Klein.

"Detective Klein, can I ask you something?"

"Ask away, Matthew, and it's Alex."

"Why's Parker called 'the Deacon?'"

"First of all," Klein told me, "never call him that to his face. He doesn't like it and the detective who tagged him with it is now walking post in the Western, after working as morgue liaison for six months. Parker is an elder of his church. Plus he's never been known to tell a lie."

"Never?" I hadn't been with the department long but one thing I'd learned was that every one lied — bad guys to cops, cops to bad guys, officers to supervision and command to everybody.

"Never."

"Are you sure he's a cop?"

"He's one hell of a cop. Just try to stay on his good side."

I'd try, but somehow I didn't think that it'd be possible.

The next morning Klein came down to the Mobile Unit office looking for me. "Want to take a ride, Matthew?"

"We going out to look for clues?"

"Something like that. Yesterday Darryl and I talked to Sarah DeMarco, she's Fairweather's girlfriend, ex-girlfriend now I guess. She told us that after spending Friday night with her, he left early Saturday afternoon to spend some time with his friends, 'his buds' as she put it."

"Did he mention anything about buying crabs along the way?"

"I asked. She then told me what a cheap s.o.b. he was and that the only time he'd ever brought crabs home was when picked up a stripper from the Block. She did give us the names of his buds. We're going to check them out now."

"And you want me to come? Are you sure they'll be home?"

"They will be if they know what's good for them. Darryl called them last night and told them it was home or here. All three picked home."

"Why not here, Alex?"

"You'll see, Matthew."

It turned out that my job was to wait until Klein and Kates were inside a suspect's house, then go around to the back and check their trashcans for crab shells. If I found any I was to recover them, ideally without attracting the attention of anyone in the house. Of course, part of Klein's job was to keep the suspect busy while I burgled their garbage. Once again I was glad I always carry plastic gloves with me.

When we got to the first house I waited until the detectives had gained entry then got out of the car. Counting houses to make sure I got the right one, I walked to the end of the alley. Then I started looking in all the trash cans, not just the suspect's. Had anyone asked, I was going to show them my ID and tell them a story about looking for a gun from a previous night's shooting. Like I said, everybody lies.

I can't say I came up empty. By the time I finished I had a very good idea of what the people in the 600 block of S. Kenwood Ave. ate, drank and considered disposable. Nobody had had crabs that weekend. If they did they'd buried the remains.

It was easier at the second suspect's house. He didn't believe in cans and had just left his trash in plastic bags at the end of his yard. Thanks to Baltimore's ever present population of dogs, rats and crows, both of his bags were ripped open, their contents spilling into the alley. This time I ignored the rest of the houses and went right up to his. My notebook in hand, I'd be an inspector from the Sanitation Department if anyone asked. I checked the refuse as thoroughly as possible — TV dinners, fast food packaging, more than his share of pizza boxes, but no crabs.

And the same with the third suspect's house, where I'd walked the alley again supposedly looking for a gun that probably wasn't there.

"No luck," I told Klein as I got back into his car. 'What about you guys, anyone confess?"

"No," Kates said, "they told us just what we expected them to — that they hadn't seen their good buddy Randy all weekend."

"Not exactly," Klein corrected, "the first one, Jimmy Hill, told us that he talked to Randy Friday at work, and asked him about catching the Oriole game on the tube. Said that in turning him down, Randy was quite graphic in describing what he'd hoped to do to Miss DeMarco that night. And of course that was the last time he saw Randy. Hill said he spent part of Saturday night at a bar, and the rest at home listening to the Birds on the radio."

"Wasn't it Hill was said that he'd called Randy Sunday morning and didn't get an answer?"

"Be a thing if he had, wouldn't it, Darryl? No, that was third guy, Joe Riley. Riley said he last talked to Randy Thursday. Called him to see if Randy wanted to spend the day at the Shore."

"What about the second guy?" I asked, just for something to say.

"Mickey Childress?" Alex answered. "If we'd been looking for clams instead of crabs we'd be done. A lot of 'yeahs', 'nos' and grunts that could have gone either way, but in the end he didn't see Randy either. He wasn't too clear on where he was, but it involved playing cards and drinking heavily."

"Well, that clears them. I'm sure nobody ever lies to the Baltimore PD."

"Grace, you are too new to be that cynical. Where to now, Alex?"

"Back home, Darryl. We'll write up the interviews and plan our next move."

Something still puzzled me. "Tell me again why this field trip. I understand going through the trash. But wouldn't it have been easier if the suspects were down in your office?"

"Matthew, think about how poor Randy was found, wrapped in cloth and plastic like you'd wrap crabs in newspaper. When Darryl and I went in each house, we took a good look around, checked the paint job to see if it matched the spatters on the tarp. About midway through the interview, one of us asked to use the bathroom. That gave us an excuse to see if our suspect had a new shower curtain, or better still, none at all. And once upstairs we peaked into the bedrooms to see if the sheets matched. And of course, Darryl had to throw his gum away."

"Which gave you an excuse to check out the kitchen trashcan for crab parts. Good thinking, I guess you guys really are detectives."

"It would have been good thinking if it worked, Grace. Right now let's hope that Trace or Latents came up with something. If not, we talk to those three again, this time in our house."

After Alex dropped me off, I checked with the analytical units. Latents had found mostly smears on the curtain, rust colored smears that smelled faintly of spice and vinegar, confirming that whoever had wrapped and bagged Fairweather had been eating crabs too. The few suitable prints that they developed were either not detailed enough to run through the computer or belonged to someone who wasn't in the system yet. Trace had also been busy — they provided a detailed list of how many crab shells had been in what layer of binding, and the color of each spot of paint on the tarp. They were still working on the bedsheet.

It was still far from quitting time. Crime doesn't stop in Baltimore just because there's an unsolved homicide. I finished what paperwork I had to do then hit the streets.

Three burglaries and a bank robbery later I was back in the office. There was a note from Klein that Parker wanted an update first thing in the morning. I got the lab sheets together and made a note to check with Trace again before going to the meeting. I'd also have to see if Klein's three suspects had records and make sure their prints were run against the ones found on the shower curtain.

I got in early the next morning, went over everything yet again. I started thinking about my trips through the alleys the day before and the cover story I didn't have to use. I wondered how Parker did it, stuck to the truth at all times and at all costs, in a world where no one else did. It made me glad to be on the forensic side of things, where the evidence may sometimes be misinterpreted but at least never lies.

It came to me in one of those "Oh Hell" moments, when you realize just what you missed and that it's probably too late to do anything about it. I found Ed, my supervisor, and told him I was checking out a van.

"Don't you have a meeting?" he asked.

"Yeah, call the Deacon and tell him I'm going to be late."

"He's not going to like that," is what I thought I heard Ed say as I ran out the door.

I probably was too late but I had to try. I was heading for a certain house on O'Donnell St., one whose address I had written down in my notes. It's normally a fifteen minute drive from Headquarters to Canton. Taking full advantage of the fact that, despite being a civilian, I was in truck with "POLICE" written big on either side, I did it in ten, which wasn't fast enough. As I pulled into the alley, I saw the garbage truck pulling out.

Damn, I had lost the race. I could still go back with my theory, but having some evidence in hand would have been better. Parker and I hadn't hit it off very well so far, and missing his meeting wasn't going to make things better.

I got out of my van. No cover story this time. No wanting to go back empty handed, I went up to house, checked the empty cans and found that sometimes the gods smile on desperate crime lab technicians.

As I packaged my find, my radio crackled my call number. "1815," I answered, fully expecting it to be Ed. It wasn't.

"6410 to 1815." The 6400 unit numbers were reserved for Homicide. The "10" marked a supervisor. I didn't need three guesses as to who it was. "You are holding up my meeting. Bring your notes, your reports and a good explanation." He gave me fifteen minutes to get there. I made it in twenty.

When I walked into the conference room I was met first by silence, then Parker's anger.

"Technician Grace, when I call a meeting I expect everyone to be present. Just what were you doing that was more important than working this case?"

I had gone into that room with all the intent in the world to apologize for being late, and then to calmly explain the reason why. But it was something about the way Parker looked at me, and yelled at me, and was so sure that he was right and I was going to be wrong. So instead I said, "I was out looking for clues. That is what I'm being paid to do, right?"

The frown on Parker's face deepened. "And did you find any?"

I ignored him. Instead I turned to Klein. "Alex, where were you when you talked to Sarah DeMarco the other day?"

"She wasn't home, so we interviewed her at work."

"So you wouldn't know if her bathroom had that new shower curtain smell or not?"

Klein looked stunned. He looked at Kates and said, "Damn, of all the simple things to miss."

"It didn't occur to me until this morning, until I remembered that in police work, everybody lies — present company excepted," I added with a nod toward Parker.

"And what was the result of this revelation, Technician Grace?" The sergeant asked, his frown gone, for the moment.

Explaining how I had just missed beating the garbage truck, I produced the evidence envelope in which I had stored the few bits of crab shells that had been left in Sarah DeMarco's trash can.

"DeMarco doesn't have a record," I said, remembering my notes. "We'll need her prints. And I'll call Trace and have them check the bedsheet for body fluids."

Parker wasn't listening. Instead, he was barking orders. "Detective Klein, bring that woman in here. Kates, get to work on a warrant for her house. I want this thing wrapped up today, before any more civilians have to do your jobs. Mr. Grace, how long before the DNA comes back off the sheet?"

"Assuming it's there, a few weeks at least."

"And unless she volunteers them, we can't take her prints without more than we've got."

"Judge Devereux may not approve a warrant on what we've got," Kates added.

"Then let's get more. And Grace ..."

"Yes, Sergeant?" For some reason I was expecting something like "good job." Foolish me.

"The next time you get a good idea, share it with others. If you had, Detective Klein might have been able to get a patrol car to the DeMarco house in time to catch the garbage truck. That's it, gentlemen."

Trace found some promising stains on the bedsheet, some of which matched Fairweather's blood type. We'd need a blood sample from a suspect to compare against the ones that didn't. And any conclusive results would take a few weeks.

As Kates predicted, Judge Devereux refused to grant a warrant based on our evidence. "What you have," he quoted her as saying, "is the suspect's blood type on the sheet he was wrapped in, and crab shells. If I were to sign a paper based on crab shells, you could lock up half of Baltimore on any given summer night."

Klein did manage to bring Sarah DeMarco in for questioning. She was in the box when I brought him the lab results, such as they were. While she hadn't asked for a lawyer, she was maintaining her right to silence.

"Alex, Hill and Childress had records, nothing serious, just the usual."

"Thanks Matthew. But let me guess the rest, the prints you got from the shower curtain don't match with either of them."

"Right, and Riley has so far managed to avoid arrest."

"So it's possible that he and DeMarco are in it together."

"Him and DeMarco?"

Look at her, Matthew." Alex pointed through the one-way glass. "She's not big enough to have dumped Fairweather all by herself. She had help."

Parker came up behind us. "Anything yet?"

"I'm about to go in, Sarge. Just thinking of the right approach to take."

Parker thought for a moment, then his face brightened. "Mr. Grace, have you submitted the shells from this morning?"

"Yes."

"Get them, and get the ones from Mr. Fairweather's bindings. This will be finished today."

I was back with the evidence in ten minutes. Parker took it into the interview room with him after telling Klein, "Watch, listen and learn."

"Miss DeMarco, I'm Detective Sergeant Parker," we heard through the speaker as we watched. "I understand that you've refused to be fingerprinted."

"Yeah, that's right," our suspect replied, "ain't no way you're taking my prints then saying they came from ... wherever it was you found Randy."

"Shame," Klein commented, "if she'd said 'shower curtain' that would have been the ball game."

"And I suppose you won't permit us to search your house?" Parker asked, knowing the answer.

DeMarco laughed at him. "So you can plant evidence? Again, no freaking way."

Parker shrugged. "Doesn't matter, we have enough to convince us of your involvement."

DeMarco didn't reply to this, but there was a slight attitude shift. You could almost see her thinking, "What did I miss?"

Parker showed her, bringing up the two evidence envelopes. "Miss DeMarco, in one of these bags I have shells from the crime scene. In the other, shells that we can associate with you. They match."

So, I thought, everybody lies — everybody.

The woman behind the glass straightened up a little, gave Parker her own shrug. "If you say you got shells, you're a liar. Randy was stabbed, not shot."

"And one for us," Klein said, "how did she know that?"

Parker didn't call her on it. "Crab shells, Miss DeMarco. Crab shells. Shells from a shower curtain, on which we have fingerprints. Shells from a tarp and a bedsheet. Shells from your garbage can. Crab shells. Did you know that crabs, like all living things, have their own DNA? DNA that can be matched to individual crabs? We're running DNA tests now, Miss DeMarco. So you see, I know who, I just need to know why?"

Sarah DeMarco looked at Parker, looked at him hard, somehow saw the truth in his eyes. She gave it up.

"It was his own damn fault. Him, Joey and me were eating the crabs at my house. Joey brought them over. I told Randy to let Joey have the last one, but no, Randy wanted it. So when Joey reaches for it, Randy whacks his hand with the crab mallet. Joey then picks up a knife and stabs Randy. Didn't mean to kill him."

"You could have called the police?" Parker offered.

"What, and let Joey go to jail over crabs?"

"Well, that's it," Klein said, switching off the speaker. "Now it's just routine follow-up."

"I thought you told me that the Deacon never lies."

"He doesn't, and he didn't. Even if we couldn't prove it, we knew that DeMarco was involved. And we are running DNA tests, just not on crabs."

"And what about the shells matching?"

"They're crab shells in one envelope, and crab shells in the other. It's not a good match, but it's still a match. Parker tricked her with the one thing she never expected — the truth."

"And now," Alex continued, "I have to tell Darryl to reapply for that search warrant. And a district car has to be sent for Joe Riley. As for me, I owe you lunch for solving my case for me. What'll it be?"

"What else, Alex?"

"Crabs," we said together.

CHILD'S PLAY

Murder scenes are noisy. There is the crackle and static of police radios, all tuned to different channels, all turned up so their users can hear their own. There is the professional conversation among patrol officers, detectives and technicians, discussing procedures, motives and evidence. There is the unprofessional chatter, the small talk about the job, the wife, the ballgame. If the victim was unlucky enough to die in an undignified or embarrassing manner, there are the tasteless jokes at his expense, unfunny anywhere else, nervous laughter keeping the grimness of death at bay. If the death occurred outdoors, add in the noise of the traffic and of the crowd. Murder scenes are always noisy.

Except when a cop dies.

When a cop is killed, the scene becomes a church. Radios are turned down, people talk in whispers. There is no small talk, and nothing is funny. The crowd is cautious, aware of the officers' mood, afraid of the anger waiting to be expressed.

I got to the scene shortly after Detective Alexander Klein. Leaving my equipment in the van, I walked up to the house to review the scene. As I went in, the cop at the door said, "Careful," and nodded at the floor near the stairs. There were drops of blood making a trail down the steps and into the dining room. I sidestepped the blood and went over to Klein, who was still getting the basic details from the primary officer, the first on the scene.

"She's up on the second floor, detective. You want to see her now?"

Klein noticed me as the officer was asking his question. He nodded hello, and I copied information out of his notebook as he answered, "No, we'll start at the back and work our way up."

Except for an officer at the front door and one at the back gate, we three were alone. All the other responding officers and detectives were outside. Some were canvassing the neighborhood, looking for evidence, talking to neighbors, hoping for a witness. Those not working were waiting. They were waiting for us to perform a miracle, to work magic and pull a name from what we found. With the name would come a focus for their anger, someone to pursue, someone they hoped would resist.

The house in which Clair Douglas was killed was a row house on Dundalk Avenue in southeast Baltimore City. Behind the block of houses was a large, undeveloped lot, separated from the back yards by an alley. As we walked from the kitchen into the back yard, I looked at the paved alley. No tiretracks there; maybe in the lot. Officer David Campbell began his tour.

"The phone cord's been cut." He pointed to a wire running down the back of the house. "And as you probably saw, the back door's been kicked in."

I took a closer look at the door. As the crime laboratory technician assigned to this scene, the gathering of evidence was my responsibility. I could see faint shoemarks on the lock stile and center rail. In what was left of the locks I could see no signs of forced entry, no prymarks or pick scratches. The deadbolt had held. The screws holding it had not.

Except for the back door, nothing on the first floor appeared to have been disturbed. The door from the kitchen to the basement was open. Campbell explained, "The basement door was open when we got here. We checked down there, didn't find anything."

Klein and I nodded. We would both check later.

We went upstairs, careful to avoid the blood drops on the steps. The house had three bedrooms, all on the second floor. The master bedroom was in front; two smaller bedrooms were in the rear. Campbell indicated the right rear room. As we approached, he pointed out three holes in the wall opposite the bedroom door and a bullet on the floor beneath them. I would have to dig the others out later. There were heavier drops of blood on the floor there and at the entrance to the room.

Clair Douglas was lying face down on the bedroom floor. Her head was pointing toward us as we stood in the doorway, her legs collapsed beneath her. Near her right hand was a BPD issued 9mm, a cartridge case jammed in the chamber. To her right and behind her were several cartridge cases. There were more holes in the rear wall.

It occurred to Klein before it did to me. "Where's the kid?" he asked. As he did, I noticed the room for the first time as a room and not as a crime scene. The wallpaper was rabbits, no, bunnies and ducks in blue and yellow. The bed was too small for an adult. The base of a lamp was another duck, and stuffed animals, blocks, games and toys were everywhere. A blackboard stood in the near corner, a dollhouse in the far right. There was a cartridge case on its dining room floor.

"One of the guys outside used to work with Douglas," answered Campbell. "He said she's divorced. Her ex has a real job, and he and his new wife have custody. Douglas only sees the girl on her weekends off."

"Anybody been notified?" asked Klein.

"Not yet. We made a quick search for an address book or phone numbers. Didn't find anything, but we didn't want to tear things apart until you guys got done."

Tired of looking everywhere but at the body, we moved into the hallway. Klein turned to me. "Matthew, the usual good job. Pictures, prints, anything else you can think of. Hell, everything else you can think of. You gonna need any help?"

"I think I'd rather do this one alone." Like him, I got better results working by myself. It takes longer, but it gets results.

"Then I'll get out of your way and talk to the brass."

"Try to keep them outside."

"They'll stay out. I'll have a 'biohazard' tape strung across the front door. They won't want to come near it."

Klein left to brief the command staff who had gathered. He would then talk to whatever witnesses the uniformed officers had found. I took another look around the house, got my equipment and went to work.

I photographed everything, taking overall shots of the rooms and the front and back of the house as well as close-ups of the evidence. I drew a diagram showing the position of the evidence and of Douglas. Any surface that might have been touched by the killer was dusted for prints. I had cut out the bloodstained pieces of carpet and was packaging the cartridge cases when the M.E. arrived. While the doctor was making her examination, I took the back door off its hinges and collected the severed phone cord. After the body had been removed, I was free to cut the bullets out of the wall. Finally I was done. When I left, only the officers protecting the scene were still there. Some of the neighbors were still standing on their porches, watching and wondering what was happening to their city.

It was late when I got back to headquarters. The people in the analytical units, the ones who worked "normal" hours, were getting ready to go home for the day. They stayed. The latent print examiners started sorting through the lifts I had recovered from the scene, entering the good ones into the AFIS computer. Firearms experts began examining the cartridge cases and bullets, and the Trace Evidence Unit started work on the blood evidence. Whatever their previous plans had been for that evening, no one was in a hurry to leave.

I finished my reports and everything else I had to do and went home. It was late, and I was tired, so sleep came easy, despite the day's activities. The next morning I picked up the results of everyone's hard work and got to the homicide unit just in time for the initial crime scene review and progress report.

Sergeant Joshua Parker was in charge. He was Klein's immediate supervisor. He had been on yesterday's scene just long enough to get the needed information and to determine that Klein had everything under control. He had spent the rest of the day coordinating activities outside the house. He'd just started the meeting when I came in.

"So nice of you to join us, Mr. Grace," he said politely, letting just enough sarcasm through.

"Sorry, Deacon, church ran late."

Parker was an elder at a small church in the Park Circle area. That's how he got his nickname. That and the fact that he has never been known to tell a lie, to a co-worker, a suspect, or, most surprisingly, a superior. He pretended to ignore my remark and turned to Klein.

"Detective Klein, would you please start again for the benefit of the latecomers?"

"Yes, sir." Klein repressed a smile before he continued. He knew as well as I did that Parker hated his nickname, and that only a civilian like myself could get away with using it to his face.

"Southeast got a call at 0905 yesterday morning. A neighbor walking her dog noticed the open back door. Campbell here was the first on the scene, and he found the body."

Klein paused. It was a little easier here, at headquarters, a day later, but it was still a cop who had died. That made it personal. And difficult to treat as just another case. It reminded us how routine and business-like death had become.

"According to the M.E.," Klein continued, "Death occurred early yesterday morning, sometime after one A.M. Cause was a single gunshot wound in the heart. She was struck twice more; neither would have been fatal."

"Where else was she hit?" asked another detective.

"Left shoulder and arm, both through and through. I think Matthew dug the shots out of the wall." I nodded a yes. "The heart shot stayed in. I got it from the M.E. at the autopsy."

He took a small plastic bag out of his pocket and laid on the table. The bullet inside it was a .38, the same kind of bullet some of the people looking at it still used in their guns, the kind most drug dealers have stopped using.

"Department issue?" someone asked, less a joke than a worried idea we all had. All cops are brothers and sisters, but not all families get along.

"Don't know. We'll find out once I submit it to Firearms." Klein put the bullet away.

"Describe the scene, please." Parker clearly wanted to move away from uncomfortable speculation, but there was a scowl on his face that told me we would be coming back to this subject.

Campbell started off, with Klein filling in details as he went. I passed around copies of the crime scene photographs and diagrams as they talked. There were the usual questions that we answered as best we could. As he concluded, Klein asked, "Matthew, any results from all your work?"

They all waited for the magic words. I didn't have any and told them so. "Nothing from the computer. Most of the prints were Douglas's, but there were a few unidentified suitables, mainly from the back door, handrail and bedroom door frame. Mostly palm prints. Give us a name, and we'll match them."

"You hope!" This from Rich Arnold, the newest addition to the ever growing homicide unit. His fascination with the forensic sciences had rapidly turned to disappointment when he learned how little they help to solve murders. His role in this investigation was to watch and learn, and to run the errands that Klein didn't have the time or inclination to do.

"What else've you got from the Negative Results Unit?"

I let his remarks pass. I would remind him of it one day when a witness folded and all he had left was a fingerprint to put his suspect on the scene.

"The cartridge cases in the bedroom were all from Douglas's gun. So were the bullets from the hallway floor and wall. All standard issue. No blood on any of them. I got four bullets from the wall behind her. Alexander's makes five. Of the four, I've got two that can be matched if you find the right gun. All came from a .38."

Parker leaned forward to interrupt and I anticipated him. "Nothing from the open case file either, Sarge." He leaned back again, and I continued, "Shoeprints from the back door, cut marks from the phone cord, it's the same story. Get us the work boots and cutters that made them, and we'll match them up for you."

I slid the technical information, style of shoe, type of cutter, and so forth, over to Klein.

"Finally, there was enough blood in the hallway for analysis. Trace came up with A-positive blood and a string of genetic markers. Douglas is O-positive. Trace has sent a sample off for DNA work as well."

Parker seemed satisfied that nothing had been missed. What pleased Klein and him the most, and what Arnold had missed, was that there was evidence that could not be explained away by the killer.

"What about the husband?" Parker asked.

"Ex-husband," Klein reminded him. "I questioned him about five yesterday afternoon. He called us when he heard the news on the radio. He had been on the road all day."

"What's he do?" asked Campbell.

"Sales rep, repairs for a local business machine company."

"You have a paraffin test done?" Campbell was a thirty-year man looking to make it forty. When he started, hot wax was used to collect gunshot residue from a suspect's hands. Today we use an adhesive and look at it under an electron microscope. It is much more efficient but not as much fun.

"GSR," I corrected. "I took the samples about six o'clock yesterday. Trace is running them now, but don't expect anything. They were collected more than twelve hours after the shooting. He'd probably washed his hands a dozen times, and he probably didn't do it."

"What about it, Klein? Does Mr. Douglas look good as a suspect?"

"Actually, Sergeant, his name is Jack Bracken. Douglas went back to her maiden name when they split.

"He's a suspect, of course, just because he's the ex. He says he was home in bed that night, and his wife backs him up. She would, of course. But there's no motive that we know of, and he hasn't been shot."

"You've made sure of that?"

"Well, I asked him when I picked him up at his house if he'd be willing to be examined by a doctor, and he went one better. He stripped down right in his living room. No extra holes in him."

I chimed in. "What about his wife? Could she be the shooter?"

"Again, no motive. Jealousy, maybe, if she thought Bracken and Douglas were getting friendly again. But it's not likely. Besides, no bullet wounds."

He paused for effect, watching our faces. Before any of us could ask, he continued, "No, I didn't. Not that it wouldn't have been more enjoyable than examining Bracken, and she did offer, with her husband present, but I had a female officer and a nurse examine her at St. Lucy's. No wounds."

"Just to be sure, ask them for their prints."

"Already taken, Sergeant, Matthew …"

"Latents checked this morning. No matches."

"Who else looks good?"

"Nobody looks really good, Sarge. Clair did a year in internal investigations. Rich, what did you find out from IID?"

"I checked with Lieutenant Tomin. He doesn't recall that Douglas handled any major complaints, just routine brutality beefs. Nobody lost any serious time or got fired on any of them. He's going to check. Say, listen …"

Arnold had something to add. He had been fidgeting in his seat ever since he'd looked at the crime scene photographs. Parker cut him off.

"I checked with upstairs. Officer Douglas had not filed any harassment complaints, or any other complaints, against anyone in the department, so that rules that out. Klein, you and Arnold will have to check at her district. Let's pray that this one isn't in the family."

"Amen," a few of us, including me, answered, none of us mockingly. In the pause Arnold started to tell us his idea, but again his timing was off and Parker continued.

"Who else have we got?"

Klein turned to Campbell, who referred to his notes before reporting. "We checked the whole neighborhood. Nobody heard or saw anything that could help. A few heard what they thought might have been shots, about one thirty, but either couldn't place them or didn't care enough to call them in. The house to the left of Douglas is vacant, waiting for renters. To the right live a couple in their eighties, old eighties. They wouldn't have heard shots in their own bedroom, much less next door.

"Of the people we talked to, nobody can remember any trouble Douglas had with anyone. Nobody said anything bad about her, either.

"My sergeant is back at the Southeast now. He and the property crimes guys are going over the files. By the end of the day you'll have a list of the local burglars and troublemakers."

Klein had by now noticed Arnold's attempts to interrupt. It was like Alexander not to give him a chance. New guys got treated like that. As Campbell finished, Klein started up before Arnold could.

"There are three people we've found who might have wanted Clair Douglas dead, and been able to follow through. Andrea Johnson is first. Johnson started holding drugs for a Pennsylvania Avenue drug dealer. He got killed, and she inherited the business. Douglas kept busting her, she kept getting out. Now it's personal, especially since Johnson filed a brutality complaint after each arrest. Her next trial is in two weeks, and she is looking at a long stay. Douglas is, was, the only witness. Johnson will walk, again.

"Next up is Anthony Lee. Five years ago he tried to hold up a Korean grocer in the Eastern. Douglas walked in and shot him before he could shoot her. He just got out and might have wanted a payback.

"The last is 'in family.'"

Some of us had only been half listening. Klein's last statement had all our attention. Even Arnold stopped fidgeting.

"Sarge, you were probably right when you said that Douglas hadn't filed any harassment complaints. But she did witness something between an academy instructor and a cadet when she was last up there for in-service training. Apparently the instructor put his hands where he shouldn't have. The cadet talked to Clair, who told her to file a complaint. She was to do it today. Without Clair, it's his word against hers. With Clair, his career was over and so, I imagine, were his pension and marriage."

"How did you learn about this?" asked Parker, who clearly had not liked Klein's "probably" remark.

"The cadet called me this morning when she heard the news. The instructor's name is Kevin Reynolds. And yes, he has a history. Two shootings, one of them questionable, in three years got him off the streets and into Education and Training."

"Any results?"

"Matthew would tell you that Latent Prints is checking their prints right now. Oddly enough, all three are A-positive. We'll need a court order for any further blood work. If there's a print match, we'll go ahead. If not, we'll keep looking - at them, and anyone else we can find."

One of the other detectives sitting in on the review asked, "What about Reynolds? Can't he be ordered to submit to a blood test? He's with the department."

"He's also a murder suspect," Parker countered. "We can't treat him any differently. If he is the one, and we force him to do anything, some judge might say we violated his rights and we'll lose the case. What is it, Detective Arnold?"

Surprised at suddenly being given the floor, Arnold stammered at first, trying to get all his words out at once. Finally, conscious that, except for the Crime Lab, everyone looking at him, waiting for him, was a superior, he calmed down, took a deep breath, and made his big play.

"Well, let's look at what probably happened." He stopped, expecting a rebuke, a remark, someone to tell him to shut up. None of us did. We would have reviewed that anyway; now was a good time.

"Go on, Detective Arnold," Parker encouraged him.

"Okay, Douglas was either awake, or she woke up when her killer kicked the door in. Either way she knew someone was coming in. Maybe she tries to call 911 but the phone was out. She gets her gun out of the nightstand or from someplace. Grace, you found the holster on her bed, right?" I nodded, and he went on.

"She went into her kid's room. Why? There were other places upstairs better suited for an ambush. I would have lain at the top of the stairs and shot as he came up. There's only one reason she went into that room."

He paused. He was Ellery Queen and we were the readers. He wanted us to guess. Actually, he wanted us to guess and be wrong. Then he would show us up. None of spoke, and after waiting a beat too long for effect, he let us in on his discovery.

"Look at this -" he picked through the crime scene photographs and selected two "- and this." He showed them around. One was an overall of the room, showing the toys. The next one was taken out of the bedroom window looking down on the alley.

I knew what he was going to say. I wanted him to say it, was waiting for him to say it, especially after his "negative results" crack.

"She knew who it was who'd broken in. Maybe she recognized the car, but somehow she knew.

"Look at the room, a blackboard, magnetic letters, spelling blocks. She went into her daughter's room to leave us a dying clue in case the killer got her."

The laughter that followed was not a loud, mocking laughter, but rather the low chuckling of veterans at a common rookie mistake. Arnold reddened, at first not understanding. When he caught on, it was too late to pretend that he'd been joking. Not that we would have believed him.

Parker, who had not been amused, said sternly, "Detective Arnold, when you were told to study investigative procedures, did you think that Christie and Allingham were on the reading list?"

Klein had not laughed either. It is considered bad form to laugh at your partner, however temporary and junior he might be, when others are present.

"Rich," he said consolingly, "that wasn't a bad idea. Not an especially good one, but you tried. It's more likely that Douglas went into the bedroom to see what was going on out back and got trapped in there. But if it was a dying clue, where is it? What was it?"

Arnold had no answer.

"Sorry about that, Rich," said one of the other detectives. He wasn't sorry, but it's something you have to say. "A lot of us forget we were new once, and a lot of new detectives forget that this isn't like TV.

"You know, even if Douglas had left a clue, the killer would have seen it first. He would have erased the blackboard or something like that. Nice try, though." This last was said with a barely disguised grin that didn't help Arnold at all.

After Arnold's first try at crime solving, the discussion became one of possible lines of investigation and further leads. It wasn't long before we were repeating ourselves. Parker closed the meeting.

As we were leaving, Klein asked, "Matthew, an early lunch?"

"Beats fighting crime. Give me time to report to my director, and I'll meet you out on Frederick Street. A half hour."

We ate at Nicky's, one of the many small restaurants and carry-outs around the HQ building that depended on hungry cops to keep them in business. Klein had his usual burger, fries and soda. I ate a baked potato with something that might have been cheese poured over it. We talked as we ate, about a dozen things unrelated to police work. Gradually, though, we worked our way back to the murder.

"Matthew, what would you have done if you had been Douglas?"

"Jumped out a window. I don't have a gun."

"You would have if you had been Douglas. Would you have gone into a back room?"

"Maybe, if I heard the door breaking and wanted to know who it was. The alley light is just outside her house. A car parked there could have been seen. If the killing were personal, she might have recognized the car."

"Johnson's she would have, she'd impounded it enough. I don't know if she would have recognized anyone else's car. But Rich had a point. Why did she go into her daughter's room?"

"Why not? She had to go somewhere. Maybe she figured that if the killer went into the front bedroom she'd have a better chance coming out the back. We'll never know."

"If she had been threatened, she might not have taken it serious enough to report it, but she might have taken precautions."

"Like learning what car the guy, or gal, drove, in case someone started following her."

We ate in silence for awhile. Toward the end of our meal, Klein asked, "What if Rich was right?"

"It would be a first."

"No, I'm serious. Just because the idea sounds like it came out of a British manor house doesn't mean we shouldn't pursue it. Not everything is Chandler and McBain."

"Alexander, what are you suggesting?"

"We go back and look."

"Alex, you are a very good detective. I am a very good crime scene man. We are both trained observers. If there had been a 'dying clue,' one of us would have seen it. And Danny was right. If it was out where we could see it, and Douglas didn't have time to be clever, the killer would have found it and removed it, or erased it."

"Maybe we didn't see it because we weren't looking for it. We're going back."

Okay, but don't tell Arnold."

An hour after lunch, Klein and I were standing in the room where Clair Douglas had been killed. We were looking at her daughter's toys, trying to transmute them into oracles. The blackboard had been wiped clean, as had the crayon board on its reverse side. Fingerprint powder on the crayon board failed to reveal any residual message. The letter blocks were arranged in their tray, none missing, no words spelled out. A metal board that looked like a child's school slate held several rows of magnetic plastic letters, in no particular order, again not spelling any words.

Klein spent several minutes contemplating the possible meaning of the cartridge case I had previously found in the dollhouse. When he asked me if I thought a rubber snake on a shelf could be an eel, which is "Lee" spelled backwards, I told him it was time to go. There was no hidden message, no final clue. Reluctantly, he agreed.

While I was packing my kit, Klein took a last look around. Later, the house would be turned over to Douglas's parents, so this was his last look. I picked up my bag as Klein asked, "Matthew, how many letters in the alphabet?"

"Twenty-six."

"How many on that magnetic board?"

I counted. "Thirty."

"How many vowels?"

"Eleven." Some were doubled or tripled.

"Which leaves how many?"

"Nineteen."

"There should be at least twenty-one. What's missing?"

I looked at the board, ran through the alphabet. I got as far as *K*. It wasn't there. Neither was the *R*.

I said to Klein, "I don't know what's worse, that it was him or that Arnold was right."

The warrant on Reynold's house was served while he was at the academy. He was detained and advised of his rights. The officers assigned to guard him made the mistake of treating him like a cop and not as an armed suspect. Before he could be stopped, Reynolds saved the state the cost of a trial.

I was on another scene when all that happened. Later I talked to Klein.

"We found the letters in his pocket when we searched the body."

"Why would he have kept them?" I asked him. "It would have been easy enough to put them back on the board."

"He panicked, I guess, or he was in a hurry. He might not have expected a gun battle, and all those shots did make a lot of noise."

"What happens now?"

"The usual. The department issues a statement, you know, 'Tragic events, et cetera,' and everybody but us forgets about two dead cops. You and I finish lunch and wait for our next call."

Klein was right. That's all that happened. That's all that ever happens.

A WALK IN THE PARK

Hilton Parkway is a snake of a road. Connecting North Ave. with Edmondson Ave. in Southwest Baltimore, it has more twists and turns than a well-paced thriller. Even good drivers on clear, dry days slow down when driving it out of respect for its treachery.

Susan Lancione was not a good driver. Neither was she a sober one. And it was not a clear dry day. It was instead a cold, wet Friday night in January.

Susan turned off Edmondson onto Hilton Parkway just after midnight. Driving north, she negotiated the first turn without a problem, but the alcohol in her system caused her to over steer during the second. She missed the third altogether. That sent her off the road, down a hill and into the trees of Gwynn Falls Park.

When she woke up, Susan found that her car had wedged itself between two trees, making it impossible to open its doors. She could roll the windows down, but the same trees kept her from climbing out. The back windows opened only from the side, to provide ventilation. They were too small for her to crawl through anyway. Unable to leave the car, she did the only thing she could. She went back to sleep.

Officer Kevin Miller was on routine patrol when he noticed the broken guard rail. Looking past it into the trees, he could see the red glow from Susan's tail lights. He pulled onto the shoulder, radioed for help, put on his flashers and bar lights and said a quick prayer that the driver was not too badly hurt. Then he grabbed his high powered flashlight and without much thought to his pride, clothing or possible broken bones he descended the slippery hill and followed the muddy tracks to Susan's car.

Falling only twice, Miller finally made it to the car. He quickly determined that, except for some bruises, Ms. Lancione was uninjured and that there was nothing he could do for her. He again used his radio, this time to request the appropriate emergency equipment.

By three in the morning, everyone thought that it was almost over. The crew from CP-11, the police department's emergency unit, had set up generator-powered lights and had strung a rope between the road and the trees to assist those going up and down and to keep them from getting as muddy as Officer Miller. The fire department's emergency team had almost finished cutting Susan out of her car and the paramedics were standing by to treat her once she was free. That was when the cold, the rain and the three cups of coffee he had drank that night got to Officer Miller.

Without drawing attention to himself he took a long walk back into the trees. He came back by a slightly different path and that was when he tripped over the body.

***

I was not in a good mood when I arrived on the scene. I work for the Baltimore Police Department as a crime scene technician. It's my job to document the scene and to search for and recover physical evidence. I enjoy my work, most of the time. Tonight was not one of those times. Processing the scene of a suspicious death at three-thirty in the morning, in the cold, the rain and the mud is not my idea of fun. Swearing softly, I put on my best professional demeanor and got out of my van.

The first person I talked to was Detective Alexander Klein. Klein was sitting in an unmarked car just slightly ahead of the break in the guard rail. The engine was running and he had the heater on. He looked warm and dry and I hated him for that. Seeing me approach in his rear view mirror, he rolled down his window.

"Matthew Grace, how are you this fine morning?"

"Get out of that car and see how fine it is. You got this one, Alexander?"

"No, if I had this one I'd be down in the muck. Arnold's got it. As senior man I elected to stay up here and coordinate things, staying available if he needs help."

"And if he needs help?"

"I'll use my radio and call for some, and wait right here until it arrives. This is a new suit, and unless that's the mayor down there with a knife in her back, I'm staying where it's warm and dry."

Klein did have the information I needed to get started, names, numbers, things like that. I went back to my van, put what equipment I would need in a back pack and very carefully made my way down the hill.

I disappointed everyone watching me by not falling or getting anything muddy but my shoes. Seeing Detective Rich Arnold, I walked over to him and gave him the usual greeting.

"Hi, Agatha, how's it going?"

At that time, Rich Arnold was one of the newest of the detectives assigned to homicide. A few months before this, he had been instrumental in solving Baltimore's only homicide in which the victim left a "dying clue." Someone, he rightly suspects me, hung the nickname "Agatha Christie" on him and it stuck. He is not sure how to take it. In one hand it does remind everyone of his accomplishment. On the other, very few men like being called "Agatha."

As usual, he ignored my greeting and filled me in on everything that had happened, from Ms. Lancione's accident up to Officer Miller's unexpected find.

"Really, Grace, there's not a lot that needs to be done. The body's been there awhile, there's some decomposition and the animals have been at it. If there were any shoeprints the rain's washed them away. I'll just need photos and a sketch of the scene. Recover anything that looks like it might be evidence, but don't go too far afield. It may not be a homicide. Can't tell with the shape the body's in. I'll have a man posted just in case. If the autopsy does come back murder, I'll have the academy class come down and do a line search of the area. With luck, it's just some homeless guy dead of exposure."

Lucky for us, one less case to close. Not so lucky, I thought, for the poor guy whose body was going to the Medical Examiner's Office on Penn St. Either way, I had the same amount of work to do, and the sooner I did it, the sooner I would be warm and dry.

The victim had been a big man, weighing at least 300 pounds when he was alive. He was laying face down, his face in the mud, his arms spread out as if he had tried to break his fall. From what I could see, none of his pockets had been turned out, so if it was a murder, robbery may not have been the motive.

I started by photographing the body from several angles. I always do this first, that way the detective or the Medical Examiner's crew are free to examine the body, since its original position and condition has already been recorded. I then backed up, and photographed the body in relation to its surroundings, which in this case consisted of a clearing and a lot of trees, with the generator-powered lights casting odd shadows as I walked my circle around the victim.

Not wanting to be caught on film, Arnold and the officers stayed back as I took my pictures. By the time I was finished, they had been joined by the crew from the Medical Examiner's Office.

As one of the M.E.'s people took some Polaroid photos for their records the other got ready to do her preliminary examination of the body. She put on disposable coveralls, a mask, eye shields and rubber gloves (you can't be too careful these days.) Starting from the top, she carefully felt her way around the scalp. She stopped when she got to the back of the neck.

"There's a hole here, just above the hairline. From the size I'd say about 9mm's worth."

"Damn! You sure, Sheila?"

"Detective, when you see as many bodies as I do in this city, you get to know what a wound from a nine looks like."

Arnold was none too happy about that. Now he'd have to wake up early and go to the autopsy, as well as spend more time on the scene, wet and dark as it was, then he had planned.

We waited while Sheila finished her once over of the body. She checked the back pockets. Nothing there. I stopped her before she and her partner could flip our victim over onto the collapsible cart.

"Wait. Rich, before things get moved too much more, aren't you forgetting something?"

"What now, Grace?"

"If that is a 9mm hole, there's a 9mm casing somewhere about."

"Unless they shot him somewhere else and just dumped him here."

"Look at him. He's three hundred if he's a pound and over six and a half feet long. Would you carry him if you didn't have to?"

"Sheila, what's the wound look like?"

"Good thing I got this mask on, Detective, or I'd have to charge you extra. This sucker's a couple of days gone and getting really ripe."

Sheila borrowed a high beam flash from an officer and got up close and personnel with the victim. "From what I can see, powder burns around the hole. Close contact wound. You find the gun, there'll be bits of him inside the barrel."

I looked at Arnold. He nodded agreement as he said, "Okay, somebody could have marched him out here. It would be easier than carrying him. You want a metal detector or are you going to go down on your hands and knees to look for the brass?"

"Just a minute." It's not often I get to play Sherlock Holmes, but this looked like a good time to try. Most semi-automatic weapons eject their shell casings to the back and to the right. Taking the bright light from Sheila, I stood at the feet of the body, where the victim should have been standing when shot. Turning to my right, I swept the high beam back and forth over the ground working my way backwards. I got lucky, and was rewarded with a glint of rain washed metal a few feet away from where I was. Arnold walked over to the spot while I kept it highlighted with the flash. He looked down and nodded.

"Lucky, Grace, lucky."

"Rather be lucky than good, Rich. Stay there, will you, while I get my camera and an evidence envelope."

Sheila and her partner finished with the victim about the time I finished with what I had to do in that area. I started my crime scene diagram near the body and worked outward, so that when it was time to help carry the body up the muddy hill I was at the far end of the operation. I got to watch as Arnold was pressed into service. It's a good thing he wasn't wearing his new suit.

It was well into Saturday morning by the time I finished my reports and submitted what little evidence I recovered from the scene. There was not a lot in that submission to help Arnold solve this one. A gun would have to be found to match against the cartridge case, and the soil and vegetation samples would likewise wait until a suspect was developed. Then we could compare them with similar samples recovered from his clothing, home and car. I called Arnold and left him with that cheery thought before going home.

I was off duty for what was left of the weekend. Sunday we changed shifts so instead of working 10 p.m. to 6 a.m., Monday I reported at the more decent hour of two in the afternoon. As soon as I got in, I found a note to see Klein up in the Homicide offices.

I found Klein at his desk. In a room normally occupied by eight or nine detectives, Klein was sitting alone, reading reports.

"Hi, Alex, where are Agatha and the Deacon?"

"I thought you promised to stop calling him that."

"Only to his face."

I should explain that not everyone in the department has a nickname. Klein does not have one, neither do I. "The Deacon" is Sergeant Joshua Parker, Klein and Arnold's supervisor. He got the name because, besides being an elder in his church, he also has the reputation of being the most honest man in the BPD. He has never been known to have told a lie, to anyone, for any reason.

Few people call Parker "Deacon" to his face. I used to, but stopped after the sergeant paid a visit to the Director of the Crime Lab. As Director Thomas put it, "Fun's fun, Grace, but if he wants to eat a man has to have a job."

"Rich and the Sarge had to leave. I'm supposed to fill you in and then send you off to meet them."

"New evidence in the park murder?"

Klein nodded. "They found the victim's car."

"Where?"

"On Franklintown, where it cuts through the park." Klein opened the case folder on the desk in front of him.

"We've identified the body. The dead guy is, or was, Harry Winslow, reported missing by his wife last Wednesday."

"How did you ID him? From what I saw, the fingers were pretty much gone."

"They were. We had to rely on plain old-fashioned police work, Matthew."

"Such as?"

"We searched his pockets and found his driver's license. His wife made the ID."

"Any suspects, Alex?"

"Sure, his wife, girl friend if he's got one, all of the people he worked with and half the lowlifes on the west side."

"Any real leads."

"If so, Rich has got them, it's his case, remember?"

"Alex, how is it that when you two pair up, Rich always gets stuck with the whodunits and you get the ones with the killer standing over the body screaming a confession?"

"Experience, Matthew, experience. When Rich gets it, he'll know how to dump the hard ones on his partner, which, by that time, will be someone else." Klein closed the case folder and stood up.

"Well, Matthew, you've got a car to dust. You'll find some prints, the computer will match them up, Rich will take the credit and another case will be closed."

Monday's drive to the park was definitely more pleasant than Friday night's. This time I was driving out there at the start of my shift, rather than near the end. The sun was shining, and the temperature was promising to break forty for the first time since New Year's Eve. It was a good day to spend outside.

The only two vehicles I saw as I pulled onto Franklintown were a marked patrol car and a very big Lincoln. That made sense. Our victim had been a big man, and big men need the room a big car gives them. I looked around for the unmarked car the Homicide Squad usually drives. Unless they were parked behind a tree, they were not on the scene.

The Southwest officer guarding the car eased out of her cruiser when she saw me pull up. She came over to meet me and we walked to the Lincoln together.

"Where's Homicide?"

"The Sergeant said that they had more important things to do than wait for you. He told me to tell you just to take pictures. I'm supposed to call a tow truck and have it taken to headquarters. The Sarge said you can dust and search it back there."

"So what you're telling me is that instead of spending a nice sunny day in the park with you, I get to go back to that dimly lit, poorly ventilated garage all by myself?" I gave her my best smile.

"Afraid so. Life's rough, isn't it?" She gave me what was probably her second or third best smile in return and I got to thinking that maybe I'd have plans for after work.

"Did the good sergeant say anything else?"

"Only that you were to call Homicide when you were finished."

"And what about the other detective - he say anything?"

"Not much, just asked me out to dinner." I don't know what bothered me more. That Arnold had asked before I could, or that we had the same taste in women.

"And?"

"I told him that I'd have to ask my husband and get back to him." Then she gave me her number one smile and went back to her cruiser to call a tow truck.

After photographing the car, I looked around, first inside the car, then the surrounding area. No blood, no other cartridge cases, nothing to indicate a struggle. Since it had been almost a week since Winslow had been killed, I really wasn't expecting to find anything. Still, I had to look, sometimes you get lucky.

What I did find were some foot paths from the road into the park. I followed the most likely one until it became clear that it lead away from the clearing where Winslow was found. So did the second most likely. The third trail led me straight to the murder scene.

When Klein told me that the victim's car had been found on a road through the park, I had hoped there would be some direct connection to the scene. Before leaving I had packed the video camera that had been seized from a drug dealer and now belonged to the Laboratory Division. I got the camera from my van and retraced my steps. I started recording with the Lincoln, showing where it was on Franklintown Rd., then followed the first two trails until their direction away from the scene became apparent. After that I went down the third trail, keeping the tape going until I came to the small clearing where Harry Winslow had been found face down in the mud.

I normally do not use a video camera on crime scenes. The images it captures are too fleeting. You can hold the camera on a body or a bloodstain for a minute or five minutes, but you still have to move away, and the image you want to leave with the jury is replaced by something less impressive, less threatening. A video tape shown in court is too much like television, and I'd sooner not be associated with TV crime shows, where all too often the first one arrested is not the guilty party.

A photograph stays with you. Hold a picture of a murder victim in your hand. Look away. Look back and the victim is still there. A photograph can be enlarged and placed in the courtroom for all to see. It doesn't go away. In this video age of quick cuts and sound bites, a still picture of a crime is something special.

Yet video has its uses. And today it was the best way to visually link the location of the car with the crime scene.

I left the scene when the tow truck arrived. An hour later I was in HQ garage still waiting for it to bring in the Lincoln. A half hour later the Lincoln finally showed up and was parked next to the other cars that had been towed in that day. There were two there that had been stolen in carjackings. They would wait until the next shift started and could spare the people to do them. Another car belonged to a suspect involved in a rape. That had come in the day before and we were still waiting for the detective to get the warrant signed so we could start on that. Another car or two and we'd be full up and have to put the overflow in the spaces reserved for the command staff.

With half the day wasted already, I got right to work on the Lincoln.

Searching a car for evidence is not any different from processing any other crime scene, except that everything comes to you in one nice neat package. You just have to open it up and take out what you need. I had already photographed the car in the park, but I took a few more of the interior and exterior just to show that the car towed into the garage was the same one that had been found in the park.

The Lincoln was clean. Mr. Winslow had kept his car neater than most people do their houses. Nothing on the floor but the mats, no trash in the back seat, the ashtrays had never been used. And, of course, in another more thorough search for blood, cartridge cases and possible weapons I struck out completely.

I removed the floor mats and packaged them for submission to the Trace Evidence Unit. The criminalist who received the mats would examine them for hairs and fibers that the person who had left the car in the park may have left behind. For the same reason, even though it did not need it, I vacuumed the inside of the car, trying to pick up those same hairs and fibers that may have missed the mat. I made a note to remind Arnold to get comparison samples from Winslow's body.

After everything had been collected, I was then free to dust the car for prints without worrying about the fingerprint powder contaminating any evidence. Normally, with a car the size of the Lincoln I would expect to recover between twenty to thirty fingerprint lifts. This time, with the rain having washed off the outside and Winslow's apparent cleaning fetish taking care of the inside, I finished in about forty-five minutes and came away with fewer than ten lifts. Most of these came from the driver's area - the inside door, seat belt buckle and rear view mirror. Most would probably be Winslow's.

I went back to the Lab office, finished my paperwork and then called Arnold to let him know what I had found, or rather, what I didn't find in the car. Sergeant Parker answered the phone.

"Parker, Homicide."

"Sergeant Parker, Matthew Grace. Sorry about missing you in the park."

"Technician Grace, I'm sure that you did not need either me or Detective Arnold to tell you how to do your job." Ever since his talk with the Lab's Director about the "Deacon" business, the sergeant and I have maintained a professional courtesy toward each other. We'll never be friends, but at least we work together better than we used to. There's probably a lesson in that for me.

"Did you find anything that I should pass on to Detective Arnold?"

"Just the usual, prints and evidence for Trace if and when he comes up with a suspect."

"Very good. I'll expect you at the case review tomorrow, one o'clock. Bring whatever you have."

"Yes, sir. And could you ask Detective Arnold to have someone from the family pick the car up as soon as possible? We really need the space."

Someone from the Lab has this conversation with a homicide detective almost every week. Still, Parker managed to sound shocked. "Technician Grace, do you honestly expect the widow to interrupt her grieving to pick up a car?"

I almost said "Yes" but realized that it would not help matters any.

"I don't suppose that we could have it towed out of here and to the City Yard?"

"No, Technician Grace, we cannot. I will inform Mrs. Winslow that the car will be held until she is ready to pick it up, at her convenience, not ours. I will see you tomorrow."

"At her convenience, not ours." That's easy for him to say. He's not the one who has to explain to a major why a stolen BMW is parked in his reserved space. But then again, neither am I. The major would call Director Thomas, and it would be the Director who had to do the explaining. With that happy thought I went home.

The case review started, as do all of Sergeant Parker's meetings, exactly on time. There were five of us around the table in the meeting room - myself, Klein and Arnold, Officer Miller and Detective Janet Wingate, a new addition to the Homicide Squad. We had all been early, and were sitting around talking about nothing in particular. At one o'clock, Parker walked in, sat down and without preamble said, "Tell me about the crime scene."

Klein and Arnold both looked at me. I passed the ball to Miller, who related how too much coffee had lead to the discovery of the body. I then gave Parker, Klein and Wingate a description of the scene itself, passing around copies of the crime scene photographs and my sketch as I did so. When I finished, I gave Arnold a copy of the video tape linking Winslow's car to the scene.

"So," Parker said, shifting his gaze from me to Arnold, "That's what it looked like. What happened down there?"

Arnold cleared his throat. He fumbled with his papers and cleared his throat again. He had been in Homicide for almost a year now. By Klein's standards and mine that still made him a new guy, but one would think he would be used to presenting cases in the review. He wasn't like this in court. I think Parker scares him.

"Well, Sir, it looks as if, that is, what probably happened was that Winslow and at least one other person parked the Lincoln on Franklintown Rd., walked down the path to the clearing and someone shot him in the back of the head, at close range, with a 9mm."

I had heard better presentations. So had Parker. So had Wingate and she had just started.

"Detective Arnold, Did it occur to you that since Mr. Winslow's car was still there but the shooter's was not that he may have met his killer there? The clearing in which he was found was a perfect meeting spot for those engaged in illicit activities." Arnold mumbled something about just getting to that consideration but Parker talked over him. "As for what you've said, I figured that out from Technician Grace's excellent photographs. What I had hoped you would tell me was who this person or persons were and why they put a bullet in Harry Winslow's head."

"Well, Sergeant, we are still working on that. Maybe Grace has something."

"We will get back to Technician Grace shortly. Give me what you do have on Mr. Winslow."

Klein stepped in for his partner. "Harry Winslow is, or was, an entrepreneur. Back in the seventies he had several Circus Burger franchises. When that chain folded its tents and went back to California, he took over the Leon's Lake Trout stores. Since then, he has run record stores, pizza joints and, briefly, tanning parlors. He got in on the video rental business just before it got hot, and started Fun Flicks Video. He had six of these stores going and was planning to open two more when he died.

"Winslow was not a stranger to trouble. He'd been shot once in a hold-up of a Circus Burger store. He lost the tanning parlors when a customer got stuck in a tanning booth and it took two hours to get her out. She sued, and he had to sell the business to pay off the judgment. And he's been arrested once or twice."

"Three times, actually." Everyone looked over at Wingate.

"What?" Wingate asked, "The new guy isn't supposed to talk?"

"Not at all, Detective Wingate. Please tell us how you know the deceased."

"Thank you, Sergeant." She was poised and in control, not at all like the rookie detective she was supposed to be. She took a brief moment to decide what she wanted to say, and then went on.

"As some of you might know, I worked two years in the Youth Division before coming here. The name 'Harry Winslow' seemed familiar, so I checked our back cases. Just about the time I transferred to Youth, Winslow was arrested for a fourth degree sex offense."

"Meaning?"

"He copped a feel from a sixteen-year-old who worked at one of his video stores."

So, Harry Winslow liked young girls. I looked over as an "Ahh!" escaped Arnold. He was thinking that Wingate had handed him the start of another possible motive.

"What happened with the case, Janet?"

"It never went to trial, Detective Klein."

"Make it Alex. Why not?"

"The girl's family settled for an undisclosed sum and the charges were dropped."

"And the other two arrests, were they also on moral grounds?"

Wingate deferred to Klein. "In a way, Sergeant. Last year the Feds nailed Winslow for bootlegging tapes out of his stores. They popped him again two weeks later doing the same thing. He had a connection that let him provide videos of current movies within a week of their release.

"And what was the status of those charges?"

"Before they were abated by death, Winslow's attorney had run out of ways to stall and had just entered the bargaining phase."

"So it is possible that whoever killed Winslow did it so his," the sergeant stopped and, with a nod to Wingate, added, "or her, name would not come up in the negotiations."

"That's possible, but he hadn't given the Feds any names yet, and there are too many outfits running pirate copies for them to make a guess."

Parker stood up. "Gentlemen, and lady, we have a man who for many years has maintained a chain of stores of one type or the other. Most of these stores had a lot of traffic, a variety of customers and a rapid turnover of cash, product and employees. In taking care of these stores, Mr. Winslow did not have to be anywhere in particular at any given time. He would therefore have a logical reason for not being able to account for his whereabouts if asked.

"Now then, this is Baltimore. Take the above, and consider that this man is now dead from a 9mm bullet, and what does that suggest?"

Without missing a beat, all of us chorused, "Drugs!"

"You have three possible motives - sex, drugs and some video pirates. That should be enough to keep you busy. Technician Grace, anything from the Lab that can help?"

"Nothing back on the prints yet. As for the rest, give us something to compare my samples to, and you might get a match."

"Very well, Detectives Klein and Arnold, You have by now talked to the employees of his video stores. What have you learned?"

"Not very much, Sergeant." Arnold was now on familiar ground and sounded more confident. "Winslow dealt only with the managers or assistant managers of the stores. He didn't have much to do with the individual employees."

Janet Wingate raised her hand to interrupt. At Parker's nod she said, "That would be because of the court settlement. In return for dropping the charges, part of the deal was that Winslow had no dealings with any of the store employees, especially the pretty young girls."

"Anyway," Arnold continued, "While everyone mentioned that Winslow had an eye for the ladies, and one or two reported seeing him accompanied by different women on occasion, no one reported anything or anyone specific."

"I suppose that not having to account for your daily activities would make adultery easier. Detective Wingate."

"Yes, Sergeant."

"Go back to the stores, talk to the women who work there. They may be more willing to tell you something than a male detective."

"How about the wife, anything there?"

"It doesn't look like it, Sarge. Rich and I talked to her a couple of times. She seemed like your typical grieving widow."

"Was she aware of her husband's affairs, business or otherwise?"

"She may have been. We asked her if Winslow was having trouble at work and she just sort of shook her head and said that he didn't tell her too much of what went on. If she's like most wives, she knew more of what Harry was doing than he realized or she'll admit even to herself."

"Work on the pirate angle with the Federal agents, and get with Narcotics and see if they can link Mr. Winslow to any drug activity. Talk to the wife again.

"Is there anything else?" Parker watched us all shake our heads. "In that case, you can all go." As we got up to leave Parker stopped us.

"One last thing, I got a memo today from our captain. He had to park on the roof because there was a VW van in his parking space. It seems that the Crime Lab put it there because all of their processing spaces were full. He has ordered us to have all cars that the Lab has finished with removed as soon as possible.

"Technician Grace."

I was trying very hard not to smile. Klein was not helping. He had gotten behind Parker and was making faces.

"Yes, Sergeant."

"First of all, stop smirking. Mrs. Winslow will call your office as to when she will be here to pick up her husband's car. Have someone give Detectives Klein or Arnold a call and they will come down to sign it over to her."

"Yes, sir. Thank you, sir."

By luck I was in the office when Mrs. Winslow called. After the meeting I had advised the dispatcher that I was available for calls. Four burglary scenes later I was back in the office trying to eat my lunch while writing my reports. I had just finished a sandwich and my third report when her phone call came. Since it was my case to start with, I talked to her. She would take a cab and meet me at the garage entrance to Headquarters in twenty minutes. I called the Homicide office and caught Klein just as he was leaving for the night.

"Alex, Matthew here."

"What is it, and why do I think I should take my coat off?"

"I just got off the phone with Mrs. Winslow. She'll be here in twenty."

"And you need one of us to sign over the car. I knew I shouldn't have let Rich go early."

"Just ask one of the others to do it."

"Can't. You know the good Sergeant. 'It's your case, Detective, it's your responsibility.'" Klein actually did a very good impression of Sergeant Parker. One of these days Parker is going to catch him doing it, and Klein will be the new Morgue Liaison Officer and spend the rest of his days fingerprinting dead people.

Twenty minutes later the guard at the Frederick St. security booth called to tell me that Mrs. Winslow had arrived. I went down to meet her and escort her to her car.

The headquarters building has two entrances. The public entrance is on Fayette St, but since it was after hours, Mrs. Winslow had to enter through the garage entrance on Frederick St. I met her at the security booth, introduced myself, had her sign in, and walked her to her car.

It is a long walk up the four ramps which lead to the processing area. I am never comfortable walking people up them to get their cars. These are people I have never met, and will probably never see again. I feel like I have to make some effort at conversation, if only to break the silence as we walk slowly up the ramps. You would think that we would be able to bring these people inside the building and take the elevator to the correct level. You would think that, but the rules say otherwise. According to Security, if someone is there to pick up his car, his business is in the garage, not the building. So instead, we hug the walls, always watchful in case a speeding patrol car comes our way.

About halfway up the first ramp I finally said to Mrs. Winslow, "Sorry about your loss, Ma'am." I knew from the reports that she was not that much older than me, late thirties to my mid-twenties, but she looked ten years past that difference. So much that the "Ma'am" came naturally and not as the result of police courtesy.

She was a small woman, five two or three and weighing no more than a third of the 304 pounds her husband registered at the M.E.'s. She dressed like your oldest aunt, the one that went into business instead of raising a family, and had that air of resignation with which some women seem to be born.

She did not answer at first. I thought that she either did not hear me, or just did not want to talk. We were halfway up the second ramp when she said in a surprisingly firm voice, "It had to happen; it did."

I made some kind of noncommittal grunt to show that I was listening. I supposed that this was her chance to unburden herself, to talk to someone who already knew most of the details. It's part of the job sometimes. I only hoped that she would not start crying. I am at a loss when people cry, and always make matters worse trying to get them to stop.

"It had to happen," she repeated. "I am only surprised that it did not happen sooner. The movie people, the other things, he just could not deal with it. The women he could deal with, but they always cost money too."

We had been walking side by side, and my face must have shown surprise when she mentioned the women.

"Oh, yes, I knew about the women. I didn't mind. You've seen him, and you see me. Believe me, I really did not mind when he started to look elsewhere. It was actually quite a relief, quite a load off, actually." I did not know if the last had been an odd choice of words or her attempt at humor. I gave her a half smile that I hoped would serve in either case.

"Mrs. Winslow, if you know something about your husband's business or," I paused for the right word. I had almost said "other affairs."

" — Or if you know about his other activities, the detectives would want to know."

"They asked all right. I did not feel comfortable talking to those two. It's different talking to you. You're not a policeman, are you?" I shook my head. "You're just listening, not asking a lot of questions."

So, I decided, I would listen more, and talk to Klein later.

I did not get the chance. As we turned the corner to the last ramp, we saw Klein by the processing area. Mrs. Winslow stopped talking.

"Mrs. Winslow, nice to see you again." Klein said as we approached. He got a slight nod as an answer.

Klein had an envelope with him. "I took your husband's keys out of property." He handed them to her.

"I have my own, thank you." She reached out for the clipboard Klein had in his other hand. "Where do I sign?"

Klein pointed out the spaces on the release form for her name, driver's license number and signature. She filled in all the blanks and handed the board back to him.

"May I go now?"

"Well, Mrs. Winslow, I was hoping that we could talk for a while. There are still some things that I would like to go over with you."

"Later, maybe. I have other business I have to take care of today. Please call me sometime next week. I may be able to answer your questions then."

She turned to me. "Thank you for your kindness." Without another word to either of us she got in the Lincoln and drove off down the ramp.

"You certainly made a good impression on her, Matthew."

"It's my natural charm. I only wished it worked on women outside the job." I told him about our conversation on the ramp.

"It's a natural reaction. First, Rich and I bring her news about her husband's death. Then we have to ask questions about her possible involvement in that death. As part of the job, we suggest that she may have killed her husband, then ask if he did anything to anyone else that would deserve killing. She has to deal with us while trying to mourn. Of course she resents us. Most of them do.

"But, Matthew, from what she told you, Rich and I will definitely have to have another talk with her, at our convenience, not hers. She may know something that will help."

As we walked from the garage into the second floor of the building Klein stopped and looked back toward where the Lincoln had been parked.

"Matthew, what did we just see?"

Not sure what he was talking about, I said, "We saw Mrs. Winslow get into a car and drive away."

"That's what I thought we saw."

We got in the elevator and rode up to our respective floors. I got off at the fifth, got my stuff together and went home. Klein rode up to the sixth. Except for a two-hour nap that he caught in an interview room, he worked through the night.

The telephone woke me up at eight o'clock. A groggy Alexander Klein greeted me when I answered it.

"Matthew, Alex."

"Alex, you sound terrible."

"I feel worse. Staying up all night will do that to you."

"I hope you're calling to brag."

"I wish I was. I've been at work all this time. I'll tell you about it when you get in. I'll meet you here at nine." He hung up before I could object.

There was never any question of my not going in. Klein would not have called unless it was something really important, like the close of a case. I made it to Headquarters with a few minutes to spare, wondering what his big break had been.

I talked the day shift supervisor out of a Lab van and loaded it up. Then I went up to Homicide. Klein and Arnold were waiting.

"Morning, Rich. Alex, you look better than you sounded an hour ago."

"The close of a case and three cups of cop coffee does wonders." He started putting on his coat. "Ready?" He waved a piece of paper in his hand.

"Where are we going, and how did you get a warrant signed this early?"

"Matthew, do you know how few judges are willing to answer the phone at two in the morning? And only one would let me come over to get this signed."

"Devereux?"

"Who else?"

Judge Gertrude Devereux was every cop's friend. In the courtroom she made life miserable for the prosecution, defense and anyone else who came in unprepared. She was scrupulously fair to both sides, and ruled as much for one side as the other. Still, when a guilty verdict came down on somebody who really deserved it, that somebody went to jail for as long as legally possible. She also believed that it was part of her job to be available to officers and detectives when they needed her to be, and not on an eight-to-four basis. She would not sign just anything put in front of her, but she listened and if you had good probable cause, you could call her, as Alex had done, anytime, day or night. Of course, if your reasons for wanting a warrant were too shaky, or just plain non-existent, you got a chewing out that you would remember three years after retirement. Then you got fined the equivalent of four hours overtime for "bothering up a judge for no damn good reason." Then you got the lesson in writing warrants that you should have received in the police academy.

Klein went ahead of us, rushing to the elevator. I walked with Arnold. "So, where are we going?"

"He wouldn't tell me either. Said it was a surprise. He's driving, you're supposed to follow."

As Klein led the way, I tried to figure out where we were going. I tuned my radio to the various district channels hoping to hear a unit dispatched to meet Homicide and the Crime Lab at a particular location. It was not until we turned from Northern Parkway onto Liberty Road that I began to catch on.

We were well into Baltimore County when we turned onto Buckingham Rd. We pulled in front of an address I recognized from the police reports. It was where Harry Winslow had lived before he had taken his last walk in the park.

Two patrol cars from the Baltimore County Police were parked in the driveway. They were blocking in two other cars. The Lincoln I was familiar with. I supposed the other, a Dodge passenger van, belonged to Mrs. Winslow. Parked on the street was a tow truck, no doubt waiting to take the van back to headquarters to be searched.

"What did I miss?" I asked Klein as we met in front of the house.

"I'll tell you later, business first." He moved to rap on the door, but Mrs. Winslow opened it before he could do so.

"May I help you gentlemen?"

"Doris Winslow, I have a warrant for your arrest for the murder of your husband, Harry Winslow. I also have a warrant to search your house, cars and grounds for evidence related to that murder." She stepped aside and let us in.

As it was really Arnold's case, Klein let him read Mrs. Winslow her rights. As she listened, she looked over at me, silently accusing me of betrayal. Had she really expected that I would not tell Klein and Arnold of our conversation in the garage? Didn't she realize that, civilian or not, I still worked for the police? And what was it she said that had tipped Klein to her as the killer?

We found the gun in a shoebox in the front bedroom closet, a common enough place to hide one. As Arnold and I continued the search for additional evidence or any other weapons, Klein went through the papers he found on a desk in a first floor office.

During our search, Mrs. Winslow sat on the living room sofa, kept company by the Baltimore County officers. Other than indicating that she had understood her rights and did not want an attorney, she had said nothing to anyone.

In the basement Arnold and I found a pair of women's shoes that had been left on the work bench. They had probably been left there to be cleaned. The dirt on the sides and bottoms looked as if it would match the soil samples I recovered from the clearing where Winslow had been found. More of that same dirt would probably be found when I vacuumed the van in the driveway.

Klein was in the living room when we came up from the basement. He made a show of unloading the gun, removing the clip, ejecting the cartridge in the chamber, before putting it on a coffee table in front of Mrs. Winslow.

"Anything you want to tell us?"

She gave a sigh, and sat back on the sofa. "I suppose it doesn't matter now. It was as I told the young man," she nodded toward me, "Harry just couldn't handle things. He opened these businesses, made these deals, but just did not have the sense to see them through. I handled the monies. I had to, or else we would have been broke."

"Why did you kill him?" Klein asked softly.

She looked at him oddly. "I just told you. He could not handle things. Every sweet young thing he got involved with was always too young and not that sweet. There was always a payoff. And the movie deal. Instead of doing the time like he should have, Harry was going to name all of his partners, except me of course."

"And his other partners would not have liked that?" prompted Arnold.

"No, they would not have. They would have killed both Harry and me. So that night, I left word for Harry to call me. When he did, I told him to meet me at the clearing."

"Why the clearing?"

"Well, Mr. ... Klein is it? That clearing was where Harry and I first, well, let's just say it was a romantic spot for us. I told Harry that I had a surprise for him. And I did, just not the kind he expected."

"Once you got him alone, in the clearing. What did you do?" Klein wanted to nail the confession down.

"I got him turned round and shot him in the back of the head."

Arnold whispered to me, "No rush on doing the van, Grace." Actually, with the confession, gun and shoes there was little need to do it, but we would anyway, just to be thorough.

"And why did you drive the van back, instead of the Lincoln you came in?" The question startled not only Mrs. Winslow, but Arnold and myself. Mrs. Winslow spoke before Arnold could ask.

"I don't know how you found that out, Mr. Klein, but yes, Harry had the van that day. The Lincoln had been in the shop for something or other. I picked it up that afternoon."

"And why did you leave it in the park?"

"It was Harry's car. If I had left the van and then reported him missing, it may have looked suspicious, him having the wrong car."

Mrs. Winslow went back to headquarters with Arnold and Klein. I waited for the tow truck and followed it back. It was not until lunch that I caught up with Klein.

"Arnold says I shouldn't tell you, just to get back at you for all the times you called him Agatha."

"You'll tell me or I'll lose the property receipt for the gun."

"You were there, Matthew, you saw the same thing I did."

"Alex, that bit is only entertaining when Holmes does it to Watson." I realized that he was referring to our watching Mrs. Winslow leave the garage. "All I saw was Mrs. Winslow get in her car and drive away."

"And what didn't you see?"

I was stumped and he knew it. He paused, enjoying the moment and then said, "You didn't see her adjust the seat. She just got in the car and drove away without taking any time to move the seat up, which she would have had to do if her husband had last driven the car."

"Which meant that she had left it in the park, not him."

"Which puts her on the crime scene."

Doris Winslow's confession held up. With that, the gun and the soil from the clearing matching that from her shoes and van, the State's Attorney had an easy time convincing a jury of her guilt. After the trial, I had to tell Rich Arnold that I could no longer call him "Agatha." I explained that since he needed his partner to solve his cases for him, he no longer deserved the name. He's still not sure whether to be relieved or disappointed.

OPEN AND SHUT

One o'clock, thirteen hundred by the 24-hour clock, almost the end of the shift. It had been a slow day as far as those of us who worked in the Crime Lab was concerned. By slow I mean that we weren't called to any crime scenes other than what you'd expect on an October morning in Baltimore.

We began our tour at six a.m. with no calls pending. That didn't last long. By seven the B&E calls started coming in as business and shop owners got to work and discovered that burglars had struck overnight. At eight the requests came in from the School Police. Vandals had hit three different schools. By nine the impound lot called with a list of recovered stolen cars that had to be dusted for prints. Ten o'clock brought the first of two bank robberies that went down that day.

We handled them all, finishing one call then responding to another until the backlog was cleared. By noon only Max Hammond was still out — on the second bank hold-up. As I said, it was a quiet day by Baltimore standards — no rapes, no shootings, no serious assaults and no dead bodies. That is until Karen Johnson got a DOA call up in College Town.

Baltimore City has more than its share of colleges and universities. The University of Maryland Medical School System is located near the Inner Harbor and the Camden Yards stadiums. The Peabody Conservatory is closer in to downtown, off Charles St. Go north on Charles and you'll pass Johns Hopkins University, Loyola and the Notre Dame College for Women. Turn northeast from there and you'll find Morgan State University. Head south and west and there's Coppin State.

If you follow sports at all, especially basketball or lacrosse, you've heard of some of these schools. Most find their way into some playoff or the other. And all are even stronger in academic achievement than they are in sports.

There are smaller colleges too, ones you've never read about in the sports pages. Most are specialty schools, designed to teach just one discipline — the Culinary Arts Institute for one. Others are devoted to incorporating a philosophy or system of beliefs into the academic life, such as St. William's Academy in Guilford, a very conservative Christian college tucked in among the homes of some of Baltimore's wealthier citizens.

With all these schools and all the students who attend them there comes a major problem — housing. Not everyone lives on campus. Not even the bigger schools have room for all the students who attend. And some of those who could find dorm space prefer the less restricted life off the college grounds.

Some of the smaller schools have no housing — St. William's especially. It is an older school, having been well established before most of its neighbors moved in around them. As the school grew, what dormitories it had gave way to classrooms. With no room to expand, student housing had to move off campus.

What we call "College Town" is where most of the off-campus students wind up. It's the Charles-St Paul-Calvert St. corridor from 28th St north up into the exclusive homes of Barclay and Guilford. Being centrally located, students from most of the schools mentioned above can be found there. They live in homes that were once three story family dwellings, now cut up into rooms and apartments. Some of the houses are devoted to students from just one school, and are in fact owned and rented by that school. Others are privately owned and are open to whoever can come up with the first and last months' rent.

DOA's in College Town are not that unusual. Every school year produces its share of suicides, drug and alcohol overdoses and death by stupidity. Last year a sophomore bet that he could chug-a-lug a quart of malt liquor while hanging out a third floor window. He lost. The year before that a junior built a homemade howitzer from compressed air and PVC piping. It was designed to shoot potatoes and similar vegetables across great distances. When it didn't fire right away he looked down the barrel to see what the problem was. Only then did it go off. The M.E.'s report on "Death by Potato Gun" was reprinted in several forensic journals.

At first Karen's case looked to be one of these cases. The 911 caller reported hearing a shot come from behind his housemate's closed door, a door locked from the inside. The caller said that they had forced the door in and found the deceased lying on the floor.

All this we got from the dispatcher who had given out the call. "Looks like another over-achieving high school student who couldn't handle the shock of getting B's in college," Karen said before leaving. To the supervisor she said, "Ed, I'll call if I need help." No one expected her to call, not on a suicide.

After she left we sat around and waited for the clock to tick down to quitting time. At twenty minutes to the hour we went down to the garage to unpack our personal equipment from the trucks. It was just as I got back in the office that the phone rang.

"It's for you," my supervisor said, looking right at me. I didn't like the grin on his face.

"Technician Grace, how are you this fine afternoon?" It was Detective Sergeant Joshua Parker of the Homicide Unit. Parker and I don't get along very well, so I knew this wasn't a social call. There were no pending court cases that involved both of us. And the fact that he was making an effort to be polite meant only one thing — I wasn't going to go home on time that day.

"Just fine, Sergeant. How are you and how can I help you?"

"I'm on the Calvert St. scene. We have need of your knowledge."

Now I was confused. Calvert St. was the location to which Karen had been dispatched. If the scene was that complicated or involved, or if it had proven to be homicide and not suicide, she would have called Ed directly, and not gone through Parker. Besides, she knew the rules — this close to quitting time, you waited until the next shift came in to call for help.

"Sergeant, Karen's on the scene, she's every bit as good ..."

"As you, Technician Grace? Actually, she's somewhat better. And it's not your crime scene skills I need. I'm also calling Detective Arnold, you can ride up with him."

"What did he want?" Ed asked after I had hung up the phone.

"He wants me at the DOA scene, Rich Arnold too."

"I guess you better go then," Ed said, putting on his coat. "See you tomorrow."

Rich Arnold was a homicide detective under Parker's supervision. Like me, he had been getting ready to go off duty when Parker called.

"Do you have any idea what this is all about?" Arnold asked me as he stopped to pick me up at the garage entrance.

I threw my equipment bag into the back seat. "None what so ever. I haven't done anything to tick him off lately. You?"

"There's more red than black on my side of the board."

The names of all the homicide victims go up on a big board — names in black are closed cases, those in red are unsolved. It's an ever present reminder of how well you're doing, or how badly.

Rich Arnold had been in Homicide for about eighteen months. During that time he had been partnered with Alexander Klein, in the hope that some of Klein's genius for solving cases would rub off on him. With Klein's help Arnold had managed to maintain a decent closure rate. Klein, however, had been detailed to a combined DEA/FBI/BPD taskforce for the past three months, and the column under Arnold's name had started to look like someone had slit its throat.

Normally I wouldn't let a comment like Arnold had just made go without some kind of smart mouthed reply — at the least I should have said, "So what else is new?" That would have given him the opportunity to rag me about some less than stellar moves I may have made lately — not that I make that many, mind you, but no one's perfect. I let it go this time. I was busy puzzling over why Parker might need me, but not my crime scene skills. Surely it wasn't for my sparkling wit or charming personality. He didn't appreciate either. I decided that there was probably a lot of evidence to be carried from the scene and Parker had selected his two least favorite people to do the donkeywork.

As Arnold pulled onto Calvert St. from 29th, I started counting the police cars that were parked in front of the scene. That's a way of judging how serious a scene is before you get to it. You get a call for a shooting. You pull up and there's only one patrol car there, then most probably someone shot himself in the foot. However, if you pull up and there's more than a half dozen all with their flashers and blue lights on, well, cancel any plans you had made for that evening.

There were only three marked cars parked on Calvert St, about right for a suicide. They would belong to the primary officer, his sergeant and the officer called in to guard the entrance and take the names of all those who enter and exit. There was one unmarked car, Parker and whichever detective had caught the call. Finally, Karen's Crime Lab van was double-parked in front of the scene itself.

"Who's got the call?" I asked Arnold as he pulled in front of Karen's van.

"Wingate." Janet Wingate was newly appointed to Homicide. This would be one of her first solo cases.

"She's good," I offered, then waited for Arnold's opinion.

"Better than me," was the surprising reply. "Give her a few years, she'll be better than most of us."

We got out of the car, walked up to the house and introduced ourselves to the officer at the door. He took our names and unit numbers, then directed us to the second floor. "Top of the stairs," he told us as we walked past him.

I'd been in this neighborhood before, on burglaries mostly, but also on some more serious calls. I was familiar with this type of house. A long hall led back from the front door. Midway down the hall was an open doorway to a big living room. At the end of the hall were stairs and a shorter corridor taking you to a sizable dining room and from there into an equally large kitchen. There was another open doorway between the living and dining rooms.

The stairs, of course, lead to the second floor. There'd be three bedrooms — one in the front and two smaller ones in the rear — a bathroom, and yet another flight of steps that went to the third floor. Up there would be either two more bedrooms or attic storage.

Being careful not to touch anything Arnold and I climbed the stairs. At the top we found Parker, Wingate, Karen and another uniformed officer. All four were gathered in the front bedroom.

Parker greeted us with a nod and a "Gentlemen." I nodded back as Arnold asked, "How can we help, Sergeant?" Neither of the women said anything. I didn't know about Wingate but from the looks I was getting from Karen they were no happier about our being there then we were. The officer looked like a child who had just witnessed a major argument between his parents. He was staring out the window and trying very hard to pretend that he wasn't in the room.

There was no body in the room. With Karen's camera bag and equipment case on the bed and two police style clipboards on the dresser this didn't look like a crime scene.

"Where's the body?" I asked Karen.

In reply I got an icy stare. Finally she pointed to Parker and said, "Ask him, we're not expert enough for this case."

Parker answered my question just as I was about to ask him what he had said to get the normally placid Karen so mad at him. "The deceased is in the left rear bedroom."

"My left or your left," I interrupted. He almost answered me but then he noticed we were both facing the same way. Ignoring me, Parker continued, "His name is Brian Rice. He was a student at St. William's Academy, as are the three young men waiting in the living room. All four live here. The three men downstairs were sitting at the dining room table this morning when they heard noises from upstairs."

"Noises?" Arnold asked, emphasizing the plural.

"Yes, two of them, the first louder than the second. One of them," Parker looked at his notebook, "Jason Prisca, came up to investigate. Rice's door was locked. He knocked and got no answer. He called up the other two, Donald Meyers and Jared Wallace. When they failed to get an answer the three of them decided to break the door in."

"Did they?"

"Go back and see for yourself, Technician Grace. You too, Detective Arnold. Then tell me what you think."

The room was what I expected. Despite being one of the two smaller bedrooms, it was still larger than most college dorms, more so when you consider that Rice hadn't had to share it. Giving the lie to most movies about college, the room was reasonably neat. A made up bed was against a wall in one corner of the room, a computer station in the opposite corner. There were no clothes strewn about the floor, and the flat surfaces of the bureau, dresser and computer table were mostly free of books and papers. These were presumably in the bookcase and small file cabinet that made up the rest of the room's furnishings. Everything was as it should be, except for the forced open door and the body on the floor.

While Arnold went to look over the now late Mr. Rice, I checked out the door. It was covered with black powder from Karen's fingerprint brush, so it was safe for me to play with if I had to.

I didn't. It was a standard inner door — one passage lock, one bolt lock. Both were more for privacy than preventing theft. The passage lock in the doorknob was hardly damaged by the forced. No surprise there. In the Crime Lab we don't even consider a door locked if it's secured with only one of them. The bolt lock was a little better. I knew that type of lock, used them in my house. It had a half inch barrel that would withstand a quarter ton of force. Put it on a good door with a good frame and you'll need an axe to get past it. In this case, the cheap wooden frame split before the lock gave.

Arnold looked up at me. "Death by natural causes," he said.

It was an old joke, one I'd heard the first week I'd been a technician. "Sure," I replied, "Shoot yourself in the head, it's only natural that you die. One shot or two?"

"Just the one. The first shot they heard must have been a hesitation shot. The second did the trick."

I looked around. No bullet holes in the wall or furniture. I started to get an idea of why Parker asked for us specifically. I looked around for something else I suddenly knew would be missing. I didn't find it.

I stuck my head out the door. Parker was waiting in the hall. "You rolled him?"

No one is supposed to touch a dead body before the Medical Examiners arrive. That rule didn't stop most detectives, and particularly Sergeant Parker. Once the crime scene photos are taken, he's got his gloves on and the corpse at an angle so he can see what's beneath it. He then very carefully lowers it back to its original position.

Knowing what Parker's answer would be, I waited for the nod of his head then asked the big one. "There's nothing underneath him, is there?" This time he gave a half smile and shook his head no.

"Should I tell him or wait until he gets it himself?" jerking my head back toward the room and Arnold.

"Better tell, him, otherwise we'll be here all day."

"No bullet hole," Arnold said as I came back into the room. "Must have been an echo."

I don't know if he was talking to me or to himself, but I interrupted and asked, "Rich, where's the gun?"

He looked around, checking under the bed and every other piece of furniture in the room. "Under the ..." he started but stopped as I shook my head.

"Parker says no."

"Then someone's lying to us."

"If you go by their story, all three are lying."

"That's what I thought too," came Parker's voice from the doorway. Standing against the shattered frame, he went on, "But then I thought that these are college students, and all three couldn't be so stupid as to fake a suicide and forget the gun. So it's possible that only one of them did it."

"And there's the matter of the second shot." I added. "Why would they make that up?"

"Exactly, Grace. So before we take all three downtown and start working on them, I thought it would be a good idea to explore all possibilities."

Parker looked at the two of us. "So now you know why I called you two in particular. In addition to being fairly competent at your respective jobs, the two of you are overly fond of mystery stories. That gives you a unique perspective over those of us with better ways of spending our time. It also gives you your big chance. Here it is, gentlemen — a locked room with an unexplained gunshot. You are not to leave this house without some idea of what went down in this room. Once I have that, I can surprise whichever one of those kids who thinks he's smarter than we are." He turned and left us to our puzzle.

Arnold gave me a "Now what do we do?" look and started searching the room. For what, I don't know. Maybe he hoped he'd find the gun some place where no one bothered to look. Either that or a note Rice left detailing exactly how he'd done it. Me, I decided to examine the door.

"Locked room" puzzles are nothing new to me, or to any crime scene investigator who's been on his share of burglaries. How the burglar entered is always the first question you ask yourself. Where did he come in, and how did he get through? Most of the time that's an easy question to answer — the window's smashed, the door's kicked in, there's a big hole in the wall. Sometimes it's not so easy and there's no apparent point of entry. Think of it as a locked house problem.

The first thing you do is check the windows — are they all shut and locked? If not, how easily do they open? The door locks are next. Can they be unlocked from the outside without a key? Most deadbolt locks can't be. Passage locks, the kind in most doorknobs, are way too easy. One of my favorite crime scene tricks is to ask the victim to lock me out of the house. Then, using only the small blade of my pocketknife, I show them how easy it is to get back inside. In most cases, I can usually open the door faster with my knife then they can with their key.

If the doors and windows don't pan out, you look for other means. I've had cases where the burglar was able to reach though the mail slot to unlock the door. Thieves have been known to enter maintenance rooms and break into adjoining apartments through closet walls. Once inside, they pile shoeboxes and clothing over the hole to cover it up.

None of this helped me in this case. This was a room, not a house. A brief glance out one of the windows showed me that they were too high to climb up to, and there was nothing in the alley below to use as a climbing aid.

No answers came from the door either. The deadbolt lock could only be locked from inside. The door was hinged from the inside, and so couldn't easily be removed and replaced.

Discounting trap doors and secret panels, I mentally reviewed all the cases I'd been on and the stories I'd read. I recalled one shooting scene I'd processed where a bullet accidentally fired in one room had passed through the ceiling and killed a woman in an upstairs bedroom. I looked at the hole in the deceased's head. A close contact wound on the right side of the head. The bullet had gone straight in. Rice would have had to be lying with his head on the carpet with the shooter pressing the gun against the ceiling and that still didn't allow for the powder burns. Just the same, I went downstairs and checked the ceiling for bullet holes. I didn't find any.

"I got it, Grace," Arnold almost shouted as I came back into the room. Without my asking he pointed to a thick book sitting on the computer table, which had apparently also served Rice as a desk. It was the Doubleday edition of *The Complete Sherlock Holmes*.

I watched as Arnold walked over to the body. He stood where Rice would have been before the shot. Making a gun from his right thumb and forefinger, he held it to his temple.

"BANG!" Arnold shouted. Then he turned to the window and said, "Bang!" again, but in a softer voice. "It has to be," he muttered, taking the two steps to the window and opening it up. "Yes!" he yelled, pumping the air with his right fist.

Arnold ran out of the room to get Parker, as he passed me he said, "Thor Bridge, Grace, Thor Bridge."

No, it couldn't be. I looked over at the Holmes book. Then I thought of the two "gunshots," one louder than the other. The second could have been the window slamming shut.

I raised the sash, looked out the window and saw what I had missed in my previous cursory glance. I waited and watched from above as Arnold had Karen photograph and recover his discovery. Then I went downstairs to witness Arnold's triumph. Damn, I hate it when he's right.

They were in the dining room. Parker was shouting at the uniformed officers, "Well look again. Make sure it isn't stashed some place."

I started to ask what he was looking for, but he wasn't yelling at me and I didn't want him to start. Instead, I looked at what was displayed on the dining room table.

There was a long piece of twine. Around one end was tied a brick, the other end was frayed, as if something had been pulled or cut off. Tied in the middle of the twine was a wooden dowel, long and thick enough to have held the window open. Next to this assembly was a broken piece of plastic, the kind used to make pistol grips.

Karen started taking pictures of the display as Arnold played Great Detective. "'Thor Bridge' is a Sherlock Holmes story in which a woman commits suicide but makes it look like murder. She makes something like this," he gestured toward the arrangement on the table, "and shoots herself on a bridge. When she releases the gun, the weight of the rock, which was hung over the side of the bridge, pulls it and the gun into water.

"In this case," he continued, "the brick was tied to the dowel and hung outside the window. Rice kept it from falling by holding on the other end of the string, which was tied to the gun. After he shot himself, his hand relaxed and he let go of the gun. The brick fell, pulling the gun out the window and the window shut."

"And why," asked the uniform who had greeted us at the door when we arrived, "would he go through all that trouble just to kill himself?"

Karen spoke up. "In some religions suicide is a sin. You can't be buried from the church or in holy ground."

"Or maybe," Wingate added, "He wanted to get his roommates in trouble. Or he just thought of it as one last joke on the system."

Someone had to ask, so I did. "Where's the gun?"

Arnold pointed to the broken plastic. "That's all that's left of it. This is Baltimore, Grace. The life expectancy of a gun on the sidewalk or in an alley can be measured in minutes. Sometime between Rice shooting himself and the uniforms' canvass, someone came along and snatched it up. This piece must have broken off when the gun hit the alley."

"It will turn up, probably after a murder or two. Good job, Detective Arnold," Parker said. "Detective Wingate, time to call the ME. Ms. Johnson, you'll want to photograph and recover the book."

"Yes, sir, right after I secure this stuff."

To feel at least partly useful, I offered to help. "Karen, if you give me the camera I'll take care of the book."

"Sure thing, Matthew," she said with a smile, handing me her Nikon. Now that I had failed to solve the crime we were friends again.

Something started bothering me as I walked back up the stairs. I put it down to Arnold having solved the problem before me. I told myself that another five minutes in that room and I would have spotted the Holmes book and made the necessary connections. Even if that were true, it didn't help the feeling.

Back in the room I took an overall photo of the room, making sure to include the computer table and the book in the picture. A close-up photo of the book followed. That was all that was really needed, but I was feeling particularly useless just then and decided to do a little extra. Wearing gloves, I opened the book to the Table of Contents and photographed the entry for "The Problem of Thor Bridge." Then I turned to the proper page and took a picture of the beginning of the story, making sure to get the dog-eared flap that Rice had used to mark his place. With any luck the prints of his thumb and forefinger would be found on either side of the flap, icing Arnold's cake.

For good measure I decided to take a picture of Rice's bookcase just to show from where he had gotten the book. I looked toward the bookcase — it was full, no gap to show where a book the size of the Holmes should have been. He could have borrowed it from one of his housemates, I thought. Then I started looking at what kind of books he did have.

Half the shelves were devoted to his textbooks and what had to be assigned reading material. The rest were filled with popular novels, a few Westerns, some horror and what seemed to be every Star Trek book ever written. No mysteries, unless you counted a Western by William DeAndrea. I pulled a few books off the shelves and leafed through them.

That's when I realized what was really bothering me. I walked over to Rice and repeated Arnold's actions — shooting myself in the head with my finger, imaging the gun falling from my hand, the now released brick falling to the ground outside, the window slamming shut.

"Sergeant Parker, get up here," I shouted, then used my radio to call the afternoon shift supervisor. There were a few things I needed.

An hour later, those of us who could fit were crammed into Rice's room. The ME had come and gone, taking the deceased away. That gave us a little more room. Karen, Parker, Wingate, Arnold and the primary uniformed officer were all watching me set up my demonstration. At my suggestion, Prisca, Meyers and Wallace had been sent to wait in their rooms.

"Are you sure about this, Technician Grace?"

"Frankly, Sergeant, no. But look at it like this — if it works you got a closed case. If not, I'm going to look like a fool. Either way you can't lose."

"I'm betting on number two." Arnold wasn't happy about my suggestion and the need to recreate the crime. If I was wrong he'd never let me forget it.

The video camera I had asked the supervisor to send was set up on its tripod, ready to record my success or failure. I picked up the other things I had sent for — a brick similar to the one used, a wooden dowel, twine and a red gun.

The red gun was a disabled .38, used by the Police Academy for training in loading and unloading weapons. The firing pin had been removed for safety purposes. The barrels and grips of weapons of this type are always painted red so that everyone knows that it's a "safe" firearm. I asked for a red gun to be sent because no one cared how beat up they got.

I talked as I set things up. "When I came up here to photograph the Sherlock Holmes book, I noticed that there was no place for it on Rice's shelf."

"So what, Grace," Arnold interrupted, "Maybe he borrowed it."

"Be quiet, Detective. Let him make his speech."

"Thank you, Sergeant. As I said, there was no shelf space for the Holmes. Not only that, there are no mystery books on his shelf."

Karen was closest to the bookcase. She looked it over. "He's right."

"Also," I continued, "The first page of the 'Thor Bridge' is bent down to mark the spot. I looked through some of Rice's books. None of them are dogged-eared."

"So what?" asked the uniform. He probably wasn't an avid reader.

Arnold was. Suddenly interested, he knew what I was getting at.

I was ready. I tied things together the way they were supposed to be — brick to dowel, dowel to gun. I put the dowel in the window, holding up the sash. The brick I left on the windowsill. I handed the gun to Arnold.

"Walk over to where Price was found," I told him. "Keep the tension on the string."

Arnold did so, being careful not to step in any blood. When he was in place, I eased the brick out of the window, slowly letting it down by the string.

"Are we all agreed that this is how things had to have been set up?"

Everyone nodded. "You don't just start turning down corners right before you're going to kill yourself," I said. "And why would someone who's not a mystery fan use an elaborate locked room scheme to take the short way home?"

I hit "record" on the video camera. Then I yelled, "BANG!"

Arnold let go of the gun. It dropped to the floor and laid there. The dowel, held firmly in place by the weight of the sash, stayed where it was, the brick dangling from the window.

A click and a flash told me that Karen had been photographing the whole thing. She took a close-up of the gun lying on the floor. No one else spoke or moved. If I was expecting applause I didn't get any.

"Once I realized that it wasn't Rice's book and that he probably hadn't turned the page down," I continued, "it suddenly occurred to me that this was a set piece, that we were supposed to make the Thor Bridge connection. Then

I realized that the dowel would probably support the brick whether the gun was released or not. And that means Rice didn't kill himself, not like this anyway."

"Good thinking, Matthew," Karen said.

"Yeah, good job," Arnold added. A more gracious loser than I am, he sounded like he meant it, too.

"Couldn't have done it without you, Rich. You thought of Thor Bridge. I probably wouldn't have."

Parker spoke. "Detective Wingate, let's you and I let the college boys know they're not as smart as they think. Grace, nice idea having them go back in their rooms."

"What did he mean by that?" Karen asked after the two had left.

Arnold answered her. "They have a right to privacy in their bedrooms. With them waiting in the living room, we couldn't go into their rooms without a warrant. But now we can go in and get them out. And at the same time look around to see who's got a large collection of mystery books, and no Sherlock Holmes."

It all came out in questioning. Prisca was the mystery fan. The Thor Bridge scheme was his idea. He came up with it after Wallace had accidentally shot Rice with what he thought was an unloaded gun. Meyers had bought it from "a guy he knew" following some burglaries in the area. Wallace found the gun in Meyers's room. After being assured by Meyers that it was unloaded, he took it saying, "I'm going to have some fun with Brian." When Meyers heard a pop, he remembered that he had meant to unload the gun, but hadn't yet done so.

Prisca had the room on the third floor. By the time he had run down to Rice's room, the other two had already decided to make it look like a suicide. That's when he got his idea. He set the Thor Bridge scheme up, tying the gun and brick to the dowel and throwing them all out the window. He then locked himself in Rice's room. The other two broke down the door.

"But why?" I asked Wingate over my steak. Parker was making her buy Arnold and me dinner for solving her case for her. No matter that he had called us in. (By the end of the meal she "let" us talk her into separate checks.) "A locked door, a dead guy, a gun nearby — instant suicide."

"Because he's a stupid college kid. He's read so many mysteries he though they were real life. He assumed that we'd somehow see through a 'locked room' death and start looking at them. It wasn't Rice's gun, he had no reason to kill himself. So he came up with an idea. He'd make it look like a murder that looked like a suicide. When they were accused, he'd find the book, then 'solve' the case. And if we found the book and figured it out, so much the better. He didn't count on us having our own mystery fans."

"He also didn't count on someone taking the gun away," Arnold added. "With the piece from the broken grip and the bullet from Rice, it will be easy to match once it's found. If it used in a crime Parker plans to charge Prisca and maybe the other two as accessories for making the gun available."

"Will that stick?"

Wingate answered me. "Long enough to mess up their lives for a while. Some justice for Price at least."

"You know," Arnold said, "It's a shame that Prisca didn't take at least one physics course, he might have fooled us."

I couldn't let that go, not with having The Great Detective looking over our shoulder this whole case. "But, Rich, Prisca did take physics back in his old school. Failed the class, of course, but he did take it."

He bit. "What school was this, Matthew?"

"Elementary, my dear Arnold. Elementary."

LAST OF THE LATIN ALTAR BOYS

The blood will never come out. That's what I remember thinking as I sat in the front pew and looked up at the altar. They'll wash it off, but there'll be a pink stain on the marble floor, and some of it will settle into the cracks. A year from now, two years even, a blood test will still give you a positive reaction.

I knew this from past experience. A man was found dead in an alley behind an apartment building. Despite a thorough cleaning by the recently departed tenants, traces of his blood were found between the floorboards of the only vacant apartment. And there was the woman who witnessed a fatal struggle between her husband and boyfriend. When the winner went to hide the body, she cleaned up all traces of the fight. Six months later she called the police after her boyfriend threatened her. Drops of her husband's blood were found up under the chair rail in the dining room. Thoughts of these cases and more came to me as I waited for the Medical Examiner to come for the priest whose body lay in the sanctuary. Even if you think you've cleaned it all up, the damned spot is always there.

By then I'd been in the church for several hours, ever since the call came in for a DOA at St. Brendan's Catholic Church. It was my old parish. I'd grown up not far from there. It was where I had gone to school, where I was baptized, confirmed and made my first communion. I had even served there as an altar boy, though these days most of my friends would find that hard to believe. Naturally when the call came in I took it.

A homeless person, I thought as I loaded my camera bag and equipment case into my Crime Lab van. Someone who sought shelter from the cold November we were having and instead found a final release from this life's sufferings. It had happened before. Not at St. Brendan's but at libraries, shelters and other places in Baltimore where the doors were open to any who cared to come in.

When I pulled up in front of the church I knew I was wrong about the victim. There were too many police cars parked there for this to be any kind of natural death. It seemed as if half the Southeast District was standing around waiting for orders. A major was talking to a colonel, and the public information officer was standing by, waiting to brief the press that was sure to gather.

Camera case in hand, I ducked under the yellow tape and climbed the twenty stone steps to the big oak doors. Despite the reason for my being there, I couldn't help but remember sweeping rice off those steps after weddings. They don't throw rice anymore. It's bad for the environment or the birds or something. They blow bubbles instead. It's not the same.

Once inside, an officer took my name and unit number and recorded them in the crime scene log. Then I looked for the detective in charge to find out just how bad things were.

They couldn't have been worse. A dead priest, struck down at the altar while saying Mass. Not only that, but I had known the man — Father Sean Murphy. He had retired from the active priesthood long ago, and was still in residence at St. Brendan's.

Father Murphy had been the priest in charge of the altar boys when I had joined up. That was back in days when the Mass was in Latin and the priest faced front instead of looking out over his congregation. Father Murphy was a hard taskmaster who had to have been a drill sergeant in a previous life. In six weeks over the summer he turned a pack of unruly fourth-grade boys into well-choreographed ministers of God, or so he called us. Every movement of the Mass was rehearsed until we could do it in our sleep. (And at the six a.m. service that's how most of us did it.)

Father Murphy loved being a priest. Mostly he loved the Mass. A part of him was lost after Vatican II changed the language and ritual from Latin to English.

It was the Saturday before the change. He'd just finished his last Tridentine Mass — the Latin Mass in the old style. The next day would be his first Sunday Mass in English. I was his server. As we finished and walked into the sacristy, he said, "And that's done and ended, Matthew. Remember this day. You are the last of the Latin altar boys. From now on it's English, and farewell to the mystery and beauty and glory of it all."

The next day he did his best with the new rite, and only once did a "Dominus Vobiscum" slip out in place of "The Lord be with you." Later it was rumored that he would still say Mass in the old way for a few of the older parishioners. If true, no one ever officially caught him at it.

Detective Alexander Klein had the case. He was standing in the vestibule as I walked in, talking to a worried-looking middle-aged woman. I waited until he finished with her.

"The cleaning lady," Klein said after we had made our hellos. "She found the body. Matthew, you're Catholic. Tell me, is it usual for a priest to say Mass this late in the morning?"

"Not for Father Murphy," I replied, then told him of my past relationship with the priest.

"You can opt out of this if you want," he offered, "if ... you know."

"I know, Alex, and thanks. But I know the victim and the scene better than anyone here. And it's too personal for me to leave to anyone else."

I did call for some help, though. I knew it would take a few hours to draw a proper crime scene diagram of a church the size of St. Brendan's, so I called someone else to take care of that while I took the photographs and collected evidence. That done, I said to Klein, "Well, let's get to it."

"First, Matthew, tell me about the late morning Mass."

"My sister still attends mass here. From what she tells me, age and failing health finally caught up to Father Murphy. He had to stop saying the regular Masses. Still hears Confession, and assists at Mass, but he moves too slow and speaks too softly to officiate by himself. But Murphy was always a bit stubborn. Every now and then, with the church locked up, he'd say a Mass by himself, for himself. It didn't matter how long it took, and he knew he'd be heard even if he whispered."

"Heard by who?" In reply I looked toward the altar, then up. "Oh," Klein said, nodding in understanding.

We walked up the aisle as Klein filled me in. "This is how the cleaning lady found him," he said as we came up on the body.

Father Murphy had been struck twice, both vicious blows to the head with something heavy. He was lying on his back in front of the altar, blood pooling around his injuries. So hard had he been hit that the top and front of the altar were spattered with his blood.

"Hit once while standing up," I said, reading the blood pattern evidence before me. "Again as he started to fall. But with what?"

I looked at the altar. It was undisturbed. A paten held the wafer that would become the Host. Cruets were still filled with wine and water. Murphy's chalice was still covered. Both candles were still there, both were still lit. Neither had been used as the weapon.

I looked around. All the other candles were in place. In fact, there was nothing out of place. Nor was there any sign of a weapon anywhere on the altar.

Later, after the pictures were taken and evidence gathered, a more thorough search of the church would be made. But I knew nothing would be found. The killer had taken away whatever he had used.

I paused to say a prayer for the repose of Father Murphy's soul, not that I thought he'd need the help. But it wouldn't hurt, and who among us can say for sure what our final reward will be. After my amen I got to work.

Photographs first. I started at the altar, overall shots and close-ups of Father Mur... No, he was the victim now. After my prayer he became "the victim," just another part of just another crime scene. It was the only way to work it.

As I said, I photographed the victim, next the altar area. I was about to shoot the sacristy and then the rest of the church when Klein came back up on the altar. He looked worried.

"Something wrong, Alex?"

"You mean besides a dead priest? Besides the fact that I've got a police commissioner, two deputies, a colonel and a district commander outside waiting for this poor Jewish boy to perform a miracle in a Catholic church. Did I mention the Cardinal's here?"

"Probably a bishop or two as well. Let Parker deal with them." Sergeant Joshua Parker was Klein's immediate supervisor.

"I wish. He's in court. That means I'll be outside as much as I'm in here."

"It's just another red ball case, Alex," I told him. "You've lived through them before. You'll live through this one."

"Yeah, but if I don't leave here with something solid they'll make me wish otherwise." He let out a sigh. "Oh, I talked to the cleaning lady again. According to her, because of recent thefts in the area, the church is locked up after the eight a.m. Mass. I figure the assailant must have hidden in here before then, in one of the confession boxes maybe."

"Confessionals," I corrected absently. "It's possible. No one would have bothered to check."

"So he waited until the place was empty. Then when he came out to rifle the poor boxes he found the priest saying Mass. There was a confrontation, then a struggle. Murphy went down and the thief …" Klein tensed up.

"What's wrong?"

"The church was locked up. He's still here."

"Calm down, Alex. Even if the doors are locked they still open from the inside. It's a safety feature. And I'm sure that the uniforms searched the place."

Klein relaxed. "I'm going to leave you to your work, Matthew. Let me know if you need anything."

Klein walked off to talk to his partner, Rich Arnold, who had just come in.

I used a lot of film that day. Finishing with the altar, I went up in the choir loft, taking overall photos of the church. I took some more when I came down, from the back toward the altar and from the altar back. I stood in each corner and shot outwards. Along the way I kept looking for the weapon. I didn't find it.

When I came down from the choir I ran into Max Hammond, the crime lab tech who had been assigned to help. As usual, he answered my greeting with a complaint.

"Could this place be any bigger," he said looking around. "And you expect me to draw it?"

"It's either that or do the dusting."

"What needs to be printed?" Max was trying to decide what was less work.

"Max," I said, pointing to the altar, "That is a dead priest. And you saw the brass hats in the crowd out there. What do you think needs printing?"

Shaking his head, he let out a sigh, "Everything." He handed me the drawing board and tape measures. "I'll get my print kit," he said.

We worked steady for the next hour or so — Max fingerprinting anything an intruder might have touched, me sketching a floor plan of the church and taking measurements so that later I could make a to-scale drawing of the entire scene. We stopped when Klein brought us some lunch from the corner store. We ate outside at the top of the stone steps.

By now the crowd had thinned out. All the commanders had left, as had all but the most curious of the bystanders. The news crews were still standing by, waiting for the M.E. to come and take the body away — that always made for good TV.

We talked as we ate, filling Klein in on our progress, or lack of it. "Any prints?" he asked hopefully.

"Sure, lots of them," Max said through a mouthful of meatball sub. "And everyone probably belongs to some honest, church-going citizen."

Alex nodded, he hadn't expected much more. "Matthew, in your sketching did you happen to find ...anything?"

"Two rosaries, a prayer book, somebody's hat and eighty-five cents in change. The change is going in the poor box, the rosaries and book on the statue of St. Anthony and I'm going to recover the hat just in case. But no, nothing even close to a weapon."

We finished lunch. Klein walked over to the uniforms to ask about the neighborhood canvas. Max and I went in to finish our work.

"St Anthony?" Max asked me once we were inside. A good Methodist, Max wasn't up on the saints.

"He's the saint you pray to when you lose things. There's a poem my grandmother taught me. 'Oh, St. Anthony, please come around. Something's lost and can't be found.' Of course for it to really work you have to turn the statue's face to the wall."

"What does that do?" Max asked.

"He stays that way until you find what you're looking for."

Max shook his head. "Remind me never to convert." Then he had a thought. "Can he find the pay raises we haven't gotten for two years?"

"Wrong saint. You need St. Jude."

"Who's he?"

"Patron of lost causes."

"Yeah," Max actually laughed. "Well, turn him to the wall and get him working on this case."

Max got back to dusting for prints. I was done with my sketching so I went up to the sanctuary to do the blood work. I had just finished when Max met me there. "You get your blood samples yet? I still got to dust the altar."

"All done," I said, showing him my swabs and vials. I left him to his work and sat myself in the front pew.

Max finished his fingerprinting. "I'm going outside for a cigarette," he said, packing up his print kit.

"South stairwell to the lower church," I replied idly, another memory coming back to me. That was where the so-called "cool kids" went to sneak a smoke during lunchtime.

"What?"

I waved him off. "Never mind. If you see Alex out there tell him we're ready for the M.E."

Max nodded and looked at his watch. "Shift change. It'll be a half hour before they get here."

"I got nowhere to go."

And he left me there alone in the church to think dark thoughts about dead men and bloodstains.

After a while my mind came back to the current case. I mentally reviewed all we'd done and tried to think of something else to do. I replayed the crime in my head.

Father Murphy standing at the altar, saying a quiet Mass for an empty church. The silence fools the intruder into thinking he's alone. He comes out of hiding. Father looks up and sees him, maybe shouts something to him. What then? The intruder panics and rushes the sanctuary. Father comes around the altar to meet him. There's a struggle, a blow — possibly fatal. The second one surely is. Father falls and the intruder flees, taking with him whatever weapon he used.

Except — the best and only hiding places were the confessionals, and the closest was nearer the door than the sanctuary. The intruder wouldn't know that the sacristy was empty, that it was just the two of them. Certainly Father wouldn't have offered any threat. He would have welcomed the man. Any struggle would only increase the intruder's chance of being caught. Most probably, he would have run to escape.

By now I was out of the pew and back in the sanctuary, trying to make sense of things, looking for a new theory of what happened. Standing in back of the altar in the priest's position for saying Mass, I looked back toward the pews and at the confessionals along the walls. No intruder I decided. I had lost faith in that belief.

Then I looked down and saw what I should have seen from the very first.

The chalice was to my left, missal to my right. That was wrong. I had served enough Masses with Father Murphy to know they should have been reversed. They were in the wrong places — if he had been using the modern ritual. I opened the missal. The text was in Latin. I remembered enough of it to be able to translate the opening prayer:

Introibo ad altare Dei. Ad Deum qui laetificat juventutem meam. In English it meant, "I will go up to the altar of God. To God who gives joy to my youth."

He'd been saying the Tridentine Mass.

And why not? It was just him and God. And saying the Mass that way brought back to him one of the joys of his youth.

Of course that meant he'd had his back to the rest of the church the whole time. If there had been an intruder Father wouldn't have seen him.

I took another look at the blood spatters. They didn't tell me anything different from the first two times I'd looked at them. Father gets hit while standing at the altar, the blood splatters across the marble top. He falls, and there's spattering across the front. He gets hit once more when down. More spatters, on the floor and lower down front of the altar.

It still didn't make sense. According to his wounds and the spattering, Father could not have fully turned to face his attacker. And he had been assaulted from the front, not the side. That was only possible if...

I put myself in Father's place. Stood where he would have been standing to start Mass. I turned as he would have turned, and found myself facing the doorway to the sacristy.

"Matt?"

I jumped. Max had come back in and I hadn't heard him.

"Everything okay?"

I started to nod yes, then stopped. "No. Yes. Maybe. Go get Alex, bring Arnold in too if he's still there." Max just stood there, wondering what was wrong with me. "Now!" I said sharply to get him moving. As he hustled out I grabbed my flashlight and went into the sacristy.

It was luck that I saw it so fast — a spot of blood on the doorway leading from the sacristy out into the hall. It was the first thing my flashlight lit up when I began to look around. Why the hallway? It only led downstairs to the lower church. Then I remembered the tunnel.

No, not the mythical tunnel that supposedly connected the convent with the rectory. Anyone who saw the aged nuns who had taught me would know that had to be a lie. This tunnel connected the lower church with the school.

Lower grade students weren't allowed to use the tunnel, not that any wanted to. It was long and dark and dimly lit by naked, low wattage bulbs strung along the ceiling, a place of mystery and legend. If two or more fourth grade boys were left alone in that part of the school basement that led to the tunnel, one would inevitably dare another to go partway in.

I almost took that dare, once. I was still gathering my courage, convincing myself that all the stories I'd heard about what was in there were just that, stories, when Old Joe came out of the tunnel's mouth.

Old Joe was what we called the school janitor — not to his face, of course. No one ever talked to Old Joe, except the nuns, who just called him Joe. Joe had been part of the school for forever, and was the only one there who looked older than the nuns. We avoided him as much as we did the tunnel.

I was in fifth grade when I learned that the tunnel was nothing more than part of the physical plant that serviced both buildings. I was in my first year as an altar boy. It had started raining during the eight o'clock Mass. I had brought neither raincoat nor umbrella and was looking at a good soaking when I walked back to school. After Mass, the eight-grader I'd been serving with led me though it.

"Better than getting wet," he said when I showed some initial reluctance. Then he added, "You ain't scared, are you?"

Of course I wasn't, I lied, and followed him in. Up until then, it might have been the bravest thing I'd ever done. And as in most cases, reality failed to live up to expectations, and my first passage through the tunnel was uneventful — which came as both a relief and a disappointment. After that the tunnel became just another way of getting from church to school.

And now over twenty years later I was going back in. I hadn't meant to — I was just following the blood trail, drop after drop, not realizing that each drop took me further away from the upper church, further away from Max and Klein. My only thought at the time was how many more hours this discovery was going to add to the processing of the scene.

There wasn't a lot of blood, only a drop here and there, each one about ten feet from the other. It could be that the assailant had himself been injured. Or else he had gotten more of Father's blood on him than is usual. I followed the trail to the back of the lower church. From there, there were two ways to go — up the front stairs to the main vestibule, or into the tunnel.

I looked at the door that would take me to the tunnel. Then I turned toward the stairs and found — nothing. No trace of blood, no trace of anything that might be blood. Reluctantly I went back to the tunnel door. There was a spot of blood on the knob. Suddenly I was back in the fifth grade, about to go through for the first time again.

You're right, I should have waited. I should have gone up those front stairs and found Klein, Arnold, a uniformed officer or even Max. Don't ask me why I didn't. To this day I don't know. I think maybe I heard that eighth-grader's voice asking, "You ain't scared, are you?" I went in.

It was smaller than I remember, but still long and dark. The bulbs weren't any brighter either. Fortunately my flashlight gave me more than enough light, its heavy three-cell weight a comfort in my hand.

I walked the tunnel all the way through to the school, coming out in a large open area of the basement. The first grade and kindergarten students played here when it was raining. It was the same as I remembered it. Ahead of me were two corridors, marked "Boys" and "Girls." These went through to the other side of the building and the first grade classrooms. In the middle of each corridor were the bathrooms. Behind me and to my left was the kindergarten. Over to my right was a cinder block room used for storage and as the janitor's office. At least it had been. For all I knew it was now the teacher's lounge.

There were three ways I could go, four if you count going back through the tunnel. Past the kindergarten was a short flight of stairs that led to an exit. I could look there. Or I could see if there were any traces of blood in one of the corridors. Or I could check out the storage room.

I went to the exit first, hoping to find a red stain that would tell me that the assailant had left the scene that way. No luck. I was reluctant to search the corridors. A strange man looking around school lavatories, even if he does work for the police, could create too much unwanted excitement. That thought caused me to realize I'd been gone too long. Klein and Max were no doubt wondering where I was. I'd go back and let them know what I'd found.

But first I wanted a look at the door to the storage room, just to be thorough. Not having seen anything of evidentiary value since entering the tunnel I didn't expect to find it now.

At first I mistook the red smear on the doorframe for paint. Another look, close-up with my flash right on it, told me that it was probably blood, left there by whoever had gone into the room. And who very likely was still there. It was past time to leave. I had just decided to go back into the tunnel when the door opened.

He was big, six-nine or ten to my five-seven. Twice as wide as me too, or so it seemed at the time. I didn't look that close. I was more interested in the lead pipe he held in his bandaged hand. The pipe was long, about two feet in length and sawn off at both ends. As close as I was I saw that one end was ragged, cut off rough enough to cause the bleeding that had brought me there. The other end, the one nearest me, still bore blood and matted hair from the assault on Father Murphy. Lucky me, I'd solved the case.

I saw all this in an instant, the instant before I decided that my continued good health depended on my leaving as quickly as possible, but casual enough not to seem to be running away. That might make him chase me. The trouble was for every two steps I took away from him, he took one towards me. Since his stride was longer the distance between us hardly changed.

It was too late to pretend I was a visiting parent, looking for whatever classroom my child was in. He'd already glanced down and looked at the ID clipped to my shirt.

I gripped my flashlight tighter. It was almost as long as the lead pipe he was holding, the three batteries inside the metal barrel meaning I could at least make a fight of it if I had to. It wouldn't be a long fight, and the outcome wasn't in much doubt, but maybe I'd get in a blow or two that would cause him to leave more blood behind. Strangely, I found myself wondering how difficult it would be for the Trace Evidence Unit to distinguish the pieces of me from those of Father Murphy if the pipe were ever found.

A quick prayer and I resigned myself to the only plan I could think of — running away and fighting if caught. That's when he spoke.

"He said, he said he was going to tell," the man said in an almost childlike voice. Not the voice of innocence, but of innocence lost — the voice a child uses when he first discovers that someone he trusted has told him a lie. "He was going to tell," he said again, as if explaining something to me. "Priests aren't supposed to tell."

I went with it. "He told us already. He told me, he told everybody. Everybody knows." I stressed the "everybody," hoping he'd think that taking me out of the picture wouldn't solve his problems.

"Everybody?"

I nodded then waited. For some reason I was hoping he would just shrug and drop the pipe. He didn't. He swung it at me. I managed to duck but lost my flashlight and footing. Hitting the floor, I rolled out of the way and heard the sound of metal striking cement. Again I rolled, not really knowing whether I was moving away from him or toward a savage beating.

There were shouts, then voices.

"Grace!"

"Matthew!"

"Drop it, drop the pipe!"

"Don't do it! Stop!"

Loud popping sounds, two of them, then the thud of a large body falling hard.

"Matthew, are you all right?" Someone pulled me to my feet.

"Timmy!"

Timmy?

"You, sir — stop right there!"

I stood up and looked around. Rich Arnold was standing there, 9mm in hand, two cartridge cases by his feet. Max was back in the mouth of the tunnel. Klein was next to me, holding me up. A skinny man with too many keys on his belt was over by the bathroom corridors. He was trying to get to the man lying at my feet, but was being held back by a uniformed officer.

The gunshots had brought other officers. Seeing a sergeant, Arnold handed his weapon to him, as per procedure in a police involved shooting. I walked over to him.

"Rich, thanks." I held out my hand. "Thank you more …"

Arnold cut me off. "I shouldn't have had to, Grace." Ignoring my hand, he walked away.

"He's right, Matthew." Klein came up beside me, turned me toward the dead man. "You got lucky. The kind of luck you only get once." To Max he said, "Hope you weren't planning on leaving anytime soon. Go get what you need — now. And call for some more help. Matthew's going to be — unavailable."

After Max left, Klein again turned to me. "What happened?"

I started with my finding the blood in the sacristy and ended with the big guy coming out of the store room and attacking me. He cut me off as I was explaining how I got caught up in the search.

"Do something this stupid again and you won't be taking the crime scene photos, you'll be in them."

Klein then turned his attention to the man by the bathroom. He waved to the uniform to bring him over.

"This is about over in the church, isn't it?" the man asked, looking everywhere but at the body on the floor.

"Yes," Klein said simply. "And who are you, sir?"

"Fred, Fred Rambowski. I'm head of maintenance for the school. Timmy, his real name's Timothy Sofius, works, worked for me." Rambowski paused. He looked at the body, then toward the store room. "There's something you gotta see." He led us through the open door.

There was a desk in the room. Behind it were two lockers. Rambowski opened one of them. Inside were magazines and pictures of children, most young enough to have been enrolled in the school. They were doing things that only consenting adults are supposed to do.

"I know I should have said something right away," Rambowski said in a tortured voice, "but I wanted to help him, not get him arrested. While I tried to figure out what to do, I sent Tim to talk to one of the priests, told him to confess and ask for help." He slumped in a chair, near tears. "I should have told," he cried, "I should have told."

It was apparent to me what had happened. Timmy had done what his boss told him — confessed to Father Murphy. Then, afraid that Father would tell, went looking for him and found him in the church. On his way over he picked up an old piece of pipe that had been left in the tunnel. Suddenly, I didn't feel so bad about the dead man lying out there on the cold floor.

Klein was quiet. He looked at me, then the locker, then at Rambowski. "Matthew," he said without expression, "what exactly was it that Sofius said to you." I told him. "That's word for word?" I assured him it was.

Klein got on the radio, called for Max. "Get back down here, bring your print kit." He sat behind the desk. "Have a seat," he told Rambowski, motioning him to chair in front. To me, Klein nodded toward the door. I stepped outside it and waved a uniform over, just in case. Then I went back in.

"… going to have those magazines dusted for prints," Klein was explaining. "Something tells me I won't find many of Timmy's on there. What do you think?"

The guilty look on Rambowski's face said it all. Klein gave a sad smile then started reading him his rights. I went out and got the officer.

"How did you know?" I asked after Rambowski had been taken away.

"It was something Sofius said to you," Klein explained "'*He said* he was going to tell.' I'm not Catholic, but I know enough that priests don't repeat what they hear in confession. So who was the 'he?' The only other person it could be was Rambowski. So did Sofius mean that Rambowski said that he, Rambowski, was going to tell? If so, why kill the priest? So …" he paused to let me catch up.

"So Rambowski told Timmy that Father Murphy was going to tell," I finished.

"Exactly," Klein said, "Rambowski's prints are probably all over these magazines. They're his. He somehow got Sofius involved in the whole sordid mess, maybe he meant to use him to lure some of the school kids down to the storeroom."

"But Timmy got to feeling guilty, and confessed to Father Murphy," I continued. "Then he told Rambowski what he'd done. Seal of Confession or no, Murphy would have a found a way to at least get them both out of the school, and see that somehow or other Rambowski was investigated."

Klein finished up. "And Rambowski knew this, or at least feared it. So he worked on Sofius, convinced him that Murphy was going to tell, and got him to do what he did."

Father Sean Murphy was buried three days after his death at a special Requiem High Mass. With the Cardinal's permission, the Mass was said in Latin — the Modern Rite, but I don't think Father Murphy would have minded. And if the server assisting the priest was about twenty years too old for the job and kept staring at a faded pink stain on the floor — well, who knew the proper responses better than an old Latin altar boy with more luck than he deserved?

TIPPING THE SCALES

It all began when I found the gun. Late one Friday night a businessman from D.C. picked up the wrong little boy near Patterson Park. Looking for some quick sex, he was robbed, stabbed in the throat and left to die. With his car parked in a secluded spot, it took some time before he was noticed, his body finally discovered by a patrol officer who thought he had found a drunk sleeping off the night's revels.

The car was towed to the garage at police headquarters. As a crime laboratory technician for the Baltimore Police Department, it was my job to process the car for evidence. After dusting the outside for prints, I searched the car and found a gun, a .32 caliber semi-automatic pistol, hidden in the well for the spare tire. What good the owner thought it could do him in there I don't know. It certainly didn't protect him from the kid with the knife.

I was by myself when I found the gun. No one knew I had it. Wiping it clean, I hid it in my equipment bag. I knew I'd find a use for it.

For Andre Jones it began when he was acquitted of homicide. The State could prove that the body found in the vacant house had been murdered. It could prove that the knife found near the body had been the murder weapon. Prints found on the knife were matched to those of Jones. The defense, however, was able to raise that faint glimmer of doubt that Baltimore juries love so much. Jones was a free man, for a time.

Two weeks after Jones walked out of the courtroom, Dominic Trainor was shot down in a dark alley near Gold St. and Pennsylvania Ave. The bullet went through and through and was never found. There were no witnesses. Being an outside crime scene, there were no prints. The chances of Trainor's murder being solved were slim. The only evidence recovered was a .32 caliber cartridge case that I said I found on the scene.

Andre Jones was no doubt feeling very lucky. Acquitted of a murder everyone was sure he had committed, he was back on the street. Only he knew if he had been guilty and he was not talking.

I learned that he had gotten a job at a bowling alley on the east side. I guess he felt that staying away from his real line of work seemed wise. It didn't pay as well but it did establish him as a citizen. Not only that, but it was also a good place to make a lot of new contacts for when he started his drug business up again. Working the lanes makes for nice cover.

A few nights after Dominic Trainor's death Jones stayed late to help with the clean-up. Walking out to his car after the manager had closed he found it unlocked. He checked it over. The steering lock was in place, the audio system intact, the ignition not damaged.

"Damn," he said out loud, "this honest work is making me careless."

Detective Janet Wingate became involved with a telephone call. The anonymous voice was one she'd heard before but she couldn't place. It told her that Andre Jones had killed Nicky Trainor in an argument over, what else, drugs. Supposedly, he still had the gun.

I imagine Jones was surprised to see Wingate and the two uniformed officers who accompanied her at his apartment. I'm sure he didn't think he had done anything to have attracted the attentions of the police. When questioned, he denied ever knowing Nicky Trainor and graciously allowed Wingate to search his home. It had been searched so many times before that the police knew more of what was there than he did, and he had learned long ago not to keep anything at home that he did not want found. He also allowed Wingate to search his car. He was more surprised than she when she came out holding the .32 pistol that had been hidden under the front passenger's seat. If he remembered the unlocked car door from the night before he didn't bothering mentioning it to the officers who took him into custody. Why bother? Who would believe him?

A firearms expert matched the cartridge case recovered from scene with the gun found in his car. Shortly afterwards, Andre Jones was again charged with murder.

As the technician who found the cartridge case, I was called to testify at his trial. While on the stand, I saw Detective Sergeant Joshua Parker sitting in the back of the courtroom. As a supervisor in the homicide unit it was his job to monitor murder cases. He had sat in on Wingate's testimony and stayed for mine.

Parker and I had never got along. He thought I was rude, arrogant and insubordinate. I found him bossy and domineering. Only our mutual respect for each other's abilities allowed us to work together on crime scenes. After today all that would change.

That morning Parker had developed a sudden interest in the Jones case. I learned later that at the lunch break, Parker had had a chat with the young public defender representing Jones. He made two suggestions that surprised the lawyer. When court resumed, I admitted under cross-examination that, yes, more than one shooting had occurred at Pennsylvania and Gold and, yes, the cartridge case could have been from one of them. I also allowed the "possibility" that the gun found in Jones's car could have been planted. After court was adjourned for the day, I saw Parker trying to talk with the Assistant State's Attorney prosecuting Jones. Whatever he wanted, he was clearly rebuffed. The lawyer had seen him talking to, and apparently helping, the defense earlier, and wanted nothing to do with him.

The defense rested without calling any witnesses. This time, despite the doubt raised by his lawyer's questions, Andre Jones was convicted of murder.

It all ended the next day. When I reported for duty on the afternoon shift I was told by my supervisor to report to the office of the Crime Laboratory's Director. There I found, in tribunal array, Sergeant Parker, Detective Wingate and an Assistant State's Attorney I didn't know. The Director was absent. My supervisor quietly slipped out of the room.

I knew what was about to happen. A part of me had always been expecting it, but I had always listened to the part that told me that it would not happen "this time." Well, this time was now the last time. I could only hope that I had figured the final odds correctly. As I sat down I wondered what mistake I had made.

Without preamble, Parker played a tape. First there was the telephone tip that Janet Wingate had received on Andre Jones. Next there was a conversation that he and I had had a few days before about an unrelated case. Not a big mistake, I thought, but big enough. Parker turned off the player.

"It took a while, Grace," Parker said, "but I finally found the tape of the telephone call that had led to the arrest of Andre Jones. Detective Wingate didn't recognize the voice, but I did when I played it back. That's when I made a call of my own, and taped it."

Then the ASA sitting next to Parker spoke up. "When Sgt. Parker first came to me I had trouble believing him. But the sergeant has a reputation for honesty. He convinced me to make the necessary arrangements."

Parker picked up from the lawyer. "I've had the voices analyzed, Grace. You made the first call."

"So, I'm a good citizen."

Parker gave me the look that he usually reserved for murder suspects. "Mister Grace, what you and I both know that most others do not is that Andre Jones did not kill Dominic Trainor. I know it because Andre Jones was meeting with a supplier at the time that Trainor was killed. This I know because a sometime informant decided to call and tell me this the morning the trial started. Now, I do not necessarily believe informants, and it took me until yesterday to find the supplier and verify the story. By then it was too late for Jones. You know that Jones is innocent because you planted the evidence. What I want to know is — why did you frame Andre Jones?"

I ignored him and turned to the State's Attorney. "Am I correct in that the second recording, the one made without my knowledge, is not admissible in court?"

"A judge might so rule, but a court order could be obtained to have another made."

"Sergeant Parker, a citizen unknown to me came up to me and gave me the information on Jones. He then disappeared. Not wishing to get directly involved, I phoned in the information as an anonymous tip, which in a way it was. As for your charge that I planted evidence, go to hell, I deny it."

"Mr. Grace, there is as much evidence to convict you of perjury as there was to convict Jones of murder. You could go to jail."

Parker was right, I could go to jail. When I looked at the sergeant, and saw the determination and anger in his face, I corrected this thought. I would go to jail. Maybe there wasn't enough evidence for a conviction, but I'd be locked up until the bail hearing, and jail was no place for someone who worked for the police. Still, I wasn't behind bars yet.

"Sergeant Parker," I said, addressing him but looking at the others as well, "Andre Jones *was* guilty of murder. Before the Trainor case he had been brought to trial three times and beat the charge each time. His conviction for a murder he may not have committed is not only ironic, it's justice."

"You've answered my question then," Parker said. "You took it upon yourself to balance the Lady's scales. Well, they'll balance, despite you. You will go to jail, Jones will go free."

Again I ignored Parker. I turned to the lawyer. This was my last at bat. I had to hit this one out of the park "Would your boss be upset if one conviction were tainted?"

"Not at all. The redressing of a wrongful conviction shows that the checks and balances in the system work."

"Hypothetically, how many would upset him?"

Janet Wingate spoke for the first time, catching on before the others. "You've done this before!" There was shock and something else, admiration maybe, in her voice.

I smiled at her. She's a smart woman. "Hypothetically, of course. If I did it this time, what makes any of you think it was the first time, or that I'm the only one involved? How many technicians, detectives, patrol officers are helping the Lady balance her scales?"

I looked at the lawyer, then at Parker. "Go back and talk to your bosses. Ask them if they want every homicide conviction, no, every felony conviction for the last few years reopened. Ask them what kind of nightmares my perjury trial and the subsequent news coverage could cause. Hypothetically, of course."

I looked in the State's Attorney's eyes as the lawyer considered the possibilities. I saw when his decision was made and what it would be. Then I smiled at Parker, a smile that I know the sergeant had seen many times in the interview room. It was a smile he hated, one about which he could do nothing. It was a smile that said, "You lose."

Quietly, without fanfare or press coverage, Andre Jones was set free on a special pardon. No one noticed. Dominic Trainor's killer was never found. Under pressure and a step or two away from an Internal Affairs investigation, I resigned from the BPD and, despite Parker's best efforts, became a private investigator. The nameless State's Attorney is now a very well known, highly successful defense attorney. After I left the department, Janet Wingate and I had a long talk. Privately, she admitted that whatever I may have done made sense. As for Joshua Parker, I'm sure that late at night he wonders how many more like me there are out there, and lies awake knowing there is nothing he can do about it.

THE GUILTY ALWAYS PAY

Carol Masters had the life everyone her age wanted. On a scholarship to Johns Hopkins University, she lived alone in an off-campus apartment paid for by her father. She had her own car, and a credit card with Daddy's name on it. She was smart, attractive and popular. Life for her was indeed good. Right up to the day when somebody killed her.

If she screamed the night she died, nobody heard it. The first anyone knew of what happened was the next morning when Diane Balzeck, her study partner, came over to review for their history final. When her knock opened the door, she peaked in.

At first nothing seemed wrong. "Carol," Diane called out, not wanting to startle her friend. "Carol, are you okay?" No answer. Diane went inside. The living room, then the dining room, everything there was all right. "Carol," Diane called again, this time louder. Did she oversleep? Was she with someone? Diane hoped not, hoped she wouldn't walk in on them, that would be so embarrassing. She thought about leaving, going back outside and calling Carol on her cell. But no, this wasn't like her. She never left her door unlocked, and always called if she couldn't keep an appointment. And she had told Diane that she'd planned a quiet evening at home. Diane moved into the bedroom.

Carol was on the bed, her throat gaping open from a knife wound. A second slash had cut her deep down her front, slicing away her blouse and into her abdomen, exposing intestine and muscle tissue. There were other cuts and wounds besides, ones that would take the Medical Examiner well over an hour to number, probe and classify.

But Diane didn't see any of this when she walked into the bedroom, only the body of her friend and the dark red sprays of blood that had spattered about the room. And while Carol Masters's last cries for help may have gone unanswered, everyone in the building heard Diane Balzeck's scream of terror.

What followed next was inevitable. The brutal murder of a beautiful girl, an honors student no less, one that came from a rich and influential family — the media had a field day. For days after her murder the death of Carol Masters was the lead story on every TV news program in the Baltimore area. Her picture was on the front page of every newspaper in town. Her story was told in detail, the tragedy of a promising life cut short.

Pressure was, of course, put on the Baltimore Police Department to solve this vicious crime. Detectives were pulled off of other, supposedly less important, cases to work exclusively on this one. Uniformed patrols flooded the area, despite its having one of the lowest crime rates in the city, just in case the killer decided to strike again. And the mayor and police commissioner were on the news nightly, assuring the public that every effort was being expended in order to bring the murderer to justice.

Based on evidence found on the scene, witness statements and investigations into Carol's life, suspects were developed and questioned. Known violent offenders were brought in and made to account for their actions on the night of her death. Every burglary that had been committed anywhere near her apartment in the past six months was re-investigated. All to no avail.

Two weeks went by. With no progress in the case, the newspapers moved the death of Carol Masters to the back pages of the Metro section. The TV stations found other crimes to lead their broadcasts with, and the police soon returned to those parts of the city that needed them most. The Homicide detail assigned to her death, once ten men strong, was slowly reduced, as new murders made their demands.

A month went by, then two. With no further leads, Carol's murder remained unsolved, her name written in red on the tally board of the Homicide Unit, reminding the detectives everyday that her death was yet unavenged.

Six months later — five months and thirteen days actually — her parents held a memorial service for Carol outside the apartment where she died. The service was dedicated to all of Baltimore's murder victims, but the only name mentioned more than once was Carol's, and hers were the only parents who spoke.

The day after the service, her parents came to see me.

My name's Matthew Grace. I'm a private investigator. It wasn't so long ago that I was a member of the BPD, assigned to the Laboratory Division and working as a crime scene investigator. I resigned just a few steps ahead of an Internal Affairs investigation. It seems my methods of closing certain cases were not looked upon with favor by department supervision or command and I felt quitting preferable to being fired.

After leaving the department, I tried honest jobs, but a nine-to-five life style didn't suit me after ten years of shift work. So when a defense attorney offered me good money to consult in a murder case, I took it. One thing led to another and soon I had my private license.

I knew who the Masters were, of course. Even if I hadn't been following the case in the papers I'd have recognized their name. Evan and Barbara Masters were one of Baltimore's more prominent couples — she was always in the society pages, he was a major player in the city and state political arena. They gave generously to a number of charities, social causes and to the campaigns of most of the area's elected officials.

Like I said, I hadn't been in business that long. So when Evan Masters's secretary called and made the appointment, my first thought was "Why me?" Oh, I knew what they wanted, I just didn't know why they wanted to hire me to do it.

The Masters arrived on time, walking through my office door just minutes before ten. I gestured towards the clients' chairs. He held one chair for his wife then sat down beside her.

"Thank you for seeing us on such short notice, Mr. Grace."

"You're welcome. Mrs. Masters, but as I told your husband's secretary, I would have been happy to come to you."

"Well. Evan and I were both downtown and this was so much more convenient."

"What my wife means, Mr. Grace, is that she's never seen the inside of a private eye's office before and wanted to see if it was anything like the movies."

What did she expect, a bottle of Scotch sitting on a corner of my desk and a .38 in a shoulder holster hanging from the coat rack? "I'd give you the tour, but this is it," I spread my arms to indicate the office, "except for a small lab set up in the back room. Now how can I help you?"

"I suppose you read about our daughter's murder," Barbara Masters said calmly, trying and mostly succeeding in keeping the emotion out of her voice. Maybe that was the real reason they'd come to my office, to discuss a difficult matter on neutral ground, away from any place with memories of their loss.

"Yes, very tragic. My sympathies."

"Thank you. Mr. Grace, Evan and I want to hire you to investigate our daughter's death."

A high profile case, rich clients, a chance for some major publicity — every PI's dream. And poor honest me, I was going to try and talk them out if it.

"Mrs. Masters, Mr. Masters, first of all, thank you for coming to see me. But are you sure this is the right course for you to take? The police are still actively working your daughter's case, and I don't know if I could do anymore than they have already done."

"They haven't done anything," Evan Masters snapped. "It's been six months and they're no closer to finding Carol's killer than they were on day one. What's needed is a fresh approach."

"Then the next question is 'why me?' There are much larger agencies in town. Why come to my little one man show?"

The wife answered that one. "You did some work for a friend of ours." She mentioned a name, one I'm sure you'd recognize if I were free to drop it. She was married to a cheating husband. Now she's on her way to being a divorcee with a sizable settlement. "She said that you were honest and discreet."

"Then there's the fact that you used to work for the police," Evan added.

"A lot of private investigators are ex-cops, Mr. Masters."

"Yes, but now many are former crime scene technicians?" So he'd had me checked out. "You have a unique perspective, Mr. Grace. You're familiar with homicide scenes and their investigation. If nothing else, once you review the file you can tell us if the police have done everything possible to solve this case."

"Given the circumstances, I'm sure they have. But you should know one thing; my parting with the department wasn't amicable. I'm persona non grata with most of the detectives. I doubt if I'd get any cooperation from them."

"Oh, I wouldn't worry about that," Mrs. Masters said with a slight smile, a smile that had more than just a bit of steel in it. Something told me that I didn't want to be on the wrong side of this lady.

"Tell me about your daughter."

I got the basics of her life. There was nothing remarkable about it. Carol Masters had grown up rich and privileged. She moved out when she was accepted at Hopkins, no doubt wanting the freedom that comes from living alone. And she did live alone, no roommates, male or female.

There wasn't much more they could tell me. If she had boyfriends, she didn't share the details with her parents. The police hadn't been that forthcoming either. They had kept the Masters apprised of the investigation, but had kept the specifics of suspects and evidence to themselves.

The business arrangements done, I promised them a report within the week. "Call me," Mrs. Masters said, "if you have any trouble with getting the police reports." I asked her who on the department she had been dealing with. She told me. "I'm going to have trouble," I assured her.

I called the Homicide Unit the next morning. A voice I didn't recognize answered. "Boyous, Homicide."

"Sergeant Parker, please."

"Ain't no Sergeant Parker here."

That was not possible. Parker was Homicide. "Sergeant Parker," I repeated, "Joshua Parker."

"Oh, you mean the Lieutenant. Yeah, he's here. Who's calling?"

"Matthew Grace."

"Matthew Grace. Oh." Whoever Boyous was it sounded like he'd heard of me. He put me on hold. A minute later he was back on line. "The lieutenant says for you to go to hell."

"That's impossible. Parker doesn't swear."

"For you he makes an exception."

I should explain. Parker was the reason I was no longer a crime scene technician. Part of the reason, anyway. Toward the end of my career I got tired of seeing guilty men walking away from crimes everyone knew they'd committed. Evidence would be thrown out, witnesses would recant, and the case would be dismissed. And sometimes juries would acquit even with sufficient evidence and eyewitness testimony. So one day I did something about it and made sure that somebody who richly deserved it went to jail. And I got way with it. And I kept getting away with it until Parker caught me.

He tried to have me arrested. Not wanting a scandal that would cause it to retry every case I'd ever worked on, the Department, as I hoped it would, covered things up. I left when Parker decided to press IAD charges.

"Tell him it's about Carol Masters," I told Boyous. He put me on hold again.

"Parker here," I heard when the hold tone clicked off.

"Lieutenant, congratulations on the promotion."

"Shut it, Grace. What about Carol Masters?"

"I've been hired to …"

Parker hung up.

I'd expected that. I made another call. An hour later I was in Parker's office. He was not a happy man.

"Grace, the only reason you're here is that the Chief of Detectives called me. The Police Commissioner had called him. That's after the mayor called the commissioner. So who called the mayor?"

"Barbara Masters."

"You're a window peeper, Grace. Why would she hire you to investigate a murder?"

"I've got a nice smile, that and the right background."

Parker thought about this for a moment, then nodded to himself. "So that's it. She's not so much interested in your solving the case than in checking us out. So what are you going to do, Grace? Read the file then tell her how many ways we messed up?"

"Lieutenant, you and I never got along. You never liked me and I never much liked you. But I always respected the work you and your men did. I fully expect to read the file and tell Mrs. Masters that you guys didn't miss a trick, that you did everything possible. And if I do find something you missed, I'll tell you, not her. She hired me to find her daughter's killer, not to make you look bad. So, where's the case folder?"

I don't know if Parker bought my little speech or not. I hoped so, I'd spent the drive to headquarters composing it. Not that that it mattered if he did. After all those phone calls he had no choice but to cooperate. Still, things would go smoother if he didn't think I was looking to put him in a jackpot.

Parker handed me a three-inch binder. "Here it is — police reports, lab results, photos and sketch. You get one look at this. You'll make no copies, you'll take nothing out. If I find anything missing, I'll arrest you for petty theft and obstruction of justice. Is that clear?" I told him it was. He directed me to an interview room, left me alone and locked me in.

I looked at the crime scene photos first. It was worse than what the media had let on. Carol Masters had suffered multiple stab wounds, many of which could have been fatal. If they hadn't, the slice across her throat was deep enough to have done the job. With the way her blood had spattered around the room, it would have been impossible for the killer not have gotten some on himself or his clothing.

This wasn't a burglar, the part of my mind that was still a crime scene tech told me. Carol's death was too violent for it to have come from the hands of a stranger. No, this was a crime of passion. The killer had strong feelings toward her — love denied, love turned to rage. Why? Jealousy, rejection, betrayal? And she had let her killer in, the photos didn't show any signs of forced entry. Or else he'd bullied his way past her when she answered the door. Still, she wouldn't have opened the door to a stranger, would she?

There was no weapon shown in the photos. There was a shot in the kitchen, one showing a knife rack with an empty slot. Looked like the roast knife was missing. Eight or nine inch blade, curved at the tip. That would have done the job.

There were a lot of photos of blood spatter, ones showing their angles and directions. There were, however, no photos of visible prints in blood. Had there been I wouldn't have been needed. The killer's prints in the victim's blood, even an L.A. prosecutor could get a conviction with that kind of evidence,

Putting aside the photos, I looked over the lab reports. All of the blood samples collected proved to be Carol's. Fingerprints? Mostly hers, some identified with Diane Balzeck, a few with her parents. There were also fingerprint IDs with a Leon Klaus as well as a Kevin Beacham. The last name was familiar. I'd heard it somewhere, but couldn't place it right away.

As far as physical evidence from the scene, that was it. The bed clothing was clean — no hairs, bodily fluids, or anything else that didn't belong to the victim. And no other trace evidence was found that might lead to a suspect match later on.

Results from the autopsy weren't much better. There had been no sexual assault, so no evidence along those lines. And while Carol had suffered some defensive wounds, she hadn't gotten close enough to mark her attacker — no skin under her nails.

I turned to the police reports. Nothing unusual there. One from the first officer on the scene. He'd arrived, saw the body and secured the place for Homicide and Crime Lab. Apartment and neighborhood canvases from other officers. Only one witness who saw a white male, apparently in his early twenties running from Carol's apartment building late that night. Beyond seeing that the man had dark hair and may have been of greater than average height, he couldn't provide much of a description. I read ahead. Klaus and Beacham both fit. It could have been either one, or someone else entirely.

I was just starting the suspect interviews when Parker came back into the room. "Finished yet, Grace? We just had a double shooting that might go bad and we're going to need the room."

I handed him the case book. "A few quick questions, if you have time, Lieutenant. If not, I can always come back."

Parker sat down. "If it will get you out of my unit faster, what?"

"Beacham or Klaus, who do you like better?"

He shrugged. "Either one, both. Klaus as the new boyfriend, Beacham the old one. Word from the Balzeck woman was that Masters broke up with Beacham because of his drug use."

"And Beacham didn't like that."

"Not in the least."

"What about Klaus?"

"New boyfriend, but the jealous type, the very jealous type."

"So either one could have done it?"

Parker nodded. "One of them probably did do it, but which one. Neither has an alibi, they both said they were home studying all night, and we couldn't find anyone to say anything different. We questioned them extensively — I questioned them extensively, and came up empty."

"What about the witness? Where was he?"

"He lives in the apartment near to the victim's. He was going in when he heard a door slam. He looked around to see someone run out."

"And of course he couldn't ID either of your suspects."

"Of course not." Parker stood up. "And that's it, Grace. Now leave and don't come back. And if you do come up with something, I want it first."

I got up to leave. "One last thing, Lieutenant. The name Beacham, I've heard it before."

"That's Beacham as in Judge Wendell Beacham. Kevin Beacham was his son."

"Was?"

"Kevin died of an overdose two months after Carol Masters was killed."

Poor Parker, I thought sometime later back in my office, here he had a ready made fall guy — a junkie ex-boyfriend who was conveniently dead — and he couldn't use him because the guy was the son of a judge. Not that Parker was the kind of cop who'd go that route, but if it hadn't been for the other suspect Klaus, the temptation to drop this one in the "Closed — abated by death" file would have been very tempting.

Beacham being a judge's son was probably the reason Parker kept a lid on his suspects' names, not even telling the Masters. My clients not knowing was the key I needed to get in to see His Honor.

I called the judge's chambers that morning for an appointment before his court docket started. His schedule was full until I asked his clerk to mention that I was working for Evans Masters. That got me thirty minutes before the start of court.

"Why should I tell you anything?" Judge Beacham asked when I told him why I'd wanted to see him.

"To help clear your son's name of suspicion of murder," I offered.

He frowned. "My son is dead, as you well know. He's beyond caring what anyone thinks of him. Besides, the only ones who know he's a suspect are you, me and the police."

"That's true," I said, "for now. But the Masters are my clients, and I plan to make a full report to them. What they do with the information is up to them."

Judges are supposed to apolitical. That's bunk and everyone knows it. They are periodically reappointed and have to stand for reelection like everyone else who holds public office. Someone with enough political pull could make things difficult for a sitting judge, if he had a good reason.

"Evan Masters wouldn't blame me for his daughter's death."

"Who's to say who a grieving father would blame, or would want to punish? And should the press find out ...?"

The judge gave me a funny look. "That sounds like ... blackmail, Mr. Grace," he said, his voice catching at the end.

"As they say, Your Honor, blackmail's an ugly word. All I'm asking for is a little mutual cooperation."

"Very well," he said absently, as if his mind were far away. Maybe he was thinking of his late son, lost first to drugs and then to him.

We went over the same questions the police had asked him. Has he ever heard his son threaten Carol Masters? When before the murder had he last seen his son? After the murder? Had he seen his son wearing or washing bloody clothing the day after her death? I got the same answers — no, a week before, a few days after and no.

I asked the final question. "Your Honor, did you son ever tell you that he had killed Carol Masters?"

"No," he said flatly.

"Did you ever ask?"

"No." This one was a little weaker.

"Why not? You had to know that he was a suspect."

He nodded. "The police told me. And I think you know why, Mr. Grace. My son was a drug user. I know from my experiences on the bench that such people are capable of anything. I didn't ask because I didn't want to know."

"And had you known?"

He got that far away look again. "To be honest, I think the father in me would have been stronger than the judge. I would have protected my boy."

"Not to mention your job?"

A look of anger suddenly came over the judge's face. It passed just as quickly. "A fair question," he looked at his watch, "and it will have to be the last one. Think about it, Mr. Grace. A judge who protects his son from a murder charge is liable not only to lose his seat but to face arrest as an accessory. But one who turns his son in would be seen as totally incorruptible. But he wouldn't be much of a father, would he?"

I had the sense that there was something the judge wasn't telling me, something he knew that I didn't. Maybe it was just fear that his suspicion of his son's involvement was justified, and that I'd find something out to prove it.

"There's another father out there trying to do right by his child, his daughter. Doesn't he have a right to know, even if it's off the record? As you said, Kevin's beyond the law now, and Evan Masters knows how to be discrete."

There was pain in Judge Beacham's eyes as he looked at me. "I really wish I could help, Mr. Grace, that I could tell you something. But I can't." And he hurried out, leaving me alone in his chambers.

Leon Klaus was my living suspect. I thought that getting an interview with him might be difficult, but when I called he invited me over that evening.

"I don't know how many different ways I can say it, Mr. Grace, I didn't kill Carol Masters. Why would I?"

"Maybe because you were jealous. That's gotten you in trouble before."

We were sitting in his living room, each of us with a beer in his hand, like old college buddies. Klaus was surprisingly open and friendly, considering I was all but accusing him of murder.

Klaus smiled. "Yeah, I kinda get possessive when I've been drinking, and that's what that trouble was about. I was with a girl and some guy starting hitting on her right in front of me. Well, being drunk and stupid I started hitting on him, first with my fists then with the bar stool. I got a year's probation and was sent to an alcohol treatment program."

"And were you drunk and stupid the night Carol was killed?"

He shook his head. "Like I told the police, I was home studying for a final. Just like Carol was supposed to be doing. We had met in that class." He got up and walked into the kitchen, came back with another beer, his third. I was still working on my first. I guess he didn't graduate from his alcohol classes with top honors.

"So why weren't you studying together?"

"Because we wanted to get some work done. When we were together the last thing we thought about were the books."

"You don't seem too broken up about her death."

I'd hit a nerve. The beer can he'd been holding slammed down hard on the coffee table. "Dammit," he yelled. I shifted my position in my chair, the better to dodge out of the way if he came at me. Instead, he banged the can down again, causing most of it to spill from the top.

"You and the cops. You think it was some big love affair. We'd known each other a couple of months. We'd been dating about two weeks. We had some laughs, the sex was good. It was fun, but that's all it was. I'm sorry she's dead, but she was just some girl I knew."

He looked down at his beer-covered hand. Without a word he got a rag from the kitchen and cleaned up the spill. He also brought back a fresh can

"Did you know Kevin Beacham?" I asked as he cleaned up the spill.

"The loser she dated before me. She dumped him because of drugs, didn't she?"

And maybe, I thought, she was dumping you because of your drinking. I kept that thought to myself, not wanting him to violate his probation by sending me to the hospital. Instead I asked, "She ever mention him?"

"No." He answered too fast and too sharply for me to believe him.

Klaus took a long drink of his beer. "Look, Mister, I'm done telling you and the cops anything. It's bad enough that, that, never mind. I'm done talking. Now leave me alone."

I stayed in my chair, not making any move to leave. Klaus didn't try to make me, just sat in his chair, drinking his beer and ignoring me. After a while, I left him alone with his thoughts.

Carol Masters sure could pick them, I thought on the drive home. She traded in a druggie for a drunk. The drunk had one arrest for assault, but who knows how many unreported fights he'd been in. The druggie may have been picked up a few times for possession in drug buy stings, but having a father who's a judge is a good way to keep your record clean.

Either one could have done it. I could imagine Klaus sitting at home, brooding, Carol Masters having just dumped him over his drinking too much. He opens a cold one, then another, then kills the six-pack. Drunk and stupid, he goes over to her place to show her who's boss.

Or Beacham could have gone over, looking to get back together, ready to swear to get himself clean. She lets him in, but he's got just enough of an edge on when she tells him she's seeing someone else. Then he picks up the knife and …

Who was I fooling? I had no idea which of them did it. I was going through the motions, but this wasn't my game. I had been good, very good at crime scene work, and now I tracked down cheating husbands and thieving employees. Homicide investigation was the big leagues, and maybe I just wasn't ready to play like the pros. Had I asked the right questions? Did I miss an answer? Whatever I had, I needed more, and wasn't likely to get it. Maybe the best I could do was call the Masters and tell them that Parker and his crew had done everything right, expect maybe they should have gotten Leon Klaus drunk before questioning him.

Still, I wasn't ready to quit just yet. I wanted to talk to the witness who may have seen the killer running from the scene. Maybe, just maybe he remembered something he hadn't told the police. I also wanted to look over the apartment where the murder had taken place.

I didn't expect that seeing the apartment would solve the case for me. I did hope that walking though it would, along with my memories of the crime scene photos, help me better understand just what the scene had actually looked like, and what had happened the night Carol was killed.

The apartment was, of course, occupied by a new tenant. The young lady who rented it, Dawn Rogers, was very understanding but a little confused by my request. Yes, she had known about the murder, but no one from the police had talked to her before this. I suppose I should have corrected her mistaken belief about my status in the case, but I figured that as long as Parker didn't find out, there'd be no harm done.

Ms. Rogers let me look over the entire apartment. I checked the locks on the front and balcony doors, walked from the living room, past the kitchen and into the bedroom, mentally substituting her furnishings for Carol's, moving the players around in my head, coming with a theory of how the crime had occurred.

Beacham, or Klaus, had come for a visit. He and Carol were in the living room. Were there glasses on the coffee table? I thought back to the photos, I didn't remember seeing any. Then it hadn't become a social evening. Maybe he arrived drunk or high, and she told him to leave. Then she said something, something that in his altered state caused him to grab the knife from the kitchen counter and go after her, catching her in the bedroom where his rage took over.

Or maybe I was chasing my tail and it was a knock-and-rob gone bad.

I must have been standing and thinking for quite awhile because I heard Ms. Rogers say, "Officer, are you okay?" I assured her I was and went to recheck her door locks.

"Did they replace the locks when you moved in?" I asked.

"New locks? You kidding? From what the other tenants tell me management hasn't made any improvements since the place was built back in the seventies. I had maintenance rekey the doors but that's all they did."

"Did you move in right after the incident?"

"About a week after, when you guys released it and management cleaned up."

I had seen all I needed to. I thanked her.

"Can you do me a favor?" she asked before I could say good-bye.

"If I can."

"There's this creepy guy in the building across the way. I think he watches me from his window at night. Any way you can get him to stop?"

She took me into her bedroom. Pointing out of her window, she showed me which apartment the creep lived in. I told her I'd do all I could.

On my way out I thought about this Peeping Tom. If he'd been living there when Carol was murdered and had been spying on her as well, he might be another witness, one who didn't come forward because he didn't want anyone to know how he got his kicks. Now that's something Parker didn't turn up, I thought, feeling better about how my investigation was going.

I left Ms. Rogers's place, the front door closing gently behind me, and I looked around for the building where Parker's witness lived. It was the same building as the creep's. Two for one, I'd save some time. I took a step toward it and stopped. Something wasn't right. It took me a minute or two to figure out just what.

I hit the bell for Dawn Rogers's apartment again.

"Yes?" came her voice through the intercom.

"This is Matthew Grace, again. Can you hit the buzzer?"

"Did you forget something?"

"Just one more question."

No, she hadn't remembered anyone working on the front door since she moved in.

Before I left the second time I played with the building door. The door's closer had been adjusted so as to close slowly every time, to keep it from slamming. I tired slamming it and couldn't. Unless it was broken that night, and from what I recalled from the crime scene photos it wasn't, it would have closed quietly then too.

So Parker's witness, this Andy Brock, couldn't have heard the killer leave like he said he did. The front door didn't slam causing him to turn. It could have been a car door he'd heard. Or maybe he'd just lied for the attention, or for the hell of it. Or maybe, I thought, looking up at the window that Dawn Roger's creep looked out of, he saw it all from a different perspective.

Of course, if Brock was a peeper, that opened up another possibility. He might have liked what he saw, and wanted to do more than look. And so one night, after taking a good long look to make sure that she was home alone, he goes over there, talks his way in. Professing his love, he's rejected, dismissed, told to leave. Then he goes into the kitchen and picks up a knife. Afterwards, he makes up the story about seeing someone to distract the police.

This theory made me think twice about questioning Brock. I'd done something stupid like that toward the end of my career as a crime lab tech. It nearly was the end of my career as I was almost beaten to death by a murder suspect. This time there wouldn't be any backup to save me.

Then again, Brock didn't have to know he was a suspect. As far as he was concerned, this was just another routine follow-up.

I felt better when Brock opened the door. I'm average weight and a little over five-seven. Brock was smaller and lighter than me. He looked like he'd have trouble battling a good stiff breeze. He didn't look like the murdering type. Carol Masters would have likely slapped him silly before he could use a knife on her. Still, he may have caught her by surprise. I decided I'd pay attention so he couldn't catch me in such a state.

I thought it best to stick with my original line of questioning, so after he let me in and we'd parked ourselves in his living room, I took out photos of my two suspects. "You know these two men?"

Brock took a quick look. "If I hadn't seen them before I'd know them now. Kevin Beacham and Leon Klaus. The police showed me their pictures often enough, each time trying to get me to say one of them was the man I saw on the parking lot."

"Any chance your memories improved since the last time?"

"Not a one."

I tried a different tack. "Did you know either one before the murder?"

"I'd seen them around, saw them going into Carol Masters's place a few times. This one," he pointed to Beacham's photo, "stopped coming shortly before the other one started showing up."

For a casual neighbor not even in the same building he knew a lot about Carol's visitors.

"Ever see Beacham after Klaus started visiting?"

He shook his head. "No, I think I'd have noticed." I'm sure he would have.

"Did you know them by name, or just from seeing them go in and out?"

"Leon I already knew. We had a class or two together at Hopkins."

"What about Beacham?"

He shrugged. "I knew of him. Campus gossip had him as a junkie who stayed out of jail because his father was a judge."

What I wanted now was a look at his bedroom. Using an old police trick, I asked to use his restroom.

Brock's bedroom was across the hall from the bathroom. Fortunately for me, the door was open.

Brock was the creep. A quick peek into his bedroom showed me a window with an excellent view into Dawn Rogers's apartment, a camera with a zoom lens in plain view nearby.

"Thanks," I told Brock, resuming my seat on his sofa.

"Hey, when nature calls you gotta answer."

I asked a few more questions but I wasn't really interested in the answers. My interest now was his apartment, how to get in and out without being noticed. Q&A was over. It was time for the sneaky stuff.

When I first went private, I did some lab work for another PI. Instead of cash, he paid me with some codes and passwords for certain databases in the Baltimore area. Back then, computer security wasn't as tight as it is these days and working those databases got me access to even more. So it was that I was able to hack bank accounts, credit card statements, financial reports and, in the case of Andy Brock, college transcripts.

Brock was an okay student. He'd never make the dean's list, but he was far from being put on double secret probation. The one course of study he followed was of particular interest — every semester he took a photography course or two. That would give him darkroom privileges, allowing him to develop his nasty little pictures himself without having to find a kindred pervert at the one-hour photo booth. It was a good bet that he had pictures of Carol, by herself and with Beacham or Klaus. And just maybe he had photographed a murder.

If he had this information wouldn't he have told the police? They'd certainly be willing to overlook a little voyeurism to solve a murder. But instead he had lied to the police for no reason. Or maybe he had a reason. I hoped to find the answer in his apartment one day when he wasn't home.

Using my access to his college schedule, I picked a time when Brock would be on campus all day. Dressed in overalls and carrying a clipboard and a toolbox, I sat in my borrowed van waiting for someone to approach his building. When I saw a woman heading that way I hustled over there myself, timing it so I would arrive just as she did.

"It's about time they started fixing this place up," she said opening the door for the both of us.

I gave her a smile and went up to Brock's apartment.

Good security on the outside usually meant poor security on the inside, and Brock's building was no exception. He hadn't spent any money on a deadbolt and my ten year experience processing burglary scenes meant that I slipped past his simple passage lock in no time. Had anyone seen me it would have appeared that I'd used a key.

Since he had no one to hide them from (he thought) I found his special photo albums right away — in the bottom drawer of his night table. They were full of what I'd expected — Dawn Rogers undressing, Dawn Rogers undressed, the same for Carol Masters. There were shots of Carol and Beacham and Carol and Klaus. The latter weren't very good as far as details, but you could tell that something intimate was going on. Maybe that was enough for him.

The money shot wasn't there. I hadn't expected to find one of either of my suspects holding a bloody knife but it would have been nice. At least I'd found something I could turn over to Parker. He could now pressure Brock into telling what he had really seen the night of the murder.

To be thorough I looked at Brock's camera. A new roll. And as long as I was there I decided to go through Brock's desk and check out his financials.

Interesting. In addition to his paycheck from a part time campus job, Brock's statements had deposits of $500 here and $100 there, all on a more or less regular basis over the last six months.

I knew it meant something, but I didn't figure it out right away. Instead I picked up the camera, trained it on Ms. Rogers's window and zoomed in. Had it been dark and had her windows been open, I could have seen everything that went on in there. From the window I looked toward the ground. A perfect view, not of the front door, but of the side of the building. There'd be little lighting at night, and someone fleeing from his crime would have sought that darkness. And the bushes along the wall would have been the perfect place to have thrown a bloody knife carried from the scene in a panic. The police had searched those bushes, came up empty. Maybe somebody beat them to it.

Then it hit me. What had I said about the money shot? Maybe Brock had taken it, and maybe he had a photo of a bloody knife to go with it.

There were no negatives in sight and I didn't have time to search for the knife, assuming my theory was right and it was even there. Besides, I didn't want Brock to know he'd had a visitor and a thorough search would have meant tearing the place apart. I'd leave that to Parker and his gang once they got a warrant. But before I gave anything to Parker, I had a murder I wanted to solve.

The payments into Brock's account had to be coming from somewhere. As I got back to my office and accessed Leon Klaus's and Judge Beacham's accounts, I was hoping that those monthly payments weren't coming from Mommy and Daddy. They weren't. Judge Beacham's account showed withdrawals of $500 just a few days before the same sums appeared on Brock's statement. So the judge was paying off to keep people from finding out his little boy was a drug-crazed killer. At least that's what I thought until I pulled up Klaus's bank records. They showed $100 withdrawals at the same intervals, again just days before Brock made deposits. The s.o.b. was double-dipping.

At that point I could have gone to Parker and laid it all in his lap, giving him the killer and telling him where the evidence might be found. But given the circumstances everybody might lawyer up and the wrong guy could go to jail. Not wanting to take that chance, I decided to make a few things happen.

I first called Dawn Rogers. When I told her what I wanted her to do she said, "You're crazy!" Then I told her why. "You're crazy," she said again, then agreed to do it.

I next called Leon Klaus, asked if I could come over, told him I had important news for him. I took over a six-pack of Natty Boh.

"Here," I said handing him the beer when he answered the door.

"What the hell's this?" he asked, taking it anyway.

"A peace offering, can I come in?"

"Sure." He stepped aside and waved me to the sofa.

Klaus popped a can and sat next to me. "You said you had good news."

"Leon," I said in my most sincere tone, "you're finally off the hook. The beer's my way of apologizing for suspecting you of murder."

That actually got him to stop drinking. "You mean you decided the judge's son did it? That no-good junkie, I thought so." He finished his can and opened another one.

"Wasn't him, either. It was some guy in the building across the way. Turns out he was spying on her, on you too sometimes, from his bedroom window. Watching Carol got him so hot and bothered that one night I guess taking pictures of her just wasn't doing it for him anymore. He went over there, she said no, and, well, you know the rest."

When I mentioned pictures Klaus stopped drinking again. "What do you mean ... pictures?"

"Pictures, Leon, photographs of Carol in the buff and what have you. The creep was taking them from his window, probably has a whole album of them for the police to find when they serve the warrant tomorrow."

Klaus crushed the third can in his hand and started on his fourth. "What did you say this creep's name was?"

"I didn't, and I really shouldn't tell you, but what the hell. Tomorrow it'll be all over the news anyway. It's a guy named Brock, and he lives in a building near Carol's, the one next door on kind of an angle." There, I'd done everything but draw him a map. "Well, I've got to get going. Enjoy the beer."

I hoped he would, at least to the point of finishing the six-pack. I needed a head start to get Brock out of his way. Parker would never forgive me if I got his star witness killed.

I got to Dawn Rogers's in plenty of time, time enough for her to get into something sexy and revealing. When she did she stood in front of her bedroom window and called Brock.

"Hi," she purred into the phone, "I know you've been watching me. I like it when you watch. Are you watching me now? If you like what you see, I'm waiting for you. Come on over."

For Brock it had to be a dream come true, a fantasy he'd lived in his mind, and elsewhere, time and time again. Now it was really happening. He rushed right over and into Dawn's apartment only to find that she had changed into jeans and a sweatshirt and that I was blocking his way out.

"Hi, Andy," I said, locking the door behind me, "welcome to the party."

"What ... I ... I mean..." he rambled on until I interrupted.

"You know, Andy, they say blackmail is an ugly word. But then so are words like accessory after the fact and accomplice to murder — but maybe the police will settle for simply withholding evidence."

"What, what are you talking about?"

"Let's go into the bedroom and watch. That's something you're used to, isn't it?"

We sat in Dawn's bedroom and waited with the lights turned down low, watching Brock's apartment. Brock had rushed over in such a hurry that he'd left his lights on, and we had a clear view of the upcoming show.

We didn't have long to wait. Soon a drunken Leon Klaus drove up, parked his car (sort of) and stumbled to the front door of Brock's building and started pressing buttons until someone was annoyed enough to let him in. We next saw him in Brock's apartment, having broken in with a lot less subtlety than I had.

"Make the call," I told Dawn, who called 911 and reported the burglary, then I called Parker. I'd talked to him previously that day and told him that I might have something for him later.

"What is it, Grace?" he growled at me. He hadn't liked being kept waiting.

"You know your witness, Andrew Brock?"

"What about him?"

"Well, Leon Klaus just broke into his apartment and is trashing the place." I hung up before he could demand how I knew this.

"You can leave now," I told Brock, "although I don't know where you'd go." I pointed out the window across to where Klaus was tearing through his bedroom. "You can go home, but if you did, the cops wouldn't have to convict Klaus for Carol Masters's murder — they could just arrest him for yours. Or you can wander the streets until the police find you. Or you can just stay here and watch the fun."

Without much of a choice, he decided to stay.

It was quite a show. The patrol units got to Brock's apartment just as Klaus had finished with the bedroom and had started taking apart the living room. He got roughed and cuffed then sat on the sofa, apparently to wait for Parker, who arrived not ten minutes later.

I gave the uniforms time to explain what had happened then called Brock's apartment. When an officer answered I asked for Parker. I watched as the cop made an "it's for you" gesture and handed him the phone.

"Hello, Lieutenant. Look out the window." I flipped on the bedroom lights and waved. "Brock's over here. You want to send someone over to get him. I'm sure he has lots to tell you."

A uninformed officer came over to collect Brock. That left me alone with Dawn. "You're not a real cop, are you?" she asked.

"Never said I was," I countered, then I explained about being hired by the victim's family.

"Well, at least you took care of that creep like I asked you to." Then after a pause added, "Can you stay for a while?"

A memory of her in the silky number she wore to lure Brock out of his apartment hit me. "I'd love to," I said, then I remembered Parker. "But something tells me I won't be able to."

I was right. Within ten minutes another uniform came and collected me, and soon I was sitting in the same interview room where I'd originally reviewed the case folder. This time Parker was sitting next to me.

"Tell me about it, Grace, and don't leave anything out."

There was no reason not to, so I laid it all out for him. How Judge Beacham had almost choked on the word blackmail, Klaus's excited comment about something being bad enough, the withdrawals, the deposits, the door that wouldn't slam and Peeping Andy.

"And then you just couldn't come to me. You had to get cute. What if Klaus had just stayed home?"

"Then I would have come to you."

"And what if Brock had stayed home, and was there when Klaus came over? What if Klaus had killed him?"

"Small loss, but I didn't think there was any danger in that." I picked up one of the photos Brock had taken of Dawn, showed it to Parker. "Be honest, Lieutenant, would you turn this down?"

As far as anyone knew, Parker hasn't told a lie since he made sergeant, so he didn't say yes. And he definitely didn't want to say no. So he changed the subject.

"What made you decide on Klaus as the killer?"

"The judge paid off at first to protect his son, who he thought might be guilty. Then probably to cover the fact that he had paid off to protect his son. Had Klaus been innocent he would have either ignored the blackmail demand or else reported it to you. The guilty ones always pay."

"So," I added, "you find the knife yet?"

Parker shook his head. "We're waiting on a warrant, but Brock told us where it is — wrapped in plastic on the top shelf of his hall closet."

"What about Klaus?"

The lieutenant actually smiled. "Angry, drunk and caught in a felony. Best kind of suspect to question. Plus one of my detectives led him to believe that being blackmailed is a mitigating circumstance. He's giving it all up."

"So, Lieutenant, do I get 'a job well done?'"

He almost said it. Instead he stood up and said, "Go home, Grace. You'll be contacted if you're needed for trial."

While Parker and his unit got full credit in the press, he did have the decency to tell my clients that I was "instrumental" in solving their daughter's murder. The Masters got the full story when I made my report. They were very grateful, and generous, and promised to recommend me to their friends. Also, through their influence, Judge Beacham's name was kept out of any official reports that might be released to the public. Brock got a deal — no charges in exchange for his testimony against Klaus, no public statements on his part and he had to move to a basement apartment and find a new hobby. No one expects him to stick to the last part of that deal and Judge Beacham is just waiting for Brock to get caught peeping again. He won't hear the case, but one of his friends will.

Leon Klaus was tried for homicide and went away for manslaughter, a Baltimore jury deciding that he hadn't gone to Carol Master's apartment with the intent to kill. I guess being drunk and stupid sometimes pays off. Her parents were devastated at the verdict. However long he spends in jail, one day Klaus will be free and their little girl will still be dead, and there's nothing their money and influence can do to change that. The guilty might always pay, but sometimes it's not enough.

PAST SINS

As I woke up, the radio told me that it was snowing and that I wouldn't have to go to school today. I hadn't been to school for twenty years so I hit the snooze alarm and went back to sleep. When I woke up again, it was still snowing. The DJ announced that a snow emergency had been declared and that all vehicles on the street would need snow tires or chains. That didn't bother me, I'd be walking to work.

I read the paper while drinking my morning tea. People were still fighting in several parts of the world and there had been the usual number of natural disasters. On the local front, jury selection was continuing in the trial of two "alleged" associates of the local mob boss. Since they were on trial for killing a juror who had held out for convicting the boss at his latest (mis)trial, jury selection was expected to take a considerable amount of time.

Baltimore is a funny city in the snow. When the sidewalks get covered, they close the schools. One inch and they declare an emergency and warm up the snowplows. I walked to work in what was considered near blizzard conditions — slushy streets and four inches on the ground. The city seemed closed.

The only car on 25th Street was parked in front of my office. It was a black limousine that had been there awhile. There was an inch of snow on the windshield and very little under the car. The car was empty.

I walked toward my office wondering who belonged to the car. As the owner and sole operative of Matthew Grace Investigations I'm used to a wide variety of clients, few of whom could afford a limousine. Those who could would expect me to come to them. And few people in Baltimore would be out in the snow at 8:30 in the morning if they didn't have to. People who own limousines usually don't have to.

My office door was unlocked. I hadn't left it that way. Two large gentlemen wearing suits with 9mm bulges were standing on either side of my desk. Sitting behind my desk was the employer of the men I had read about in the morning paper. (Concerned as I am about my continued good health, I'm not about to use anyone's real name. I'll call the guy at my desk "Louis.")

Louis looked at me with disapproval. "You are late," he said. "I have been waiting for you since 7:55."

"It's snowing," I said. "Besides, what's the use of running you own business if you can't sleep in when it snows? What are you doing out in this weather?"

A man not accustomed to answering other people's questions, he paused before replying. "I attended 7:00 mass at St. Leo's. I came straight from there. You are usually in your office by 7:45. You complete your previous day's reports and conduct telephone inquiries until noon. You then have lunch before doing your field investigations. Unless a case demands it, you seldom vary this routine. You did today. Why?"

"Mr. Louis, I am, of course, aware of whom you are, but you're in my office. If I wanted someone to answer to, I'd get married. Now, if you have business with me, step around to the customer side of the counter."

Part of me was hoping he'd get mad and leave. Another part was afraid he'd get mad and wouldn't leave, but have his bookends teach me manners. The rest of me was wondering what he needed a PI for with an organization capable of the research job he'd had done on me.

He didn't leave. I didn't lose any teeth. To my surprise, he left my chair in favor of its twin on the other side. As he sat down, he said to his shadows, "Leave us, wait in the car." As they left, I got two looks that said, "Touch him and we'll see how many times you can be folded."

I got down to business. "How can I help you, Mr. Louis?"

Without his bodyguards, Louis looked liked a hundred other clients, nervous, worried, afraid that the man they came to for help may not be honest. Echoing my thoughts, Louis said, "I think that I can trust you. Your discretion regarding the demise of our late mayor is proof of that. Tell me, if you can, how did you get the Fireside Girls to agree with the 'official' story?"

"Cookies. The public school cafeterias will be serving lots of cookies in the years to come." I wasn't surprised that he's heard the real story. Only the public hadn't.

He smiled, I think. Then he got down to business. "Mr. Grace, I am being blackmailed. I would like you to find out by whom." I started to interrupt. He continued, "I assure you, the incident in question was not illegal, and investigating it you should learn nothing which would endanger your health." As neat a veiled warning as I'd ever heard.

"I hope you'll forgive this question, Mr. Louis, but considering your reputation, what's left to blackmail you with?"

Distaste and regret showed in his face. "Two years ago I had an affair with a young lady. It lasted several months. I ended the affair when I realized the damage the discovery of my infidelity could cause to my marriage and to me. I made generous provisions for the lady in question. I have come to realize that, whether or not they would have been discovered, my actions were not those of a good Catholic or an honorable man." He paused. I let the "good Catholic" remark slide.

He continued. "Two months ago, I received a letter in the mail. It was neatly typed. The author threatened to reveal his knowledge of my affair to my wife. He promised his continued silence in exchange for continuous payments."

"How much money is involved?"

"Ten thousand dollars a month, for now."

"How are the payments made?"

"I send the money addressed to a mail-forwarding service, and before you ask, theirs is a most secure operation. Several 'research' operations have failed to turn up a name or address."

I then asked the question I'm sure all of you have been thinking. "Why not tell your wife? Take your lumps and be done with it?"

"That is not the problem, Mr. Grace. The one person I cannot tell is my wife. When we were young, our marriage was arranged by our parents. As in former times, it was a marriage designed to unite two warring 'families.' I gave my solemn word back then to remain faithful, and I have kept that word except for this one affair. There was belief in honor then, there is little now. Two people who still believe in that honor are my wife and her brother. My wife's brother is a business rival. If my wife were to learn that I had been unfaithful, she would tell him, and he would feel bound to take the actions he believed necessary to redeem her honor. These actions would lead to an escalation that would keep the police very busy."

Little is known about the true activities of Baltimore's Mob. It is believed that organized money lending, prostitution and gambling are controlled, more or less, directly by its competing factions. Also, those factions serve as banks and laundries for the independent drug gangs. A war on any scale, added to the usual violence in Baltimore, would make things very messy indeed.

I spent the rest of the meeting getting the details of the affair, where they met, where they went, who knew about the affair, who didn't. Louis assured me that I would not have to question his bodyguards of that time. They had been retired. I didn't ask, but I don't think they got gold watches.

As Louis stood to leave, I asked, "Do you still have the letter?"

"I was wondering when you would ask. I have it here. I will leave it with you to conduct whatever analyses are necessary. When you are finished, I will trust you to destroy it." He then gave me a telephone number which would eventually reach him and turned to go.

I stopped him with one last question. "Mr. Louis, why a private investigator? Couldn't one of your people look into this for you?"

"Very few of my people know about this incident. I cannot afford to have it known that I am being blackmailed. It would involve a serious loss of respect and thus a loss of authority. I feel more secure trusting you that my associates. I believe you to be trustworthy. I know that they are not." With that he left.

I was surprised that he would leave the letter with me. When I read it, I understood. All it said was, "You know what happened at the Lorre Hotel. So do I. Others will know unless you pay my price . . ." It went on to detail the financial arrangements. As written, there was nothing to indicate what had happened. If his wife saw it, Louis could always tell her that he'd had someone killed. That she would understand.

In the back room of my offices I maintain a small forensic laboratory. It's not as elaborate as the Baltimore Crime Lab, but I don't work for them anymore. The first thing I did was to photograph the letter, just in case I found a printer for comparison. After that, I sprayed, dusted and even fumed the paper with glue vapors. I found a few fingerprints which looked suitable for comparison. Later that day I had an acquaintance who still worked at the Crime Lab run them through the identification computer, no questions asked. The next day he called back, asked me if had ever heard of the man I am calling "Louis" and expressed concern for my continued good health.

So as not to give the lie to the report that Louis's associates had prepared on me, I spent the rest of the morning conducting telephone inquiries. Actually, they were computer inquiries. Using a computer and a few codes and programs I wasn't supposed to have, I traced several runaway spouses by tracking their credit card use. (Yes, some people are that dumb.) One guy had left a bank card trail through almost every massage parlor and sleazy motel from Baltimore's Block to Miami. I caught up to him just as he had checked into a reputable (for a change) hotel on the beach. His wife took the next flight south.

After lunch I started the work for which Louis was to pay me generously. My first stop was the mail-forwarding business the blackmailer was using. Louis was right, the place was secure. I tried bribery, chicanery, even resorted to honesty, to no avail. Since burglary (i.e., "research") had already been tried and had failed, I eliminated the business as a source of my quarry's name.

Interviewing witnesses, accomplices, whatever, is not what I do best. My interview technique was once described by a colleague as walking up to someone and asking, "Did you do it?" and taking "No," for an answer. I've gotten better since then but not by much. I'm a lot better at night surveillance, paper chases, unauthorized entries for "research" purposes — you know, the sneaky stuff. Only when that fails do I resort to asking questions.

Turning again to my computer, I checked the bank accounts of all of my suspects. Only one, Louis's accountant, showed any deposits large enough to suggest guilt. The accounts of the other suspects were as clean as money coming from their line of work could be. The rest of my computer search, credit records, purchases, vehicle registrations, provide no further information. No one, except the accountant, had cleared any old debts, or purchased any new cars, boats or other toys. At least, there were no records of their having done so. People in their line of work don't always leave records. It's not in their natures to do so.

The snow had stopped, so I walked home, got into my car and started my drive-bys. I drove past the homes of all my suspects, the ex-girl friend, Louis's chauffeur (who, unlike the bodyguards, had not been "retired") a man whom Louis had described as his "counselor," the accountant and the hotels where all of the action had taken place. Doing these drive-bys helped to give me a feel for the kind of people who lived in the homes, and gave me a preliminary look-see in case "research" was called for.

After the drive-bys, I stopped at the hotels. Both establishments were the kind that the average big spending tourist would ignore. There was no glass, glitz or glitter. Neither was anywhere near Baltimore's Inner Harbor. Still, both did a steady business, specializing in comfortable surroundings, discrete service and failing memories.

No one at either hotel remembered Mr. Louis or his friend. At least, not until I started mentioning certain key phrases like "Grand Jury", "ongoing investigation", "search warrants" and, my favorite, "scandal." After that, I got all the cooperation I wanted and the names of several current and former employees to check later. A funny thing, though. As I left, the managers of both hotels called me "Officer." I wonder where they got that idea.

The computer checks on the hotel employees were negative. Several were cheating on their taxes and one was selling the hotel's guest list to a mailing list firm, but they were clean as far as I was concerned. Phone calls to their homes complaining that their account at the mail-forwarding business was overdue were met with uncomprehending remarks.

I called on the former girlfriend next. The elaborate story I had prepared went to waste when I found out that she was in the eighth month of a two-year world cruise. The "counselor" was likewise out of the country. He had suddenly been called to Rome, to assist in the legal defense of some business associates. I was running out of suspects.

Saving the accountant for last, I made arrangements to speak with the chauffeur. Yes, she remembered driving Mr. Louis to the hotels. No, she did not know what he did there or whom he met. Yes, it probably was some sort of business conference. No, she definitely did not hear any gunshots or see anything that would suggest violence had occurred. I left her with the impression that someone had been retired at one of the hotels. I didn't want anyone else thinking blackmail.

The accountant was easy, disappointing and exactly what I'd expected. He was my best suspect, but accountants don't have to blackmail you to steal your money. After arranging an interview, I walked into his office accompanied by two of Louis's nastier employees. I said to him, "Mr. Louis knows what you have been doing. He would like to see the books."

Until then, I had never seen a person wilt. He did. He shrank into his chair, trying to find a back door in it. "A confession will make things go easier," I lied. He believed me.

I left his office alone, leaving him with my companions. I presume he has since been retired.

Most blackmailers are easy to find. Their immunity lies in the unwillingness of the victim to have his secrets revealed. This was a different case. The suspects I had were either unavailable or had been proven innocent (of this crime anyway). What few doubts I had were resolved by night time visits to the homes of whomever Louis had invited for dinner that evening.

By now, Louis was becoming impatient. Another demand had been made and he wanted results. I began to get the feeling that if I didn't produce I was going to meet his old bodyguards. And I was out of ideas.

One night I sat in my darkened office reviewing all I knew and didn't know about the case, starting with my finding Louis in my office. The click came as I remembered our conversation. There was someone I had left off of my list of suspects. A few phone calls. A computer check and I was sure. The next morning I called Louis and told him where to meet me.

The afternoon sun was soft through the stained glass, St. Brendan's was quiet, almost empty. Group penance services have cut down on the number of people who regularly go to Saturday confession. I looked around the church, at the new organ, the new speaker system, the fruits of one man trying to make evil do some good.

Louis was parked outside. Except for his chauffeur he was alone. I wondered what this "good Catholic" would do to the priest to whom he'd confessed his sins of the past three years.

I entered the confessional. The door slid back. "Bless you, Father, for you have sinned. This will be your last confession."

BY THE SWORD

As usual, I was late for lunch with my sister. At least this time I had a good excuse, or at least a better one than I usually give her. And I was not too late, just under twenty minutes this time.

I found Susan sitting at her favorite table at "Uncle Jack's," currently the trendiest of all of Baltimore's restaurants. I gave a wave to the fancy dressed man who controlled the seating and sat myself down next to her, carrying my excuse.

"Matthew Grace, you're late again."

"Sorry, Sis," I said to her frown, "but I just solved the Phillimore kidnapping."

"Didn't Sherlock Holmes do that?"

"Well, yeah, he did, but he only found Phillimore," I said as I held up my treasure, "I found his umbrella."

It was a very nice umbrella, and it could have come from the era in which the first of us private investigators worked. It was made from the finest materials, from its ivory handle to its very sharp metal point. And it did have the initials "J.P." engraved just below the handle. So who knows? It could have been the object for which Phillimore turned back into his house, only to disappear. To me it was an antique I had been hired to find and retrieve, no questions asked. The value that my client placed on it, and the difficulty I had in retrieving it, meant that I was not going to let it out of my sight until our meeting sometime tonight. I did get funny looks from people I did not know. I just pretended to be British and ignored them.

"I figured you would be late, so I ordered for you and told the waiter to start it cooking when an extremely rude person came crashing into the restaurant."

"Well I hope that person hurries up and gets here, I'm hungry."

"The food will be here soon. I ordered your usual, bacon cheeseburger with fries and a root beer." She said this like there was something else to eat for lunch.

While we waited, we talked of family things, who was getting married or divorced, who was pregnant, who was mad at whom and why — all the best gossip. I asked after her family. Everyone was fine, she admitted after some hesitation, then asked about my social life. (None of your business, thank you very much.)

It was after the food had come and had been mostly put away that I asked the big question. "Well, Susan, what do you want?"

"What makes you think I want anything?"

I had heard that tone before. She used it on Dad when we were growing up, still does in fact. She would use that voice when she wanted something, then he would unwrap himself from around her little finger and give her whatever she had asked for. She tries it on me every once in a while, just to see if it will work. It seldom does.

"Sis, we meet for lunch four times a year. We meet on my birthday, you pay; on your birthday, I pay. In December we meet to discuss Christmas plans and in May to discuss the family vacation. For you to treat me to lunch, in Uncle Jack's no less, in the middle of April means that you want something."

"What makes you think that I'm treating?"

"If you want something, you're treating."

"I'm treating."

Over dessert and coffee she told me her problem.

"It's Bill, and no, he's not cheating on me so get that look out of your eye. He's having trouble at work, and it might cost him his job."

"What did he do, or is it being done to him?"

"It's being done to him, and what he did was trust somebody he shouldn't have."

"Start from the beginning, this sounds complicated."

"It's about his promotion, the one I mentioned at Mom's last month."

"The one he was sure to get."

"That one, but now he's not so sure."

"What happened, Susan?"

"You know Bill, he's never been a political type. He's always believed in hard work, a good attitude and treating people fairly."

"Are you sure he's a lawyer?"

"I keep telling you, Bill's an attorney, not a lawyer. He handles contracts, not cases. The last time he was in a courtroom was to plead guilty on that speeding ticket and pay the fine."

"I offered to have it fixed. I know the judge."

"Anyway, he approaches his job in the same way. No office gossip or politics. He helps anyone who asks, always gives credit where it's due, and never goes out of his way to promote himself. The only reason he's gotten to where he has is that he is very good at his job, and his bosses know that."

"He's head of his section, isn't he?"

"And until now the only candidate for department manager."

"And now?"

"About six months ago, the firm hired several new associates. One of them was assigned to Bill's section, a Sharon Manchester," Susan all but spit out the name. "Well, as usual, Bill went out of his way to make her feel welcome, helping her on some projects, giving her some good contracts to work on, that sort of thing. She's good at her job, and Bill made her look even better. Now it looks like she's going to steal the promotion out from under him."

"How, if she's only been there for six months."

"She's been with Bill's firm for six months. She relocated to Baltimore from Philadelphia. I understand that before Philly she lived in Pittsburgh and Boston. Altogether she has about eight years' legal experience."

"A little more than Bill, but he's been with the firm longer."

"Right."

"So, what's the big deal? Bill's better than she is, or at least as good, and his standing with the company is better. And if she is that much better than he is, Bill would be the first to admit she deserves the promotion."

Susan gave me the look I deserved, but I had to say something to get her to the point.

"This has nothing to do with merit or ability, Matthew, it has to do with, well, first, she's an attractive, hard working, seemingly talented woman in a law firm top heavy with men.

"Second, she's gone out of her way to get to know all the partners, you know, running errands, making small talk, asking for advice on points of law when she knows more than they do."

"In other words, sucking up." She did not like that expression but agreed with my point.

"Right, something Bill doesn't know how to do, and wouldn't if he could. Finally, she's taken sole credit for some projects on which she and Bill both worked, and on working those projects, she learned of some of Bill's other ideas, plans he was working on to improve office productivity and accounting procedures."

"And she jumped the gun and presented them as her own ideas."

"Right, and since Bill hadn't talked about them at work, he couldn't very well claim them, it would make things worse."

"So, this Sharon has used her looks, gender and personality, Bill's help and trust, and a personal amorality with which I can identify to make herself a viable candidate for promotion. I can see why you're worried. She's a shark, Bill's not, and predators almost always win." She saw my point and finished my thought.

"And when they win, they eliminate the competition."

"You're right again. If she gets the job she'll make partner and then find an excuse to get rid of Bill. That way, if she proves to be less than the ideal choice . . ."

"Not 'if,' when," Susan corrected.

"OK, when," I agreed. "When this happens, there will be no one who can easily replace her, and the firm is that more likely to retain her."

"So I need a bigger predator."

"Meaning me?"

"Meaning you."

"Susan, I would do anything to help you and your family, if only to keep you from having to move in with me. But I'm not quite sure of what you think I can do to help Bill. By now the matter's pretty much decided, isn't it?"

"It may be decided, but it won't be official until after the partners' party, which is in two weeks. They usually make big announcements the Monday after the party, to keep anything from spoiling the mood."

"And you expect me to . . .?"

"I expect you, Matthew, to look under beds and into closets, to turn over rocks and look under them for whatever slimy secrets Ms. Manchester has hidden. And then to use them to keep her from getting, or accepting, that promotion."

"And if she doesn't have any 'slimy secrets'?" The look she gave me said it all. I pretended to ignore her unspoken suggestion that I manufacture some evidence against Ms. Manchester and agreed to look into the matter. That ended lunch as far as Susan was concerned and she called for the check.

As we left, the waiter called out to me, "Sir, your umbrella."

The fee I earned for finding and delivering the antique umbrella to a grateful collector meant that I was able to afford to spend a few days digging into Sharon Manchester's background in the hopes of digging up enough dirt to bury her chances of promotion. In prehistoric times (B.C. - before computers) this would have meant spending hours, maybe days, knocking on doors and visiting government agencies, working to keep my face straight and my lies believable as I convinced people to give me information which I really should not have. Now it's easier. After spending one afternoon at my keyboard, hooked into systems I had no right to be in, I knew a hell of a lot about Sharon Manchester. I knew where she banked, who had issued her credit cards, how much she owed on those cards and where she had used them. Thanks to that information, I learned where she spent her vacations, bought her books, rented her videos and shopped for clothes. I knew her tastes in literature, movies and fashion. I could tell you how many traffic tickets she had had in the last five years and her mother's maiden name. And none of it did a damn bit of good.

If I were Marlowe or Spade, or at least living in their times, the fact that Ms. Manchester had once spent a week in the Bahamas with a man not her husband would have been enough. The fact that some of her video rentals came from that back room restricted to adults would have been more than enough. Actually, if this were Sam Spade's time, the problem would never have come up. No matter how good she was, Ms. Manchester would have never been considered for any position of authority in a male dominated business.

How good was she? If Susan was to be believed, good enough to threaten her husband's job. But if she was that good, why was she now working for her fourth law firm in eight years?

I previously had done some work here in Baltimore for a Philadelphia-based lawyer. I called him up and got the name of a good Philly PI from him. A friend in New York gave me the name of a Pittsburgh agency that he trusted. Boston was taken care of by a cop friend who had moved there and gone private himself. I hired all three to look into the background and work history of Ms. Manchester and hoped that Susan would be willing to pay some of the expense, or at least would buy me a bigger Christmas present than she did last year.

There was little I could do until the reports came back. I did not want to talk with her neighbors or co-workers until I had more to go on, for fear of alerting her that an investigation of some sort was taking place. I did manage to verify that, since coming to Baltimore, she had not been arrested, admitted to the hospital under suspicious circumstances, or had done anything to suggest she was leading a less than wholesome life. I also drove by her rented home in the Owings Mills section of Baltimore County a few times, once faking car trouble a few houses away from hers, just in case an unauthorized visit while she was at work was called for.

Finally, after several days and two or three phone calls from Susan, the reports came back.

Sharon Manchester went from law school to a firm in Pittsburgh. Four years later she moved to Boston. Another year found her in Philadelphia. She lasted there three years before coming to Baltimore. All of the moves appeared to be voluntary on her part, but she had not gained any sort of advantage by any of them. In each case, she accepted the same sort of job at about the same salary level as she had at her old firm.

Her work records did not give the reasons for her various departures. Officially, in each case she left for the always popular "personal reasons." Her move to a new firm in a new city was always accompanied by a polite, somewhat non-committal letter of recommendation from a mid-level partner of the old firm. And once again, there were no records of any kind to suggest any sort of shady dealings in any of the three cities.

Fortunately, where the official records failed, gossip came through. My fellow PIs had been sharp enough to question not only the personnel offices and the bosses, but also the secretaries, mail room clerks and coffee ladies, the ones who always know what really goes on in the office.

A secretary in Pittsburgh remembered a Ms. Manchester who had moved up rather rapidly in the firm, a bit too rapidly for a lawyer fresh out of school. Her promotions came at the recommendations of the man assigned originally to act as her mentor, and who later requested that she work in his department. They often worked late. Ms. Manchester left that firm shortly after her mentor's wife filed for divorce.

In Boston, a security guard recognized Sharon Manchester from a photograph. He had had to escort her from the building on her last day of work. "Kicking and screaming all the way" was how he described her departure. He later learned that, mistaking a friendly gesture for carnal interest, she had offered a senior partner a weekend of passion for a better assignment and a higher salary. That law firm, having just successfully sued a major oil company for sexually harassing one of their clients, quickly fired Ms. Manchester, later changing the records to reflect a resignation, so as to prevent a suit on her part.

She behaved herself in Philadelphia, for a while. She earned her two promotions the old-fashioned way, by hard work and a legal talent that even she did not know she had until she tried to use it. Sadly, one afternoon a promising, good-looking law student asked her to recommend him for a position with the firm. She recommended several positions, and they were trying out the third or fourth one when a partner walked in on them. She was allowed to resign. The law student, who was quick to claim sexual harassment, was hired and now has Manchester's old job. He does quite well at it, but he is never too busy to talk about old friends with curious private eyes, as long as no names are mentioned, of course.

And, of course, I could use none of this. Not only would I get the above-mentioned people fired, but the law firms in question would deny any knowledge of her actions. Still, it was something with which to work.

I was still trying to figure out how to use what I had learned when Susan called, again.

"Matthew, any progress?"

"Susan, I told you this morning, and last night, and the night before last that I was doing my best. I have made some progress, but I am going to need time to develop a plan on how to use it."

"Time is what we don't have, Matthew. The partners' party is this Saturday, which gives you just four days to do something."

"Like what, Susan? Plant some drugs in her house and then call the cops? How about I shoot a senior partner and hide the gun in her desk?"

"Shooting a partner is going a bit too far, Matthew. But the drug idea is a good one. Maybe you could put some in her desk. I could tell you how to sneak in."

I have never been above planting evidence where it will do the most good, which explains why I no longer work for the Baltimore Police Department.

But I do insist on the person being framed having been guilty of some sort of violent criminal act. As much as I loved my sister and her family, I was not going to risk jail for her husband's job. I told her this and she hung up on me.

The notion of a frame stayed with me, though. I sat down and worked with it for a while, until I finally developed it into a wild idea. I called Susan back.

"Hello."

"Susan, if you hang up again, I'm off the case."

"I'm listening."

"Who makes the final decision on the promotions?"

"Quinn Manning, the business manager. He reviews the candidates, reads the reports and then makes a recommendation to the other senior partners. They generally go along with his decision."

"Will he be at the party?"

"Of course. Matthew, what is this all about?"

"Never mind. Is he married, and are spouses invited to this party?"

"Yes, and yes. Matthew . . . "

This time I hung up on her.

That afternoon I made an appointment with Ms. Manchester.

"I want to thank you for seeing me so early in the morning, Ms. Manchester."

"That's quite all right, Mr. Grace. How can I help you?"

"As I explained yesterday, I am a private investigator. I have recently been retained to investigate a case of possible sexual harassment involving a member of your firm."

When Manchester heard the words "sexual harassment" her eyes narrowed as looked at me. Knowing her history, I could only guess that she was reviewing her own past actions to see if she had made a slip along the way, or if old sins were coming back to haunt her.

"And your client is . . .?"

"My client, Ms. Manchester, would like to remain anonymous, at least until I have established whether there is a need for further investigation. As an attorney, I am sure that you appreciate the need for confidentiality."

"I certainly do, Mr. Grace, but I don't see how I can help you. I specialize in contract law, and I am certainly not the person to talk to if your client wishes to make a harassment complaint. You would do best to see one of the partners."

"You, Ms. Manchester, are exactly the person I want to talk to." That worried her a bit. Was she my target? Time to let her off the hook. "Ms. Manchester, I'll be frank. I don't want to talk to one of the partners. I want to talk, to you, about one of the partners."

"Which partner?"

"Quinn Manning."

"Mr. Grace, I really do not think this is the time or the place to be discussing senior partners. Nor am I the person you want to be talking to. If there has been an accusation against Mr. Manning, you should bring it up with him, or with house counsel."

"I haven't said anything about any accusations. To tell you the truth, I don't know if there's any basis for accusations. And if you'll give a few more moments of your time, I just might be able to spare your firm some messy publicity."

"All right, Mr. Grace, a few more minutes."

"Ms. Manchester, I did some research into your firm and its personnel before coming to you. I know that you are one of the most recently hired women to join the staff, and thus potentially one of the most vulnerable. Has Mr. Manning ever suggested to you that your position in this firm could be improved if you were 'nice' to him?"

"You mean if I would have sex with him. I'm a big girl, Mr. Grace, I don't need euphemisms."

"No, of course not. Has he? Or have you heard any gossip along those lines, any warnings from any of the other women?"

"There are too few women working in this firm to give warnings, and I do not engage in gossip. But to answer your question, Mr. Manning has never behaved improperly toward me nor have I ever seen or heard of him behaving improperly toward anyone else. Now, if there's nothing else, I do have other work to do."

"No, there's nothing else. Thank you, Ms. Manchester, for your time. If there's anything I can do for you, please let me know."

I gave her my card and she saw me out. I left quickly, before my brother-in-law got to work.

After planting the seed, I decided to water it. I was owed several favors by more than one newspaper reporter. It was time that I was repaid for the tips I had given them. I decided to let Murphy help me.

Murphy was the crime and scandal man for the Baltimore Sentinel, the city's newest daily. It had rushed in and filled the void left when the Baltimore Sun stopped publishing its evening edition. Hitting the stands at about three every afternoon, it was a tabloid devoted to the more sensational happenings in Baltimore. Little national news and a lot of local dirt made the Sentinel the paper to read if you wanted to keep up with the office conversation the next day.

I had steered Murphy toward some good stories, and away from some that would have buried the fledgling paper with lawsuits. He repaid part of his debt by calling a friend of his at Bill's firm and warning him about a certain trouble making PI who was out to make life difficult for them on behalf of a money hungry client.

Shortly after lunch my frantic brother-in-law called. What was I up to and why had the word come down not to have anything to do with me? I reassured Bill that nothing I would do would reflect badly on him and reminded him that for the sake of both our careers not to let anyone know we were related. He reminded me that he was as proud to be related to a private eye as I was to be related to a lawyer and that settled that.

There was nothing more to do. The fish were in the water and all I could do was wait to see if the shark took the bait. I called Susan and told her that on Tuesday she was treating me to lunch again, this time at Elmer's, the best burger joint in Baltimore.

This time she was late. For someone who only comes down to Baltimore's Inner Harbor once a year (for the Fourth of July fireworks, and her husband drives) finding a place to park can be an adventure.

"Do you know what I've gone through today for the privilege of buying you food?" That's my sister. No "Hello," no "How you doing?", just complaints if things do not go her way.

"Let me guess. You paid at least ten bucks to park in a garage. Then after a ride in a smelly elevator, you had to walk several blocks to get here." Her frown told me I was right. I pointed out the window at my car parked at the curb. "You should have parked at a meter. A dollar an hour and you don't have far to walk. So tell me, how was the party?"

"The party was fine, just like all the parties the firm gives. Now, what's this news you have? Have you figured out how to sink Manchester?"

"Nothing happened at the party?" I love it when a plan comes together, but I was getting the feeling that this was not one of those times.

"Nothing unusual. Harry Jones spilled wine down his wife's dress, but he does that every year. We've starting taking bets on when."

"Sharon Manchester, how did she behave?"

"Like a, well I won't say like a lady, but she was okay. She came in, batted her eyes at all of the partners, mingled, ate, drank, mingled some more and left early. She didn't attack anybody, if that's what you're thinking."

No, that was what I was hoping.

"What about the promotion? Any word?"

"Bill came home yesterday and said that word had come down that the announcement would be made next week. The delay is part of your plan, I assume?"

"That's a good assumption." It was not true, but it was a good one, and it got me off the hook. I quickly changed the subject, telling my sister that the less she knew about my plan, the less she could spill to her husband.

We finished lunch quickly, talking about family matters and the few friends from the old neighborhood with whom we still kept in touch. Susan occasionally tried to pry a part of my plan out of me. I did my best to hide the fact that I did not have one anymore. We parted with my sister thinking that the meeting had been my way of getting a free lunch out of her.

I went back to my office to figure out what went wrong. Given Manchester's past history and what I had said about Manning, she should have made some kind of play for him at the party, even if it was only some discreet hip action during a slow dance. Old eagle-eyed Susan would have caught that, no matter how subtle Manchester tried to be. No, something had not worked.

True, it hadn't been much of a plan, but it had been *my* plan, and I hate to lose, especially to someone who doesn't know she's playing the game. Or maybe she did know she was playing. Sharon Manchester was an intelligent, very competent person. Bill would not have kept her in his section if she wasn't. She used sex to get ahead, but that did not lessen her intelligence. She may have thought, and in some cases may have been right, that sex was her only stairway through the glass ceiling.

Manchester could have seen through my plan. A little research on her part would have established the connection between Bill and me. Or maybe, she had learned her lesson the last time, and was now trying to get by on her ability. If that were the case, I did not want to bring her down. She had beaten Bill (and me) fair and square, and deserved what she got. I would call Susan later in the week, treat her to lunch, and tell her that I had done my best, but it had not been enough. Damn, I hate to lose.

I had one more thing to do before I could put this case behind me and go back to working for paying clients. I called Murphy at the Sentinel.

"Murph, Matthew Grace here."

"Grace, how you doing? Got the goods on the new comptroller yet?"

"Matter of time, Murph, matter of time. We got the last one, didn't we?"

"I got the last one, you got the head of the Housing Authority Police."

"Well, she shouldn't have checked into that hotel with the comptroller."

"What can I do for you this time, Grace?"

"Not a thing, just calling to thank you for the favor last week."

"No problem. Caught the guy right after his three o'clock meeting and warned him about you. I made a friend, and you won't be getting any business from that law firm ever again."

"That's not a problem. I've never done any work for that firm. I work exclusively for . . ."

"Grace, are you still there?"

I had been about to hit Murphy with the old joke about the law firm of "Dewey, Cheatem and Howe" when a bell went off inside my head.

"Grace, are you there? Grace?"

"Sorry, Murph, something just came up. Look, I've got to go. Lunch is on me next time."

We said our good-byes and hung up. I sat down and pondered the implications of what Murphy had said.

Murphy had not called his friend until after three. Bill had called me just after noon. The word had gone out before Murphy's call. Manchester must have alerted the firm. But to do that, she would have had to go through Bill, her immediate superior. Since Bill did not know about my visit, she had bypassed the chain of command. But why? Reporting my visit may have opened the doors to her own past, which she would not want to do so close to a promotion. I made a call.

"William Scott's office, how may I help you?"

"Lawrence Fine, of Dewey, Cheatem and Howe, for Mr. Scott."

"Just a moment, Mr. Fine."

I was on hold for a few minutes when Bill answered.

"William Scott."

"Bill, when did you get an office? I thought you just had a cubicle bigger than the rest."

"Matthew, I am not supposed to be talking to you, not at work."

"You're not, you're talking to Lawrence Fine. My partners would like to know who put out the word not to talk to me."

"Why?"

"If I've offended someone, I would like to make amends."

"And the Democrats will lower taxes."

After some persuasion, he told me.

I spent the next few hours with the computer going through credit card statements, hotel reservations and airline records. I spent the rest of the day matching what I found to what I learned earlier about Sharon Manchester. The next morning I went back to Bill's firm, although to a higher floor with a better view.

"May I help you?"

"Matthew Grace, to see Mr. Manning. And before you call security, please give him this." I handed her a business card with a date and name on it. She took it in to her boss. She came right out.

"Mr. Manning will see you now."

Manning was sitting behind his desk. Without waiting for his invitation I sat in front of it. He was not glad to see me.

"Well?" he growled, "What the hell is this," he gestured to the business card, "and what does it have to do with me?"

I picked up the card and read the back. "Lorre Hotel, March 18."

I threw the card back on his desk. "You had dinner there, charged it, paid enough for two, not enough for three."

"So, what, I was entertaining a . . ." He stopped for a minute, and then remembered that this was his office. "I do not have to justify my actions to you."

"Not to me, but your seeing me on the strength of this card means you may have to justify them to someone." I had copies of other records and receipts. As I spoke, I tossed them one by one on his desk.

"That night, you paid for dinner, Sharon Manchester paid for the room. A month before, you made the Bahamas reservations, she bought the food, and the firm was charged for a 'business' trip. And did your wife like the emerald ring you bought her? Or wasn't it her size?"

He was angry. All of sudden this was not his office anymore. His anger came from his not being able to do anything about it, and his fear of not knowing what I could do.

"All this," he waved at the papers on his desk, "can be explained."

"Maybe. Maybe your firm will want to believe whatever story you could give them, maybe your wife will too. Maybe Murphy of the Sentinel won't do a story on sexual harassment in the city's top legal firms, and maybe I won't spread the story all over town." I gave him my best "You Lose" grin. "You know, these days, with all these computers around, it pays to use cash."

"What do you want?"

"Now you're thinking like a lawyer."

When it was over, Bill had his promotion, with a larger raise than he had anticipated. Sharon Manchester was going to get a lateral transfer, away from Bill and into criminal law. What she and Manning did on their own time was no longer any of my business. I called my sister and gave her the good news.

I had some other business downtown, so it was late afternoon when I got back to my office. When I got there, there was a bouquet of flowers waiting for me. Thinking it was a "Thank you" from my sister, I opened the attached envelope. There was no card inside, just a piece of legal stationary "From the desk of Sharon Manchester." On it was written,

"I owe you one. SM."

It ought to be fun collecting that debt.

CASHING IN

The five people in the office had once been millionaires. They were now as poor as they had been last week, before they bought the lottery ticket that had given them instant wealth. Their problem was that while you had to pay to play, and had to play to win, you needed the ticket to cash in, and that was what they wanted me to find.

Actually, they wanted me to find the man who had the ticket. Adam Thornwald was the accountant and office manager of Northside Designs, the firm in whose offices I sat. As the money handler it naturally fell to him to purchase the twelve biweekly lottery tickets that the six of them bought in common.

"None of us ever really expected to win," explained Peter Newton, who started as spokesman for the group. "It was just something we started last year. The jackpot had hit ten million, so we each threw a buck in the pot and Adam bought the tickets. When it hit eighteen million, we upped it to two dollars each. We didn't win that time but kept on buying the tickets." He was remarkably calm for a man who had just lost one-sixth of twenty seven-million dollars.

"If Thornwald has the tickets, how do you know you won?"

"He, um, Mr. Thornwald, um, you know, gave us all, um, copies . . . of the tickets." Jane Simpson was the firm's secretary. The only subordinate in an otherwise small group of equals, earning much less than half of what the others made, for her the last few days must have been a theme park ride. Friday she had been the go-fer for five people she could not call by their first names. Saturday, she had been rich, an annual two hundred grand for the next twenty years. Monday, when Thornwald did not come to work and the nervous jokes turned into serious worry, she was back to serving coffee and typing memos. Now she was on edge, hoping that I would be good enough at my job so that she could quit hers.

The other three were acting better than Simpson but not as cool as Newton. Cecilia Weston and Anthony Kerper sat together in a corner couch, huddled for support, clearly a pair. Neither said it, but they wanted me to stop asking questions and go out and find Thornwald, preferably before lunch. Kerper kept looking at his watch as if he had something better to do than help me find him a whole lot of money. Weston just sat and stared.

Deborah Hall paced the room in intricate patterns. Now and then she would glance down the hall from the first floor lobby where we were meeting toward the back door. The way she fiddled with the pencil she had in her hand made me sure that as soon as I was finished she would be out of that door and lighting up.

Except for Ms. Simpson, all of them were successful commercial artists and designers, comfortably well off even without their missing winnings. The extra money would have bought nicer cars, longer vacations and bigger homes, but would not have significantly changed their lifestyles, not the way it would have if only one or two of them had won. They did not need the money the way that Jane Simpson did, but they all wanted it just as bad.

"Ms. Simpson, after you learned that your number had come in, what did you do?"

"I, um, really didn't know, not until, you know, Ms. Weston called me, oh, about nine. She asked me if I had heard from Mr. Thornwald. She told me we had won, you know, the big money, but she couldn't get him on the phone. After that I was, um, so excited I really don't remember much. I hardly slept that night and spent most of Sunday in a daze. And yesterday, um, well, you know . . . " This speech was accompanied by much fidgeting and sideways glances at her bosses, hoping for approval, hoping she did all right.

"What about your family? How did they take the news?"

"I'm, um, not married. None of us are."

The others confirmed this. All were unmarried, all but two lived alone and those two lived together. They were young, single and, except for Ms. Simpson, more successful than I hoped to be ten years from now. And here I was trying to make them richer.

I addressed the group as a whole. "I take it that everybody called everybody else Saturday night?" They all nodded. "Did anyone talk to Thornwald?" Head shakes this time. "How about Sunday?" More shakes.

"I tried calling his mother, thinking he might be visiting there. She hadn't heard from him since Thursday."

"Thank you, Ms. Hall. Did you tell her about the ticket?" She shook her head. "Did anyone tell anyone else?" Some had, some had not, but no one let on who actually held the ticket.

"Yesterday, when all of you got to work and realized that Thornwald was not going to show, what did you do?"

"Panicked!" Newton spoke for them all. "We weren't really worried until about ten. Adam goes away for the weekend a lot, and sometimes comes in late on Mondays. When he wasn't here at ten we joked about it at first, you know, about him taking off with the ticket. We called him a few times, just got his machine. Hell, we called him a few hundred times. We also tore his desk apart, then his file cabinet. That afternoon we decided to call you if he didn't come in today."

"Why me?"

"Cecilia suggested you."

"Ms. Weston?"

"You did some work for a friend of mine, Andrea Conners. She recommended you."

"How is Ms. Conners?"

"Very well now that her son is back. Have you heard if the boy's father ever recovered?"

"No, I wouldn't know." Actually I did know, and if there is any justice in this world he will never recover. Ms. Conners had talked more than she should. I quickly got back to the current case.

"Did anyone go to Thornwald's home?"

No one spoke. There were not even any head shakes or nods. It was a simple thing, so simple that they had not thought about it. Just as well, I needed the work.

"We figured that since no one answered his phone, and the machine was on, he wasn't home."

"It's like Pete said," Kerper added, "if he was home why wouldn't he answer his phone?"

I tried to lead them into it. "He could have celebrated way too much and has not yet recovered."

Deborah Hall did not like this idea. "Oh no, Adam doesn't drink much, and he has never done drugs."

"Well then, he could be very sick and unable to answer the telephone." They all agreed on that one. "Or . . . " I left it hanging.

"Or?" Ms. Weston really wanted to know.

"Or he could be past sick." One by one they caught on.

The apartment in which I hoped Thornwald was still living was on the Boston St. waterfront, one of several condominium and townhouse projects crawling east from Fells Point like Carolina kudzu. After some discussion it was decided that I should pay the place a visit and check on his health. Kerper and Weston wanted to come with me, no doubt worried about whether I could be trusted with a multimillion dollar piece of paper. I pointed out that if Thornwald had passed on I might have to do things of which the police would not approve in order to secure the ticket, so, I asked, did they want to be listed as accessories or accomplices? I went alone.

It was three forty-five by the time I got to the tower. Deborah Hall had given me the access code to the building and there was no security at the door, so I had no trouble getting inside. As my elevator called out the floors I said a silent prayer that all I would find, Ms. Hall not withstanding, would be a very happy man coming off of a three day debauch.

No such luck. I rapped once just to be polite then tried the knob. It turned easily and I was inside.

Thornwald lived in one of those no wall apartments. It was one big living space except for a kitchen alcove and a bathroom. There were no closets, his clothing kept in heavy wardrobes and dressers to the right in the sleeping area. Opposite that was the designated living room and work space, a computer desk pushed against the window overlooking Baltimore's harbor. The monitor had rabbits hopping across it, a screen saver program happily working.

The middle of the apartment made up the dining room, in the center of which was a large oak table, its top clean but not too well polished, all of its chairs but one pushed in.

I saw none of this when I first walked in. The first thing I saw was Adam Thornwald hanging in place just to the left of the table over the pulled out chair, an off-center chandelier whose lights had gone out.

I did not bother going through the motions of checking to see if he was dead. After ten years with the BPD's Crime Lab and three in private practice I knew dead, especially when it had been hanging for a day or two.

I stared up at him, adjusting to the new situation. Following the rope from his neck up I saw that it went up and over one of the fake rafters that was supposed to add charm to the place and which definitely added 10K to its price. The rope was secured in the sleeping area, tied around a heavy wardrobe that probably had taken three men to bring in. A lot of work for someone who could have just opened a window and had a nice view of the harbor on the way down. Maybe he had been afraid of heights.

I had to call the cops, but I still had a few minutes before my delay became unreasonable. I used that time to see from what the computer screen was being saved.

A note, of course. I touched a key and up it came. "I am sorry," it read, "I let you all down. I lost it. Forgive me." He never got around to printing it out.

I next made two calls, one to the police, one to my clients. I told them more then I did the police.

I still had time. No one hurries to a suicide. I used it to take a roll of pictures with the pocket camera no good PI should be without. It was one of those with a zoom so I got some nice shots of the rope and knot at Thornwald's neck. By the time Baltimore's finest arrived I was standing by the telephone like the good citizen I usually am.

There was the usual "who are you, what did you do, what did you touch, why are you here?" questions. I explained that I was a private investigator who had been asked to check on Mr. Thornwald's well being (or lack thereof) by his concerned partners. I did not mention the lottery ticket. That was mine to find. The police would probably keep it for evidence, or let the family claim it.

The technician from the Crime Lab came in just as I was finishing my initial statement to the officers. She brought some good news, good for me anyway. Two separate double homicides on the east side and a drive-by shooting in south Baltimore meant that no one from Homicide was coming if everyone on the scene was sure this was a suicide. That meant that I would get home early and that I could sneak back the next day to look for the ticket. I walked over to the computer, displayed the note and printed a copy for the grateful technician. (She wanted to go home early, too.) Fortunately, no one asked how I knew it was there.

Despite hearing "Thank you, Mr. Grace, you are free to go," several times I stayed and waited for the Medical Examiner's people to arrive and take down Thornwald's body. I explained that my clients wanted to make sure that everything possible was being done and that I was just covering my butt. That the officer understood. What I was doing was looking around, trying to find some place a lottery ticket could have fallen that the apartment's owner could not find it.

The Medical Examiner's crew showed up on their way to one of the double homicides. After some discussion as to the method, the two of them stood on the table holding the body while the officer loosened the rope. The officer loosened the rope too soon, and Thornwald came down hard, his shoes marring the surface of the table, already dirtied by the shoes of the ME team, who did their best to keep Thornwald from falling to the floor.

Once down, Thornwald's body was quickly taken away and with him gone so was our reason for being there. I left with everyone else, planning to come back as soon as I had my photographs developed and I could make a good guess as to where Thornwald had lost the ticket.

I had dinner and went back to my office. I had promised Newton and the rest a report first thing in the morning and I wanted to give them something hopeful but not too promising. As I worked on the report something started to itch the back of my mind, something I must have seen but did not yet understand. I had the feeling that if I could scratch the itch I would find the ticket.

As I was driving home to do some reading and to get a little sleep, the click came and the itching stopped. I had tuned to the very oldies station, you know the one, the only station in town that plays your kind of music, but the one you hate to listen to because it is too close to admitting your age. Nancy Sinatra's boots were walking and I thought about what Thornwald's shoes had done to his table.

Until his shoes and those of the ME team had dirtied it, the dining room table had been clean. So where were the shoemarks from climbing up and jumping off? Maybe he cleaned up before he jumped. Maybe the maid had come in and just had not noticed him. Maybe hanging there had not been his idea and right now one or more of his co-workers was trying to figure out how to cash in the ticket without arousing suspicion.

I did not get much sleep that night. I turned around and drove back to the office to pick up some equipment. Within the hour I was back in Thornwald's condo. This time I made very sure that no one saw me go inside.

There were two possibilities. (Three really, but the table was too slippery for socks.) The most probable was that whoever had hung Thornwald had noticed his, or her, shoemarks and just wiped them off. The other, well, that's why I brought my print kit.

Working in the dark, not wanting to show a light, I used fluorescent powder and an ultra-violet light source to make it glow. The powder stuck to the dirt on the table and gave me ghostly images of the ME team and Thornwald's rapid descent. It also gave me something I had hoped to find but had not really expected. Some were obscured by the shoeprints, but I found a few prints from a naked foot, the ridge detail of the toes clear enough to make an identification.

Whoever belonged to that foot probably was not strong enough to have done the job solo. For good measure I scattered some powder on the wardrobe that had anchored the body. I got one good thumb print near the bottom. I hoped that it did not belong to the officer who had dropped Thornwald.

After taking enough photographs to make sure that I got good copies of the prints I found I cleaned up and left the apartment as carefully as I had arrived.

I got a few hours sleep in my office, waking up in time to fax my report to Northside Designs. I followed it up with a phone call promising further developments that afternoon. I made sure that everyone had come into work that day and was expected to stay there.

I then called Karen Johnson who, like me, had once worked for the Crime Lab. When she left, she started a personal protection service. I asked for the services of Lucy and Abbey, my favorites of her specialized crew.

That done, I took my film to a friendly photographer, one who was, by now, used to the kind of photographs someone like me takes. He is a crime buff who does not ask too many questions in exchange for thinking that he is on the "inside" of an exciting business. You know, someone who watches too much television.

The detail work was done, most of it. Any of them could have killed Thornwald, taking advantage of his absence on Saturday night to visit him Sunday and make sure he did not see Monday. All I had to do was to figure out who, that and break into four homes.

Having worked in the Crime Lab for far too many years, and having investigated far too many burglaries, I have developed considerable housebreaking skills. Even so, illegally entering four separate dwellings and leaving without being accompanied by the police taxed my skills. Still, I got in and out easily and did what I had to do.

I worked in their bathrooms, using black powder to look for foot and toe prints. I got a nice variety off of the tiled floors and tub edges. I lifted them with tape and transferred them to white cards, not having the time to bother with photographs.

That afternoon I picked up the photographs. It took another hour to compare the prints and learn who had killed Thornwald.

When I picked up Lucy and Abbey I asked Karen to double check my identification. With her verification I went to Northside Designs to play Great Detective.

The back yard of the business was surrounded by a fence high enough that Lucy and Abbey would not be disturbed. I quietly let them in and made sure that they had the back covered before going in through the front. As before, we met in the first floor front lobby.

I suppose that I should have started off with "I guess you are all wondering why I called you all together" and then proceeded to dazzle them with a leisurely explanation of my reasoning followed by the exposure of the murderer. But this was no manor house and I was in a hurry.

Making sure that I had the front door blocked I cut to the chase. "How about it, Ms. Simpson? Who helped you hang Adam Thornwald, or do I print everyone here?"

Surprised, she looked not at me but right at Anthony Kerper. He wasted no time but pushed Cecilia Weston out of the way, ran down the hall and out the back door, leaving a shocked Cecilia with a horrid look of betrayal on her face. I wonder where he told her had been last Sunday.

Newton cried out, "He's getting away!" and started on the chase I had cut to. I stopped him.

"No, he's not."

Because I was listening for it, I had heard the back door shut, then heard another hard thump as something slammed against it. Kerper probably. I went out the front and around to the back to avoid disturbing the girls at their work.

I was not disappointed. Kerper had his back against the rear door, being watched by a very large, very black Great Dane. That was Lucy. Abbey, a much smaller dachshund, was barking at his heels. With Lucy growling softly, Kerper was almost glad to see me.

"Anthony, I'll say this once. Abbey here, " I pointed to the dachshund, "is trained to go for the throat and hold on tight. But she's short, and can only reach halfway up." He got the idea. "So, where's the ticket?"

To Abbey's disappointment he had it in his pocket.

I brought Kerper back to the office. I gave Peter Newton the ticket and explained the facts of life concerning evidence. Immediately Newton, Hall and a still shaken Weston left me with my suspects and went off to cash in.

TEN MINUTES AT A TIME

As a private investigator I meet all kinds of people and hear all kinds of stories. Most people want me to find somebody - a missing daughter, a cheating spouse, a thieving employee. This is what pays the rent and buys the groceries. Still, there are some who come into the offices of Grace Investigations whose stories would not be run on tabloid TV on a slow news night. Me, I believe them. I believe them all, at least for the first ten minutes. When they walk through my door, I always start out believing them.

When a woman came in and told me that she was God and bade me go forth and prove it, I worshiped her, for the first ten minutes. And for ten minutes I believed the guy who wanted protection from the space aliens who watched him from light sockets. I even believed the couple who told me that Elvis was buried in their basement. So when a woman walked in and told me that her baby, who had died at birth, was still alive but had been stolen, I was ready to believe her, at least for the first ten minutes.

"They took my baby, they took her and told me she was dead." She had started talking as soon as she sat down. "Miss Martin sent me over, she said you found her son, said you would help me."

I had not really found him. I had merely located that part of Interstate 83 over Eastern Ave. in which he had been buried. The people for whom he had worked had placed him there after he had stolen from them a considerable amount of money and drugs. Twice a month Miss Martin takes a drive and throws out flowers at the appropriate mile marker.

Gladys Baker was using up her ten minutes and I still did not know what she was talking about. She was still going on about her baby. First he was dead, then she was alive, but either way she did not have the child and she wanted him or her back.

I managed to interrupt, finally. "Ms. Baker . . . Ms. Baker . . . " It took three more "Ms. Bakers," at increasing volume, to quiet her. "Good, now relax. Take a few deep breaths. Good. Now, I'll get you a cup of tea and you tell me your problem."

The breathing helped. She calmed down. I got her the promised tea and she sipped it as she spoke.

"All I ever wanted was a baby, but I waited until I could support one to do it. I was so happy when I found out I was expecting."

"How did the father feel about it?"

"He knew, didn't care. Anyway, I did everything right. Gave up drinking and smoking, and that other stuff too — but I never really did too much of the other stuff. I went to all of my clinic visits and everything. Two months ago, just about on time, I went into St. Lucy's, that's where my doctor wanted me to go. I didn't like going there, it's kind of far, but I went and I . . . had my baby. I passed out when I did, just after, only heard her cry once. When I woke up, they told me, you know, that he had . . . "

She could not finish, she did not have to. She sat there, on the edge of tears, squeezing her mug while she fought for control. I waited, still thinking this was a ten minute case.

Gladys was about twenty-one, a little old for the South Baltimore girls who usually have a baby just to fill the hole where a family should be. I knew she was from South Baltimore because that is where Rebecca Martin lived, and people down there stay close. Her going to St. Lucy's was a surprise though. That hospital is up in Park Circle in northwest Baltimore. It does have a decent obstetrics department, but it is far from Ms. Baker's Pigtown. (No, that is not a slur. They used to run pigs from the Camden freight yards to the market through her neighborhood — hence the name.)

"I'm better now, thank you."

"Ms. Baker, what makes you think that your baby . . ."

"Kimberly, I'm going to name her Kimberly."

"OK, what makes you think that Kimberly is still alive? Wasn't there a body, a funeral?"

"There was a body, but he wasn't my baby."

Her ten minutes were almost up. "I thought you said that you had a girl."

"I did. Look, when I woke up and the nurse came in, she told me that my baby had died. I was wrecked — crying, screaming, heavy sedation. When I woke up the second time, I guess I had accepted it. I was better, sad but, you know, resigned. They took good care of me. The doctor wrote off part of his bill. They even set up counseling, near my home and all. They offered to help with, you know, the arrangements for 'my boy', my 'son' who had died. So I thought I had heard wrong at first. It wasn't until I was leaving the next day that I knew I had heard right the first time."

"Heard what right?"

"It was when I heard the crying that I knew that my baby had been a girl, not a boy."

It had been a long ten minutes, but I had nothing better to do that day so I went on. "What crying?"

"When I left my room with my girlfriend, she had come to pick me up, I heard *my* baby cry. I'd only heard her once before, but it was the same cry. I knew it when I heard it, and when I heard it I remembered something. I must have forgotten it when I passed out, but just after that last push, when the baby came out, I heard a nurse say, 'What a beautiful little girl.'"

That did it. She had me. I still did not believe her, but her story was definitely worth more than ten minutes.

"What did you do when you heard the cry?"

"Tried to kill the first nurse I saw."

"And then?"

"Decked the nurse that tried to help her. After that it's a blur. I think they sedated me again. Only fair, I knocked out one of them."

"What happened then? They call the cops?"

"Nope, no cops, no lawyers. They told me that they understood the pressures I had been under and told me to get counseling. Then two orderlies escorted me out."

After that we got down to details. I learned the names of all of the "theys" she had been talking about. A few nurses, the doctor, the baby's father. She had had a sonogram, she had even been given a photograph from it, which she said she would bring me the next day.

"Don't bother," I told her. "I'll be down your way tomorrow on business. I'll pick it up then." The business I had was checking her out with Miss Martin, but she did not need to know that.

"Thank you, Mr. Grace. Miss Martin told me you would help. She told me that you'd do more than listen for ten minutes and politely show me out, like the lawyers and police I've talked to. They didn't believe me."

"I'll be honest, Ms. Baker. I believe that you believe what you're saying, but you may not have the story, or the facts, right." She started to protest, but I quickly went on. "I do think you have enough of it right to look into and let you know if I can help."

"About you helping. I know this is your job, and I'm not a charity case, and I know that only TV detectives work for free, but I don't know ... "

"We'll work something out. Let me see what I can do first."

I showed her out after promising to stop by and pick up the sonogram the next day. Then I sat down and started listing all the things wrong with her story.

I started out with St. Lucy's. Many years ago it was just a regular hospital, ably serving, along with Provident Hospital down the street, the needs of the community. It had been built by an order of nuns, who had as their patron the original St. Lucy, on the site of what had been first an amusement park and then a drive-in theater.

Times changed. Provident Hospital is now Liberty Medical Center. As the fortunes of her order declined, so did St. Lucy's hospital. It was about to close for good when a group of investors, made up primarily of doctors, lawyers and others who profit from misfortune bought it from the good Sisters. They changed its nature. They added high-tech research and upscale treatment. They increased security. St. Lucy's still functions as a regular hospital, but its patient list is more of a who's who of Maryland's elite, rather than a reflection of the community. If your disease calls for exotic treatment or experimental therapy, if you need a transplant without waiting on a list, or you just want the pampering to which your bank account entitles you, go to St. Lucy's. Otherwise, walk further down Liberty Heights Ave. and wait to get into the Medical Center.

So I could not understand why Dr. Gordon Williams would have treated Gladys Baker at St. Lucy's. Their obstetrics program was good, but not that much better than the hospitals closer to Pigtown. Her insurance plan was not that good either and, from what she told me, hers was not a high-risk pregnancy nor did he subject her to any exotic treatment.

There was also the way she was treated - "they" were just too nice to her. Her doctor cutting his bill, no charges after she assaulted two nurses, and no lawyers. There were still a few of St. Lucy's nuns working there, but I doubt if their good examples extended that far.

The baby was another concern. Did Ms. Baker have a boy or a girl? Hospitals pack their delivery rooms close together, so she may have overheard comments from the next room over. If she had heard correctly, why was she told that she had had a boy? Nurses are supposed to be able to tell the difference. Unless the baby boy looked like a girl because of some genetic defect Williams had not picked up on and which lead to its death. It would have been nice to have examined the body.

What had happened to the body? I had asked Ms. Baker about it but she had never answered and, trained investigator that I am, I had never followed through.

Ms. Baker had just arrived home when I called and asked what, if anything, had been done with the infant.

"Nothing as far as I know. Why should I care? It's not my baby."

"Did the hospital contact you at all about it?"

"I got a letter from them about claiming it. I tossed it."

The contract she had signed authorized me to act in her behalf. I explained to her what I wanted to do and why. She reluctantly agreed.

The next day, dressed in my second best suit, I presented myself at St. Lucy's morgue. (They call it the "Biological Repository.") I had with me my cousin Jack, who owns and operates a funeral home. I identified myself as Ms. Baker's representative there to claim the body of Baby Boy Baker.

"It's about time," complained the attendant. "That freezer's just cold enough to slow things down. It don't stop the natural processes. Another day or two and the kid would of been out of here."

I did not ask what would have happened to him. I suspected that it had something to do with intense heat.

"Is that hospital policy, or has someone been pushing for you to dispose of the body?"

"Naw. Nobody cares about me or them. Most people don't even think about us. Most are usually claimed in a day or two, or shipped to the Medical Examiner's. Them that nobody wants stays until they get ripe, just in case there's a call for them."

I ended this delightful conversation by signing for the body. Jack took it away in his black station wagon. He knew what samples I needed, and his freezer was very, very cold. Before he left, we both checked to see if my theory was correct. It was not. Baby Boy Baker had definitely been a baby boy.

After Jack left, I tried to do some real detective work. I wanted to interview the two nurses that Ms. Baker had attacked and someone from administration. As I said earlier, St. Lucy's had improved security. I was not a patient, visitor, employee or anyone else qualified to wear white within her walls. I was asked to leave.

That did not bother me, much. If the tests came back as I expected there would be no need to talk to anyone. If not, "they" would be coming to my office, waiting to talk to me while Ms. Baker and I called in the lawyers.

After getting thrown out of, or rather, escorted from the hospital, I kept my promise and picked up the sonogram from Ms. Baker. I also took a sample of her blood and found out where her ex-boyfriend lived. While in the neighborhood I stopped by to chat with Rebecca Martin. She assured me that Gladys Baker was ". . . a good girl, a little wild at times, but a good girl." She was sure that I could ease her mind about the death of her baby. Since I was going that way I promised to throw some flowers on I-83 for her.

I had learned to take blood samples when I worked in the BPD's Crime Laboratory. While there I also learned about the limitations of traditional blood tests. I decided that once I convinced Tony Marcheski to part with some of his blood I would send all three samples (blood from the mother and father, tissue from the baby) for DNA analysis. That would tell me if Baby Boy Baker deserved his last name.

It took me a few days to find Marcheski at home. At first he was not thrilled about shedding his blood for an old flame.

"Why should I? I gave her what she wanted — a baby. I don't owe her nothing else. And ain't nobody gonna make me either."

"You're a real man of the Nineties, Tony." He missed my sarcasm and took this as a compliment. "I can see why you might not want to cooperate and, believe me, I don't want to force you to do anything you don't want to." This was true, since Marcheski was at least a head taller and fifty pounds heavier than I. Had I tried to force him, I would have probably given the blood sample. "So I'll just leave you with this and be on my way."

"What the hell is this?"

It was an attention getter that I had prepared back at the office for just such an occasion.

"That, Tony, is a bill for your share of Ms. Baker's current medical and psychiatric expenses. You'll be getting one just like it every month until she has recovered from the loss of her child. It shouldn't be any longer than a year or two. As the father of the child you *are* responsible for half of her expenses."

We settled out of court for a tube of blood.

I stopped by Jack's, picked up the samples he had obtained and delivered them to a private laboratory that specialized in DNA work. They assured me that they would rush the analysis, which meant results in three weeks instead of the usual two months. In the meantime there were paying clients who needed my attentions.

Not that I was idle on Ms. Baker's behalf. A doctor I consulted told me that there was no way of determining, from the sonogram, the sex of her baby, who had been turned the wrong way when the picture was taken. She also informed me that St. Lucy's had started making its records available, to authorized people, online. So I spent much of an afternoon trying to convince St. Lucy's computer that I was authorized. I also checked the records, financial, legal, etc. of Dr. Williams and his staff. That was easier, I already had the codes needed to do that.

The record checks told me that no one involved had been arrested and that they all had their decisions to go into medicine justified by their bank accounts. Dr. Williams was a very generous employer to be paying his employees so well. Of course, according to his bank statement he could afford to be nice to his staff.

Melting St. Lucy's computer ice was difficult. I worked long enough to determine that, while it could be done, any intrusion would eventually be detected. I would probably get one chance, and I would have to know for what I was looking. I decided to wait for the results of the DNA testing.

Ms. Baker was patient. She only called once a week to check if there had been any progress. It was right after her third call that the results came in. Whether she had had a boy or a girl, the baby in my cousin's freezer was not hers.

I could have stopped there. Armed with my report Gladys Baker could have attracted any big name lawyer in the state, and all of the media. Everyone involved would become part of the tabloid circus, with Gladys in the center ring. She would probably even make some money out of it, maybe enough to pay my bill. But it would not get her baby back, if that were even possible. Before the TV lights came on, I wanted the truth.

Three people knew what had happened in that delivery room. Two of them worked for and were well paid by Gordon Williams. Before telling Ms. Baker what I had learned I wanted to do some more digging. I also wanted to talk to the good doctor. Fortunately, he lived alone.

People feel safe at home, even these days. They think that bars and alarms will keep out someone truly determined to get into their home. They come home after a long day at work and they begin to relax. You would. You would be looking forward to dropping the working day's cares and worries and slipping into a more comfortable routine. The last thing you would expect would be to find a stranger sitting in your favorite chair, waiting for you in the dark. Dr. Williams was properly surprised to see me when he turned on the lights.

"Tell me about Gladys Baker's baby, Doctor." I already knew but I wanted his version. He stood there, not moving, not speaking. I continued. "Three months ago Gladys Baker gave birth, with your assistance, to a healthy baby girl. Several hours later she was told that her son had died at birth. Now, we both know that boy was not her son. Where is her baby?"

He had had time to adjust to the situation. I was not a burglar and had not, so far, moved to harm him. As he spoke, he tried to move subtly to his alarm system's panic button. I let him. I enjoyed watching him trying to be subtle.

"I do recall someone was asking questions about that some time ago . . ." He reached the panic button and stabbed at it.

"That was me, Doctor, and I disarmed that before you came home. You may call the police, if you want it all to hit the fan, and the papers." He decided not to use the phone. "Have a seat, and tell me the truth."

Seemingly defeated, he sat on the sofa opposite me, a guest in his own home. "I should have known it would not work, that it would have to come out. But at the time it seemed the easiest thing in the world, a clever idea actually."

"What was it?"

"Gladys Baker's child, a baby girl, did die that night. She died because of something I forgot to do, a simple test that would have revealed a correctable defect. She lived about an hour. At the same time a woman came into our ER about to deliver. Her child died at birth, from a congenital problem that could not have been prevented. I had attended both births, as had my nurses, so we switched the babies. If the Baker woman insisted on an autopsy we would have been covered in any lawsuit."

"What about the other woman, couldn't she sue?"

"No, she had no pre-natal care at all, not at St. Lucy's. I only attended the birth."

"So, this was just a scheme to protect your malpractice rates?"

"Yes. Of course I realize that I was wrong, and I will gladly make a generous settlement, one that will be more than fair."

I believed him, for all of ten minutes.

Williams may have been a good doctor (at one time at least) but I had been lied to by lawyers, politicians and other experts. He had nowhere their skill. Besides, I already knew the truth.

I had anticipated the "switched babies" story and had done some checking. Like births, deaths are public records.

Linda Horn was a drug addict who had given birth at St. Lucy's the same night as had Gladys Baker. She had not wanted the baby but had kept putting off doing something about it until it was too late. The relief she felt when she learned of its death was enhanced by the cash settlement offered by Dr. Williams and his offer to "take care of everything" in exchange for a signed release. It had taken me half a day to find Ms. Horn and an hour (and some cash) to get her story.

"I talked to Linda Horn before coming here. Very generous, Doctor, to pay for something that was not your fault."

His explanation given, Williams was once again master of his house. "I have told you what happened, now leave or I will call the police."

"Call them. There are no signs of a break-in, your alarm system will show no signs of tampering, and I'm not armed. It's your word against mine that you didn't invite me in."

"Just as it's my word against yours that things happened the way I said they did, and my staff will back me up."

As I said, I had considered a baby switch, but could not figure out why. Williams's insurance would have covered any mistake he made, and he had had no reason to have paid off Linda Horn, not until she yelled "Lawsuit!" anyway. I had been thinking about an adoption scheme until I remembered that hospitals did things other than deliver babies. I also remembered Ms.

Baker hearing her baby's cry, maybe its last one, the day after it had "died" an hour after birth.

After deciding what to look for I broke into St. Lucy's system. An upscale hospital like St. Lucy's would naturally deal with other upscale hospitals across the country, all of them filled with patients able to buy whatever they wanted, or needed.

"What do you do, Doctor?" If he had not heard the sarcasm in that title before I made it clear then. "Do you select certain women based on anticipated need, and then run complete profiles on them? And what do you do when a junkie's baby doesn't die at the same time?"

"I have not the slightest idea to what you are referring."

"Los Angeles, the day after Gladys Baker gave birth. An infant born there with congenital defects received a heart/lung transplant, the new organs coming from St. Lucy's Hospital on a release signed by Linda Horn. The next day, a generous sum was deposited, from an L.A. bank, into your account. I just hope you eased the child gently into death before harvesting her organs."

His outrage was almost believable. "You can't prove any of that."

"I bet I can, but then again, why bring the law into this?" He relaxed, his relief almost tangible. He was willing to pay blackmail, at least until he could figure his way out of this. He was probably planning to blame his nurses.

"No, not the law, but there is justice. A street robbery gone bad, a bullet in just the right spot. A traffic accident, carefully arranged so as to cause death, but not do damage to any major organs. Your driving record shows that you are an organ donor. It might just even the scales if you were to make good on that pledge."

I left him with that warm thought and went off to confer with, and console, my client. A phone call on the way and Rebecca Martin agreed to meet me there.

We let Williams worry for a week and build up a nice case of paranoia. Just when he should have started to relax we held a press conference and called in the lawyers.

When it was all over, everyone involved from the hospital went to jail, lost a lot of money, or both. Williams did try to blame his nurses, but they turned on him right after the first newscast. With their help, he went away for homicide.

Gladys Baker became rich, you may have seen the movie, but never adjusted to her loss. Baby Boy Horn was given a proper burial and his mother even got a slice of the financial pie. Me, I went back to work trying to solve other people's problems. I still believe everything they tell me, sometimes for longer than ten minutes at a time.

SERVING JUSTICE

I sat in the back of the courtroom watching the man who killed my niece get away with murder. Three months ago, Judy had been coming home from school. She was crossing the street when a car driven by Richard Szold blew a red light and hit her. She was thrown up onto the hood and into the windshield. She was dead before her body hit the street. Szold tried to flee the scene but crashed into a telephone pole before he had the chance.

Szold was arrested on the scene and charged with automobile manslaughter while intoxicated. The case against him began falling apart as soon as the trial started.

The arresting officer had been a rookie when the accident occurred. On the scene he had failed to administer the proper field sobriety tests. On the stand his testimony was shaky during direct examination and got worse during the cross. After he stepped down, the defense moved to suppress the results of the breath test administered to Szold immediately after his arrest. The test had shown Szold to have been well over the legal limit for intoxication. After arguments that no one in the courtroom, including the State's Attorney, really understood, the judge ruled that there were enough ambiguities in the arrest procedure and the advice of rights read to the defendant for him to conclude that Szold had not voluntarily taken the test. The State was not permitted to introduce the breath test results. There were no other witnesses. Because of Maryland's double jeopardy laws, no other traffic charges had been filed. With no real evidence against Szold, the judge granted the defense motion for dismissal. Richard Szold walked out of court without even a point on his license.

I had expected this. When a well-paid Towson businessman with experienced legal talent goes up against an overworked, understaffed State's Attorney's Office, the people with the time and money are going to win. I quietly walked out of the courtroom while the TV vultures were trying to get a good camera angle on Judy's distraught parents.

Tonight is the Saturday after the trial. Tonight, like the three Saturdays before this, Richard Szold has gone pub crawling in Baltimore's historic Fells Point. Tonight he has a real reason to party. Tonight I broke into his home.

Szold lives alone. His wife left him about the same time he killed Judy. Still, I called his house before breaking in. His answering machine told me that there was no one there. I broke in through the back door, using a tire iron to force it open. Wearing gloves, I ransacked his bedroom and piled all of his video equipment in the kitchen. The police would think that Szold's return, several hours from now, had scared off the burglars. I did what I had come to do and left.

I do not know how long it will take. Maybe Szold will need a drink before calling the police. Maybe he will wait until after their investigation. He may be too tired and will wait until tomorrow. It doesn't matter. Sooner or later he will need a drink.

Ethanol is only one kind of alcohol, the only one you can safely drink. Methanol is another kind. It doesn't take much, but drink enough methanol and you will die. Drink almost enough and you won't die, but you will be blind for life. I added some to each of his bottles. I hope he drinks almost enough.

LADY KILLER

There are two types of PIs in this world. The first are the noble kind, who will only take a case that's worthy of their talents, a case that involves a great social injustice or one in which an innocent person is at risk. They don't care about being paid, and wouldn't stoop to hiring themselves out to do what is now called "domestic surveillance." You can usually find them on television.

The other kind of PI is the one who actually makes a living at his craft. All he looks for is a paying client and a job that's just this side of legal. What the job is doesn't matter. Do you need somebody to go undercover to find a thieving employee? Pay him and he's there. Does somebody owes you money and is it worth the expense to track him down? He'll find him for you. Your husband or wife stepping out? He'll check out cheap motels and peep through windows until he get you the pictures you need for that big divorce settlement.

My name's Matthew Grace. I'm one of those PIs who isn't on television. People come to me with problems they can't solve themselves. I don't worry much about whether the problems are worthy of my talents — if I can help them, I help them. If that means following a husband who keeps forgetting what that band of gold on his finger is for, that's what I'll do.

The woman who came into my office a few weeks ago told me that she had one of those husbands.

"What makes you think your husband has been unfaithful to you, Ms. Trilling?" I asked after the preliminaries were out of the way.

While no Hollywood knockout, Gloria Trilling was a reasonably attractive woman. She was a brunette of average height, her hair cut short but fashionable. With the business suit she was wearing it was hard to tell but she seemed to have a decent enough figure, with everything in its right place and nothing either too big or too small. When she was dressed up for a night out there would have been plenty of husbands who would be glad to have her as the other woman. But who knew? She might be hell to live with, or else not as affectionate as her husband might like. Or else her husband was just a jerk, the kind who cats around because he thinks he can. Either that or he's bored, and just wants a little variety. There could be a hundred reasons, but none of them my concern. He wasn't the one paying me.

"I was doing the wash, and found some hairs in his undershorts." I waited, sometimes clients bring these things in with them. When she didn't pull a pair of jockeys out of her purse, I went on.

"Hairs in a man's underwear are not that unusual, Ms. Trilling."

"They were red, Albert's hair is brown."

I granted that that was unusual, then asked, "Was there anything that caused you to look at his laundry that close, or did you just notice the hairs?"

Ms. Trilling sighed, as if the hairs were enough proof. If they were, she wouldn't have needed me, but I didn't explain that to her.

"He's been working late, at least once every week or so. He's been too tired to . . . " she paused, looking for the right euphemism. "Let's just say he's been very tired lately. There have been phone calls to the house, the caller hangs up when I answer. And the other day I found this in his car."

This time she did reach into her purse. She pulled out a pack of matches and threw it on my desk. The cover read "The Avalon Motel — Rt. 40 West, Ellicott City." I had never heard of it, but Ellicott City is two counties away from Baltimore.

I picked up the matchbook, opened it and looked inside. A few matches were missing. "Does your husband smoke?" I asked her. "Do you? Does he ride to work with anyone who does?"

Ms. Trilling shook her head. "No, *she* had to have left them there. Probably dropped them when they were doing God knows what."

"Any idea of who *she* is?" The job's a lot easier if you know all the parties involved.

"If I did, I wouldn't be here. I'd have the lawyers working already."

I got the particulars from Ms. Trilling — where her husband worked, his usual schedule, how often he varied from that schedule. She thought to bring a recent picture of him, one of them as a couple from their last vacation. We came to a financial agreement and I told her that I'd call as soon as I had something to report. She picked up her copy of the contract we had both signed, gave me a nice retainer check and left.

I spent the next hour making sure that the woman who had just left my office was Gloria Trilling, that she was married to a guy named Albert, and that their pictures matched the one she had given me. When a friend at the MVA faxed me file copies of their driver's licenses and they both matched the vacation picture, I went to work.

Using codes that nobody's supposed to have but almost everybody in the business does, I first checked Albert's credit history. There were no unusual charges on his credit card statements — nothing to the Avalon, no recent jewelry or lingerie purchases, no expensive dinners at fancy, out of the way restaurants. My client had charged some lacy things and perfume at a few of the mall boutiques, probably trying to relight old fires, but Albert hadn't.

Of course, Albert could have been using a corporate card. I checked those records and still came up with nothing. Maybe Ms. Trilling's suspicions were wrong, and Albert was being a very good boy. It was more likely that Albert was being a very careful bad boy.

The rest of the day was taken up in doing work for other clients. After supper and the rush hour were over, I decided that it was time for a drive in the country. I scanned the photo Ms. Trilling had given me into the computer. Once I had it on the hard drive, I digitally cropped it to give me a close-up of Albert. I printed out a few copies and set out for Ellicott City.

The Avalon Motel was on Route 40 West, but not exactly in Ellicott City. It was, rather, a few miles past it. To get there I had to pass the remains of the Enchanted Forest, an abandoned amusement park from too long ago. It was popular in the days when there was only one Disneyland and no one used the phrase "theme park." Plaster statues of dwarves and elves, fake castles and teacup rides couldn't compete with killer roller coasters and high tech carousels. The Enchanted Forest closed shortly after I graduated high school. I've only been back once, looking for a young man who had run away from a group home. I found him hiding in the remains of Snow White's cottage. With the rides gone, and the buildings crumbling, the park had an eerie feel to it, like a fairyland war zone. The fairies had lost, the ogres had looted the place and everyone had taken off for somewhere else.

Seeing a part of my childhood left to ruin that way had depressed me for days. As I drove past the park the feeling returned. I hoped it wasn't an omen of things to come.

I got to the Avalon shortly after seven. From the outside, it had clearly seen better days. You'd bypass it if you still had hopes of finding a nicer place to stop somewhere down the road. But if you were hungry and tired, and the kids were driving you nuts, you'd pull right in without worrying too much. An effort had been made to keep it a step up in class from the "no tell motels" that lined Route 40 all the way back into Baltimore. There were no neon signs advertising hot tubs, water beds or "by the hour" rates. The exterior was painted and the parking lot clean. There were no scantily clad women strolling the lot waiting for some lonely man to ask them for a "date."

I parked my car out of sight of the desk clerk and walked into the glass-enclosed office. There was a bowl of matchbooks on the counter, all of them matching the one my client had showed me. I waited while the clerk checked in a tired-looking salesman.

"Been on the road all day, didn't sell a thing," the salesman complained.

"It's like that sometimes," the clerk, who had "Ned" written on his uniform shirt, said in routine sympathy.

"Anyplace I can get something to eat around here?"

Ned directed the salesman to a diner further west, then asked, "Anything else you might need tonight?" with a leer that any male over the age of sixteen would have understood.

The salesman looked disgusted and said sharply, "The room will be fine." He left clutching his sample case.

It was my turn. Ned asked me, "Need a room, mister?"

"No, just some information." I identified myself as a PI and showed him some credentials. Out of habit, I waved my license too fast for him to read any of it. "Are you the regular night man?"

"Yeah, what of it?"

"Have you ever seen this man here before?" I showed Ned the picture of Albert Trilling.

"Never saw him," came Ned's quick reply. He hadn't looked at the picture.

"Maybe if you took a closer look," I suggested. I knew where this was heading. I had the money ready in my front pocket. The only question was how much I would have to give him. I let Ned start the negotiations.

"It wouldn't matter," Ned told me, in the same tone of voice in which he had offered the salesman an evening companion. "The motel's clients expect a certain amount of confidentiality. I wouldn't feel right about betraying their trust."

I took a twenty out of my pocket and laid it on the counter. I kept my hand on it. "I can understand and appreciate your feelings. But I would also appreciate any cooperation you could give me in this matter."

Ned looked down at the twenty. "I don't know," he said. I left the twenty on the counter and put my hand back in my pocket. I took out another twenty and a ten and held them up.

"The twenty's for looking at the picture. You get the rest of the fifty if you can help." Ned looked at me then at my pocket, wondering how much more I had to offer.

Fifty was my tops in the bribe department, at least today. I played the card that Ned himself had dealt me. "How's the out-call business going, Ned? How many honeys do you have on speed dial? Or do you use an 'escort' service?" I waited a beat, then added, "Does the management know about this sideline?" His look told me that his boss did. The local cops probably knew about it too. "How about the State Police?" Bingo!

Ned's hand snaked out and grabbed the twenty off the counter. "Let me see the picture," he mumbled. I handed it over to him and hit the start button on my pocket recorder.

Wanting the other thirty, Ned studied Albert's photo hard. "Yeah, I know this guy. He comes in here every couple of weeks or so."

"With a redhead?" I asked.

"Redhead, blondes, brunettes — a different one every time. Some are real lookers, others, well, I could get him better." He looked at the phone. "He came in once with a girl young enough to be . . . well, she looked too young, know what I mean? I questioned him about that one, I have some standards, and kids are o-u-t out. He waved her over and in the light I could see she had some years on. I guess he was into fantasy that night."

"He ever use your service?"

"Never had the chance to offer it. He always brought his own. He didn't even try to hide them like some of them do. I guess he should have, huh. What happen, wife catch on?"

"Something like that," I admitted.

I thanked Ned and gave him the other thirty. I told him I'd probably be seeing him again. Which I would. If Ned had told me the truth, it would be to our mutual profit. If not, if he had just shined me on for the fifty, one day the state boys would run an undercover on his little out-call racket. I'd be there to watch and remind him that honesty is usually the best policy.

I stopped at the diner Ned had mentioned to the salesman. I had a cup of tea, a piece of pie and a few words with the waitress. She didn't recognize Albert's photo. Neither did the cook. I went back to Baltimore with only Ned's word that Albert had been to the Avalon.

The next day I called my client. I told Ms. Trilling that progress had been made but that there was nothing definite yet. I asked her to let me know the next time her husband called to say he had to work late into the night.

While waiting for her call, I made the rounds of the bars and lounges near Albert's office building. I bought drinks, tipped big and showed his picture to as many bartenders as would talk to me. Only the bartender at Lenore's recognized Albert.

"He comes in here," she told me. "Sits at the bar, checks out the women. Usually leaves with one."

"Same one every time?"

"No, he spreads it around. I don't know what he's got, but it must be something. He scores more than the Ravens."

"The way they've been playing lately who doesn't? He ever hit on you?"

She gave me a strange look. "Funny, with the different types he goes after you think he would have, but no, he never has. Not that I'd go out with him, but it would be nice to be asked. Maybe there's something wrong with me."

I had looked her over when I came in. She looked good to me. Nice figure, pretty face, nothing visibly pierced but her ears. She had a pleasant attitude and a friendly way about her.

"Nothing wrong that I can see," I said quickly, not wanting to give the impression that I had to think about it. "Why wouldn't you go out with him? Don't you date the clientele?"

"Depends on the clientele." She gave me a smile that told me that a few follow-up questions would be more than worthwhile. "But not him. He's a slut."

I quickly got off the topic of Albert Trilling and on to more personal matters. After that, I didn't worry about the Trillings' problems for the rest of the evening.

The call came Wednesday of the following week.

"Albert told me this morning that he'd be working late tonight," Ms. Trilling told me over the phone. "An out of town client's coming in and he has to entertain him." By the tone of her voice I could tell that this client could be Santa Claus as much she believed in him.

"Did he say who the client was or where he was from?"

"No, just that and the usual 'Don't wait up.'"

"I'll take it from here," I told her. "I'll call back tomorrow with the news, good or bad."

Late that afternoon I took up my post in Lenore's. I sat at one end so that I could see the comings and goings. In between her serving customers, I chatted with Brenda, my new favorite bartender. Then Albert came in. He ordered a drink and took a booth. After about fifteen minutes, he sent a drink to a blonde sitting at the opposite end of the bar from me. The blonde accepted and soon joined him at his table.

"That's him, isn't it?" Brenda asked. I nodded and she added, "I ask you, Matt, what do men see in women like that? She's just a cheap floozie."

The bar was dark and I couldn't get a good look at her, but cheap was not a word I would have used. Her over-the-face hairstyle must have set the blonde back a few hundred, and maintaining the dye job must have cost as well. The size-too-small sweater cost at least as much as her hair-do, and if what was outlined by the sweater was factory equipment I was not the trained observer I thought I was. Floozie she might be, but not cheap.

To Brenda I said, "It takes all kinds, I guess." I quickly finished my drink and got ready to leave. The topic of blondes with big breasts was not one I wanted to discuss with her.

"You mean he takes all kinds," she said. "See you later."

I had already told her that I'd be leaving abruptly if Albert hooked up with anyone. I wanted to beat him to the Avalon. "Not tonight," I said as I was leaving, "I have to work late."

As I left Albert had ordered himself and his companion for the evening another round of drinks. That gave me a fifteen to twenty minute head start. At this time of day, the beltway would be packed. So I drove up Charles St. and made my left on Franklin, which is one of the aliases Route 40 uses when it's in the city. An hour later I was at the Avalon.

"How you doing, Ned?"

Ned was very glad to see me, or at least the money he figured he was going to make from me. "It's Mr. Detective. What can I do for you tonight?"

"How much do rooms rent for, Ned?"

"It's a Wednesday in the off season, fifty a night."

"How'd you like to make a hundred?"

His greedy eyes lit up with that question. "What do I have to do?"

I took a fifty out of my pocket and laid it on the counter. "This is for you, for your trouble." I followed it with a hundred. I kept my hand on both bills. "This is for two rooms next to each other, the kind with connecting doors. You do have two like that?"

"Yeah," he said, eyes on the two bills. He checked his key board. "104 and 105. Where's the other fifty come in?"

I looked at my watch. I figured I had about ten minutes before Albert and his new lady friend pulled up. I had to make this fast. "In a few minutes this guy is going to show up." I showed him Albert's picture. "Remember him?" Albert nodded. "When he does, rent him room 104. Pocket the money."

Ned wasn't sure. "You're not going to hurt him, are you?" I had the feeling it would be okay if I were, it would just cost more.

"No, just make a movie to show his wife. Deal?"

"Deal."

Ned gave me the keys to both rooms. I made sure that he had a spare to give Albert when he checked in. I went up to my rooms hoping that I had time to set up.

I did. Albert and his lady must have had a third drink. Thirty minutes after I had set things up in 104 I was still waiting. With three drinks in him, I worried that Albert might have been stopped for DWI and was now phoning my client from Baltimore's Central Booking Facility. I kept checking the parking lot from my post in 105. Finally, I saw his car pull up.

I had hoped to slip a fiber optic scope under the doors connecting the two rooms and watch the two come in. No such luck. The carpet on either side was too thick to slide the flexible cable underneath them. I made do with opening the door on my side and keeping my ear to other one.

In the good old days of private eyes, when Marlowe and Spade worked for twenty-five dollars a day and expenses, I would have left the other door unlocked and waited for the two to get comfortable. When I heard rusty bedsprings going up and down, I'd open the door and snap a few pictures with my trusty Speed Graphic. Then I'd run like hell hoping that the wayward husband was too twisted up in the sheets to run after me and give me the beating I probably deserved.

But that's not necessary these days. As soon as I heard them come into the room, I hit the remote for the small video camera hidden inside the clock radio I had previously placed on the dresser. I had it positioned so as to catch all the action on the bed. It was a small digital camera, and copied nicely on to VHS tape. It would give me one hour's worth of sound and color pictures, which beat the hell out of anything Marlowe could have done. Then again, Marlowe had been too noble to go husband chasing. I hoped they'd leave the lights on. The camera does have light gathering capability, and would record in the dark, but the quality isn't that good.

After hitting the remote, I took my 35 mm camera out to the parking lot. I snapped some nice shots of Albert's car, making sure to get the big "Avalon Motel" sign in the background. After that, I went to the office and paid Ned another twenty for the registration card that Albert had signed. My work for the night finished, I went back to my own room, watched one of the in-room movies that wasn't pay-per-view and soon drifted off to sleep.

My watch alarm woke me up early the next morning. By that time, Albert and company were long gone. It was time to for me to leave as well. Getting into 104 before the maid, I packed up my hidden camera and headed back to Baltimore.

Once I got back to my office, I took the camera out of its radio shell and popped the videotape into the player for a quick look. I watched Albert and his temporary friend come in, hop into bed and start undressing each other. That was enough for me. I rewound the tape, hooked up the VHS recorder and made a copy for Ms. Trilling. Then I called my client at her work number and gave her the news that her suspicions had been correct. She or her lawyer could pick up the evidence at my office, along with my written report, anytime after noon. I promised to bill her for my time and expenses and hung up. Ms. Trilling picked up the tape and report that day after work. She even paid my bill on the spot. Another client satisfied, another case closed.

Or so I thought at the time. A week later I was reading the morning paper. The police had been busy the night before. Two men on the east side were gunned down in a drive-by. A hold-up gone bad resulted in another death. And a fourth was murdered in a downtown bar.

As I read of the last death, I realized that the murder had taken place in the lounge where I had met Brenda when I was trailing Albert Trilling. The story said that an unidentified man had been killed, and that no one else had been hurt, so I knew that Brenda was probably all right. Still, my hand was stretching toward the telephone to call her when it rang.

Thinking it was her on the line, I picked up the receiver before the first ring had stopped.

"Hello," I said anxiously, not bothering with my usual "Grace Investigations."

"Mr. Grace, how nice to talk to you again." The voice on the other end of the line wasn't Brenda's. Instead, it belonged to Lieutenant Joshua Parker, Homicide Unit — BPD.

Parker had been a sergeant in homicide when I still worked for the Baltimore Police as a crime scene investigator. He was largely responsible for my leaving the department. Back then, Parker's idea of seeing justice done had not extended to planting evidence to convict someone who truly deserved to go to jail. It still doesn't. Mine, on the other hand, did and still does. Hence our conflict. He tried, but couldn't stop me from becoming a PI. Despite our working together on a few cases since, he still doesn't trust me, and would happily throw my butt in jail if he could.

"Lieutenant, what a nice surprise," I said as I tried to figure out why he wanted to talk to me. I wasn't currently involved in anything involving murder. Maybe he had another rogue cop.

"Mr. Grace, if you are free this morning I would like to stop by your office and talk to you."

That was a good sign. It meant that he only wanted to talk. If I were a suspect in something, I would have been invited down to Police HQ. If I refused I would have been escorted downtown. The lieutenant has had me escorted twice before. I did not want to make a third trip.

"For you, lieutenant, I'm free all morning. When will you be here?"

"I'm outside your building right now, Grace. In two minutes that will be me knocking on your door."

"Don't bother to knock. For you the door is always open."

I had less than two minutes to figure out why Parker had come to see me. A glance at the newspaper still spread out on my desk gave me the answer. I suddenly knew who the man who had been shot down in the bar was.

I was setting up the VCR to copy the videotape when Parker came through the door. I gestured toward the client's chair and he sat down. As soon as he was comfortable I asked, "So who put me in, Ms. Trilling or Ned at the Avalon?"

Parker looked down at the paper on my desk. If he was disappointed that I stole his thunder he didn't show it. "Both of them, actually. Parsons didn't know your name, but he did describe you fairly well. Gloria Trilling told me that you might have some information that would help solve her husband's murder."

I don't as a habit lie to the police, nor do I withhold evidence from them unless there's a very good reason to do so. In this case I couldn't think of any. I hit the "Record" button on the VCR.

"What happened to him?"

"He got killed. Ms. Trilling said something about a videotape."

I ran it down for him. My client's suspicions, the Avalon motel, Albert's meeting the over-developed blonde at the bar. I told him everything I saw and did at the motel, down to the movie I made and how much I paid Ned Parsons for his help. Parker's eyes did light up when I told him about Ned's call-in sideline.

"Don't get too excited, lieutenant. Ned told me that Albert never used it. For him it was always BYOB."

"Bring your own . . . ?"

"Bimbo. And now that I've been a good little PI and told you all I know without your having to throw me in jail or threaten my license, why not tell me what really happened?"

"Grace, if you're planning to involve yourself in this . . ."

"Why should I? I was paid to get dirt on the husband. Now he has six feet of it coming to him. My job's done, and unless you're here to hire me, nobody's paying me to do anything else."

Parker thought about it for a minute, then relented. "Okay, your girlfriend will probably tell you all about it anyway." I tried not to show surprise that he had connected Brenda and me. The slight smile on his face told me that I had not entirely succeeded.

"Yesterday evening about five-thirty, Trilling was sitting in the bar, no doubt waiting for a pick-up. A man came in and walked up to him. The suspect then pulled a revolver and fired twice, killing him.

"Where was he shot?"

"In the head, both times. After shooting Trilling the suspect ran out of the bar. Nobody followed him. By the time we arrived he was gone."

"Description?"

"The usual — white male, average height, average weight, dark hair. Your girlfriend saw the whole thing, she gave as good a description as anyone. She's fine, by the way," Parker added before I could ask.

"The shooter say anything?"

"Just, 'I told you to leave my wife the hell alone.' Then he started shooting."

That did put it down to a jealous husband. I printed Parker out a copy of my report, and gave him my copy of the registration card. I hit the eject button on the VCR and handed the tape to him.

"Here you go, lieutenant. One dirty movie, freshly copied."

Parker didn't take it. "That's a copy?"

"Yes."

"I'll take the original."

"I think you'd rather have the copy." I offered it again.

Parker shook his head, as if saying to himself that he knew I'd pull something like this. "The original, Grace."

I put the VHS tape down and ejected the original. I handed it over.

"Thank you for your cooperation, Grace." He stood to go. Neither one of us offered to shake hands. "I'll call you if I need anything else."

As he was walking out of my office, I called a friend at Homicide and got the number of Parker's cell phone. I considered waiting until he got back to his office before calling him, then decided the longer I waited the madder he'd be. I did look out the window and wait until he got in his car, though. Just before he could start it up I dialed his number.

"Parker here."

"Lieutenant, Matthew Grace. Tell me, lieutenant, has the BPD invested in a digital VCR or camcorder yet? If not, how are you going to play that tape?"

There was a pause, then what sounded like mild cursing. I think that he almost called me a dirty name. Ten minutes later we had traded tapes and he was back in his car.

Despite the notoriety and increased business that a murder will bring to a bar, Lenore's was closed that evening. Most of the staff had been kept late at police HQ giving statements, and the mess left from the killing still had to be cleaned up.

Back at her apartment, Brenda gave me her version of the murder. She had been through the story more than a few times with the cops, and one more time wouldn't upset her that much, or so she said. She wanted to talk about it, she told me, to work it out of her system.

"He walked right in, Matt," she told me. "I didn't take much notice of him at first. He just sat at the bar and looked around. Then he walked over to, what was his name, Albert?" I nodded and she went on. "He walked over to Albert. He said something to him. Albert smiled, and said something back. From the way he was standing, it looked like the guy was hitting on him."

"You sure?"

"Yeah, I've watched that dance too many times not to know the steps."

"What was Albert's reaction?"

"He wasn't offended. I thought that maybe he had been through enough women and was switching sides. That's when the guy pulled the gun and shouted what he did."

She stopped there, and I didn't push her to go further. I changed the subject to more pleasant matters and we got down to enjoying one of her rare evenings off.

Later Brenda asked me, "Are you going to investigate?" I shook my head and she said, "Why not? I thought that's what all you private eyes did when something happens to your client."

"Only on TV," I told her. "To begin with, Albert wasn't my client, his wife was. Secondly, she's not my client anymore. I did a job for her, she paid me, we're quits. Finally, the BPD is on the job. They do it much better than I could and they're getting paid to do it. Besides, I've been told repeatedly that they, or rather, Lieutenant Parker, don't appreciate my interfering with police matters."

We left it like that. However, despite what I had told Brenda, by the time I got home I couldn't help but think about what steps I would take if I were investigating the case. I wondered if the killer was married to the blonde from the Avalon, or if he was just Albert's past catching up with him.

Back in the office the next day, I found myself putting the tape in the player and sitting down to actually watch Albert's last tryst.

The first thing I noticed was that I had been right about his date's dye job. Once she had fully undressed I saw right away that blonde was not her natural color. I was wrong about the breasts, though. Oh, they were no more natural than her hair color. In fact, they were less so and came off with her bra. If Albert was upset or surprised he didn't show it.

After the night's activities had begun, I noticed something else. This was not a first time pick-up. The awkwardness that comes with a couple's first time wasn't there. These two knew each other's likes and dislikes. They had been together before. Maybe the jealous husband with the gun was married to the blonde.

I never got a good look at the blonde. She kept her head down most of the time, and when she did lift it up her hair covered her face. Neither did the audio help. The only things said were related to what was happening at the time. No names were mentioned. They knew each other's, and talking about one's spouse is just not done at a time like that.

There was nothing on the tape that would help the cops, except to help direct their attention to the blonde. With nothing else to do I took out my reports and notes from the case and went over them. I read Ned Parson's comments about the types of women that Albert had brought to the Avalon. I thought about the overage schoolgirl and then about the blonde who was not quite as advertised. Ned was right, I guess Albert did go in for fantasy.

Then it hit me. I suddenly knew who the blonde was, and who the man was who had put an end to Albert Trilling. Or least I thought I did. After a few hours work with my scanner and the facial composite software that had put so many police artists out of work, I was ready for my final trip out past Ellicott City.

Ned was still on duty. I waited until two John Smiths had checked in with their "wives" and walked up to the counter.

"Oh no, I'm done talking to you."

I didn't bother with a bribe. "You can talk to me, Ned, or I'll call Lt. Parker and he'll have your butt dragged down to Baltimore. It will be tomorrow afternoon before you get back, if he doesn't find out about your rent-a-date sideline." No need in letting Ned know I had already spilled those beans.

"What do you want?" he asked reluctantly. " I thought that guy you were following was dead."

"He is." I threw a stack of computer printed photos on the counter. "Recognize anybody?"

There were twenty photos in the stack. Ned identified five of them, including one that looked very much like the blonde, as maybe having checked in with Albert at one time or the other. I wasn't surprised when he told me that he had seen the blonde only once.

I thanked him and left. When I got back into Baltimore I drove straight to Lenore's. On her break I showed Brenda the composite photo of the blonde. She nodded, agreeing with Ned that it might be the woman Albert had left with. Then I showed her one other picture.

"That's him!" She shouted loud enough to attract the attention of some of the patrons at the bar. The newly hired bouncer looked her way. She waved him off.

"That's him," she repeated in a whisper. "Who is he?"

"If I told you, you wouldn't believe me." I told her, she didn't.

My last stop of the night was at the home of Gloria Trilling. She wasn't there. I let myself in using the skills I had picked up investigating far too many burglaries for the Crime Lab.

I used my time constructively while waiting for my former client to come home. By the time her car pulled in the driveway, I had found the blonde, red-haired, and black wigs she had worn to cover her own shade of brunette. The schoolgirl clothes were hanging in the back of the closet, next to a man's suit that would have been too small for Albert. The only thing I didn't find was the gun. If she still had it on her I was in trouble.

By the time Trilling walked through her door, I had it most of it laid out on her living room floor. I gave her time to take it all in, then stepped out from the dining room.

"It was the schoolgirl outfit that did it." I told her, not giving her a chance to speak. "The night clerk at the motel suggested that your husband was into fantasy. That combined with the too-fake blonde you had me follow led me to think that it was all fantasy, that all of Albert's women were just you."

I handed her the composites I had made after having scanned the vacation photo she had given me into my computer. I had isolated her face, then used the identification software to give her a variety of looks. The one of her as a man was the one Brenda had identified.

"You and Albert had been playing this game for some time. I'm guessing it started out as a way of spicing up your marriage. When you decided that you wanted him dead, you used it, and me, as a way of sending the cops down a false road. Why'd you do it?"

If she still had the gun now would be the time she'd use it. Instead she just looked at me for a minute, then said, "It was cheaper than a divorce."

Without saying another word, she dropped the composites and started gathering up the stuff on the floor. "By the time the cops come, this will all be gone," she told me. "As for these," she kicked at the photos scattered at her feet, "they don't mean a thing. Everybody knows that with a computer you can make anyone look like anyone else. You can't prove a thing."

"I know," I said, surprising her. "I just wanted you to know that I knew, that you didn't fool everyone." I walked past her toward the door.

"You're not turning me in?"

"For what?" I asked. "Like you said, there's no real proof except some made up computer photos. Besides, you were my client. I took your money, not the cops'. That gives you a certain amount of confidentiality. Let them do their own work." I didn't know or care if she believed me.

As I opened the door to go, I turned with a warning. "Parker's no dummy, neither are the men he commands. One of them will figure it out. When they do, well, you may not be convicted, but the legal fees will make you wished you had divorced him."

"I'm not sorry I did it. I'll take my chances."

I closed the door behind me. Her chances didn't look good. Parker and his men were pulling up as I left. I handed him the recorder that I had used to capture her confession. Out of another of my pockets came the tie she had worn when she killed her husband. It still had a small bloodstain that she hadn't noticed or bothered to wash out.

"Thanks for the call," Parker said grudgingly. "I thought you weren't going to get involved."

I shook my head. "Yeah, well, every once in a while I think I'm on TV."

A HOUSE DIVIDED

The phone was ringing when I got into my office. The machine picked up the call before I could. A woman's voice came on.

"Matthew, I need you. Call me right away."

I knew the voice. The woman it belonged to was tall, very attractive and financially well off. And she needed me. Every single man's dream. Except that this woman's interest in me was solely professional.

Sharon Manchester was a lawyer, one of the best, no — the best defense attorney in Baltimore. We had a past, she and I. A case I was working ended up with her being forced out of her corporate practice and into criminal law. A break for both of us. It turned out she had a talent for keeping people out of jail, and, once she'd forgiven me, she called on me whenever she needed the services of a good investigator.

I called her back on her private number.

"About time," she barked into the phone without greeting. Caller ID has ruined telephone courtesy for some people. But not for me.

"And good morning to you too, Ms. Manchester. What's the problem and how can I help?"

"Murder," was all she said before hanging up. She always did know how to get my attention. Twenty minutes later I walked into her office.

Sharon was at her desk. As the man sitting across from her stood up I saw the scratches on his left cheek and a mark by his right eye that would be a bruise in a few hours.

"Matthew," Sharon said, again ignoring the pleasantries most of us use to get through life, "this is …"

"I know," I said, recognizing him from the papers. "His name is Legion …"

The man smiled and completed the phrase, "For we are many."

His name wasn't really Legion, it was Doe. First name, well, that depended on just who you were talking to.

Starting life as Brian Drake, in his twenties Doe was diagnosed with Multiple Personality Disorder. Putting it simply, his mind, his psyche, was fragmented into many different personas, each with its own purpose, each with its own role to play in how Drake dealt with the world around him.

The diagnosis came as a relief to Drake, whose behavior up until then had been considered the result of anything from drugs to paranoid schizophrenia. "I was glad to know," one article quoted him, "that the voices in my head were just me talking to myself, that they really were there."

Once diagnosed, Drake began the usual therapy for such patients, that of gradually merging his various personalities into one unified whole. It was a long process, taking up many hours of therapy. A year after it started, Drake was down to five main personas.

That's when the fun started. One of the personalities decided that he liked things just the way they were. During a time when he had conscious control of Drake's body, he hired a lawyer, our very own Ms. Manchester. In court, Ms. Manchester argued that her client, who for the purposes of the trial used the name "William Doe," was a person in his own right and that integration would cause this person to "cease to be," in effect, killing the entity known as William Doe.

The other four personas fought the suit, claiming that "William" was merely part of a fragmented whole and therefore had no individual rights.

But you know all this. How could you have missed it? Reporters from magazines, newspapers and every local and national network in the country descended on Baltimore, everybody with cable access watched the trial on a daily basis — they all wanted to see a man sue himself for custody.

Everyone had an opinion, and those with degrees made money renting themselves out as experts to the media outlets. Attorneys discussed the possible legal ramifications of having two or more people inside the same body. Political experts argued whether Drake/Doe was entitled to one vote or five. And the only thing the army of psychologists that were paraded by us agreed upon was that Drake's condition was not schizophrenia.

Aside from watching both the "right to life" and "right to choose" groups trying to figure out whose side they were on, my favorite part of the whole mess was the sight of Drake changing seats in court. Ms. Manchester would question a witness. Before the defense could cross, Doe would leave the plaintiff's table and walk over to the defense side, his expression and mannerisms changing subtly as he gave way to one or another of his other personas.

The ease with which Drake switched personalities amazed some mental health experts. Some argued that this was evidence that he was faking the whole thing. Others said that it was a tribute to the treatment he had received so far that the different facets of his mind were able to cooperate to such an extent. In fact, this was a key defense point — that Drake's ability to "change his mind" so readily argued in favor of the fact that he was nearly wholly integrated, and should be allowed to complete the process.

In the end it didn't matter what any of the experts or special interest groups thought. It came down to the opinion of one woman in a black robe.

Ruling from the bench almost immediately after closing arguments, Judge Gertrude Devereux ruled that "It is this court's decision that the persona of William Doe, currently housed in the collective body of Brian Drake, is a legal entity in his own right." She then enjoined the remaining personae from continuing any treatment that would lead to William's melding with the other four.

After her ruling, Judge Devereux waited for the inevitable "Notice of Appeal" by the defense. Instead, the defense presented the court with a petition to name "Brian Doe, Drake Doe, Charles Doe and Rachel Doe," (that's right, one of the personas was a female) legal entities as well, all residing with William Doe in a collective body. The judge agreed and five people walked out of the courtroom on one pair of legs.

In his press conference afterwards, the defense attorney explained what had happened. "My clients, having just sustained the expense of hiring two legal teams, simply could not afford to continue with an appeal. Their petition to be named as persons in their own right was done simply to protect their interests."

It should have ended there. After the books and the movie and the failed sitcom loosely based on their life, the Does should have faded from public consciousness. And they would have, if William hadn't decided to run for a seat on Baltimore's City Council, his slogan — "Five for the Price of One."

The other four stopped William the only way they could, they all ran against him. With the vote split five ways, their opponent won easily.

And now here I was standing in a lawyer's office with the Does, and the subject was murder. It looked very much like they were going to be in the public eye again.

"So who'd you kill?" I asked Doe as he sat back in the chair. I took the one next to him.

Before answering, Doe took a pack of cigarettes from the left inside pocket of his suit coat. Lighting up without asking either of us if we minded, he inhaled and let out a puff before answering, "I didn't kill anyone."

I took a guess based on what I'd read about the Does and saw during the trial.

"And what about your roommates, William?" The look he gave me told me I'd been right. Before he could ask, I added, "I am a detective."

"Let me tell it, William," Sharon said from behind her desk then turned to me. "Last night William had a social engagement with a young lady. He spent the night, or rather, he fell asleep in her bed. Charles woke up first.

When he did he saw that the woman was on the floor. She'd been beaten to death."

"Any chance of an intruder? Husband, jealous boyfriend?" I didn't think there was, but it's best to get the obvious questions out of the way first.

William shook his head. "The door was bolted. Besides, Drake's a light sleeper. He would have woken up. It had to have been one of us."

"And you don't know which one?" Another shake. "Why not? Don't you all look out the same pair of eyes?"

It's not like that," William said. "We're not always conscious all at the same time. At times, the only one aware is the one in charge of the body. The rest of us are — well, it's like a light sleep, call it dozing. Other times, one or more of us are awake but just watching."

"And who's awake now?" I asked.

"We all are. It takes an effort, but we can do that when it's something important going on."

"Like now?" He nodded. "And what about last night? Any onboard voyeurs?"

"It's hard to tell just who's awake, but we do try to respect each other's privacy. No one likes an audience. I really don't care, but it bothered Doris."

"Doris was the …"

The look on his face — sadness, regret, guilt? It came and went so fast I couldn't tell. "The …" he paused for the word.

"Doris Randall, the victim." Sharon said matter of factly.

"And how'd you find out she was dead?"

"Charles woke us all up."

"And you didn't kill her?"

"No!"

"And you don't know who did? Nobody let anything slip while you were all waking up?"

William sighed. "No. We had dinner, we went home, we made love, we fell asleep. That's all I know. I cared for Doris. If I knew who killed her I'd tell you."

"Let me talk to Drake. Wait." I turned to Sharon. "They're all your client now?"

"Yes. All of them, even if I only get one fee from the lot."

"Okay, Drake. Come on down."

Doe changed. Slowly, William gave way to Drake. His face became softer, less angry looking. His whole body relaxed. He gave me an amused grin, "Like I haven't heard that one before." Drake's voice was higher than William's, much higher.

He looked at the cigarette in his right hand. "Nasty habit," he muttered, and stubbed it out in the ashtray on the corner of Sharon's desk. He smacked his lips, grimacing at the taste left in his mouth. Reaching into his right coat pocket, he took out a mint and popped it into his mouth, throwing the wrapper next to the butt.

Legs crossed, hands cupped on his knee, Drake said, "For the record, I didn't kill the girl. In fact I had nothing to do with her. My tastes don't run that way."

I shrugged. Big deal. "Must be nice then, living with three other men."

Drake smiled, "They certainly don't enjoy my nights out. Rachel does, however. As I do hers. We share."

"Your bed partners don't mind?"

"Who tells them?"

I changed the subject back to the murder. "What do you know about last night?"

Drake gave me a look of disgust and a small shoulder shrug. "Not much. I had the body that afternoon, I had some work to finish. William took over for his date and I went offline. I did wake up briefly last night."

"What time?"

He shrugged again. "Couldn't tell. It was dark and I was in a strange bed."

"Alone?"

"I'm never alone, but I know what you mean. There was a body in bed with me. Knowing who it was, I went back to sleep. The next thing I knew, Charles was waking us all up."

"What did you do then?"

"Got dressed and left right away."

The key to interrogating suspects in a murder is to question them apart, then compare stories, see what doesn't match. I thought about this while I was talking to Drake. They were all in there, watching and listening, no doubt editing their versions of what they did and saw based on what each one said. Still, you played the hand you were dealt even when the deck was stacked and hoped you were the better cheat.

Brian Doe wasn't any help. Aside from spitting out Drake's second mint and lighting up his own brand of smokes — menthol versus William's unfiltered — he claimed to have "gone away" right after fixing dinner that night. (It was his turn to cook.) Like Drake, he was unaware of the murder until alerted by Charles.

Saving the one who found the body for last, I next talked to Rachel. Like the others, her appearance was accompanied by a complete change in mannerisms. Passive to William's aggressive, features animated compared to

Brian's complete lack of expression, she was most like Drake. But where his effeminate movements and body language seemed affected, Rachel's were much more natural. Talking to her and listening to her high toned voice, I briefly felt like the only man in the room.

"I really wish I could help you, Mr. Grace, I do. But I really was not paying attention that night. What William and that woman were going to do, well, despite the situation I find myself in I'm not really into women."

"Drake says you and he sometimes share."

"Drake's a horrible gossip and more than a bit of a bitch." That said, Rachel's eyes rolled slightly back into her head. "Yes, I meant that," she said to herself. "Well then, go ahead." When her eyes rolled back to me she said, "He's sulking. We probably won't be hearing from him the rest of the day."

"Did you hear or see anything last night, Ms. Doe?"

"I did wake up once. Not in control, just for the ride, mind you. William and that woman were, well, let's just say they weren't sleeping. I went right back out. And the next thing I knew, Charles was shouting us awake."

"Okay, let me talk to him."

Another complete change. When Charles took over, Doe became the kind of man you trusted right away. Leaning back in the chair, he relaxed completely, looking me right in the eye, nothing to fear, nothing to hide.

"It's about time," he said, but with a smile to let me know he was just joking.

"Saving the best for last. Did you kill Doris Randall?" I gave him a smile back. If he thought I was joking, fine.

"No," he said simply, not taking offense at the question.

"Do you know who did?"

"If so, you wouldn't be needed."

Good point, which reminded me of something I had to ask Sharon. But I wanted to finish with Charles first.

"How did you find the body?"

"Dead. Sorry, poor joke. I woke up early, I often do — I'm the morning person of the group. When I woke up, thing the first thing I noticed was that the bed was wet. Now I, or rather, we, haven't wet the bed since the age of seven, when our body finally got tired of the beatings. I switched on the light and saw the blood. Doris was on the floor. She'd been beaten rather badly." Charles held up his hands, showed me his knuckles. They were badly bruised, with partly healed lacerations. "No question that one of us did it."

"I take it that's what you're hiring me to find out — which one?" I asked Sharon.

"Exactly," she confirmed.

There were a number of questions still open, I'd get to them later. But first I asked, "What's the police view on this?"

Sharon sighed, "They haven't been called yet."

"What!" I shouted loud enough to startle whoever was in the next two offices. "Why the hell not?"

"Matthew," Sharon said calmly, "my obligation is to my client, or clients as it were. We all know that as soon as the murder comes to light, the investigation will lead back to the Does. They'll be arrested, despite the fact that only one of them is guilty. If you can discover which one did it, this can all be resolved quickly, and without another media circus."

"Resolved how?"

"Just go to the scene, find out what you can. When you come back, we'll talk some more."

Lawyers. If they weren't such a source of steady income, and if I didn't need them to keep myself out of jail from time to time, I'd have nothing to do with them.

On my way to the crime scene, I tired to figure out just why Sharon needed me. Doris Randall's body was bound to be discovered sooner or later. (Hell, there was a better than even chance the police were already at the scene.) After Randall was found, it wouldn't take the police long to connect her to the Does. And the circus Sharon was worried about would start.

There was no way the Does were not going to be arrested. I knew the head of the homicide unit, had matched wits with him several time. Detective Lieutenant Joshua Parker would not listen to Sharon's "You can't arrest the guilty person without locking up four innocent people." To Parker, they'd all be guilty. He'd lock them all up and let the courts sort it out.

In court Sharon would no doubt make the same argument, that it's better for a guilty man to go free than for four innocents to be jailed. The great State of Maryland would argue against Judge Devereux's civil ruling — that the Doe collective was legally one person. With that Sharon would have the Does pull out five drivers' licenses, five voter and library cards and five social security numbers. With that the state's argument would fall apart, and the Does would go free, killer and all.

Which led me back to why Sharon needed me. Surely not knowing was better, reasonable doubt and all that. Maybe she thought my discovering which persona was the killer would give gave her an edge. If so, that was okay. I had an edge too. I already had a fairly good idea who it was.

To my surprise, there were no patrol cars surrounding the Park Ave. apartment where William and his friends had left Doris.

Using the access code Charles had given me I let myself into the building. His key opened the door of the apartment.

Taking out my digital camera, I snapped photos from the doorway. I wanted a visual record of what the apartment looked like before Parker accused me of tampering with evidence. Once I had the living room recorded I did the same for the dining room and kitchen. No signs of disturbance yet, but I knew the main show was in the bedroom.

It was as advertised. The bedroom was neat, clean and well ordered, except for the body on the floor. After taking my photos from the doorway, I walked over and took a closer look.

Before becoming a private investigator, I'd been a crime lab technician for the BPD. In the ten years I worked crime scenes I'd seen many a horrific sight — burned bodies, dead children, slaughtered families. For shear savagery this was right up there — her face battered beyond recognition, the bruises on her torso and arms telling me of the beating she'd taken while still alive.

I knew then what I had to do. I took one last look around the apartment, photographing what I saw — Doris's body, the spatters on the wall, the blood covering the sheets. That done, I called the police.

I know what you're thinking — good little PI's aren't supposed to do that. They're supposed to wipe down all surfaces, remove the one critical piece of evidence that would convict their client, then get the hell out of Dodge, leaving the police to find the body on their own. Well, maybe on TV and in the books you read, but in real life that kind of behavior only gets you the top bunk in the Grey Bar Hotel.

But what, you ask, about my responsibility to my client? Which one, the killer or the four who just may be lying about knowing what happened. Or the lawyer who was going to use me to see that a killer walked free? No, right just then my responsibility was to the girl on the floor, to see that somebody, somehow paid for her death. Right or wrong, that was what I was thinking when I took out my phone and called Parker's office number.

It would take time for Parker to have a patrol unit respond to the building, even longer for them to get from the lobby to the eighth floor. Time enough for what I had to do. When the uniforms came in, I was sitting at Doris Randall's desk with my hands neatly folded in my lap. The two cops checked my ID, searched me for weapons (I didn't have any), then proceeded to make certain that the rest of the apartment was secure, stopping to look at the dead body along the way. Besides asking who I was and could I prove it, neither talked to me.

Parker showed up with his detectives twenty minutes later.

"Good morning, Lieutenant," I greeted him when he arrived. (It was still slightly shy of noon.)

He gave me a head nod and uttered a surly "Grace" then went into the bedroom. When he came out he looked at me and asked, "You touch anything?"

I tried to look shocked and insulted. "I know better than to disturb a crime scene."

"I know you know better, Grace. That doesn't mean you wouldn't do it."

The man knows me all too well, even if this time I was innocent. "Lieutenant, I called you, remember? If I was going to fiddle with evidence, I wouldn't have hung around."

"We'll see," he grudgingly acknowledged. "Tell it."

I gave him the digest version. "I was called this morning by a lawyer whose client reported that a murder had taken place in this apartment. The lawyer hired me to check things out and proceed accordingly. Things checked out, and I called you."

"And the names of the client and lawyer are …"

"Privileged." Parker gave me an "I might have known" look and was deciding on how mad to get with me when I added, "for now."

"What do you want?"

"I stay and watch your investigation. What you learn, I learn. Afterwards, I'll tell you everything you need."

"And if I decide to take you downtown and put you in a little room until I get back?"

"Then this and any further conversation we might have are over. And a killer just might go free."

Parker didn't like me very much, but he knew me, had known me from when I worked scenes as a crime lab tech. He decided I wasn't bluffing.

"Okay," he agreed, "you can stay. But first," he held out his hand, "give it over."

"I'm unarmed, ask them," I said, pointing to the uniforms that had first responded. "They do a nice frisk."

"You may not carry a gun, Grace, but you're never without a camera. Give it over." Parker hand was still out. Reluctantly I handed him my digital.

By now the lab techs had arrived. I didn't recognize either of them, new hires I guessed. If they had heard of me at all it was probably the cautionary tale of how and why I left the department and would have been warned to stay away. Parker called one of them over and handed him the camera.

"What's on here?"

The tech powered up the camera, pressed the right buttons to display any photos I may have taken. None showed.

"Empty, Lieutenant."

Again Parker held out his hand. "Don't make me ask again, Grace. Or I will have you strip searched right here and now."

The last time Parker caught me on a crime scene and confiscated my camera he settled for removing the flash card, not stopping to think that I may have switched it for a new one. It seems he learned from his mistake. I took an envelope from my jacket pocket and handed it to him. He passed it on to the tech.

The lab tech took out the flash card and loaded it into the camera. She then displayed all the photos I had so carefully taken. "Nice work," she said, handing me the camera back but keeping the card. Parker had trained her well.

"Nice try, Grace." To the lab tech he said. "Mr. Grace is going to watch. If he touches anything, shoot him. Or rather, call me and I'll shoot him."

Parker left me to see what, if anything his detectives had come up with. I followed the crime lab techs around. They photographed and sketched the scene. Then one of them dusted for prints while the other started to collect evidence. Using tweezers he carefully picked the cigarette butts from the bedroom ashtray and put them in small envelopes. Small pieces of clear plastic from the floor went into a separate envelope. He looked around, except for the bedclothes and the blood samples, there wasn't anything else. That was okay, I'd seen everything I needed to see.

An idea had started forming when I saw the tech collect the butts. Things gelled when he picked up the plastic. I suddenly had a clear idea of what had happened last night, and why.

"Lieutenant," I called. Parker came into the room. "Let's take a ride." I hoped I was in time to prevent what might be another murder.

On the way back downtown, much to his surprise, I leveled with Parker — about Sharon hiring me and who her clients were.

"Damn," he swore softly. He knew as well as I did the legal difficulty of convicting twenty percent of somebody and the national press coverage the attempt would bring.

"Hey, at least your job is done with the arrest. It's the State's Attorney's office that's got to win in court."

"Grace, you should know my job isn't done until the killer's locked up for good. And from where I'm sitting, the only time the s.o.b.'s going to spend in jail is however long it takes for him to make bail."

"Maybe not." And I told him what I thought was going to happen, what, in fact, had probably happened right after I left Sharon's office. Then I told him what he could do about it. It was enough to make him almost like me.

We walked into Sharon's office without waiting to be announced. The Does were still there. I thought they'd be.

"Matthew," Sharon said in surprise when I walked through the door, "what are you ..." Surprise changed to anger when Parker followed me in. "What is he doing here?"

"Sorry, Sharon, couldn't help it. The good lieutenant twisted my arm."

Parker, who I've never known to tell a lie, remained silent. Sharon looked at me doubtfully. I don't think she bought my attempt to hide the fact I'd changed sides.

Ignoring them both, I went over to our clients. Coming up close and looking them in the eyes, I said, "I want to talk to William."

I watched as a variety of expressions passed over the face in front of me — Brian's nearly blank stare, Drake's amused superiority, Rachel's animated features, Charles's directness — all of them went by at least once. It was as if they were trying to decide who was going to talk. No where did I see a trace of William.

They settled on Drake. "So you guessed it, William was the killer."

"It was no guess, gentlemen and lady," I said, knowing they were all listening. "I knew before I left this morning."

"I don't see how." Still Drake.

"Matthew," Sharon said in warning, nodding towards Parker.

"It doesn't matter, let him listen," I told her. Then to the Does I said, "William said that he and Doris shared dinner, then her bed. Afterwards, he fell asleep and didn't wake up until Charles sounded the alarm. Yet Rachel said that during the night she woke up to find Doris and one of you having sex. If that someone was William, there was no reason for him not to mention it. Since he didn't, it must have been another one of you."

"So someone got a freebie, big deal."

"So it gives us motive. Maybe Doris knew who it was, maybe not. But while she was with whoever, William woke up, didn't he?"

Not waiting for an answer, I went on. "William woke up, and didn't like what he found. Doris was his, and one of you took her from him. Since he couldn't take it out on himself, he took it out on her."

This time I waited. Eventually Drake said, "Hard to prove."

"Then let William come out and deny it."

There was another long pause. "He can't," Drake finally said. "He's gone."

"What!" Sharon shouted. There was no reaction from Parker. I'd told him to expect this.

"Explain."

Drake sighed. "Of course we knew it was William. Like he said, I'm a light sleeper. I woke up when he started beating her. I tried to stop him, but he was too much in control. I woke the others but even together we couldn't stop him."

"So you came here, hoping Ms. Manchester could find a way out, lying to protect William, right?"

"Right, we thought if no one knew which of us it was, the police couldn't make an arrest."

'The rest of you," I said, trying to look past Drake, "is that true?"

Drake faded, Charles came out. "Speaking for all, yes."

Parker, who had been uncharacteristically silent through this, finally spoke. "So what happened to the William part of you?"

"We thought that by keeping quiet we'd stay out of jail. After Mr. Grace left, Ms Manchester pointed out that …"

"Just a minute," Parker interrupted. "Anyone mind if we do this by the book?"

"What do you mean, Lieutenant?" Sharon asked.

"Well, since it's clear that your client, or part of him, anyway, did kill someone, I'm going to have to arrest him. So I think Miranda would be a good idea right about now."

"As a matter of law, Lieutenant," Sharon replied, "the killer may no longer be here. If so, then any arrest may subject you to a civil suit."

Parker smiled. I'd seen that smile before. Sharon hadn't. If she had, the interview would have been over. "I'll take my chances, Ms. Manchester." He then read the Miranda warnings. To be absolutely sure, he read them four times, insisting that each persona come out and acknowledge that he or she understood the rights as read.

"Are you done?" Drake again, obviously the group spokesman. "Well, as Charles was about to say, Ms. Manchester told us we would be going to jail no matter what, and that it might be some time before she could get us released. That changed things."

Drake paused. Collected his thought. "Before William sued us, we were close to unification. Only the court order forced us to live together. When it became clear that it was either all of us or William …"

I finished for him. "You ganged up on him. The four of you used his guilt combined with your strong desire to be one and what, divided him among you?"

"Something like that. Anyway, he's gone."

"And so is your killer, Lieutenant," Sharon added. "So go ahead and arrest them. I already have the writ of habeas corpus drawn up for Judge Devereux. With William gone, all you have left are four innocent people."

"Maybe," I said quietly, "maybe not."

"What do you mean, Matthew?"

I stood, walked over to her computer. "May I?" She nodded. I logged on to the Internet, then to an online email service. Entering my user name and password, I brought up the mail I'd sent myself from Doris's apartment and downloaded the attachment. Thumbnail photos of the crime scene came up.

"Grace!" Parker was none to happy with me.

"Before you ask, Lieutenant, I had some time before you guys arrived. While I was waiting, I downloaded the pictures from my camera into Ms. Randall's computer, then emailed them."

Parker gave me a cold stare, realizing that there was no way he could stop me from doing the same thing the next time. "I should have just taken the damned camera," he muttered, loud enough for me to hear. I got the message. I could have my fun, but it would cost me.

Clicking on the photos, I gave Sharon a tour of the crime scene, talking as each image came up. "As I said, I had William pegged as the killer from the start. I went to the scene thinking I might find something that would change my mind. I didn't."

I brought up a picture of Doris's beaten body. "This was done in anger. A stranger couldn't have done this ..." a close-up of her face "... or this ..." zoom in on her split lip and broken teeth, "... or this ..." around the eyes ...

"Okay, Matthew, we get the point." First time I ever heard Sharon get emotionally upset. I guess lawyers don't like to see what their clients are capable of.

Back to a general shot of the room. "Yeah, that's enough. You can see why I didn't want anyone from this group to get away with anything. But while I waiting for the police to arrive I started thinking about the one who had sex with Doris — the other one, not William. Why? Why would one of them do something that he or she had to know would upset William to such a degree? And granted, maybe one of them couldn't have stopped him, but surely all of them working together could have. And we know I was right about that."

I pulled another series of shots. "This ashtray," I zoomed in, "There's William's brand, but those other two, they're Brian's menthols, aren't they?" Another photo, zoom in to the floor. "And aren't these candy wrappers from the mints Drake eats to kill the cigarette taste?"

I looked at the client, wondering which one was running things now. It didn't matter.

"You planned it, probably had been planning it for some time. What did you do? Watch William and Doris get it on, then wait until they fell asleep? The rest of you stayed up — long enough for a few smokes and a couple of mints. Then one of you woke Doris, and while he was having his fun another one woke William."

"How could we know how he'd react?" one of them asked, Charles maybe, it was his tone of voice.

"Because when everything's considered, he was a part of you. You knew where his trigger was and you pulled it."

"But why would we?" Higher pitched voice, nervous, Rachel. If they were truly different people I'd separate them and work on her. She'd break first.

"Because you're tired of living in a time share. You want unity, and William and the court order kept you from achieving it. But now, William's gone. You used his emotional distress and your collective will to do what otherwise could only have been done in therapy, therapy the law would not allow."

I gave that a moment to set in, then went on. "And all you had to do was provoke William into killing someone, then wait to be arrested. That would give you an excuse to get rid of him, and the law couldn't touch you, because the 'person' responsible would no longer exist."

"A nice theory, Matthew," Sharon said once I'd finished, "but of course there's no way to prove it. And even if you could, so what? Regardless of the provocation, it was William Doe and William Doe alone who killed Doris Randall."

It was time to drop the big one "A nice summation, Sharon. If I were a juror, I'd acquit. But you forgot one thing. Everyone in this room heard your clients admit to destroying the persona of William Doe who at the time was legally a separate human being, entitled to the protection of the great State of Maryland. Lieutenant?"

Parker did the honors. Standing up and walking over to where they were sitting, he said, "Charles Doe, Rachel Doe, Drake Doe, Brian Doe — you are all under arrest for the murder of William Doe." Five minutes later, he was leading them out of the office.

Much to the dismay of every paper, news magazine and TV network, there was no trial. Faced with being tried as four people for the "death" of William Doe, or as one for the murder of Doris Randall, the four plead out on the condition that their therapy be resumed. And soon there was one — Brain Drake, together again, looking forward to a new life, which he'd be able to enjoy in about ten to twenty years.

MESSAGE IN THE SAND

They wait until just before the sun goes down, when most of the swimmers and sunbathers have gone in and all that's left on the beach are a few surfers hoping to catch a decent wave or two. It's then they come out, old men mostly, equipped with sand pail shovels and plastic cups, a hip pack around their waist, and most importantly, a metal detector, the magic wand with which they hope to find buried treasure.

For some it's exercise, a way of taking a walk without it seeming a waste of time. For others it's a way out of the condo, their time alone without the bother of the wife and grandkids, a peaceful time between the activities of the day and yet another round of miniature golf. But some have bought into the dream, the fantasy that somewhere buried beneath the sand amid lost keys, soda cans and dropped pennies lies a real find, something worth, well, maybe not a fortune, but a thing to show off, a story to tell about how one day they found something marvelous.

Each one has his own idea of what that marvelous object would be. To one it's a rare coin, carried by someone as a good luck piece until he lost it, and the good luck waits to be passed on to the finder. Another's on the lookout for jewelry — a necklace or a ring. For George Balinski it was a watch. Not just any watch, but a Rolex. One day, he would think as he walked barefoot in the sand, one day I'd like to find such a watch. I'd clean it up and put it on, and it would run perfectly. And whenever somebody saw it on my wrist, he'd say, "Nice watch," and I'd say, "Found it on the beach, just lying there waiting for me."

But George was realist enough to know that fantasies were meant to be enjoyed for themselves alone, and not because they'd one day come true. When he was younger he'd had lots of fantasies — of what kind of job he'd have, what kind of wife and house. None of them came true either, but he was happy nonetheless.

What George forgot was that sometime wishes do come true. He and the wife had had the condo for two years now. It was a nice place on 40th St. with two bedrooms and a foldout sofa in the living room, plenty of room for everybody. And of course, everybody was there. And to get away from them all — the wife, the kids, their kids — George started taking the metal detector out in the morning as well.

On the day it happened, George was just walking along, enjoying what to him was quiet — the cry of the gulls, the sound of the surf, the occasional ping that told him his detector was working. Two nice looking young women passed him on the beach. One of them smiled at him. And just as his thoughts of buried treasure gave way to a different kind of fantasy, the pings of his metal detector got louder and more frequent. He'd found something. George stopped, got out his shovel and dug into the sand.

Never had George expected to find anything of real worth in the sands of Ocean City, Maryland. And he certainly never expected to actually find a Rolex. But sometimes a wish comes true, and on that day, it did for George. But you have to be careful for what you wish, and how you wish. For even though George had always dreamed of finding a Rolex, he had never imagined that when he did, it would still be attached to the arm of its former owner.

And it was just the arm, the left arm of an adult male. At first it was thought that arm had come from the victim of a boating accident or shark attack, but no accident had been reported or any shark sighted. It was only when the investigator from the Medical Examiner's Office observed that the arm appeared to have been severed by a very sharp blade that the State Police crime scene technician said aloud what everyone had been thinking.

She looked first at the spot from which George had exhumed the arm, then up and down the beach, then at the spot again. And then she asked, "If the arm was buried here, where's the rest of him?"

Despite closing the entire Ocean City beachfront for the first time in recorded or remembered history, despite bringing in body-sniffing dogs, sophisticated sonar and ground radar devices, despite a massive sand-sifting endeavor, the rest of the victim never did turn up.

The next day, fingerprints identified the arm as belonging to a Peter Bondello. This ID created another flurry of activity, since Bondello was a prominent organized crime figure, a very active member on the Baltimore mob scene.

I know, Baltimore's not supposed to have a mob, not in the criminal syndicate sense of the word that is. But the Outfit is everywhere, and anyone who thinks his city is immune from its influence is just fooling himself. There's a branch in every decent sized city — supplying product to the drug runners, organizing loan sharking and prostitution, and sinking hooks into legitimate businesses under the guise of "protective services."

The identification of the arm as Bondello's brought in the FBI, DEA, ATF and assorted other alphabet agencies. Brenda and I arrived in Ocean City a week after they did.

I wasn't there for Bondello. I'm just Matthew Grace, a simple PI from Baltimore. Looking for newly one-armed gangsters is not on my list of job services. I knew about the Baltimore mob, of course. Its head man had even hired me once or twice when he needed a job done legally (mostly) by someone he could trust. I'd also worked against the mob on one or two small matters, managing to get the jobs done with no hard feelings. (Well, there was that warning shot fired through my office window, but that may have been an old girlfriend.)

No, I was in Ocean City for a more prosaic reason. I'd been hired by Mike and Betty Tauber to find their daughter.

In addition to being Baltimore's favorite vacation resort, Ocean City is often a teenager's first real taste of freedom and responsibility. Fresh out of high school, he goes down the ocean (or as we say in Baltimore, "downy oshun"), finds a job and a place to stay, and is on his own for the first time in his life. In a very short time, he learns about paying bills, cooking, cleaning, getting along with roommates and what it's like to work for a living. Not the little after-school and weekend jobs he had while in high school, but a real, forty hour a week job, one that leaves him too tired at the end of his shift to hit the beach or clubs like he thought he'd be doing before he drove the 150 miles from home.

Some of these kids handle the pressure and by the fall are more than ready for college. Others can't take it, and run home to their old protected lives. Others just quit their jobs but stay in OC, getting by however they can.

Smart, blonde and attractive, Darlene Tauber drove down to Ocean City with three of her friends just two weeks after graduation. They'd rented a place together, a walk-up apartment on Caroline St, just a few blocks off the ocean. Her one friend, Tiffany, knew somebody who knew somebody who could get all of them jobs flipping burgers or making pizza at Friendly Bob's — one of many such carry-out places that line OC's Boardwalk.

Darlene called her parents as soon as she got settled in her apartment. She called again the next day, and the day after that. But soon the calls started coming every other day, and sometimes every third day. But when a week went by the Taubers started getting worried. That's when they came to see me.

"Did you try calling her?" I asked the worried couple as they sat in my office.

"Yeah," Mike Tauber said as his wife nodded. "Thursday night. Her roommate said she hadn't seen her for a few days. Said she didn't know where she was."

"What did you do when you heard that?"

"Drove down there myself. Betty stayed up here in case Darlene called. I took the cell so she could let me know if she did. When I got there, her things were still in her room. Checked with where she was supposed to be working, but her boss said she'd quit two days after she started. After that I didn't know what to do. I got a room and just walked around looking for her — the beach during the day, the Boardwalk at night. When I came back Sunday Betty and me talked it over and figured it was time to call in a pro at this sort of thing."

"Did you call the police?"

The anger Tauber had been holding inside came to the surface. "Of course I called the police," he yelled, "I'm not stupid."

"Michael." His wife put a calming hand on his shoulder, but he shrugged it off. There was a rage inside him that had to come out.

"Of course I went to the Police, first thing after leaving her place. Do you know what those bastards told me?"

I knew. It was what I'd probably have to tell him in a week or two.

"They told me there was nothing they could do. When I gave one of them her description, you know what he said, 'Female, eighteen, blonde and good-looking. Yeah, she'll stand out down here.' Then that son-of-a-bitch suggested that she'd probably moved in with her boyfriend and that she'd call after 'the thrill was gone.'"

That was a possibility, but you don't suggest to an angry father that his sweet little girl is shacked up with some guy. I'd ask Mrs. Tauber later, or better yet, Darlene's girlfriends when I got down there.

They gave me a picture of Darlene and we came to a financial arrangement. Tauber wasn't happy when he learned that he'd be paying for my motel stay. "Money for this has gotta come out of Darlene's college fund," he grumbled. I stayed quiet as he wrote a check for my first week's fee and expenses. I promised to leave the next day and report back as soon as I had news, or in a week if I came up dry.

"So when do we leave?"

That was the first question Brenda asked when I called her at home to tell her about my new case. I'd known Brenda for several months, met her on a roving husband case that turned into a lot more. We'd been dating ever since.

"What's this 'we' stuff?"

"We, as in you and me. You're getting a free stay down Ocean City. Any room you get will come with a double bed. Get the picture?"

"I'll be working. This isn't a vacation."

"It will be for me. I'll be tanning."

"All day."

"Same here."

"And maybe all night."

"That much I knew — double bed, remember?"

How could I say no? Brenda drove down with me.

I checked in with the Medical Examiner's Office before we left. No unidentified females matching Darlene's description had been received. Same story with the Eastern Shore hospitals and police departments. I also checked with the Delaware cities of Rehoboth and Bethany Beach. Plenty of blondes picked up on charges ranging from DUI and public indecency up to and including assault with intent to maim. All of them identified, none of them Darlene.

We checked into a moderately priced hotel on 1st St. Brenda wasted no time changing into the few bits of cloth she called a swimsuit and hitting the beach. I already had on my OC work clothes — jeans and a polo shirt — so I decided to visit Darlene's apartment to see if maybe her roommates would tell me something they weren't willing to tell her dad.

After calling ahead to make sure one of them would be there I took the bus down to Caroline St. (Ride all day for two dollars — beats trying to find a parking space). It was a second floor walk-up over the Swim-n-Surf, a store where you could buy boogie boards, suntan lotion, swimsuits and other beach necessities for twice what you'd pay in Baltimore. Tiffany, the girl who'd organized the whole thing, met me at the door and, after carefully checking my ID, let me in.

The apartment wasn't much — a small living room, smaller kitchen and two closets someone forced mattresses and box springs into and called bedrooms. Unlike the place I stayed in when I was eighteen and on my own, everything was clean and orderly. But then, four girls were staying here and not three guys whose idea of doing laundry was to go for a walk in the rain.

"Tiffany," I said after the preliminaries were over, "I know you told Darlene's father that you didn't know where she was, but maybe she's someplace she doesn't want her father to know about. He doesn't have to know."

"You mean, like, with a guy, or something, Mr. Grace?" She shook her head in the way that girls her age do, the way that drives boys her age to distraction, the deferential way she called me "Mr. Grace" only serving to remind me how far away I was from being that age. "No way, she wasn't like that. And if she was, she'd tell me, we're almost best friends. And after her father left, I'd have called her and, like told her, call home or something; give 'em a story and let 'em know you're okay."

"Darlene have a cell?" I asked. According to her mother she didn't, but she might have picked one up.

"Don't know. If she does, I don't know the number. Or it might be in there." Tiffany pointed to some copier paper boxes in a corner. One of them had Darlene's name on it in blue marker. "Not much storage space," she explained. "We keep our things in there. Clothes we leave in our suitcases or in the closet."

I went over and took a quick look in the box. I didn't see a cell phone but there were several cameras there, a well used Nikon and several disposable ones.

"Like, if you want to take that with you and look through it I guess it's okay, you working for her father and all."

The Nikon was empty. The disposable cameras hadn't been used yet. There was nothing else of interest in the box. I was hoping for some pay stubs.

"I'd like to look through her clothes."

"Eh, sure," Tiffany said and showed me which coats in the closet and which suitcase were Darlene's. "Eh, I sort of borrowed this top from her. Do you need it back?"

"I'm not going to take them, Tiffany, I just want to go through the pockets to see if can find a name, phone number, address — anything that could tell me where she might be." I started looking through the pockets of Darlene's jackets. "When did you first notice she was missing?" I asked as casually as I could.

"I didn't. I really didn't know until her father called. With her working a different job, and with me on all kind of hours at Friendly Bob's, we really didn't see each other that much. I thought we each kept missing the other."

"Where's she working now?" I was coming up empty with Darlene's coats and starting to get a bad feeling. I opened her suitcase. There seemed to be too many clothes for a girl who may have moved without notice.

"Don't know. She didn't stay at Bob's long. Her hours sucked — three p.m. to eleven. The work's so hard you're too tired to do anything after, and you're still tired in the morning so you sleep in. You wake up in time for work but not the beach. Darlene left Bob's and got a job at a pancake house. That was all morning work so she had time at night. But the tips weren't that good and she missed going to the beach. Last time I talked to her she said was going to quit there too, that she'd found a job perfect for her. But she didn't say what it was."

I finished with the suitcase. The bad feeling was getting stronger. "Tiffany, do me a favor. Go through Darlene's things — closet, suitcase, that box and her bathroom stuff. Let me know if it's all there, if there's anything missing except what she might have been wearing the last day you saw her."

Tiffany did, starting with the box and finishing in the bathroom. "It's all here," she said when she came out, "clothes, toothbrush, hair dryer, make-up. Why would she leave without taking ... oh no!" Suddenly Tiffany had that bad feeling too.

"She's probably okay," I quickly lied. "And wherever she is, I'll find her. That's what I do." That's what I was being paid to do. It didn't mean I'd succeed. I gave Tiffany one of my cards. "If you or your friends see her, or hear about her, or remember anything that could help, call my cell."

Tiffany nodded, on the edge of tears as she started to imagine all the wrongs that could have happened to her friend, wrongs that the Taubers were no doubt imagining as well. She'll blame herself, I thought, for not noticing sooner. I started to tell her not to, then realized it wouldn't do either of us any good. Instead I took the easy way out and said a quick goodbye.

The on-duty manager at Friendly Bob's didn't remember Darlene.

"Maybe," he said when I showed him her photo, "So many kids come through here. Some of them are hard workers, putting in as many hours as they can get, trying to make as much money as they can before college. Others," here he shook his head, "others come thinking it's going to be one long vacation. They're shocked when they learn they're actually expected to work." He handed back the picture. "Sorry, I can't help you, but feel free to ask around."

I did. One of the waitresses, a girl named Lauren, remembered her. "She worked with me the first day or two. After that she never came back."

By the time I got to the pancake house it was closed. It was strictly a breakfast and lunch kind of place. I'd try the next morning, both there and back at Bob's. Darlene's other roommates were scheduled to work then and might know something. Somehow I doubted that they'd be able to tell me anything more than Tiffany had.

I was right. Like Tiffany, neither roommate had even realized that Darlene had been missing. "She was in and out all day, working some kind of crazy schedule," one of them told me, but working where she couldn't say. I had the same kind of luck at the pancake house. Like at Bob's, Darlene had come and gone so fast she didn't leave behind any impression.

After that it was a long day down the ocean. Darlene hadn't opened an account at any of the local banks. The police had no record of her filing any kind of complaint or being charged or detained for anything. I was left with going store to store, showing her picture, saying her name, hoping that sooner or later I'd find the place she'd gotten her perfect job.

I got back to the hotel about five. Brenda's swimsuit was hung on a drying rack near the window. I could hear the shower running. I hoped that Brenda wasn't planning on a big evening out. After the day I had, all I was up for was a quick burger and then back to the room and some quality time with my laptop, checking for any activity on the credit cards Brenda's parents told me she had.

I opened the bathroom door and poked my head in. "I'm back," I said to the silhouette behind the shower curtain.

"Rough day?"

"I've had better."

"Well, there's a present for you on the night table. Now close the door, it's getting chilly in here."

I went to look for my present, presents actually, since there were five of them — telescope pictures.

Telescope pictures have nothing to do with bringing things closer. Imagine a small four-sided tube, about an inch on one end tapering to a half inch at the other. Hold the small end to your eye, there's a lens to look through. Hold the big end to the light. There's a picture inside. The pictures are taken by "scope" guys and gals who walk the beach. You call them over and they take your photo. Later that day you go to the scope place and they sell you a telescope with the picture inside, a lasting memento of your trip down the ocean. Mostly they snap kids and grandkids, young couples who've just started dating and newlyweds. This time the pics were of Brenda, posing provocatively in her all-too-brief bikini.

"See anything you like?" Brenda asked from behind me as I was trying to decide which of her five poses was my favorite. I turned and there she was, wearing only a robe, her hair still wet from her shower. The burger and laptop could wait, I decided, putting down the scope in favor of the real thing.

Later, with Brenda sleeping quietly and me at the desk running Darlene's credit cards, my mind drifted back to the telescope pictures. There was something I'd almost thought of before Brenda had come out of the shower. Not of Brenda in her swimsuit, but of how nice it must be to spend your summer walking up and down the beach, just taking pictures and getting paid for it. For someone who likes the sun and has an interest in photography, it would be the perfect job.

Ocean City had three scope shops. I got lucky with the second one.

"Yeah," the manager said, looking at her picture. "She worked here."

"Worked?"

He nodded. "Hasn't been in for a while. Shame too. She was a hard worker. Took lots of pictures. Good ones too, always in focus with nice exposure. Never got the customers in shadow or against the sun. Just about everything she took sold."

"She make a lot of money?" I asked, hoping he'd know where she cashed her paychecks.

"The harder a kid works, the more money he makes. She worked hard, pulled in about $45-50 a day, and at a dollar a scope that's a lot of hustle. And before you ask, we pay in cash."

So much for the bank idea. I tired another angle.

"Why'd she leave?"

He shrugged. "Who knows with these kids? Here one day, gone the next. One night she was all excited about the job, the next day she's a no-show."

"When was this?"

He thought a moment. "I think it was the day before the break-in, or maybe right before."

"What break-in?"

"Somebody smashed the back door, went through the racks with the scopes in 'em."

I looked at the wall behind the sales counter. It was lined with bins holding bags of scopes waiting to be picked up. "What was taken?"

"Not much. We don't keep cash here overnight. Just some of the scopes. Who would want somebody else's pictures?"

Who indeed? The bad feeling that had been growing since my t... Tiffany suddenly got worse. "Your photographers, are they assigned s... areas of the beach to work?"

"Yeah," the manager told me. "Each of the scope stores takes a third of the beach. My crew's got from 28th St. up to 75th. Darlene worked between 35th and 45th."

"Any of her pictures left?"

"None of the store's. They went missing along with some others in the break-in. But we have some of hers."

"Hers?"

"Yeah, she always carried her own camera with her. She saw something she liked, she's snap it. Sometimes she'd take an extra pic or two of a customer — cute kid, good looking guy, something like that. Most people never knew she'd switched cameras. We'd develop them for her at cost overnight. In fact …." He disappeared into the back of the shop. Came out with a manila envelope, handed it to me. "We had these in the developer the night of the break-in. You find her, give 'em to her. Tell her she's welcome back anytime."

I thanked the man and left.

On the bus ride back to the hotel I resisted the urge to look at the photos. With recent events, Darlene's interest in photography and the area she worked, the break-in, the fact that there were no photographs to go with the cameras found in her apartment, I knew with a cold certainty what I'd find on at least one of the pictures in the envelope. And the longer I waited to look at them, the longer I had to decide just what to do about it.

Someone had been watching him, probably followed him from Baltimore. Watched as he checked into his hotel, was behind him when he walked the Boardwalk and was close enough to him on the beach to see him have his picture taken by the scope girl. He wouldn't have been the subject — no, he wasn't that stupid, none of them were — but he'd be in the background of one of the shots Darlene took on that beach. He may not have noticed, but the man who followed him from Baltimore, the man who was waiting for just the right time and place to do his job and leave his message, he would have seen. And this man would have acted, would have made sure that this photographic evidence would disappear.

No doubt he followed Darlene back to the scope shop, then followed her home. Her apartment had a simple lock, easy enough to pass through without any signs of tampering. Take the film out of the camera, take any used disposables and any developed prints. Break into the photo shop and steal the scope pictures Darlene took that day. Oh yeah, and somewhere along the way, snatch up Darlene herself, just to be on the safe side.

All this ran through my mind as I looked through the last set of pictures Darlene had taken, the ones the man on the beach, just like her customers, didn't realize she'd snapped. Hoping I was wrong, I looked at each one through a magnifying glass, looking at the people in the background, looking for a familiar face, one that had been in the paper just about the time Darlene had gone missing.

I found Peter Bondello's picture midway through the stack of twenty-four exposures. His was with some woman I didn't recognize. They were laughing, sharing a joke maybe. His arm was around her — the same arm that George Belinski later found buried in the sand.

The picture confirmed it. I was too late. It didn't matter that it was too late by the time the Taubers had hired me. I'd taken their money and promised to get their little girl back. They'd put all their hope in me and now the best I could do for them was maybe find her body.

For a while I just stared at the picture wondering what to do. Going to the police was an option, just not a very good one. True, tying the disappearance and possible death of a young girl to the brutal murder of a mobster was sure to generate a public outcry, massive news coverage and increased efforts by the police, but it would also drive those involved deeper underground than they already were. The woman in the photo, if she wasn't already sharing a landfill with the rest of Bondello, would disappear just as Darlene had. And after all the publicity died down, Darlene would be just another missing teenager and Bondello an unsolved piece of OC history. I didn't care too much about Bondello, but Darlene deserved justice.

No, the police were out. I'd make arrangements to be sure they'd get a copy of the photo in case the plan I had come up with went wrong, but for now Darlene's connection with the case was my little secret.

Brenda and I left Ocean City that day, stopping at the scope place and the post office before we did. I called the Taubers when we got back to Baltimore, telling them that although I hadn't found Darlene, there were still a few leads to follow that might tell me where she was. I hated myself for the false hope I left them with, but I couldn't have them going to the police, not yet anyway.

The call I was expecting came the next day. The whispered voice mentioned a place and time, and strongly suggested I be there. My package had arrived.

When you think of meeting with a mob boss, your imagination no doubt conjures up images of Italian restaurants, dark warehouses or the backroom of a neighborhood bar. Sometimes it's like that, but my meeting with the man I call "Mr. Louis" was just outside the Pratt St. pavilion in Baltimore's Inner Harbor. I arrived a few minutes early to find him sitting on a bench, watching the tourists go by. As I approached him (slowly), a large man in a "Charm City" T-shirt moved to intercept, but at a nod from Mr. Louis he let me proceed.

"Mr. Louis, thank you …"

"Shh," he interrupted me, looking at his watch. He pointed to the U.S.S. Constellation, a naval sloop from the Civil War whose permanent berth is now in Baltimore. "Any minute now."

A cannon went off and white smoke erupted from the bow of the ship. Had the cannon been loaded with shot or ball, pieces of Federal Hill across the harbor would now be missing.

"Everyday at one o'clock, they fire it. A demonstration for the tourists. It used to be louder, but the hotels complained about the noise rattling their windows. Now they just use a half load."

Must be convenient knowing exactly when a noise like a gunshot was going to go off. I kept this thought to myself and instead said, "You got my presents?"

Mr. Louis reached into his pocket and brought out two telescopes, one in light blue plastic, the other pale green. Both had "Souvenir of Ocean City" written in gold on their sides. Without looking through either he said, "Yes, thank you for thinking of me. I have some of my granddaughters when they were younger, but these, these are quite different."

They should have been. The green one had Bondello's face on it, cropped from the photo I'd found. The blue one was the unknown woman. As attention-getters they couldn't be beat.

"What is it you want of me, Mr. Grace?"

I had to phrase this carefully. I needed this man to be in my debt, and not me in his. "To do you a service, Mr. Louis. A young girl is missing. Her parents hired me to find her. In looking for her I found a photograph she'd taken of Peter Bondello with this woman. Realizing there was a connection, I came to you rather than … going elsewhere."

Louis knew exactly where "elsewhere" was — a big building with men in blue uniforms.

"And how does this concern me?"

"Make no mistake, Mr. Louis — I will do whatever it takes to find out what happened to this girl. Make as much noise as I have to. But I thought that, given the circumstances, maybe you'd prefer it if things were done quietly."

Louis took his time replying. He sat there for a few minutes, toying with the scopes, watching people go by. Finally, he nodded and turned to me with a smile.

"As you say, Mr. Grace, quiet would be better — for both of us. And you have done me a service, but not how you think. Until now, what happened to Peter was as big a mystery to us as to you and the authorities. There had been no approval of … well, let's just say that Peter's name had not been discussed. And the way it was done …" Louis shook his head "… such a gesture is now for others."

He held the blue scope up to the sun. "I have not seen this woman, but perhaps others have. I will ask. Please wait for word from me before ... making noise."

"You have my word, but I can't speak for the parents. A day or two more, and they're likely to go public."

"I understand. And thank you, Mr. Grace."

Mr. Louis got up and slowly walked away, leaving me on the bench watching the tourists and hoping I'd played my hand right.

The next meeting was in a bar, one of those neighborhood places whose name changes every few years as the guy who bought it realizes that running a bar is way too much work and not as much fun as Sam Malone made it look on television. So he sells the business and license to another guy with a dream and if he breaks even he considers himself lucky.

I got to the bar a few minutes early. Mr. Louis was already waiting for me in the back room. He was sitting at a table which had two other chairs around it, his ever-present bodyguard standing alertly in a corner, one that provided a clear view of the room and an even clearer line of fire.

Louis gestured for me to sit down. "You have news?" I asked him.

He shrugged. "Maybe, I believe so. We will know for sure once our guest arrives." Louis looked at his watch. "He will make it a point to be late, as a demonstration of his independence."

"But that won't change the fact that you called and he came, right?"

"It is sometimes best to let people ignore the strings that bind them. You have the photograph, and the negative?"

I passed them over. This was the part I didn't like. To find out what had happened to Darlene I was giving up the only evidence I had, the only evidence anyone had that would tie her to Bondello's death. Sure, I had kept a print for myself, and had scanned the image, but without the negative either could be dismissed as photo manipulation. Still, it was the only chance to find out the truth. And tonight that was all I was interested in.

As Louis predicted, our guest arrived twenty minutes late. He entered without knocking. As he moved to our table he shot a glance over to Louis's bodyguard, sizing him up as if deciding which of them could take the other, then smiled as he figured that he'd probably be the one to walk away. He sat down without any apology for being late.

"You wanted to see me?"

"Yes," Louis sad quietly, "thank you for coming, Mr. Wills. This is Matthew Grace. Mr. Grace, Derek Wills."

I'd heard of Wills. His name had been in the paper a few times. He was usually mentioned as "allegedly" being involved in Baltimore's drug trade. He'd been arrested several times but never convicted. Witnesses against Wills tended to disappear or suddenly change their testimony on the stand. Word on the street was that if it was illegal and could be sold — narcotics, guns, flesh — Wills had or wanted a part of it.

Wills gave me the same scrutiny he's given the bodyguard then asked Louis, "What's up?"

Louis handed Wills the photograph of Bondello and the woman. "I believe you know this couple." It was a statement not a question.

Wills looked at the photo, shrugged, and threw it back on the table. "Knew them, you mean. She was my lady, before she took off with this piece of dirt." He smacked the photo, his hand hitting Bondello's image.

"I take it then that you are responsible for what was found on the beach?"

Wills started to answer, then looked my way. It finally occurred to him that I might not be part of Louis's organization. "He okay?" he asked Louis.

"Mr. Grace came to me with this photograph. He could have gone to the police. And he promises not to go to them if you will answer some questions."

I hadn't promised any such thing, but if that was the price I guess I'd have to pay it.

At Wills's hesitation, Louis prompted. "We are both of us in his debt."

"Yeah, what the hell. Bondello took what's mine. Nobody takes what's mine. When I heard they were going down the ocean I followed them. Saw them on the beach, watched as they went back to their hotel. That night, I did them right in their room, nice and clean."

"The police never found his room," I said.

"Yeah, like any of us use our real names. She probably checked in while he sat in the car."

"The arm, that only drew attention," Louis pointed out.

"That was the point. You put a hand on what's mine, you lose the hand. Some people needed to know that. Now they do."

"And their bodies?" Louis asked before I could.

"Lots of dumpsters in OC. Who's gonna notice a few more trash bags?"

That was my cue. "Is that what happened to the girl?" Before he could ask "What girl?" I added, "The one who took this picture."

Another smile. "Saw her snap the pic. Couldn't take the chance that it'd turn up on the front page of the Baltimore Sun. Tried to get it back, when I couldn't I snatched her up, just in case."

"And where's her body, another dumpster?"

Wills smiled, then laughed out loud. "Who said she's dead. Nice piece like that, it was a shame to waste it. Gonna turn her out, make some money."

I went dead inside. Until then I thought that the worse news I could give the Taubers was that their daughter was gone and that the man responsible was beyond the law. Now I'd have to tell them that for just for taking a picture she'd been sentenced to a life of disease and addiction. To myself I swore that somehow I'd get her back. If she was in Baltimore, I'd find her. If not, I had contacts in other cities. One way or the other I'd get her back. She wouldn't be their little girl anymore, but I'd bring Darlene back to her family. And once she was safe, Wills would pay. If Louis had to go down too, so be it. I'd pay the price when I had to.

I barely heard Louis ask me if I had other questions. I mumbled out a "No" and he said, "Thank you, Mr. Wills." There was a hard edge to Louis's voice, an iciness that hadn't been there before. "I believe that will be all."

Wills stood up. "A pleasure, gentlemen." After another challenging look at Louis's bodyguard, he walked out. The pictures he left on the table.

When we were alone, Louis asked me, "Mr. Grace, are we done here?" It was the way he said it that made me think we weren't, that he was waiting for something. I looked at the photo on the table and I knew what it was.

"Mr. Louis, did you mean what you told Wills? About being in my debt?"

"Of course, Mr. Grace. If I said it, I meant it, and I always pay my debts."

"What Wills did, he should have gotten the okay first?" Louis nodded. I picked up the picture. "The girl who took this was just eighteen. Your granddaughters, they're about that age now, aren't they?" Another nod. I called in the favor. It was the one Louis was waiting for. He was happy to oblige.

Derek Wills disappeared from the streets that night. I understand that after some intense questioning, he told of an abandoned motel off of Route 1 in Bel Air where several girls were being held, pending their sale to the highest bidder. Because the condition of the merchandise was an important part of the negotiations, none had suffered more than some rough handling, mild starvation and the fright of their young lives. An anonymous tip led the State Police to them. Darlene Tauber was one of those girls.

A week after Darlene was returned to her parents to try to resume a normal life another anonymous tip led police back to the motel. There, in the same room where the girls had been kept, a severed arm was found, its fingers grasping a crumpled photograph, a message for those that needed to know. The rest of Derek Wills's body never turned up. There are plenty of dumpsters in Baltimore too.

HOW THE STORY GOES

It's every private eye's dream. There you are, sitting alone in your office, wondering where your next job's coming from when she walks in through your door — the beautiful young blonde in the tight red dress. She slinks up to your desk and sits down, slowly crossing her nylon covered legs, giving you a teasing glimpse of the promise that waits above. Then she begs for your help — she's in trouble and you're the only one who can save her.

Of course you take the case. You take it without thinking, without even a mention of payment. You take it even knowing that it can only end one way, in death and heartbreak. You take it because you're an urban knight and she's the damsel in distress. You take it because of the girl.

That's the dream, and sometimes the reality comes close. My name's Matthew Grace, and the blonde who walked thought my door one fine spring day wasn't that young and she wasn't wearing a tight red dress. Instead she was on the far side of fifty and wore a form fitting jogging suit designed more for fashion than exercise.

It fit her well, flattering a shape a woman twenty years younger would be glad to have. Now whether that shape was due to nature's gifts or a surgeon's skill was an open question, but it wasn't up to me to ask. My bet was on nature, since her face bore lines of a life well lived, lines that could easily have been lifted out and allowed her to lie about her true birth date.

"Mr. Grace?" she asked as she sat in the client's seat (without crossing her legs, I should add).

"Yes, and you are …?"

"Sarah, Sarah Freedman."

"And how can I help you, Ms. Freedman?"

"Make it Sarah. My pussy's missing."

She said this with a smile, a challenging smile that told me that she knew exactly what she was saying and had said it anyway, just to get my attention.

She had it. "And when did you last see your pussy?" I asked, playing along.

"Last night when I undressed for bed."

"And this morning?"

"It was gone when I woke up."

"And was there anyone with you that could have taken it?"

She gave me another smile. "I do on occasion let people play with my pussy, pet it even, but I assure you, Mr. Grace, I was all alone last night."

"If we're going to talk about your pussy, you should call me Matthew, and we are talking about a cat, right?"

She gave me a winner's smile. "Of course we are, what else could we have been talking about?"

I wasn't going to answer that one, so I nodded my head in defeat and asked for details.

"My cat's name is Sam. Not very original but he looks like a Sam. And as I said, I last saw him when I was getting ready for bed. I turned out the lights and went to sleep. Sam went off to do whatever it is cats do when they're alone in the dark. This morning when my alarm went off he wasn't there. He's always there, sitting on my covers and meowing until I wake up. Then he relaxes, knowing that sometime soon he's going to be fed."

"And you looked for him?"

"A rather silly question, Matthew. Of course I looked for him — up and down, down and up, inside and out. He's nowhere on the house and grounds."

"Any idea how he got out?"

Sarah shook her head. "Not a one. None of the windows were broken and all the doors were locked. I live in a safe neighborhood but I make sure to keep everything locked tight. There's no way Sam could have gotten out, but he did."

So that was it. Sarah was worried about more than a missing cat. If Sam had gotten out of her locked house, then maybe someone had come in.

"Did you call the police?"

"And tell them what? My cat is missing, come right away. They'd come because of where I live. They'd pretend to look around, not find anything and file a crazy lady report. If I'm going to be called crazy I'd rather pay for the privilege."

I asked where she lived. She gave me an address in Guilford — very safe, and very expensive. Up there the police respond faster for a missing cat than they do for a murder on the west side.

Has it finally come to this, I asked myself — Matthew Grace, Pet Detective? I thought about all the things I could be doing other than looking for a lost cat. A long list came to mind. Then I looked at Sarah. There was something — her manner, her approach, herself — I found myself attracted to. I liked her, and wanted to help. Like I said, you do it for the girl, even if she does have twenty years on you.

I told her I'd be out later that morning.

"Thank you, Matthew. Barbara's always talked about how you helped her."

She could only be talking about one person. I had solved her daughter's murder, and later she hired me to get the goods on her husband in what proved to be a very ugly divorce. "How is Ms. Masters?" I asked.

"Living the good life down in Florida, spending what's left of her husband's money."

"Good for her. And speaking of money." We came to a financial agreement that pleased us both, me more than her.

"And you'll be over later, right?" She asked as she gave me a check and I gave her a copy of the contract.

"Right," I assured her.

"Bet this is a first for you?"

"What is?" I asked, knowing full well what was coming.

"Being paid to look for pussy." She left before I could come up with a good reply.

By the time I got to Sarah's town house the cat had come home. She met me at the door with Sam in her arms. Obviously an indoor cat, the black and white tom looked like he'd spent a bad night roughing it.

"He was waiting for me when I got home," Sarah said after inviting me inside.

"So am I out of a job?"

She made a rude noise. "Don't be ridiculous, Matthew. We both know I didn't hire you to look for my ... cat."

She gently dropped Sam to the carpet. I reached down to scratch him. He hissed and ran away. "Sam doesn't take to strangers." Sarah explained. "He'll stay out of sight until you leave. Now then, someone was in this house last night, I want to know how and who."

The how was easy. Calling on experience gained from ten years as a crime scene technician, I went through the house looking for signs of a forced entry. The first thing I noticed was that Sarah didn't have an alarm system. The next was that there was only a passage lock on her upstairs balcony door. A closer look showed me bright scratches on its strike plate. I looked outside — easy access from the ground with the climber hidden from the street.

"Did you find any doors unlocked this morning?" I asked after coming back downstairs.

Sitting in a living room chair, Sam in her lap (I guess he thought I'd gone), Sarah closed her eyes as she retraced that morning's activities, one hand moving and finger pointing as she mentally moved through her house. Finally she opened her eyes and said, "The deadbolt of the back door was unlocked."

I looked over the lock. No prymarks or fresh scratches. I opened the door and flipped the barrel of the deadbolt out. It held firm when I tried to push it back in.

"Your burglar got in through the upstairs door. However long he stayed, or what he did while he was here I can't tell you, but he left through your kitchen door. Sam must have left when he did, then wandered too far."

While Sarah went through the house to see if anything was missing, I called 911 and reported a break-in. A patrol officer arrived, followed by a crime lab technician. The officer took a report, and the tech dusted both doors for prints, not finding any.

"Now what?" she asked after the police had left.

"Now I call a locksmith and have him change all your locks, just in case your intruder picked up a key. And then we see about having an alarm put in."

I stayed until the locksmith had come and gone. The alarm people wouldn't be out until later in the week.

"You should be okay now," I told Sarah as I got ready to leave.

"Matthew, why do you think he didn't take anything?" There was a tremor in her voice that hadn't been there before. Maybe it finally occurred to her that she'd been alone in her house with a stranger, a stranger who had maybe watched her as she slept and could have done whatever he wanted while she lay there helpless.

I shrugged. Nothing had happened and I didn't want her dwelling on what could have. "Who knows. He was probably just looking for stuff he could stick in his pocket — cash, watches, jewelry, credit cards. Or maybe Sam chased him out. Or," I paused, putting a big grin on my face, "maybe he heard you sleeping and realized there was someone home."

"Maybe," Sarah said, then caught my implication. "I do not snore," she protested.

"Okay, you don't snore," I said in a patronizing tone.

"I don't," she said with make-believe hurt in her voice, then she added "but if you don't believe me, there's one way you can find out." This last was said somewhat in jest, but I got the feeling she wouldn't mind if I stayed over, if only to sleep on the couch to protect her from any intruders.

I declined graciously. "I'd love to, but I'm afraid old Sam would sneak up on me while I was sleeping and suck the breath from my body." I then promised to stop by after the security system was installed and went on my way.

That should have been the end of it. Of course, it wasn't. Two days later I got a call.

"Matthew, it's Sarah." She sounded worried. "Can you come over?"

There weren't any clients in the office and I didn't have any urgent business just then. I was working on another case but it was a nighttime thing. "I'll be right there," I told her.

The drive from 25th St. to Guilford takes fifteen minutes. I made it in ten. When I got there Sarah was on her front porch. Sam wasn't anywhere to be seen.

"What happened?" I asked.

She waved one arm toward the rear. "I came home from shopping and found, well, just look around back." Whatever worry had been in her was gone. Now she was just mad. I walked to the rear of her house.

The new lock had held. The frame hadn't. The door had been forced, the wood of the frame splintered from where it had been pried. I sensed rather than heard Sarah behind me.

"Bastard," was all she said. I hoped she was talking about the burglar and not me.

"Have you been inside?" She shook her head no. I handed her my cell phone. "I'm going in. If you hear any screaming or shouting it will be me. Call 911 and tell them an officer needs help." A little white lie, but it was the fastest was to get the cops there.

Being careful not to touch anything, I entered the house. Nothing out of place on the first floor — stereo, TV, DVD, all the electronics still there, same for the silver in the dining room. The second floor started out the same, until I got to Sarah's room.

It wasn't much, just a single drawer not closed right, but all of the others were shut tight. From the bit of lace sticking out I made a guess as to its contents, but I'd wait until the crime lab had done its job to be sure.

The rest of the house checked out. Nothing disturbed, no burglar hiding anywhere. And still no sign of the cat. He was either hiding or had escaped again.

Another report, more fingerprint powder on the back door and the dresser drawers in Sarah's bedroom. "I'm worried about Sam," was all Sarah said to me after she had toured her house with an officer to see what might be missing or disturbed.

The cops left. I took Sarah up to her bedroom. The drawer I'd found disturbed was now fully opened, showing its contents.

"Do you keep anything in there other than underwear?" I asked.

Sarah's anger at having her home violated was still there, and she was still glancing around hoping that Sam would show up, but her mood was improving. She blushed, just a bit, then gave me a sly smile.

"Just some ... personal items, for when I have ... company, and one or two for when I don't but would like to. Why, want to see?"

"No thanks." I think my cheeks might have reddened as well. I quickly added, "No papers, money, or other valuables?"

"Just some very expensive bras and panties. The less there is, the more it costs. But nothing other than lingerie."

"Check and make sure it's all there."

She did. "Hard to tell," she said when she finished. "What's not here might be in the laundry. Why is this important?"

I told her. "I'm assuming the same guy broke in twice. Now maybe the first time he just looked around to see what he could find, and he came back today to check out the one room he hadn't gone into — yours."

"I sense a 'but', Matthew."

"Yeah, a big one. It may also be that the first time was just to look around, to get an idea of the layout of the house. This time when he came in, he ignored the big money items and went right to your bedroom and rifled stuff very personal to you."

"So in addition to being a thief he's a pervert."

"He's some kind of freak," I said, then gave her the bad news, "And he might be targeting you."

On my advice, Sarah fortified her house. Workmen were called in. The back door was repaired and all the door frames either strengthened or replaced. Strong but decorative gratings covered the downstairs windows. The security company was called and offered a premium to immediately install an alarm.

While this was going on, I called everyone I knew in the BPD — the burglary unit, the sex offense squad, what few friends I had left in the crime lab — no one knew anything about a house creeper in Guilford. I had Sarah call the Northern District Station and ask, no demand, increased patrols in the area. At first the duty lieutenant wasn't interested, but then Sarah repeated her address and started dropping names and soon got what she wanted. It's good to be rich.

"I hate this," Sarah said when all the work was just about finished, "I hate feeling like a prisoner in my own home."

"Welcome to life in the big city. At least you have the resources to do protect yourself. There are plenty who don't. All you have to worry about is maybe one sick little weirdo. There are no drug dealers standing on your corner or sitting on your stoop at night, no stray bullets fired through your window by gang bangers doing a drive-by. And when was the last time anybody in this neighborhood looked over his shoulder when taking an evening stroll?"

She gave me a funny look. "Matthew, you are not going to make me feel guilty about being rich. My parents and two ex-husbands worked hard for my money and I'm going to enjoy it. And I think I have a perfect right to be afraid of 'one sick little weirdo' and to hate what I have to do to stop him from coming into my house. Now let's take a walk and look for Sam. He's probably somewhere out here hiding from the workers."

We didn't find the cat.

"Ordinarily I'd say leave the door open for when he comes home but …."

"No, that wouldn't be a good idea, would it, Matthew? Are you sure you won't stay and help protect a poor old lady?"

"You're not that old and certainly not poor. And while you should be safe here tonight I'm not so sure I'd be.'

"Why, afraid I'd try to seduce you, or afraid I'd succeed?"

"It would certainly be an interesting and enlightening experience, but I have a policy about getting involved with my clients, or rather, my girlfriend tells me I do."

"Oh well, you're still my knight in shining armor, even if you are taken."

"Thanks. Call if anyone tries to storm the castle."

"Let them try. They'll find I've got more than locks and alarms, although I might need help in disposing the body."

With nothing more to do, I left, partly worried about her and partly feeling sorry for anyone who tried to get in when she was home and awake.

Sarah called the next day, just to let me know that Sam had come back. "I found him collapsed by the back door this morning," she said. There was something in her voice. She should have been happy. She didn't sound like it.

"How is he?"

"Not good, Matthew. He was scratched and bleeding, one ear was torn. It looks like he'd lost a few fights. I've got him at the vet's now, but it doesn't look good."

"Sorry to hear that."

"Hell, it's just a cat." That's what she said, but the catch in her voice told me she was near tears. Sam wasn't just a cat, he was her housemate, her companion, the friend she told all her secret troubles to. If she was anything like the pet owners I knew, she probably loved him more than she did most people.

I knew Sarah wanted to talk, but I was busy on a missing person case, a sixteen year old runaway the police hadn't been able to find. The parents had called me in and after three nights of exploring Baltimore's underground music scene I was getting close. Right then I was waiting on a phone call that might tell me where she was. I told Sarah to call me if she needed anything and hung up. Ten minutes later my contact phoned in and I was off to save yet another damsel in distress.

It turned out to be a long night followed by an even longer day. In the end I missed the girl, who took off for New York with a drummer and a bass player. I called a fellow PI who worked out of Brooklyn and handed the case over to him. He was between jobs at the moment and glad for the work. Then I went home and crashed, all thoughts of runaway girls, kinky burglars and injured cats forgotten.

Nothing much happened the next few days. I kept busy doing background checks and security inspections for some regular clients. Every once in a while I'd think to call Sarah and see how Sam was doing, but somehow never found the time. It was a week later that she called me.

I'd been in court all day, sitting in a drafty hallway waiting to testify in an insurance scam case. The defendant had collected big, claiming a severe back injury as a result of an accident. The insurance company, sensing fraud, paid off anyway then put me on the case. It didn't take me long to photograph the defendant in various activities inconsistent with his supposed injuries. I understand that once he was caught, he offered to pay the money back with interest. Instead, the insurance company sued to recover the payment, plus interest and penalties, then prosecuted in criminal court.

A day consisting of several hours of waiting followed by fifteen minutes of testimony is more tiring than you'd think. When I got back to the office and saw the blinking light on the answering machine I was tempted to let the two waiting messages go until the next day. But I checked the caller ID and saw that one was from Sarah and the other from a New York exchange. I hit the play button.

The New York call was from my buddy in Brooklyn. He'd found the girl. She was safe and on her way home. The drummer was in jail and the bass player was, in Jack's words, "recovering from injuries sustained after trying to assault me." Good old Jack, always able to liven up even the simplest case.

Sarah's call was strange. If a voice ever combined amusement with disgust, hers did. "Matthew, can you come over? And bring some of that fancy forensic stuff you say you have."

I grabbed a quick dinner and drove to Guilford.

After we said our hellos, I asked "How's Sam?" feeling guilty for not calling before this.

"He ... he didn't make it." Now I felt worse. I know, it wasn't my fault that the cat hadn't had the sense to stay inside, or that he had been a house cat with zero survival skills. And I wasn't the one who twice broke in letting the cat out. But I was the one Sarah had called, to protect her home and keep her safe, and so far I hadn't done such a good job of it. Her pet was dead, the burglar still not caught, and now there was some new trouble.

"I'm sorry," always seems so inadequate when someone loses a loved one, but we say it anyway, and I said it then.

Sarah tried to shrug it off. "It wasn't your fault, Matthew, and he was just a ..." She didn't finish. Instead, she all but fell into my arms and started crying. I held her tight as she mourned her lost friend.

I don't know how long we stood there in the hallway, but eventually she cried herself out. "Thank you," she said, lightly kissing my cheek as we separated. "I thought I was done with that yesterday after the vet called. I guess not."

"Sometimes you have to share the pain to be rid if it," I told her.

"Maybe, but I'd like to share the pain with the s.o.b. who did this, and be rid of him. Find him, Matthew. Find him for me and make him pay. Make him pay for killing my cat and making me cry."

"This isn't a murder case, Sarah. In some ways they're easier to solve. This is a B&E, with no clues and no witnesses. I've done what I can with locks and alarms. Maybe he'll go somewhere else. If not, and he tries again, he'll get caught in the act."

"Not good enough."

"It will have to be. Fire me if you want, but I've got nothing to go on."

"Yes you do. Do you think I asked you over just to sob on your shoulder? Come in here."

She led me into the study. There on the desk were three envelopes. One had been opened, two were still sealed.

"The opened one came yesterday. I was too upset about Sam to bother with it. The other two came in today's mail."

I looked them over without touching them. Standard padded mailers, available in any office store. Address labels printed off a computer. Postage was regular first class stamps. Judging from the postmarks, they were mailed from three separate post offices. Smart guy. The stamps and labels were self-adhesive, so no saliva for DNA. And the labels were printed, so no handwriting. And I was willing to bet that there wouldn't be any fingerprints either.

I pointed to the opened package. "What's in it?"

"Look for yourself, but put on gloves first."

I got a pair from my crime scene kit, put them on. Reaching into the envelope, I first pulled out a typed note. "Thinking of you," was all it said. A pair of panties followed. They were bikini cut, light blue and while not totally revealing, were sheer enough to tease and promise.

"Yours?"

Sarah nodded. "They used to be. One of my favorite pairs too. I'd wear them when I was expecting … well, on special occasions."

I smiled. Trying not to think of how she might have looked on those occasions, I turned my attention back to the panties. They were smeared with a white sticky substance.

"See why I told you to wear gloves?"

There was something wrong. So far our burglar had taken care not to leave anything behind. So why is he now giving us a great big DNA sample? I took another look at the sample. No, not quite right.

I took a rechargeable flashlight out of my bag, attached a blue lens to it. "Turn out the lights," I told Sarah and handed her a pair of orange goggles. Putting on a similar pair, I shone the light on the panties.

"If that's what's it's supposed to be," I explained, "it will glow in the dark." Sarah switched off the light. Nothing, whatever was on the panties stayed dark.

"So what is it?"

"Nothing naturally produced," I said. "Probably handsoap. That's what we used back in the lab when we experimented with the best way of packaging condoms."

Wearing gloves, I carefully opened the other envelopes. One of them also had panties in it — black lace in the style of men's boxers. Of course these were cut so that the overall effect was different. The other envelope held a camisole that was transparent enough not to be there at all. Both were stained with the same substance as the first.

"And I looked damn good in all three."

I ignored Sarah and read the notes that were in the envelopes. The one that came with the camisole, which according to the post mark had been mailed the day after the blue panties, said, "Always on my mind." The package with the black lace panties was mailed last. Its note read, "Still thinking of you. I have one pair left. Guess what I'm doing with it?"

"This guy's clever," I told Sarah. "He sends you just enough so that you get the message but nothing that would trace back to him. I'm betting that the police won't find any prints on the envelopes or notes either."

"Do we have to call the police?"

"Sarah, this had gone beyond simple burglary or a panty raid. I think you've got a stalker. First he prowls your house, then he steals your underwear. Now he's letting you know what he does with it. Next he'll come after you."

"Matthew, it's just that I'd rather my lingerie and what some pervert is doing with it not become a matter of public record. As you said, there're probably no prints or anything on them anyway."

It was against my better judgment, but I agreed. I'd take it all back to my office and process it myself. If I found something I could turn it over to the police then.

Meanwhile there was a more urgent problem.

"Sarah, you have a stalker," I told her again for emphasis, "someone who's become fixated on you. We have to find him before he tries anything else. Now, any strange phone calls lately?"

"No, and I have caller ID in case any come in."

"How about the stores where you shop? Anyone overly friendly, anybody offering to carry your bags home?"

"This is Guilford, Matthew. We're rich, all the shopkeepers are overly friendly. And since we drive everywhere nobody has to carry anything."

"Your emails? Any weird messages?"

"Just people in Nigeria who want to share ten million dollars with me and offers to increase my manhood."

"Do you visit chat room?"

"Please. I have a life and real friends."

"And I'll need a list of them, ex-lovers and casual acquaintants as well. They all have to be checked out. Anyone new in your life?"

"Just a good looking private eye who won't take a hint. I may have to start stalking him."

"Well, when you steal my underwear take the ones with the holes. Now about those lists."

Leaving Sarah to write her lists I went upstairs. I wanted to see what houses were visible from her second floor windows, especially those in her bedroom and bathroom. If I could see them maybe someone could see in. A lot of freaks start as peeping toms and move on to more violent hobbies.

Again, I forgot that Sarah lived in an exclusive neighborhood, where privacy was part of the reason you paid seven figures to live there. Trees everywhere except for the front. And unless the elderly couple who lived across from Sarah had a horney nephew or grandson, I was ruling them out.

Sometime serving your client means doing what's needed rather than what you're told. So despite Sarah's instruction, I called Janet Wingate. Janet had been a homicide detective back when I worked in the Crime Lab. She transferred to the Sex Offense Unit shortly after I went private. I filled her in on what was happening.

"Unless your client wants to make a report, Matt, there's nothing I can do officially. I can check to see if this guy's behavior pattern matches any known offender, and I can run it past our profiler. Maybe she can tell you what kind of a freak you're looking for."

"Thanks, Janet. I don't suppose you can run handsoap through the database?"

"No, but if you come up with a real sample, let me know and I'll run that."

After hanging up, I turned my attention to the envelopes and their contents and as I expected, came up blank. That left Sarah's lists.

Most of her close friends were women about her age. These I eliminated right away. There were few men on the list who weren't married to one of the women. Those remaining were past the age of climbing balconies and forcing doors. That didn't mean I ruled them out, just that they were on the bottom of my own list.

Her acquaintances were few — people she knew from her clubs and the charities she supported. Again, the members of her club tended to be women like her. And the charities were of the "have dinner and write a check" variety rather than the "go out and get your hands dirty" type. Sarah didn't have a job, so there were no co-workers to worry about.

That left ex-husbands and lovers. She'd had two former spouses. The first remarried, started a family and had moved to out Montgomery County, Maryland.

"Martin and I married too early," she'd told me. "We were young, foolish and in heat. Back then you waited until after you were married and we got tired of the wait. Once the novelty of playing house and getting it regular wore off we learned that we had nothing in common. We split up after about two years. Long enough for a nice settlement though."

The second was still in town, running an advertising firm.

"He was a blind date that a friend set up. Not really a bind date, I needed an escort to a charity concert and she drafted Howard. We hit it off and soon hit the sheets. Things were good there so we made it legal."

"How long did Howard last?"

"Always long enough, he was quite the gentleman. Oh, you mean the marriage. We had six good years, and one really rotten one. The rotten one was the last, in case you hadn't guessed."

"Who cheated on who?"

Sarah gave me a pointed glance. "Really, Matthew, as if I'd get caught. Anyway he cheated, not on me personally but financially. Tried to make my money his money."

"You were married, wasn't your money his money?'

"Don't be naïve. Being rich means that's it's always your money. Casual sex would have been forgivable, but he tried to take what was mine. That I don't forgive. So three years ago I went to court and took away as much of his money as I could. And now every three months he sends me more."

After splitting with her husband Sarah had had three lovers, the last a little more than three months ago.

"Brice was younger than you, Matthew, a real May-December kind of affair. But all he saw in December was Christmas."

"Just in it for the money?"

"A crude way of putting it, but yes."

"So how that break-up go?"

Sarah smiled. "He left me, about a week after I started talking marriage. Well, not only marriage but how nice it would be to have someone to care for me in my declining years, which he suddenly saw as right around the corner. He left without saying goodbye."

"Maybe he's come back?"

She thought about that. "Could be, but I can't see him prowling around or fondling my underwear. He wasn't like that. None of them were really."

"What about the other two?"

She shrugged. "Country club sex, more diversions than affairs."

"I hate to ask this, Sarah, but the country club waiters, or your gardener, or a handyman — ever give one of them a tumble?"

From the look on her face I'd shocked her for a change. "Matthew, please, not with the help."

"Maybe the help felt differently."

"I never gave any of them cause to."

Still I added more names to my list. The crew from her lawn service, pizza guys, delivery men — if any of these were on the edge of stability he could have mistaken a friendly word, a kind gesture, a generous tip as sign of deeper interest on Sarah's part.

I checked them all out. I called Janet and asked her to find out if any of them had records. Howard was clean, Martin had a few DWI arrests and was still on probation from his last one. Brice had been popped a couple of times for drunk and disorderly and resisting arrest. The rest of them — the workers, Sarah's male friends and acquaintances — were a mixed bag, some of them clean, some with minor charges like common assault and simple possession. None of them had been arrested or convicted for anything major that would make them a likely suspect.

There were two however, that rated an extra look. One of them, Neil Atkins, had twice gone down for burglary. He was one of the drivers for the pizza place Sarah used. Another, Marlon Bradford, worked for the lawn service. He'd been arrested for domestic assault and his wife still had a restraining order out on him.

"Waters isn't likely," Janet told me as she cut into a steak I was paying for. I was treating to dinner as a thank you for running the record checks. "He'd be most prone to harass his wife rather than pick a relative stranger. And from what you've told me about Sarah Freedman, she sounds like too strong a woman for him. Bradford is the type to go after someone weaker and in his own social class, someone he can dominate."

"What about Atkins?" I asked between bites of my New York strip.

"He's worth spending time on. Getting in would be certainly be easy for him. Maybe one night when he dropped off a pie Sarah answered the door in her night clothes. He could have taken that as a silent invitation and decided to act on it. Too many of you guys believe those stories you read in men's magazines. Or in your case, detective novels."

I thought about telling Janet about blonde damsels in distress and urban knights in trench coat armor rushing to protect them, but I didn't feel like getting laughed at. "Anything from your profiler?" I asked instead.

"She finds this case ... interesting was the word she used. This kind of stalker doesn't usually go to the lengths yours, or rather, Ms. Freedman's, has. He's taken extra care not to leave any trace of himself. Most times it's the other way around, they want to share with the object of their affection. She says the soap in the underwear is a new one on her. She can't wait to study this guy once you find him."

I appreciated Janet's faith that I would find him. "Did she say there was anything else ... interesting about what this freak's done?"

"It's more what he hasn't done. No phone calls. He should by now have called just to hear her voice, if only on the answering machine. Another attempt at entry maybe, if not her home than her car, to find and take something of hers that would make it more personal for him. She said it was almost as if he wasn't serious about Sarah but only playing, that she was more of a fancy than an obsession."

Now the hard work began. The postmarks from the packages sent to Sarah showed they'd been mailed from three different postal substations. However, the stations were all in the same general area of Baltimore County. Whoever mailed them either lived in that area, drove through it on his way to work or was assigned it as part of a regular route. At least, that's what I hoped.

That still left a lot to do, too much for a one man operation like mine. I thought about calling in a larger agency to help, one that had the people and resources to trace the activities of a large number of people. Whoever I called wouldn't have to know why, or my client's name, just investigate and report.

I made a note to call Sarah to get her okay for the extra help. As it turned out, I didn't need it.

I started thinking about what Janet's expert said, how the stalker's behavior was less than obsessive. Maybe there was a reason for that.

A stage magician always has a pretty girl helping him, someone for the audience to watch while he pulls off the trick right in front of them. A clever man setting a trap will set two, so that his victim will relax after finding the first. And a person hiding the truth will sometimes reveal it in such a way that it seems like a lie. It's all about distraction.

Maybe that's what was going on with Sarah. The break-ins, the stolen underwear, the soap in the panties — all of it had us thinking about sexual fixation. What if that was the distraction? To get us looking in one direction while the real danger comes from another. To keep us guarding the castle and watching for an invader when the damage has already been done.

But what was really going on? Nothing had been taken, at least, nothing I knew about or that Sarah would admit to.

I called her the next day. "There's nothing else missing, Matthew, except a tiger-striped bra and panty set I can't find. That must be what our friend is playing with."

"I don't think he's playing, Sarah. Is there anything you're not telling me? Anything private, embarrassing or less than legal taken you didn't want to admit to?"

"I don't embarrass that easily, Matthew. I haven't smoked dope in several years and the only Coke I have comes in cans."

"Then check your desk — your blank checks, bank statements, credit cards and receipts. Maybe what he was after was you, your identity anyway."

"All he would need is a number? And he could have copied that down, right?"

"Right." I told her to call her accountant and put him to work checking her finances. And that I'd be over later that day to see if her computer had been accessed anytime during the two break-ins.

I wasn't satisfied. Sarah could still be hiding something, something from one of her ex-lovers — a photo, a note, a gun — something that if revealed would cause public humiliation or land one or both of them in jail, something she thought I couldn't ignore.

Or she might just be playing me. What better distraction than to be the victim? She'd wait a day or two more and another package would arrive, one that this time would point me in the direction she wanted me to go, would aim me toward her intended target.

I didn't want to think that, but I had to consider it. Maybe despite the come-ons and the innuendoes I was just the hired help, no different from the handyman or the gardener, to be used and discarded once I'd done my part. It had happened once before, but I had seen past the false hair and fake boobs just in time to send that blonde to jail.

Not this time, a voice inside me argued. I stopped to think why not and finally came up with Sam.

Sarah loved that cat and the cat loved her. Had she forced her back door to fake the second break-in he wouldn't have left, he would have stayed by her side. Instead he followed the burglar out the back door.

Which was odd. The first time I came to her house Sarah told me that Sam ran and hid from strangers. So why did he follow this one out the door, not once but twice? Maybe whoever he followed wasn't a stranger.

That would give me two suspects — Sarah's ex-husband Howard and ex-lover Brice. Both were in the house long enough for Sam to become accustomed to them. He may have followed either of them outside.

"I don't see either one of them doing this," Sarah told me the next day. I had brought with me an expert in intrusion detection who was now making sure her computer hadn't been compromised. As he worked, Sarah and I talked.

"You said Brice left on his own. Any hard feelings?"

"None, from either of us. I was tired of the novelty and started talking marriage to scare him off. It worked. He saw old age creeping up on him from the outside and ran like a rabbit. Shame in a way. He had other rabbit-like attributes that I miss from time to time."

"What about Howard?"

"That was war. As I told you, he tried to steal from me, so I took him for all I could. He fought back, but I had better lawyers. I left him enough to start his own business, and even then I got a piece of that."

When you get past the distraction, when you stop watching the pretty girl and concentrate on the magician, sometimes it's easy to see how the trick is done. I suddenly had an idea of just what was going on.

"How's his business going?"

Sarah shrugged. "Not bad, not great. No one's getting rich these days except those of us who already are. Howard sends me a check every quarter and that's all I care about."

"You audit him?"

Sarah gave me a predator's smile. "My accountant does, every year. No one steals from me twice."

Except that if I was right, someone already had. I was betting that it was Howard, and I was suddenly afraid of the reason why.

"Do you still have Howard's social security number?" I asked Sarah.

She nodded. "In with the old tax returns in the den." Which is where my expert was. Good. I excused myself and joined him in the office.

Finding Sarah's old returns, I wrote Howard's SSN on a piece of paper.

"How's it coming, Paul?"

"No problems, Matt. No one's made any serious efforts to get in, just the usual crap off the Net and her software took care of that. I added some stuff to strengthen her defenses."

I handed him the paper. "This belongs to Howard Freedman. Find out what you can about him, in particular his financial status."

Paul smiled. Intrusion detection was his job, and he did it better than most. But hacking was fun. Like many computer experts, Paul Nicholson had worked the other side before turning pro, laying siege to systems and networks instead of protecting them. I could have it done myself, but Paul was the expert. He could get twice as much information in half the time. I left him to his piracy and rejoined Sarah.

It took Paul less than an hour to get everything I needed. "Ready," he called out from the den. I joined him there and he handed me about ten sheets of paper. "Here's the hardcopy."

I looked over the report. For a businessman in today's economy, Howard Freedman was doing okay. Not great, but okay. Enough in his savings, checking and investments to get by, and his retirement plans were healthy enough that he wouldn't starve when he got old. He owed money to the usual people — car lease, mortgage on the condo, credit card debt. The last was quite sizable, but nothing he couldn't handle as long as he had money coming in. And that was the problem. Howard's sole income was his business and while Freedman Advertising was still in the black, a projection Paul had worked up showed that wouldn't be the case in a few years. Too many companies, too few accounts.

"Without more income, there's no way he's going to be able to compete," Paul told me. "Of course if your client was willing to drop her take from twenty percent to ten, or even fifteen, he might make it. It would help her in the long run. Better ten percent of something than twenty of nothing."

"She won't. I think she'd rather see him fall, particularly if she were partly responsible for his collapse. She takes her cut for revenge's sake, not because she needs the money."

But Howard did. And he would be in better shape if Sarah's share was reduced. Even better if it dropped to zero.

"What's their business arrangement?" I asked.

"She gets the twenty percent as part of the divorce settlement."

"Insurance?"

"Dual policy, 100k on each, taken out when they got married. Howard's kept up the payment on hers, let his lapse."

That was enough for me, almost. There was just one more thing I had to do.

After Paul left, I told Sarah about my suspicions.

"Your ex is going to try and kill you."

Sarah just stared at me in disbelief. For the second since I met her, I managed to shock my client. "I don't believe you," she finally said.

"It's the only thing that makes sense," I explained. I told Sarah about what the profiler had said about the stalker's atypical behavior. I added my own opinion about how Sam had behaved.

"And from this you think Howard's going to kill me?"

"I think he's planning to try. With you out of the picture his income increases twenty percent plus there's the insurance he keeps on you. He's going to need that money to save his business, not right away but down the road. Killing you now makes sense. The longer he waits the more obvious his motive."

"But why this elaborate game?"

"To distract the police. Even if a death looks like a burglary, they always suspect the current or ex-husband or lover. Howard was giving them a distraction, a fictional pervert to chase after."

"So what now, have him arrested?"

For what? There's no proof he did anything. And you can't charge someone for what you believe he intended. I hope to have some proof by tomorrow night. Then you should be safe. First we let Howard know we're on to him. That will make him drop any plans he's made."

"And then?"

"And then we get nasty."

Before I left, I made sure that everything was locked up and reminded Sarah to set the alarm. No one would be getting in that night.

On my way home I drove by Howard's condo for a little reconnaissance. His building was right in the middle of Baltimore's eastside, where revival and rebuilding were the new catch words. Row houses that fifteen years ago sold for fifty thousand and housed lower to middle class families were being restored and marketed to upwardly mobile couples for 200K plus. Breweries and factories were being gutted and remade into high priced apartments. And espresso bars and trendy restaurants were taking the place of the neighborhood pharmacies and grocery stores. It was all very fashionable and *the* place to live. It was bringing people back into the city, but I couldn't help wonder what was going to happen to the area when the novelty wore off.

Howard lived in one of the converted warehouses. This one had a brand new 24-hour food store across the street from it, no doubt selling meals to go for the busy professional getting home late and a coffee shop to get them going the next day. Its parking lot was the perfect place to sit and watch people go in and out of his building.

Like most of these kinds of places, this one had the basic security set-up. The lobby door was kept locked. You either had a key or had to be buzzed in. There was probably a notice on the door advising the tenants not to admit anyone they didn't know. They'd also probably been told time and again not to blindly buzz anyone in, no matter how many times he rang the bell. Human nature being what it was, I counting on at least some of the residents to ignore this advice.

I was also counting on two other things. The first was that with a building the size of Howard's, no one would know everybody. So a stranger in the hall would be assumed to belong there. The second was the assumption that decent security outside meant poorer security inside.

I was right all the way around. When I went back the next morning I was dressed like a citizen — suit and briefcase. I arrived late enough so that most people, including Howard, would be at work. Waiting until I saw people coming out, I approached the front door key in hand, shaking my head like I'd forgotten something. A kind soul coming out held the door open for me. Once inside, I made my way uninterrupted to Howard's apartment. His cheap locks offering no challenge, I was soon inside and tossing the place.

I was neat. I didn't want to be. A part of me wanted Howard to know someone had been in his home, wanted him to feel a little of the worry and violation that Sarah had suffered. The rest of me didn't want to go to jail, so I was careful not to leave behind any signs of my visit.

It didn't take me long to find what I was looking for — a pair of tiger-striped panties with matching bra, souvenirs of how clever he was. They were tucked away, unstained I should add, in the drawer where he kept his own underwear. I wondered what Janet's expert would make of that.

I also found a bonus — a partly used sheet of stamps, the same kind that had been attached to the packages Sarah had received. I pealed one off the backing paper. With luck its perforations would match those on one of the stamps in the packages. Not conclusive proof, but it was the kind of evidence that, along with the panties, would convince a jury.

Not that this was going to court. The plan was to confront Howard with our knowledge of his plan, then advise him that his continued well being depended largely on Sarah's. I'd drop a few names, names of men with bad reputations and no scruples, who would be sure to visit him if Sarah so much as stubbed a toe under suspicious circumstances. Once we had him sufficiently cowed, Sarah would demand that he raise her share of his business to thirty percent. If not, she'd go to the police and I'd go to the newspapers, telling them about his break-ins, his panty raid and his imaginative use of hand soap. Even if he wasn't convicted, or even arrested, he'd be publicly humiliated. Either way he chose, he'd be out of business in a year.

That was the way it was supposed to go. A successful conclusion to a somewhat bizarre case, a case that had started as something out of Chandler — the bold and sassy blonde in trouble, threatened by a mysterious stranger, a hardboiled PI her only hope. He takes up her cause, sees that she's safe, looks for the bad guy. Along the way there's some flirting, maybe serious, maybe not, but it becomes a little more than just a business relationship. In the end, the good guys win, the bad guys lose and all's right with the world.

That's not exactly what happened.

I spent the afternoon doing work for a few other clients. I got back to the office about seven. I was tired and wanted to go home. I just had to call Sarah and discuss when and how we were going to puts the screws to Howard.

She called me instead.

"Matthew, can you come over here?" Her voice had the same tone it did when she called me about the second break-in — strained, worried, on the edge of losing control.

"Is everything all right?" As I asked this my thoughts raced with all the reasons it wouldn't be — Howard had tried breaking in again, Howard had broken in and was there, I'd been wrong and it had been the pizza guy all along.

"Yes, it is now." That eased my mind a little, but now by much. I told her I'd be right there.

There were no police cars surrounding Sarah's house. That was a good thing. Before going in I did a circuit around the place. No doors or windows opened. Another good thing. I went in and found the body of Howard Freedman lying on the living room floor. Not a good thing.

It looked like Howard had been shot once, and not from a distance. There were close contact powder marks on the front of his shirt. A small caliber cartridge case was on the floor next to him. A glance around the room showed me a purse-sized semi-automatic pistol on an end table where Sarah had left it.

All this I saw in seconds. I was suddenly glad I hadn't left any signs of a burglary behind in Howard's condo. I started to ask what happened but Sarah beat me to it.

"I was upstairs when I heard noises. I grabbed the gun I've been keeping in my nightstand. I came down to find Howard standing there. Before I could tell him that we knew what he was planning he came at me. I had no choice, Matthew."

Most of me wanted to believe her. I liked this woman, had come to think of her as a friend. There was an attraction there too, one that never had a chance to grow but it was there. Because of that I wanted to believe her.

But she'd killed a man and hadn't called the police. She called me instead. And the house was tight. The back door was closed and she had unlocked the front to let me in.

"How'd he get in?"

"He... he must have had a key. He probably took one the second time he broke in."

Except that the locksmith had left four keys, two each for the front and back and all of them were accounted for after that burglary. I know, I counted them.

Sarah must have read the doubt on my face. "Or maybe I left the door unlocked." A better story, but I was willing to bet that one of her house keys was now in Howard's pocket.

"And after he came in, he locked the door and turned the alarm on." I looked over at the blinking light by the front door. "Tell me the truth."

"I let him in. I wanted him to think I'd figured it out all by myself, that I was smarter than he was. When I confronted him he went crazy and attacked me."

"So you shot him with the pistol you just happened to have in your hand?"

"What is it you want me to tell you, Matthew?"

What I wanted her to tell me was a story I could believe. That wasn't the way this was going to go.

"Don't say a word, Sarah. Not a single word." I didn't want her saying anything I might have to repeat under oath.

I knew what had happened. She had spent all of the previous night and most of the day thinking about what Howard had done to her, and what he might be planning to do. She thought about all he had cost her — her piece of mind, her sense of security in her own home. Howard had taken away her privacy and caused the death of a loved one.

I remembered her telling me about Howard, how he had taken what was hers and that was the one thing she couldn't forgive. "No one steals from me twice," she'd said. Howard had. I looked down at his body. He wouldn't a third time. He had paid dearly for making her cry.

"Howard wanting to kill you was only a theory," I finally said. "It's not enough for self-defense."

"It could be, with some help."

So that was it, the reason why she had called me instead of the police. I was the crime scene expert, I could make it look real, like Howard had broken in and threatened her, like she had no choice but to defend herself. She was counting on whatever feelings I had for her to cover up her mess, to risk myself to make things right. But there was only so far I could go, only so much I was willing to chance.

"He would only have tried again later," she said, sensing my reluctance. "He would have waited, arranged an alibi, and tried again."

She had a point. Maybe he would have, or maybe not. Either way, hadn't Howard gotten what he deserved?

I tried to think so, tried to remind myself that it was Sarah who was the victim, that it was Sarah who was to be the target. She was the damsel in distress, I was her protector and the story was nearly over. It needed its happy ending. The only problem — "happily after ever" was for fairy tales.

And this wasn't a fairy tale — just a story about a simple private eye with a client who thought that being rich meant being right. And as I said at the beginning, there really was only one way for this story to end.

I walked over to the phone and hit 9-1-1, told the operator that there was a man down, that he'd been shot and appeared to be dead. I gave the address and hung up.

"You've got about three minutes to come up with a better story than the one you told me. Better still, don't tell them anything and let your lawyer deal with it."

For one of her minutes Sarah just stood in shocked silence at my betrayal. She spent her remaining two calling me a variety of unpleasant names, one or two of which I hadn't heard before.

The police came, sealed the scene pending a search warrant and drove us both downtown.

It took Sarah less than an hour to come up with her new story — that I had shot Howard. I'd been expecting it, and willingly submitted to a gunshot residue test, insisted on one in fact. Sarah was less than willing but wasn't given a choice in the matter. When the results came back, she needed yet another story.

A long night of questions, answers and explanations followed. It was early morning when I was finally allowed to leave.

I wasn't the happiest of PIs as I walked out of the Homicide Unit. A man was dead, my client was in jail for killing him, and I'd put her there. The feeling that I'd betrayed her left the taste of ashes in my mouth.

I was almost out the door when I was called over by Joshua Parker, the lieutenant in charge of the Homicide Unit.

"It would have been easy, Grace."

"What would have been easy, Lieutenant?"

"Arranging the evidence so that your client walked out alongside you. Why didn't you?"

Before I answered, I thought of Sarah, the woman who'd hired me to protect her, the woman who'd trusted me, charmed me, who damn near seduced me. And again I asked myself the same question Parker had. Why didn't I?

"I don't know," I answered us both, "maybe because I don't like being played for a fool. Maybe because I thought you'd catch me this time. Or maybe because it just wasn't right."

"You've played the fool before. And you're too good to leave behind anything I could prove." He almost left it like that before adding, "You did the right thing, Grace."

That shouldn't have made me feel any better, but somehow it did.

***

The trial was a media sensation, rich people, stolen underwear, a dead cat — how could it have been otherwise. Both sides subpoenaed my records, I wound up testifying for the defense. Sarah did well on the stand, charming more than one member of the jury, which hung nine to three. Right now she's out on bail waiting a new trial.

My life goes on much the same it had before Sarah walked in — stray husbands, missing children, thieving employees — steady work but nothing to write about and generally that's the way I like it. But every now and then, as the office door opens but before the client comes, I wonder if it will be another woman in trouble, needing the help that only I can give her. And when that happens, you can bet I'll take the case, even knowing how it might end. I'll take it because it's my job, I'll take it to set things right and I'll take it for the girl — because that's how the story goes.

THE CHOICES WE MAKE

Druid Hill Park sits in the center of Baltimore. Enclosed in its 700 plus acres is the Baltimore Zoo, The Conservatory, the city reservoir and numerous tennis and basketball courts. There's also a flying disc golf course. There used to be a reptile house, with the biggest snakes you'd find outside a political convention. And no doubt more than one body lies carefully hidden under the park's woods and greenery.

A nice quiet part of the park is Three Sisters Lake. It's a secluded spot just off the Greenspring Avenue entrance and is favored by nature lovers by day and romantic couples at night. And as it turned out, it's also a very nice spot to dump a body. Or two.

I'm a city boy. I like paved streets, cement sidewalks and row houses covered with Formstone and fronted by marble steps. There's only two times you'll find me in the park. The first is my annual visit to the zoo. The second is when my job takes me there. My name is Matthew Grace and when this whole mess started I was still a crime scene technician for the Baltimore Police Department. Doing that job meant I was in Druid Hill Park more often than I liked.

Usually it was for what we called a body dump. Someone's killed, and since having a dead body on your hands is somewhat incriminating, it's better to put it elsewhere. A park at night is a good place. Mostly bodies are left in Leakin Park, in southwest Baltimore, but as I've already said, Druid Hill Park gets its share.

Only once did my two reasons for going to the park coincide. A body was found in the polar bear enclosure when the zoo opened for the day. The recovery of the body was complicated by the fact that Frosty, the zoo's polar bear, had already claimed it as his personal rag doll and chew toy. Sedating Frosty was out of the question, he might have fallen into the water and drowned. So was waiting until the bear got tired of playing with the deceased. And no one wanted to go in and try and take the body away from him. The victim was finally removed when someone climbed on top of the enclosure's roof and looped a rope around his body. Needless to say, Frosty was more than a little upset and batted the body like a piñata until it was out of his reach.

I wasn't expecting anything like that when I got a call to respond to Greenspring and Druid Park Ave. for a questionable death at the lake. I was expecting a body dump or a drug overdose. Yet I had enough time on the job that I really should have known not to expect the usual in Baltimore City.

I was the last to arrive on the scene. When I got there the first thing I noticed was the quiet. There was none of the usual talking and joking that accompanies any crime scene. When people did talk, they did so in whispers.

Detective Alexander Klein met me by the clearing just before the lake.

"This is a bad one, Matthew."

"I've seen bad before, Alex."

"Not like this."

Her name was Mary Kesling. She was twelve years old and would never be thirteen. She'd been missing for two days, having disappeared while walking home after school. A jogger on his early morning run found her. No effort had been made to hide her. Whoever the killer was had wanted her body found.

Mary's body was nude, her clothes in a neat pile beside her. You can guess some of what was done to her. As for the rest, I hope to God you can't. Imagine the worst, you won't be far wrong. Even today, with my years as a crime lab tech far behind me, this scene still haunts my dreams.

What was done to this girl made us angry. Angry at the city for producing the monster that could do this. Angry at ourselves for not being able to protect innocents such as Mary. And mostly angry at her assailant. Had he been in our midst all we would have needed was a rope. We were in a park. There were plenty of trees.

What made it worse for me was that there was little I could do for her, not there on the scene. What trace evidence there was would be on her body, and the Medical Examiner would recover that. All I could do was take some photographs, make a few measurements and carefully gather her clothing.

It was while I was gathering her clothing — shoes, socks, jeans, blouse, undershirt — that I noticed that something was missing. "Alex, no panties."

"Sick bastard took a souvenir."

That made it worse, that her killer still had a part of what was hers, that he would use it to relive the moment, over and over again.

Rich Arnold, Klein's partner, came up behind me. "M.E.'s here. You done, Grace?"

I wanted to say "No." I wanted to say that there was still evidence to recover, evidence that was unique and would point directly to the killer. I wanted shoeprints, tire tracks, fingerprints — all those things I was trained to find. It wasn't that kind of scene. "I'm done, Rich, send them in."

***

"Okay, gentlemen, what do we have?" Sergeant Joshua Parker asked the next day at the case review. "Mr. Grace, let's start with you." He gave me a look as if expecting one of my usual smart mouthed replies. Sorry, Sergeant, I thought, not this time. This one's all business.

"I really wish I had something, Sergeant. Soil and foliage samples from the park. Hairs and fibers from the clothing. The M.E. will get more evidence from the victim. More hairs, more fibers. We'll get DNA from the semen left on and in her. With any luck he'll be in the Fed's database."

"And how long for the DNA?" Parker wanted to know.

"Three weeks to a month, that's if we can convince our outside lab to rush it."

"And in the meantime, a few more young girls could die. Gentlemen, tell me we have a witness."

The detectives seated around the table were silent. Finally, Klein spoke up. "Sorry, Sarge. The best we could come up with was someone who thought a dark colored sedan drove out of the park about 3 a.m."

"And what was he doing up at three in the morning. Any chance he's the one."

"No, *she's* not. Just a young lady who was out partying. She lives on Green Hill, and was just coming home when she saw the car drive past her. She thought it came from the park. That's it."

"And the plan for today is?"

Arnold answered. "We walk the route Mary usually took home from school. Then we walk the alternate routes. We talk to everyone. Maybe someone saw her being snatched up. We'll find something, Sarge."

But they didn't, not that day, or the day after, or the day after that. A week went by and there was nothing new. All we had was a missing pair of pink panties and maybe a dark car. And so we waited for a lucky break, or for the killer to strike again.

Every cop in the city was on alert. Schools were watched, and anyone near them who even looked like he might be having a dirty thought was brought in for questioning. Nothing. Dark cars in and around the park were stopped and their drivers questioned. Still nothing. Then one day there came a lucky break, or so we thought.

Officer Jesse McMullen was on normal patrol in Hampden, which is just north and east of Druid Hill Park. A dark blue sedan cut in front of him and blew through a stop sign. McMullen pulled it over and as he approached the car he noticed that the driver appeared to hide something under the seat. That happens all the time. Most of the time it's drugs or alcohol. And most of the time, the officer who stopped the car merely retrieves the forbidden item and arrests the operator for driving while impaired. Sometimes it's more serious, and there are rules for when it is. But sometimes the rules aren't followed.

After McMullen identified the driver as one Shelby Adler and checked him for wants and warrants, he called for back-up. With Adler out of his car and safely under the observation of another officer, McMullen searched the car, expecting as I said to find drugs or an open container of some sort. Instead he reached under the front seat and came out with a pair of pink panties that Adler had been fondling while driving.

Adler was taken into custody. Several hours of intense interrogation followed. In the end, he not only went for the rape and murder of Mary Kessler, but also of two other girls whose bodies had yet to be found. He refused to say where he had hidden them but did offer to produce their underwear.

Suspect, evidence, confession — that should have been the end of it. Officer McMullen was hailed as a hero and recommended for a bronze star, the BPD's highest honor. In exchange for a sentence that might let him see daylight after fifty years, Adler was willing to plead out and give up the location of his other victims. All was well, and the good guys had again triumphed.

Or so it seemed.

An attorney's job is to represent his client to the best of his ability. It's not supposed to matter if the client is a saint unjustly accused of a heinous crime or a monster who deserves everything that's coming to him in this world and more in the next. An attorney must do his best for his client.

Some attorneys balance this responsibility with the one they owe society as a whole. If they have a client whose guilt has been proven beyond any shadow of a doubt, one whose release would constitute not only a perversion of the law but would represent a clear and present danger, they get the best deal they can for them, but they make sure that the society to which they belong is kept safe. Other attorneys see only the client and despite his guilt and the danger he might pose, pour over every report, every bit of evidence, every witness statement looking for the one flaw or mistake that would put his client back on the street. Shelby Adler had one of these lawyers.

Carlton Lange was an assistant public defender. He didn't want to be, but after law school he had neither the grades, money nor connections to be hired by a big name firm. And so he took a job with the Baltimore PD's office and waited for his big break, the one case that would get his name in the papers and show him to be the greatest legal mind since Darrow and Mason. It didn't take him long after being assigned the case of State v. Adler to realize that this was that case.

He waited until Adler's court date, until all the bodies had been found and all the evidence against his client was in. And then, on the day Adler was supposed to plea guilty, Lange held a last minute conversation with his client.

"Your honor," Lange announced to the court, "at this time my client wishes to change his plea to not guilty."

The Assistant States Attorney's objection was overruled and a trial date was set. She really didn't mind. She had enough for a conviction. She had the panties, she had a confession, and she had two bodies that the defendant had personally led the police to.

"What you don't have," Lange argued at the suppression hearing, "is a warrant to have searched my client's car. And without that, you haven't got anything."

And that's when it all came apart.

Reluctantly, the judge agreed with Lange. She excluded the panties, and with them, Adler's confession, and any evidence obtained from the confession, including the bodies of his other victims. Not only that, at Lange's request, she enjoined the department from further investigation of Adler until and unless "independent evidence identifies him as a possible suspect." Thanks to Carlton Lange, Shelby Adler not only walked out the courtroom a free man, but did so with as close to legal immunity as one could get.

Word of the ruling spread quickly. Smelling blood in the water, the media sharks gathered and began their feeding frenzy. Stunned, Klein and I walked down Fayette St. back to headquarters.

"So what happens now?" I asked when I was finally able to speak.

"Nothing. Adler gets away with it. If he's stupid enough to do it again in this jurisdiction we might have a shot, but he'll probably disappear, move somewhere else, become someone else and pick up where he left off."

A thought occurred to me. "Before that happens, what if 'independent evidence' links Adler to some other crime?"

"What crime and what evidence?"

"I don't know yet. But I'm sure we could arrange something."

Klein caught on to what I was suggesting. "Don't even think something like that, Matthew."

"Why not? We played it straight and lost, and now a monster's walking free. At least this way …"

"That way leads to you losing your job, going to jail, and any good you've ever done being called into question. Let it drop, Matthew. The good guys lost this one."

I let it drop. Someone else didn't. A week later I got another call to Druid Hill Park for another questionable death. My first thought was "He did it again, and he's rubbing our nose in it." My second was to hope that there was some evidence we could legally use against him.

I should not have been worried.

Rich Arnold saw me drive up, waved and walked over. "Lovely day, isn't it, Grace?"

"What's up? Where's Alex."

"His day off. This one's mine and mine alone."

"Then who's going to solve it for you?"

Arnold shrugged. "Don't know. Don't care. This one can stay on the books forever."

As we approached the all too familiar clearing by Three Sisters Lake I soon found out the reason for Arnold's jubilant mood. This scene was decidedly different from the last. Officers and detectives alike were all smiles, and the only things needed to make this a real picnic were a couple of kegs on tap and the crack of a bat on a ball in the distance. Strange behavior on a murder scene, I thought. Then I saw the victim.

It was Shelby Adler. Twenty-three years old and destined not to see twenty-four. According to Arnold, Adler had been missing the whole week, having disappeared shortly after leaving court.

A jogger, not the same one – that one had changed his route — had found his body this morning. No effort had been made to hide him. Whoever the killer was had wanted the body found.

He was nude, his clothes in a neat pile beside him. He'd been savagely beaten but that wasn't what killed him. Rather, cause of death was exsanguination, Adler having bled out from the gaping wound between his legs, where his penis and testicles had been before someone had brutally removed them with a somewhat dull blade.

"That had to have hurt," Arnold said as we stood over the body.

"I'm sure it did. Let's hope he was conscious the whole time."

Like the last time, there wasn't much I could do. Photographs, measurements and recover the clothing. When I inventoried the latter no one was particularly surprised to find that Adler's undershorts were missing.

What did surprise us was the drawing I found in one of Adler's pants pocket. It was a sketch of a woman. The artwork was simple, almost child-like, and it showed her from the waist up. There was nothing special about the blouse she wore, and her hair style was one that any woman — old or young, black, white or Asian — could have worn. The only thing special about the drawing was her face. She didn't have one.

"Who's that?" Arnold asked, looking over my shoulder.

A cold chill came over me as I realized that this drawing had been left for us to find — the killer marking his, or rather, her victim. "I don't know, Rich, but I think it's a message."

"What kind of message?"

"I'm afraid that we're going to find out."

I was right. The day after Adler's body was found, all the TV stations and both daily papers received the same drawing in the mail. The package sent to the Sentinel also included a pair of men's boxer shorts, which DNA analysis later proved to be Adler's, verifying the sender's claim. The message enclosed with the drawing was simple. "Justice found Shelby Adler," it read. "It will find others. I am any woman. I am every woman."

The Sentinel dubbed her "Jane Doe." The name stuck and Jane Doe was adopted by countless women's groups.

Not that any of them countenanced the violence that was done to Adler, or so they claimed in press releases, but it was the message behind it, that women will not be victims any longer and stand ready to protect themselves to any extent necessary.

Soon Jane Doe ceased to be the signature of a killer and became instead the symbol of a movement. Women would attend rape trials wearing T-shirts bearing Jane's image (or lack of one) or, in some instances, a featureless mask. All to stand silent witness for the rape victim and to be a warning against her attacker.

Adler's killer was never caught. Arnold went through the expected motions but dropped any active investigation just as soon as he picked up another murder. Nobody objected.

And to its credit, the department stood by Jesse McMullen, a good cop who had made a devastating mistake. He was buried in the Evidence Control Unit for a few years and then went back on the street with little fanfare. He repaid the department's trust by becoming even a better cop, and when he finally earned a promotion to detective, asked for and received an assignment to the Sex Offense Unit. We all do penance in our own way.

What happened at Three Sisters Lake seems such a long time ago now. It was a different time, a time when it was still a game of good guys versus bad guys, and I was still one of the ones wearing the white hat.

As you know by now, that changed. It was after the Kesling case when I started seeing in shades of gray instead of black and white. Soon after that I was almost killed on the job, and Rich Arnold left the force because of what he had to do to save me. Then I put into practice the idea I got walking back from the courthouse with Alex after Adler was released. And sure enough I got caught and it cost me almost everything Alex said it would. I stayed out of jail, but I lost his friendship and my job. I picked up what pieces I could and became a PI. And that was okay for a time, too.

Then … things changed again.

***

It was a slow day in the offices of Matthew Grace Investigations. Hell, it had been a slow month. It seems like there's not much call for a private eye when the economy is down. No wives coming in looking for dirt on their husbands. No husbands complaining about cheating wives. And if there were missing persons out there, their loved ones must either not want them found or else had decided to find them on their own. Not even the lawyers were calling, asking me to prove this client innocent or that witness lying. People were solving their own problems rather than hiring someone else to do it for them.

I'd been private for about ten years. It wasn't my first slack period. After the first one I'd learned to put a little something away for when it happened again. And it always happens. You just ride it out, depending on your savings and the occasional credit checks and security inspections to see you through until the big paying jobs start coming your way again.

Only this time it was different. I'd met someone, Brenda, on a previous case, and we were getting serious. When I mentioned the slump in business, she'd suggested that maybe it was time for a career change, to start thinking about a job with regular hours, paid vacation and a family medical plan.

The word "family" got my attention. It was the first time either of us had mentioned it. And it got me thinking. You can do a lot of thinking when you're alone in an empty office waiting for business to pick up, especially when your thoughts aren't happy ones. You think about where you're going to be in a year, two years, ten years. You think about the family you don't have now but will have then and how you're going to provide for them. And you think that just maybe it's time to grow up and stop playing cops and robbers.

I had some options. Corporate security, insurance investigation, or maybe getting back into government work. There was one big obstacle to that last idea, but I'd spent the last few years and some serious effort in working my way around him.

Of course, I could just give up the field work and take Grace Investigations completely digital — online investigations, intrusion detection, computer security. I'd hacked enough systems to know how to protect them, and what I didn't know I could hire people to do.

I thought about that idea for a while. Me as the boss, running the office and letting my employees do the work. Then it hit me, what work? So I put aside my daydream of being the Old Man in charge of the Continental Detective Agency and went back to thinking about what skills I had other than shadowing wayward husbands and peeping through windows.

I had just decided it was time to upgrade my resume when the phone rang. It was that obstacle I just mentioned. The not so tender voice of Lieutenant

Joshua Parker of the Baltimore Police Homicide Unit came through the phone. "Grace, I need you at a crime scene. You willing to come or do I send a unit to bring you?"

That was strange. I was the very last person I thought Parker would want on any active crime scene. Unless of course I was face down in a chalk outline.

"And good afternoon to you too, Lieutenant. Is there a reason you want me on your scene or do you just miss me?"

"Chauncy St, in the alley behind Eutaw. Your client's dead."

Figures. First client all month and he's already dead. Since a live one wasn't likely to walk through my door any time soon, all I could say was, "I'll be there." I dropped a camera in my pocket, locked up and went to see what the good lieutenant wanted.

Chauncy and Eutaw were in the middle of the city, just a few blocks below Druid Hill Park. Cruising along Lake Dr. I parked as close to patrol cars blocking the north end of Eutaw as I could. Parker had left word, and once I showed my ID to an officer standing watch behind the yellow police tape, I was escorted to the scene.

It has been a while since I'd been a part of an active crime scene, that is, one I hadn't caused or played a major part in. Things hadn't changed. Uniformed officers still guarded the scene, canvassed the neighbors for information and advised the detectives on who was who among the local bad guys and knuckleheads. There were the usual rubberneckers, straining to see past the police into the alley where all the action was. As I was being led to the body, one of the crowd eased over to the yellow tape, slowly lifted it and ducked under. He was quickly surrounded by men in blue and led away from the scene, all the while shouting that this was his block, and he had the right to visit his friends if he wanted to. An officer sternly informed him that if he crossed the tape again, his friend would have the right to visit him in lockup.

Parker was standing in the mouth of the alley. Next to him were a detective and a crime scene tech. I didn't recognize either of them but from the crispness of her uniform and the still very bright yellow of the crime lab patch on her sleeve I could tell that the tech was a recent hire. The pale, somewhat sickly look on her face told me that this might be her first big crime scene, and gave me an idea of what was waiting in the alley.

Parker was talking to the lab tech as I approached. "I don't care what the uniforms told you, Miss Jennings, search the alley yourself. The city's paying you to be the crime scene expert, not them. Go earn your pay. Go look for clues. Detective Harris, go help her."

Parker turned his attention to me. "Mr. Grace, nice of you to join us. Come this way."

We followed the detective and lab tech into the alley. Thinking back to my first big scene I said, "You should go easier on the help, Lieutenant."

"Why?"

"You were new once; remember what it was like?"

"Grace, I was never new."

Midway down the alley was the body, covered with a thin white sheet like an old piece of furniture in a vacated house.

"Baltimore burial?" I asked.

"Not quite," came Parker's terse reply. "Uncover him," he said to the officer standing with the body. The sheet was lifted.

The victim was a white male. Whoever he was he did not die peacefully. Equal portions of fear, pain and horror were frozen on his face. He had died the worst kind of death, and as the humane part of me felt that no one should have to suffer as this man did, the cynic in me wondered what he had done to deserve it.

"Know him, Grace?"

I shook my head. Distorted as his features were, it was hard to see the man behind them. I bent down to take a closer look. "Should I?"

"We found this on his body." Parker handed me a business card, one of mine. "It was in his wallet."

"Wallet. Then you know who he is."

"Yeah, Bennie Waters. Does that ring any bells?"

I took another look. I still didn't know him. "Lots of people have my card, Lieutenant. I give them to bartenders, hotel clerks, fast food cashiers – anybody I meet on a case who might have some info I need. Maybe he was one of them and I gave it to him on a job. Or maybe he got it from somebody else. Somebody who thought he needed it. Who knows?"

Waiting on Parker, I looked around the crime scene. Jennings and Harris were walking the alley, heads down, looking for clues and earning their money. There was another crime lab tech doing the scene sketch, rolling his walking tape, taking measurements, writing them down. A couple of bored cops were just standing there. One looked at his watch and asked his partner, for the second time since I'd been there, if the Medical Examiner had been called yet.

When I got tired of waiting on him, it became clear that Parker was going to make me ask. I did. "You obviously didn't need me to ID this guy, so what's the real reason you called me down here?"

Parker sighed. He glanced up to make sure no one was paying us any special attention. "Do you have a pair of gloves on you?"

"Always, you know I hate leaving prints."

"Put them on." I did and he handed me a folded piece of paper. "We found this when we were looking for his wallet."

On the paper was a sketch of a woman, a woman without a face.

"Damn," I said softly. Now I knew why Parker had called me, why the rush to find out what I knew about the late Bennie Waters. That little piece of paper had turned this scene from a dump job in an alley to a major case.

"Damn indeed, Grace."

I looked at Bennie. The crotch of his pants was stained with blood. "Family jewels taken?"

"Probably. We won't be sure until the M.E. get here and we depants him." Before I could ask he added, "I couldn't find any volunteers to feel around down there."

"You mean you didn't order Miss Jennings to do it. That might be considered looking for clues."

"I'm mean, Grace. I'm not nasty."

"And I thought you never told a lie."

"Finally," one of the bored officers said and whatever retort Parker might have had was lost as the Medical Examiner's van pulled up.

Since nobody told me to move, I was one of the ones around the body as the M.E. examiner brought his gurney over. After taking a few quick photos with his digital camera, he started going through Bennie's pockets.

"Never mind that," Parker ordered, anxious to see if he was right. "Just get those pants off him."

Bennie's jeans were quickly slid off. The examiner took one look between Bennie's legs and said, "Well gentlemen, there's your cause of death."

No doubt he was right. Bennie's genitalia were gone, brutally cut away, after which he bled to death through the gaping wound where his penis and testicles used to be.

Jane Doe was back.

It wasn't the first time. About a year after Shelby Adler's death, another body was found, this time in Patterson Park in southeast Baltimore. The victim was the Richard Fabry, the twenty-one year old son of one of the city's more prominent families. He'd been accused of sexually assaulting several underaged girls, extremely underaged — fourth and fifth grade underaged. Of course he denied his guilt and the only evidence against him was the testimony of his victims. And that was shaky at best, given the psychological damage done to them by the viciousness of the assaults. It looked like Fabry was going to walk — until the video showed up.

No one knew where it came from. The Sentinel received it in the mail from an unknown source. It clearly showed the defendant and one of his victims and corroborated everything she claimed that he had done to her.

The police were unable to trace the sender and a search of the Fabry's house failed to turn up any similar tapes.

And that's why the tape was excluded. With no way to authenticate the video, the judge refused to allow it into evidence. Rather than risk an acquittal, the States Attorney's Office dropped the charges, hoping new, traceable evidence would turn up. It never did. It wasn't needed. Fabry's body was found just a week later, mutilated the same way Adler's had been. A video tape was left near the body, a picture of the same faceless woman wrapped around it. The video showed Fabry's last dying moments.

This time more effort was put into finding Jane Doe. After all, this time rich people were involved. The results were the same.

Since then, Jane Doe's struck three more time. Each time the same picture, the same mutilation. Bennie was her sixth victim.

"I guess guilty pleas are going to go up," I said to Parker as the M.E. examiner was taking Bennie away.

"She does have that effect," he agreed.

"So what'd he do?"

"I called Sex Offense. Detective McMullen's supposed to be here any time now."

"Meanwhile, Lieutenant, what's the tell?"

"The what, Grace?"

"The one thing that makes this one different. What'd Jane leave behind this time?"

"You've been watching too much TV poker, Grace. And assuming anything was left behind with the victim, that knowledge is need to know, and you most certainly don't. I called you here on the chance that you might know something that could help us. Which reminds me, why are you still here?"

"You haven't thrown me off the scene yet."

"Well, thanks for coming down and consider yourself thrown off." Parker walked me out of the alley. My departure was delayed by the arrival of Jesse McMullen. He was one of the few cops who didn't shun me after my abrupt departure from the Crime Lab.

"Good afternoon, Lieutenant. Grace, good to see you again. What's the story?"

Parker looked at me as if expecting me to leave. "You dragged me out here, Lieutenant, at least let me hear the good part."

Parker gave a "what the hell" shrug. "Bennie Waters, Detective. What's he done?"

"Serial rapist, likes old women." McMullen looked past us into the alley. "Bennie the dead guy?"

Parker ignored the question. "And why wasn't he locked up?"

"Proof, Lieutenant. Bennie always takes them from behind, they never see his face. Always uses a condom and takes it with him."

"So what put you on to him?"

"One scene he left the wrapper. We got his print. States Attorney said it wasn't enough." He said this last with disgust.

"It wouldn't be," I added. "Just look around. There's at least a half dozen used condoms and as many wrappers in this alley. Was the wrapper from a lubricated condom?"

McMullen looked at Parker who nodded an okay. "Yeah, why?"

"Try this. Test the swabs the hospital took from your victims. The lube should be on them. Run that against the lube in the wrapper. If there's a match, it's your connection for the States Attorney."

"Good thinking, Grace. Why didn't our lab come up with that?"

"Maybe you should ask them."

"Maybe we should hire you back. What do you think, Lieutenant?"

"I think it's moot," Parker said. "Waters's the one in the alley, Detective. He's not your concern anymore."

"Least let me look at his body. Make sure he's dead."

"Go ahead." To me Parker said, "I've kept you long enough, Grace. Thank you for coming out."

"It's not like I had a choice."

"There are always choices, Grace. You just have to be willing to accept the consequences when you make the bad ones."

"Story of my life." I turned to go. Parker stopped me.

"One more thing. Jane may have seen your business card. If so, she might think you were helping Waters. Watch your back."

Parker's warning, there was something in his voice. I'll be damned, I thought, he really means it. "Thanks for the concern, Lieutenant," I said, then added, "But if Jane's after me, it'll be my front I'll worry about."

***

It wasn't Jane Doe that worried me for the next few days. Real life was distracting me. Business still hadn't improved and thoughts of getting an honest job were more and more in my mind. McMullen's comment in the alley kept coming back to me. It had been good being on an active crime scene again. Maybe enough time had passed. For most people it probably had, but not for Parker. He'd made that clear. Choices and consequences.

It was about a week after Bennie Waters was found. I went to work as usual wondering how many more lonely days I'd spend in my office before I accepted the inevitable. As I put my key into the lock the door swung open on its own.

Home or office, I always lock my door when I leave. It's the result of having been on too many burglary scenes when I was with the Crime Lab. An inspection of the lock showed me the tiny scratches left by lock picks.

I did the stupid thing and went in, not knowing who or what would be waiting for me. I got lucky, the burglar was long gone. I was alone in my rifled office.

I should have called the police and reported a burglary. But to what point? Nothing appeared disturbed and a quick look around told me nothing of value had been taken. And I didn't need the crime lab to come out to dust for prints. I did that myself and gave up after finding a couple of glove marks on the inside door frame.

Going through my files and making sure that nothing had been taken gave me something to do other than to wonder who the burglar was. It wasn't kids or dopers; they weren't likely to wear gloves, not unless they're smarter now than when I was with the department. And they definitely wouldn't have bothered picking the lock. Kicking the door, grabbing the TV, that was more their speed. No, this was more deliberate, someone looking for something specific. But who, and what? I hadn't been involved in any cases that would attract that kind of attention in some time.

And then I remembered Jane Doe, and Parker's warning. Maybe Jane had paid me a visit to check out what, if anything, I had done for Bennie Waters. Or maybe she was looking to see what kind of information I had gathered on her since I had talked to Parker last week.

And that got me thinking. And the more I thought, the more I became convinced that I could put a face to Jane Doe. It took me a couple of days — a few phone calls, a little snooping on databases I shouldn't have access to and I was sure. The only problem was what to do about it.

Was Jane Doe a killer? Yes. Was society better off without the people who'd been killed? Another yes. Would these people have been punished in any other way? Not in this world. So who was I to interfere with the workings of justice?

I was the guy who knew who Jane Doe was. I was the one who could stop the killings. I thought about what Parker said about choices. That decided me.

I was feeling pretty good about myself on my way to work the next morning, at least I was until the back window of my car exploded. Not bothering trying to convince myself that a rock had been thrown up by another car's tires I sped away. And just as I was trying to figure out where I messed up and tipped Jane off, there was a pop and a large caliber hole appeared in my front windshield.

I drove away fast, not bothering with red lights or stop signs, weaving in and out of traffic, trusting in the reaction times of other drivers. A quick check in the rear view mirror failed to show anyone obviously following me, driving as crazy as I was, but why should it? Jane wouldn't want to attract attention and wasn't the one being shot at.

Neither was I, I realized, not right then. I slowed down to a safer speed all the while expecting another shot. It didn't come. There were too many cars around right now, too many possible witnesses. Still I knew it wasn't over. All Jane had to do was to keep behind me and wait for another opportunity. A lapse of my attention, a moment of distraction and I probably wouldn't even hear the shot that killed me. I had to end it now.

I came up with a plan that I hoped — no, prayed — would work. It's not easy to drive, worry about gunfire and work a cell phone all at the same time but I managed it.

My office is on 25th St. I went past it, turned north on Howard. Traffic thinned out, I slowed down, making myself more of a target. I said another prayer, hoping that the good choices I'd made in my life had outweighed the bad, that I had enough credit in Heaven that I could pull this off. If not, I hoped to at least live long enough to pay off the balance due.

I was on 29th St, now, heading west. Soon I'd be on Lake Dr. I could speed up, lose the tail and my pursuer might still probably know where to find me. I couldn't take the chance. I kept a steady speed — slow enough to be followed, just fast enough not to be caught — and turned into Druid Hill Park and drove straight to Three Sisters Lake.

A few minutes ago the idea of ending things where they began had seemed like a good idea. As I pulled into the parking lot and got out of my car I wasn't so sure. Had enough time gone by? Was everything in place? I'd find out soon enough.

A couple of joggers ran by. Then some guy with his dog. Nobody paid much attention to the guy at the picnic table by the lake waiting for a killer to show up. I was beginning to wonder how long I'd have to wait when a car pulled up. Its driver got out, looked around, put something inside his coat. Then he came over and sat next to me.

"Too many witnesses for you, Jesse?"

Detective McMullen smiled. "For now, Grace, for now. Should have known you'd figure it out."

"Is that why you burgled my office?"

"Thought you might be working for Parker. Had to take the chance to find out what you knew. When I heard at work you'd been asking about me I knew it was all up. What gave me away?"

"Does it matter?"

Detective McMullen shrugged. "Suppose not." A pause. "Can't let you walk away from this."

"That's exactly what you have to do. I'll call Parker. You call a lawyer and make the best deal you can."

"Don't think so. My fault that Adler got off. I fixed that. When nobody cared I realized what I had to do. Left the drawing to confuse things, lay a false trail." McMullen looked around. Still too many people for him. "They were scum, Grace. Why do you care what happened to them?"

"I asked myself that last night, Jesse. I don't care — not about Adler, or Fabry, or the others. Maybe they got what they deserved. I care about the next time, or the time after that, the time when you make a mistake and take down an innocent man, the man I'd have on my conscience by staying quiet."

"Thought you of all people would understand. Some years back you were doing the same thing. Only you didn't go far enough."

"I went too far as it was, Jesse. I might have gone farther, but for the grace of God."

"I thought Parker stopped you."

"Parker works for Him."

McMullen stood up, walked around a bit. Looking out over the lake he said, "Not turning myself in." He turned to face me. He hand was on his gun. "And I can't let you do it."

"Quite a public place to shoot someone, Jesse."

"Like they won't find a gun on you."

"I'm not armed."

"I brought a spare, just in case. Patrol will find it on you when they get here."

"My car's all shot up."

"Nothing that can't be explained."

This was getting too close. Time to end it.

The go word was "Deacon," Parker's old nickname. I said it loud enough to be heard, trusting that my prayers had been answered, that Parker had had enough time to get into position after called him from my car.

Somebody up There must have thought I was worth a miracle. Parker stepped out from the trees that had given him cover. So did two officers. All three had their guns drawn.

McMullen just looked at me, then at Parker, then back at me. He slowly took his hand from his weapon.

"You always were a sneaky bastard, Grace."

"It's what I do best."

The uniforms disarmed McMullen, cuffed him and called for a wagon. As he was being led away Parker came over and sat down bedside me.

"Time was, that might have been you," he said softly. I didn't reply. When a man's right, he's right.

"So what did tip you off," Parker asked after a minute or two.

I told Parker about the break-in. "That got me thinking. Would Jane care what I'd done for Waters? And if she was worried about my working for you, how did she know? Then I realized that when McMullen showed up at the scene, he didn't seem all that surprised to see me."

"Which meant he may have seen your business card when he planted the picture."

"Right. And the clincher was that I'd never heard of Bennie Waters. All of Jane Doe's other victims had made the papers and been on TV. Bennie hadn't. Which pointed to the States Attorney's Office or the police."

"Thin, Grace, very thin. Not enough for an arrest, let alone a conviction."

"Which is why I put myself on the line to get you a confession, instead of driving right to Central District after getting shot at. And why you let me do it. But that was the plan all along, wasn't it?"

"Was it?"

"Don't start lying now, Deacon. I'm willing to bet you never heard of Bennie Waters either. And that told you the same thing it told me. So when you saw my card, you called me in, hoping I'd get involved."

"I knew you'd get involved, Grace. You can't help it."

"So why not just ask for my help?"

"I wanted to see if you'd figure it out on your own," Parker said, then after a moment added, "and I wanted to see what you'd do when you did."

"You thought maybe I'd let McMullen walk away?"

Parker didn't lie, ever. All he said was, "I had to be sure."

"Why?"

"Word is you're looking to change jobs. Ever think about coming back to the side of the angels?"

"You'd let me back on crime scenes?"

"Never in a million years, Grace. I don't trust you that much. But the States Attorney's Office is looking to hire some more investigators. You could do good there. Besides, working with a bunch of lawyers, you'd be the most moral person in the place."

"Thanks, Lieutenant I'll think about it."

"You do that, Grace. You've heard about good intentions and that road to Hell?" I nodded. "Well, nothing says you can't step off that road onto a better path. And if that's your choice, I'll send in my recommendation."

***

A week later. Brenda and I were at Lenore's, the lounge where we first met. Brenda was working the bar, filling in for the regular night man who had called in with the flu. I was nursing a Natty Boh, talking to her between customers.

"I've made a decision," I told her.

"You're going to have a second beer?"

"No, about Parker's offer. I'm going to take it."

She nodded, like she had been expecting this ever since I told her about it. She probably had. I think she knows me better than I do.

"If that's what you want, Matt. Sure you can handle working for someone else after all this time?"

"It'll be an adjustment, but hey, it's a mostly daylight job with regular hours and benefits. Just the thing for a family man."

I held my breath as I waited for her reaction. I didn't have long to wait.

Her eyes narrowed, and she fought off a smile. "That better not have been a proposal, Matthew Grace."

"No? Why not?"

"When I say 'Yes,' I want soft lights and romantic music."

"Oh." I nodded the way all men do when they're pretending to understand a woman.

But there was a waitress waiting for that nod. I had stopped in the night before and given away more money than I should — some to her, the rest to the night bartender to call in sick. At my signal she dimmed the lights and cued the piano player who started playing one of Brenda's favorite songs. I reached into my pocket and took out a small box.

"Is this better?" I asked.

I thought about going down on one knee but realized with the bar between us she wouldn't be able to see me. Instead I just flipped the box open and showed her the ring.

"Will you marry me?"

Brenda eyes widened and started filling up. The smile she had been fighting broke loose. "Of course," she said and all but dragged me over the bar.

As we embraced I thought, and not for the first time, that I was far luckier than any man deserved. I had a new job, a second chance and a woman who loved me. All that, and I still got to play cops and robbers. I'm telling you, it's great to be me.

Coming 2010 from Padwolf Mystery!

BAD COP, NO DONUT

edited by

John L. French

from the author of
THE STARSCAPE PROJECT

MIND FIELDS

Brad Aiken

"Imagine a world without surgery. Imagine having the ability to analyze and repair damage to the human brain without making a single incision. You are imagining a nanobot, a programmable robot about the size of a single human cell."
— Dr. Sandi Fletcher, Johns Hopkins University; June 5, 2045.

    Special Agent Trace McKnight imagines a very different world; a world in which nanobots implanted in the human brain can be used to control the actions and thoughts of their host, turning any man into the perfect killing machine, even one who could assassinate the President of the United States.
    This renegade NSA agent infiltrates the lab of Dr. Fletcher to steal her nanomedicine research in order to develop his mind-control weapon, but instead arouses her suspicions. Fletcher enlists the help of Baltimore police detective Richie Kincade, and the pair soon find themselves caught up in a web of espionage that places them directly in the cross-hairs of the seditious NSA agent, a man feared even by those within his own organization.
    As McKnight's plan unfolds, Kincade realizes that he and the good doctor have just been pawns in a game that neither of them were prepared to play, but that won't stop them from playing to win.

    "In his latest sci-fi novel, Mind Fields, Brad Aiken's brilliance as a writer weaves a strikingly vivid tale of scientific advancement that leads to a terrifying vision of the future. The resulting rollecoaster ride of action and suspense kept me on the edge of my seat throughout the entire novel! " - Melissa Minners, **G-Pop**

From the pages of
MURPHY'S LORE™

FAIRY WITH A GUN

THE COLLECTED TERRORBELLE

PATRICK THOMAS

**AGAINST CLUB CRASHING VAMPIRES,
A SERIAL KILLER WEREWOLF WHO THINKS PRETTY WOMEN
SHOULD PLAY LITTLE RED RIDING HOOD TO HIS BIG BAD WOLF,
THE CORPSE KNOWN AS ZOMBIELICIOUS, A VICIOUS
TROUSER SNAKE AND THE ULTIMATE BAD-ASS
SOME WOULD SAY YOUR BEST DEFENSE IS A GOOD OFFENSE
THOSE IN THE KNOW WILL TELL THE BEST OFFENSE IS
TERRORBELLE™: FAIRY WITH A GUN**

FROM PADWOLF PUBLISHING
www.padwolf.com